CATSPAW

JOAN D. VINGE

WARNER BOOKS

A Warner Communications Company

Grateful acknowledgment is made to Harper & Row, Publishers, Inc. for permission to reprint an excerpt from CROW, copyright © 1971 by Ted Hughes.

Warner Books, Inc., 666 Fifth Avenue, New York, NY 10103

w A Warner Communications Company

Printed in the United States of America
First printing: September 1988
10 9 8 7 6 5 4 3 2 1
Book Design by Nick Mazzella

Library of Congress Cataloging-in-Publication Data

Vinge, Joan D.
    Catspaw / Joan D. Vinge.
        p.   cm.
    I. Title.
    PS3572.I53C3   1988
    813'.54—dc19   88-40082
    ISBN 0-446-51396-2   CIP
                                     AC

This one's for you, kid.
You know who you are.

(With his glared off face glued back into position
A dead man's eyes plugged back into his sockets
A dead man's heart screwed in under his ribs
His tattered guts stitched back into position
His shattered brains covered with a steel cowl)
                    He comes forward a step,
                                   and a step,
                                     and a step—

                              —Ted Hughes

We are afraid of truth, afraid of fortune,
    afraid of death, and afraid of each other.

                    —Ralph Waldo Emerson

To understand a cat, you must realize that he has
    his own gifts, his own viewpoint, even his own morality.

                    —Lilian Jackson Braun

PROLOGUE

SOMEONE WAS AFTER ME. The feeling, the knowing, was like the touch of ghost hands on my back all through the long afternoon. I *knew* it, the way I still did sometimes, picking things up like bits of song heard through static. It had got hold of me first in the bazaar of the orbiting spaceport. I'd been standing under the colored sunscreen at the jeweler's booth, letting a dark woman with long fingers puncture my earlobe with a ring. "Duzzin hurt," she was crooning, in some kind of accent as thick as the smoke from the charred meat in the next stall. "Hold still, duzzin hurt, duzzin hurt . . ." like she was talking to a child, or a tourist. It did hurt, but not much. And I was a tourist, everybody here was a tourist, but that didn't make acting like one feel any less strange to me.

I winced, and then the second of sharp pain was over. But in the second of empty whiteness that followed it, while I was waiting for more pain, I got something else: the touch, the whisper of something's interest brushing against my mind. Not someone, something—neutral, patient, mindless. I looked up and away, jerking free of the jeweler's hand as she wiped blood from my ear. But there was nothing to see, no one I knew, or who seemed to know me. Just the shifting crowd of colors that were too bright, faces that were too soft, like the crowds in an Oldcity night. . . .

I shook my head as the past slid across the present like a membrane. It still happened to me too often—that suddenly I felt like I

1

was dreaming, like I didn't know who or where I was. The green agate beads on the wire bumped the side of my jaw.

"Anuzzer—?" the woman was asking, reaching out. I pushed away into the crowds, and let them carry me on down the street under the light of the artificial sun.

Once I knew the thing was onto me, I couldn't stop feeling it —that whispering, toneless song like a hook caught in my brain. I tried to tell myself it was my imagination; my crippled mind feeling something the same way an amputee felt phantom pain. But it didn't work. I knew what I knew. It went with me along the twisting, gaudy streets that tried to hide the fact they were only going in circles; into the quiet, shadowed sprawl of the museum complex and out again; into a food bar; into the silver-fixtured hotel men's room. It watched me, only me, tuned to the electrical fingerprint of my brain, locked in. I thought about going back on board the *Darwin,* but even a ship's walls wouldn't keep it away from me. There was no reason in hell why anybody at all would put an ID trace on me. Maybe it was a mistake, a trace meant for someone else, an echo-reading. . . . If somebody wanted me, where were they? Why didn't they just ask? Why shadow me through this crowd of vacant-faced marks in their showday clothes—

"Cat—oh, Cat!"

I turned, my fists knotting up, even as I recognized the voice. My hands were slippery with sweat. I opened them, working my fingers.

It was Kissindre Perrymeade, her half-dozen brown braids dancing down over her khaki shirt, her smiling face like scrubbed ivory.

I stopped, letting the crowd flow on around me until it brought her to my side. "Hi, Kiss." Her nickname always made me smile. I pushed my hands into the pockets of my jeans. "I'm glad to see you," I said, meaning it for once.

You are? her face asked, with that mix of aching shyness and trying-not-to-stare that usually left us both acting stupid whenever we met. We'd walked the surfaces of half a dozen worlds together, along with five hundred other students in the Floating University, but I'd never really gotten friendly with her, any more than I was friends with any of the rest of them. She was a teaching intern, which made me half-afraid to say anything to her to begin with. And the fact that she was rich and pretty and stared at me only made it worse. Because the same things that made most of the others keep their distance from me pulled at her. I didn't talk like they did, I didn't dress like they did.

I hadn't come out of the same places. I had eyes with long slits for pupils, in a face that wasn't put together right by human standards: a halfbreed's face. I never talked about any of it, but that didn't make it go away.

And yet the things that made most of the others snap shut like traps made Kissindre stare. I knew she sketched my face with her stylus on the edges of her glowing noteboard, as if I was something she thought was beautiful, like the artifacts and scenic views she made painstaking drawings of—things everybody else holoed once and would never look at again. I didn't know what I was to her, and if she knew she wouldn't admit it; and that made me feel even more awkward whenever we were together.

But now, with something inhuman locked on my brain, I was glad of any face that wasn't a stranger's, more glad that it happened to be hers, even smiling that painful smile. I noticed she was wearing jeans. Nobody else on the ship wore jeans, except me. Jeans were cheap, common, worker's clothing. It hit me suddenly that she'd only started wearing them after I met her.

"Is something wrong?" she asked, glancing up at me again.

I shook my head, only partly for an answer. "Why? Because I said I'm glad to see you?" My eyes kept wandering away, searching the street. I took her arm, felt her start but not pull back. "Come on, let's take a jump, let's get out of here. Let's go see something." Thinking that if I could get away from the spaceport for a few hours, maybe I could lose the mistake that was dogging me.

"Sure," she said, brightening now. "Anywhere. It's incredible—" She broke off, as if she knew she was starting to talk too much. At least she meant it. Most of the students on the *Darwin* were too rich and too bored and only looking for a long vacation. But a few of them were really here for what they could learn. Like her. Like me. "Your ear's bloody," she said.

I touched it with my fingers, remembering, feeling the earring. "Just got this. Supposed to be a relic."

She stiffened.

"Don't worry," I said. "It's not." I didn't like the way humans helped themselves to pieces of the scenery without asking any more than she did. Maybe less. Concentrating, I tightened the fingers of my mind into a fist; something I could still do, even if I couldn't reach out. The scratching alien hum stopped. With luck, I'd just stopped existing for whoever was on the other end. But it was like holding my breath.

We made our way back to the museum, went down ten levels to the wide shadowy cavern where the shuttles squatted in patient rows like opalescent beetles, waiting on the smooth ceramic pavement to carry people like us down to the planet's surface. There was no permanent human structure of any kind on the world that lay a thousand klicks below our feet, the world humans called the Monument. The whole planet was a Federation preserve . . . an artificial world, constructed millennia ago and dropped into an orbit around a bleary orange star out here in the middle of nowhere.

The spaceport station orbited high above it, as big as a small town, which it was. The museum complex occupied about half of its core; it was a center for the study of the vanished race that had created the Monument: rooms and rooms full of artifacts and questions without answers. It was supported by the flesh and flash of the tourist resort that made up the rest of the port.

As we came out of the dark hallway under the heavyalloy pillars, three shuttles rose up together with a hum like invisible wings and circled away into the dark mouth of the airlocks. On the far side of the field the polarized hull of the station let in the sky: midnight blackness shot with stars. The orangey streetlight of the Monument's nameless sun shone in one corner; the world itself rolled silently past down below our feet. It had been left here by a civilization humans had named the Creators, because they couldn't think of anything better. The Creators had vanished long before humans ever crawled up out of their own gravity well and spread like roaches across the stars. Nobody knew where the Creators had gone to, but everyone agreed they were gone, leaving behind almost nothing except this monument to their mystery. Even the Federation respected it.

"What do you want to see?" I asked Kissindre, as we drifted up to join the usual long line of tourists and students putting in their requests at the gateway. I didn't care where we went, as long as it got me out of range. You could take tours that took only hours, or as much as a couple of days, to any part of the world. It wasn't that big a planet; its diameter was only about thirty-five hundred klicks, even though its gravity was almost Earth-normal. It was one of the things the xeno experts couldn't explain: why a world put together by aliens seemed to fit humans so well. If they hadn't been like us, then maybe they'd wanted to tell us something. But then, there were the Hydrans, who were so close to human that the differences didn't even matter on a genetic level. I was living proof of that. And what was left of the Hydran race was living proof that humans didn't listen very well.

"Well . . ." Kissindre bit her lip, staring up at the shifting images on the screen over our heads, the deep views changing, the overlying digits in bright yellow flashing the transit times and the fees. "The Moonpool Caverns are supposed to contain some of the best examples of synaesthetics . . . and if you want to dive . . ." She glanced back at me. It was an overnight trip.

"Great," I said. "Anything you want." The effort of holding my mind shut was making me sweat again. I focused on her face, concentrating on that. She was staring at me, her eyes as transparently blue as deep water, her lips parted. It made me realize suddenly that I was horny as hell. That I wanted to kiss her.

She looked up at the screen, away at the view of space, back at me again. She blushed. "Except . . ." she mumbled, "I promised Ezra I'd meet him for supper."

"No problem," I lied, glancing away this time. "Another time. Something short . . ." I stared at her back, feeling even worse than usual, and pinned my restless hands against my sides with my elbows. We were almost to the gateway.

"Yes, maybe we—"

"Kissindre!"

She jerked around as the voice—Ezra's voice—suddenly caught us from behind. I turned with her, saw her boyfriend come galloping out into the square toward us. He always moved like he was about to fall over. He spent most of his time with trodes taped to his head. His face was red as he cut into the line beside us; so was hers. Different reasons . . . or maybe not. Once I would have known for sure.

"What are you doing here?" he said, trying not to sound like he sounded.

"Studying," she said, a little too loudly.

"Studying what?" He looked at me.

"The Monument! I thought *you* were still working on your compilation—"

"I was in the resource center when I saw you out the window—"

"So?"

"So when were you planning to meet me for dinner, Kiss?" His voice rose over the muttered conversations around us. "In your next incarnation?" The black frizz of his half-grown beard quivered when he stuck out his jaw.

"Ezra . . ." Kissindre hissed, hugging her sketchboard against her with white-knuckled fingers. "You're so archaic."

"Three," I said to the gate. "Student." I let its sensors scan my databand. "Goldengate." The station was passing right over the Goldengate window. A short jump, one we might all survive. I went on through the gate, hearing my boots click on the ceramic.

After a few seconds I heard two sets of expensive magnetics follow, and more muttering. I ducked into the next waiting shuttle, and sat down. Kissindre climbed in and sat down right beside me. After a minute Ezra joined us, sitting on the other side of me. The door sealed; destination co-ords rippled across it. The shuttle lifted, so smoothly I hardly felt the motion, and spun toward the locks. I settled back as we passed through and out, beginning our drop down the Monument's gravity well. I stretched out my legs; loosened the fist I'd made of my mind, finger by finger.

Nothing. Out of range. I sighed, shutting my eyes. Now it was easy to believe it was a mistake. Or even my imagination. Paranoia was an old habit, a hard one to break, when I felt like a freak and a fraud. When every time I shut my eyes I still saw the darkness . . . I opened them again, blinked, stared; watched the world below swelling outward like a balloon across the viewscreens as we dropped toward it. If I thought about that too much, it made my stomach climb into my throat. I glanced at Kissindre and Ezra, remembering again that I wasn't alone. I might as well have been. They were still arguing, across my chest, in angry whispers.

". . . Well, I can't help it, I have to access, I don't have an eidetic memory like the Walking Data Bank here—" His hand in my face, gone again.

"Ezra—"

I looked at the screens again. We were almost down now, entering the atmosphere, our trajectory altering toward our final destination. The deceleration buffering wasn't very good. Kissindre and Ezra got quiet as it got harder to speak. The discomfort made me feel better instead of worse; at least we had brakes. Too much of the galaxy was run by things I couldn't even see. It still made me nervous.

The surface of the Monument was spreading out below us, like a painting coming into clearer and clearer focus. I stared at the view, letting the images seep in through my eyes, feeling a slow smile stretch my mouth. *It was so beautiful.* Sometimes when it was like this I felt as if I'd had a brain transplant, as if I was living in someone else's body. The fact that I couldn't prove anybody else was real by their place inside my thoughts any more didn't help the feeling.

I tugged on my earring, feeling the pain; rolling the cool, hard surface of the beads between my fingers. I'd never had any jewelry before. Never wanted any, when it only attracted the wrong kind of attention—the kind that would get your throat slit. One morning-after back in Oldcity I'd woken up with a tattoo, but even that didn't show with my clothes on. Getting the earring today I'd been trying to prove to myself again that I didn't have to be invisible any more. I tried not to remember what I had to remember every time I glanced at my credit readout: that by the time the University finished its studies here I'd be zeroed, out of money. I took a deep breath, easing the tightness in my chest, watching the view.

Anywhere you set down on this world, you'd find a scene that filled up your eyes with wonder. The air was like satin, the winds like musicians. It was as if an artist, or a thousand artists working together, had been given a whole world as clay, as lightbox, as a musical instrument. Nothing but beauty anywhere, as perfect as diamonds. Nothing. Nothing alive to disturb its stasis. Not a leaf, a bird, an insect. Not until now.

The changing view of beyond-the-walls had stopped changing. The hatch sighed and yawned. We climbed out, stretching, silenced by the sudden silence of the yellow windswept plateau that was the designated viewpoint. Two other shuttles were already there, and a bunch of gaudy tourists stood a few meters away. I could hear their voices, but the sound was thin and high, as if they were somehow farther away than they looked. It was nearly sunset. The reddening light burnished the sandstone cliffs, making the hills look like they'd been cast from brass. If you didn't know, you would have sworn that only time and wind had eaten them down into those forms. But if you looked at anything too closely—anything at all, a pebble—you might find a hidden sign, an undecipherable signature, telling you that some sentient mind had laid everything out just so, and left it that way for eternity.

I turned, stepping away from the shuttle. As I looked around me the hugeness, the sheer size of world and sky, hit me so hard I couldn't breathe. It made me feel like there was no place to hide . . . the way I always felt when I took on too much open space too fast. I made myself keep looking, feeling the wind ruffle my hair with an easy hand. I took a breath—forgot to finish it. Beside me Kissindre and Ezra sighed and said, "Oh . . ." and broke off their argument.

This ship-in-a-bottle world's foster sun lay framed inside the arch of stone they called Goldengate, as if time itself was trapped there, frozen in the moment. The black silhouette of the bridge was shot through with a pattern of bright rays, riddled with the precision of lace. And as the wind rose, lifting a pale curtain of dust, I could hear it: the thin, high piping far up in the air, the song the wind made in the hollow flute of stone. The sound reached into my chest like an invisible hand to break my heart. I started away from the others, forgetting them, forgetting everything, sunblind, stone-deaf. . . .

Loud bleeping cut across my senses, jerking me back. I stopped at the edge of a sheer drop, the boundary of the access area. I stepped back onto safe ground and waited for my ringing ears to clear. Then I stood on the edge between worlds, listening to something else. . . . After a minute I crouched down, making handprints in the burnished dirt. I picked up a smooth, striped stone no bigger than my hand. I put it down again, in a different spot; it still looked perfect. The voice of the wind turned cold inside me.

"Whatever made them do it?" Kissindre murmured, not to me but to the wind, and I realized she was standing beside me now. "Was it just for its own sake, all this beauty . . . ?"

"A ritual object," Ezra said, "part of their structure of worship." That was the answer we usually heard while images of strange artifacts poured into our heads. It meant the experts didn't know what the hell it was either, and probably never would.

"No." I straightened up, brushing my hands on my jeans. "It really is a monument."

"To what?" Kissindre asked, her eyebrows rising. Beside her Ezra frowned.

"Death," I said, feeling the word fall out of my mouth, cold and hard. "Bits and pieces, the bones of planets, that's what it's made of. That's why there's nothing alive here." The sun was disappearing beyond the cliffs. The wind was beginning to feel as cold as I did.

Kissindre caught at my arm. "Who told you that?"

"Huh?" I looked back at her, seeing sunspots where her eyes should have been.

"Who—?"

I shook my head. My thoughts felt heavy and slow, like molten glass. "Dunno. Heard it, I guess. . . ."

"I've never heard that one." She shook her own head, but it wasn't denial. She squinted out across the sea of stone, her body tightening with excitement.

"He's making it up," Ezra mumbled, without the guts to say it to my face. Kissindre began to murmur notes into the recorder on her necklace, her eyes back on me.

Still feeling like I'd been hit on the head, I bent down, trying to hide what was happening inside me. I pulled the knife out of the sheath inside my boot, straightened up. Leaning against an outcrop of rock, I reached into the pouch pocket of my tunic and found the eggfruit I'd bought this afternoon. I began to peel it, steadying my hands, before I looked up at them again.

Their faces were like two six-year-olds, the naked fear slowly draining away, leaving them slack-jawed. Like they'd never seen anybody pull a knife before.

"I don't make things up," I said finally, and then wished I hadn't, while they nodded, too eagerly. I didn't know how I knew what I'd just told them about this place, couldn't remember ever knowing it before that moment. All I was certain of suddenly was that I was an alien. Had always been, would always be.

I put my knife away. "See you." I looked back at Kissindre and Ezra for as long as it took to say the words. I started toward the waiting shuttles, and they didn't follow.

"Cat—?" Kissindre called suddenly, her voice pale.

I turned back, waiting.

She licked her lips. "Can you . . . can you really read my mind?"

So that was it. She knew I was a psion, knew it was Hydran blood that made me half a stranger. But she didn't know the rest of it. . . . Probably she wouldn't want to. "No," I said, "I can't." I went on alone.

On board the shuttle I ate my dinner, and stuffed the pit into the ashtray, next to some skagweed user's stale cud. The smell of the cud was overwhelming the air scrubbers. There was the butt end of a camph in the ashtray too. I almost took it . . . let it fall back. Still too much memory. Maybe there always would be. Maybe the monument to death wasn't falling away below me now, maybe it was inside my head. . . .

That was easier than believing that somehow I could just know things about a place. Or maybe I was just better than the rest at reading the subliminals embedded everywhere in the Monument. That made a kind of sense. Maybe the Creators had been more like Hydrans than like humans, after all. But it didn't ease the feeling of being out-of-focus that had only been getting thicker all day. I tugged on the earring again. First the tracer, then Kissindre, now this. . . . I remembered I was falling back into the tracer's electronic net right now. Humans were always making my life lousy, still hounding me, like they'd done to the whole Hydran race. . . . *Screw it. Stop acting like a shadow walker*. I unclenched my fingers, pulling them out of the holes they'd dug into the formfoam armrests.

I held my mind shut, holding my breath, the rest of the way back to the station. When we landed I stepped out again into the perfectly antiseptic, climate-controlled womb below the museum. The port's massive ceramic/composite hull was all around me, like the walls of a fortress. There were half a hundred people within reach of my voice, and none of them looked too interested in me. I let go, setting the crippled receptors of my brain as free as I could, listening: nothing. The toneless static of the trace wasn't there . . . if it had ever been there in the first place. My telepathy had gone dead three years ago, but sometimes my brain still played practical jokes.

I shrugged the shadows off my back and went on across the tiles, out through the gate with the rest of the sightseers. They flowed on into the echoing mouth of the walkway that led back through the museum's labyrinthine guts, and eventually to the lifts that would carry them on up to the port levels. I went with them, letting my shoulder hug the reassuring closeness of the wall along the edge of the crowd.

And then suddenly I stopped, staring. Spraypainted on the wall, inside a clumsy heart, was my name. CAT. CAT & JULE. People swore as they bumped into me, but I didn't care. I didn't even notice as all the rest of them passed me by; didn't notice that I was standing there all alone now, with only the sound of my breathing and the sign on the wall. I felt a kind of panic begin to rise inside me. The day had just gone from out-of-focus to completely insane. I looked back over my shoulder. Light and darkness shifted around me, flowing across the pillars and walls like water, as if they had a life of their own.

I turned, feeling a sudden bright stab of warning a split second before my eye caught real motion. Two shadows peeled off from the darkness of a passageway, and closed in on me. I caught a flicker of orange, the flaming badge of some combine's colors on somebody's sleeve. And then the cold bite of nothingness hit my neck, chemical teeth sinking toward a vein, finding it. And that was all.

ONE

I CAME TO on board a ship, but it was no ship I'd ever seen before. I was lying on a foam-padded, fold-down bunk, in a room that I couldn't mistake for my cabin or any other place on the *Darwin* if I'd been blindfolded. The last thing I remembered was a flash of combine colors on a Corporate Security uniform jacket; the gray-green garbage-can walls around me now, the stripped imitation asceticism of the single desk and chair, the storage nets, the bed, all screamed military.

I'd been bodysnatched by some combine's Security arm . . . which made no sense at all, except that here I was. I tried to sit up, and was more surprised than not when I found out I could. No binders on me, no straps. My knife was missing. I felt along my neck and stripped off the patch I found there. I'd been drugged, all right, but my head seemed clear enough now.

The door of the cabin was shut. Just then it slid open, as if they'd been waiting for me to wake up. Two men entered, probably the ones who'd done it to me. One dark-skinned, one pale. They wore interchangeable faces and interchangeable silver-on-gray duty fatigues. They stopped inside the doorway, waiting, tense. I wondered if the combines made their Corpses get face jobs so they'd match. Then my eyes found the insignia on a jacket front, and I froze. Data flowed across the ID patch below the sunblaze logo of Centauri Transport. A giddy flash of double-sight hit me. I didn't know what this was about, but I knew now it wasn't a mistake. And it wasn't good. Cold anger, or maybe cold fear, slammed though my brain. I stood up, and said, "Wha's goin' on—?"

And sat down again with my stomach up in the back of my throat. "Shid." Now I knew why there were no binders. No need. Whatever they'd drugged me with left a hell of a hangover.

The twins looked at each other and grinned, but it was more like relief than like they thought it was funny. They came across the room, as if they'd been afraid to get too close to me before. "Okay, freak," one of them said, "the Chief wants to see you." They hauled me up again, and half-dragged me out the door. I wished I'd eaten more dinner, because I wanted to see it all over them when I puked.

We were on board some kind of small scoutship; at least they didn't have to drag me far. They pushed me through the doorway into another cabin, and down onto a wall couch.

I was wrong; I wasn't on some scoutship. This was some combine vip's private cruiser. It might have been on a different world from the room I'd come to in.

"Here he is, sir. He's safe," one of the guards said beside me. I realized they didn't mean safe and sound. They meant crippled.

I'd been wrong . . . and right. "The Chief" was Centauri's Chief of Corporate Security. He was sitting in a tapestry-covered recliner behind a perfect black semisphere of desk, staring at me from across the room. He had a face like the blade of a knife, thin, sharp, and cold . . . no beard, except high up on his cheekbones in a feathery line, as if his eyebrows grew around to circle his eyes. His eyes were so dark they looked black. He was wearing a full-dress uniform—a gunmetal-gray helmet with Centauri's logo and his insignia dancing on it, a conservative business suit in silver tweed, a drape crawling with shining crap that made my eyes swim. I'd never seen so much flash on one body before. The fact that he was wearing it said either he wasn't worried, or he wanted to impress me. I didn't know what that meant, either way.

I looked away from him, because he was staring at me without blinking. We seemed to be inside a bubble, hanging out over the black heart of space. The Monolith's sun hung just above his left shoulder, like a floating lamp. I couldn't see the world itself. I looked down at my feet, glad that at least there was a rug. Sapphire blue, it had the Centauri logo shot through it in gold. Subtle. I pressed deeper against the back of the couch, waiting until my stomach caught up with the rest of my body again. Then, as carefully as I could, I said, "Wha'. Do. You. Wan'?"

"Your name is Cat. My name is Braedee." The black eyes were still fixed on me like cameras. "I'm Chief of Security Systems for Centauri Transport. Do you understand what that means?"

It meant there was probably nobody higher in the combine's power structure except the controlling board members. It meant that he was probably the most trusted man in that entire structure. Also the worst enemy anybody who crossed them would ever have. The ruling board itself must have sent him after me. Did they really know who I was? My paranoia started doing the multiplication tables. I shook my head to answer him. It was cold in his office; the sweat crawling down my ribs made me shiver.

"It means that I don't see just anybody. It means," a muscle in his face jumped, "that we need . . ." twitch, "a telepath." Twitch. "Now I'm going to explain why."

Surprise caught in my chest, then relief, and confusion, and anger. I sucked in a breath. "No." I touched my head, meeting the telephoto eyes. "Nah. Till. Fix. Dis."

"The drug blunts your psionic ability. The speech is an unfortunate side effect. Your comprehension is completely unaffected. There's no reason for you to say anything until I've finished."

"Fu' you." I stood up, turning toward the doorway. The two matching Corpses filled it up. I turned back again to face Braedee. "Fix. It!" If they knew what I was, they should know I was no more danger to them than any deadhead they picked off the street. Less— I wouldn't kill them. But from the way his face worked, I knew he was as piss-assed scared as anybody else. Maybe more, considering what he did for a living. The more someone had to hide, the more they usually hated psions.

Braedee shook his head. He said, "Gentleman Charon taMing heads the Centauri board. He ordered me to keep you drugged."

TaMing. I jerked as I heard the name. "Fu' him too," I said, trying to cover my surprise.

Braedee glared at me for a long minute, considering the alternatives, probably feeling the invisible fist of Centauri ready to come down on us both. There was something wrong with his eyes, more than just the way he looked at me; but I didn't know what it was. At last he said, "I'll give you the antidote if you'll submit to a scan." Calling my bluff.

My hands tightened, went loose again. I nodded finally and sat back down. One of the Corpses came and dropped the veil of silvery mesh over my head. I flinched and shut my eyes as it molded to my flesh, tingling like a thousand insects crawling on my face. The urge to rip it off was almost more than I could stand; the first time one had been used on me they'd had to use binders, too. At least by now I knew what was coming. I'd been through so much testing, so much therapy since the killing that I'd learned to live with it. I clenched my jaw, trying not to resist—resisting anyway, not able to stop blind instinct as the sensation began. Worms ate my brains for dinner, while somewhere the scan sequence vomited a useless data simulation of my mangled psi.

It was over in less than a minute—subjective time of about fifty years. The mesh dropped into my lap. I brushed it off and kicked it away, wanting to spit.

Braedee was staring into the air, at me, but through me. I looked over my shoulder but there was only the single wall that backed me up. "She was right," he murmured. "The shape of your profile is . . . well, see for yourself." He really was looking at me now.

I didn't see him move, but suddenly the sun disappeared behind him, and instead my scan profile flashed across space in pure light lines of red, blue, and green. Data into symbol—making it comprehensible for humans, who had to input everything the hard way. I stared at the dead end that had turned me into a deadhead, the wall I'd built myself and couldn't tear down again. "Seen. It."

The image disappeared. I blinked at the sudden reappearance of the sun. "All right. Give him the patch," Braedee said.

One of the guards stepped forward again, and stuck another patch over the vein in my neck. "Leave it there for twelve hours, or you'll regress," he said.

I nodded, and waited a minute longer before I tried to speak again. "Okay, deadhead." My voice was raw and shaky, but I heard what I expected to. "I'm ready for the reason. It better be good."

His mouth lifted, just a little, like I amused him. Then the thin, pale lips stretched over his teeth again; he pressed his fingertips into a steeple on the lifeless surface of his desk. "You were once briefly . . . involved . . . with Lady Jule taMing, who is a member of the founding family of Centauri Transport."

"A friend," I said. "I was her friend. I'm still her friend."

He frowned, at the interruption, or the implication. My own face appeared suddenly in the air behind him: a little younger, a lot thinner, hair curly and white-blond, skin brown, eyes green and slit-pupiled. The story of my life was summed up in about half a dozen depressing lines underneath it. No living relatives . . . criminal record . . . psionic dysfunction . . .

"We know all about your . . . relationship with the Lady and Dr. Siebeling, her husband," he went on, still frowning. "About their Center for Psionic Research, about the . . . service you performed for the Federation Transport Authority." He seemed to be having a hard time getting the words out, coughing slightly every time the taste got too acid for him.

"I'll bet. I'll bet the FTA would be amazed at how much you know about that." I leaned back, putting one boot up on the couch. One of the guards moved forward and slapped it down.

"That patch on your neck comes off just as easily as it went on." Braedee stared at me, not blinking. I realized he never seemed to blink. I wondered if he was really alive. I couldn't tell.

I swore under my breath, suddenly feeling stupid for saying anything. Stupid and scared again. Nobody sane crossed a combine the size of Centauri and opened their mouth about it. Just seeing a uniform was still enough to make my stomach knot. I'd had a lot of run-ins with Corpses in my life, enough to know that if they had you they always made you pay. The only people who knew where I was right now were all Centauri Corpses, and all in this room with me. And there were worse things than a speech impediment.

"All right," I mumbled, not meeting his eyes. "What do you want?"

"We need a telepath. As I said before." He leaned back in his seat, easing off. His drape flashed and shimmered as he took a deep breath. "Lady Jule recommended you. She said that even though you were young, you were . . . extremely intelligent, and . . . loyal." He shifted again. He looked like he trusted her judgment about as much as he trusted me right now. But I was here, and that meant either he did believe her, or he was desperate. Maybe both.

I thought about Jule, let her face form in my mind, the details getting a little hazy when I tried to focus on them now. The surprise was back in place, hot as coals: that Jule would tell her family anything about me; that they'd ever want anything to do with a psion. Jule was a psion, like I was. Her freak-hating family had made her life a living hell because of it, until she'd finally tried to cut all her ties with them. But blood was still thicker than water, and the taMings were a family with a long reach. They didn't like to lose something that belonged to them, even if it was flawed. They kept in touch.

"Why'd you snatch me, then?"

"Would you have come, if we'd simply asked you?"

I thought about it. "No."

He raised his eyebrows, as if that was all the explanation it needed.

"That heart sign on the museum wall . . . you think of that?"

He shook his head. "Lady Jule suggested we do something . . . unusual to attract your attention."

My mouth twitched. I jerked my head at the image in the air behind him. "You don't want me. I'm brain-damaged." The way they'd brought me here told me enough about what I could expect if I hired on as a corporate telepath. And I couldn't imagine anything they'd want that I'd ever want to do for them.

"That blockage is self-inflicted." He half frowned, as if he couldn't imagine why having somebody die inside your mind might make some part of you want to dig a hole and never come out of it again. He was right. He couldn't imagine. "It isn't irreversible. Lady Jule suggested that you might even find working for us to be a therapeutic experience."

I shook my head. "I don't believe that."

His face hardened. He was allowed to believe that I'd lie to him, but I didn't have the same right. "I have a communication from the Lady," he said. "She realized that you might be skeptical."

I leaned forward on the couch. "Let me see it."

"When I'm ready." My picture on the invisible screen behind him ate itself. The sun was back over his shoulder again. "First you hear me out. This is no ordinary security position we're offering. I'm not stupid enough to think that would interest someone like you. And you hardly fit our profile." I smiled; he didn't. "This is a matter that concerns the taMing family personally. One of them, Lady Elnear, has had attempts made on her life. So far we have successfully blocked the attacks. But we have been unable to discover why the attempts are being made."

"You mean she's such a wonderful human being she doesn't have any enemies?" I said sourly.

The frown came back. "On the contrary. There are any number of competing interests that could be considered Centauri's enemies . . . her enemies. Lady Elnear's holdings have united Centauri and ChemEnGen," as if that was supposed to mean something to me. "She is the widow of Gentleman Kelwin, and fills his seat on our board, as well as being the lynchpin stockholder of our merger lease with ChemEnGen. She also votes for our interests in the Federation Assembly."

"Oh." She was either one hell of a woman, or a complete pawn. I thought I could guess which. "And you want me to find out which one wants her dead?" If all their best snoopware couldn't track it, I could hardly believe they thought I'd have better luck.

But he nodded. "You would function as her aide, accompanying her at all times. Lady Jule suggested that using your . . . abilities to protect another person might help your condition."

I sat up straight. "The person would have to matter. Lady Elnear doesn't mean shit to me, and neither do the interests of Centauri Transport." I shook my head, starting to get my nerve back. "Anyway, I've been through enough therapy to change the lives of everyone on a planet, but I still can't keep control of my psi. I used to be good enough—maybe—to do what you want me to do, but not any more. If you really want Lady Elnear safe, find somebody else."

He didn't answer me at first. But then he said, "There are drugs that can make it possible. That can block the kind of pain that's crippling you. We can get them for you."

I looked down. "I know," I said, finally. I looked up at him again. "There are drugs that will let you walk around for days on a couple of broken legs, too."

His fingers began to move one by one, tapping a silent code on his black desktop; spelling out his impatience. He looked at me, his mouth thinning. "Centauri will make it worth your while."

I shook my head again. "Sorry. I've already got something to do. You interrupted it. Take me back to the *Darwin.*" I got to my feet.

"If you wish." Braedee leaned back in his seat and cracked his knuckles. "But your credit is down to three meaningful digits, and your tuition will be due again at the end of this term. What are you going to do then?" It wasn't just curiosity; the words were a knife blade pricking my ribs. "Yes," he said, smiling, "we really do know all about you."

I felt the helpless anger try to choke me again. I hadn't even had a rating or a databand until three years ago; hadn't even existed to the galactic Net that monitored the lives and fortunes of everybody worth noticing, from the day they were born to the day they died. Then I'd been paid off for my "service" to the Federation with a rating that made me dizzy, and the freedom of a galaxy to spend it in. I hadn't been stupid enough to think it would last forever. But I'd lived my entire life in the bottom of a sewer. I had a lot to learn, and a lot to forget, and I'd wanted to see what I'd been missing all my life. So I'd signed up for the Floating University, which cost a lot.

"No smart answer?" Braedee asked, pressing a little harder. "Did you really think that repository for the spoiled offspring of privilege was going to prepare you to live in a high-level technological society?" I felt my mouth tighten; so did he. The smile started to come out on his face again. "I understand that until about three years ago you were completely illiterate. . . . Of course, given enough time and training, you'd be marginally employable, although your lack of social skills would probably keep you in a low-level position. But you aren't just ignorant—you're also a psion. You look very Hydran. I don't have to tell you what that means."

I felt my face flush. "I don't have to work for a combine." I was fighting the fear inside me—the fear that it was all true. It was bad enough just being a psion. All human psions had Hydran genes in them somewhere. But most of them didn't have to wear it on their faces; their mixed blood was ancient history.

"Of course not. There are other jobs. Contract Labor is always looking for bodies. . . . But you know that."

My hand went to my wrist, covering it, like somebody caught naked; covering the scar that still marked the place where the bond tag had been fused to my flesh. But it was already covered. My fingers felt the warmth of the databand, solid and real. Mine. "Forget it, scumbutt. You just lost me." I stood up for the last time.

Suddenly Jule's face was in the air behind him, larger than life, so real I could almost touch her. Her gray, upslanting eyes were looking straight into mine. Her face was tired, pale, uncertain . . . beautiful. "Cat," she said, and a trace of real smile pulled at her lips, as if she could really see me. I felt my mouth smile in answer, even though I knew she couldn't. I hadn't seen her face in over two years. Seeing it again made me ache, the way sometimes a song would, triggering memories. I wondered if it would always make me feel that way.

"I'm not sure this is the right thing," she went on, glancing away at someone, and back. "It has to be your choice—I told them that— or it's no good." She brushed a long strand of midnight-colored hair out of her eyes as the breeze lifted it. There was the shifting green of leaves behind her, the wink of sunlight on spray. I felt the breeze touch my face, smelled the fresh smells of damp earth and flowers. Whoever had made this tape hadn't spared anything to make it feel real. I wondered if Jule was in the Hanging Gardens, upside in Quarro.

I felt a twinge of homesickness for the first time in my life. They hadn't taped her at the Center for Psionic Research, in the stink and the noise and the darkness of Oldcity. Maybe they couldn't take it. Maybe they hadn't wanted me to think about that. Except that it made me think about that anyway.

"They told me about Elnear." Jule's eyes darkened. "I don't understand it . . . but if you can help her, Cat, if you're willing to, do it. Please. She's the only one . . ." she glanced away again, "the only one in my family who ever loved me." Shadows moved across her face—leaf-patterns, and the darkness of past lives. Her eyes were both hard and longing when they met mine again. "She's a good woman. She needs someone she can trust. She can trust you. I trust you. I . . ." she did smile, now, "we miss you." She lifted a hand in farewell, and she was gone.

The room seemed colder without her; emptier than if I'd been there alone. But I wasn't alone. I looked up. Braedee's eyes were fixed on my face, sucking in everything that showed. I almost asked to see the tape again. I thought about him watching me watch her. I didn't ask. Remembering it would have to be enough. *All right,* I thought. *For you. All right.* And it was all right this time that she couldn't hear me think it.

"She told me not to tell you this," Braedee said, "but the Center that she and her husband run is almost out of funds too."

I felt my mouth twist. "You always go one step too far, you know that?"

"Then I have you." It wasn't a question.

I glanced out at the sun, where Jule's image had been. "You don't know how close you just came to losing me again. One day you're going to walk right off the edge."

He smiled.

"I'll do it for Jule. But I want the money. For me. For the Center too. Set up the contracts. I'll tell you if it's enough."

"Of course. Some now—more later, if you do your job. We'll settle the details as soon as we reach Earth."

"Earth?" I said, sounding a little like I'd been hit in the stomach.

"That's home to the taMings." I was amusing him again. "They are a rather conservative family."

"Home." It was a strange thought. I looked down at myself, back at him. "You know, Braedee, you're in the wrong kind of work. You should have been a blackmailer."

He shook his head. "You have a lot to learn about politics, boy."

TWO

ONCE BRAEDEE HAD FINISHED convincing me that nothing was ever free, including me, he signaled the doorway like a magician calling up tricks. When I turned around to look, I wasn't really surprised to find someone standing there: a tiny dark-haired woman who looked like an antique doll, like her body might be made of soft cloth under the cover of her dark business suit. She wore a combine logo like a brooch at her throat. It wasn't Centauri's.

I clapped my hands, once, twice, three times. "That's pretty good," I said, looking back at Braedee. "Can you do animals too?"

One of the guards made a sniggering noise. Braedee looked at him with those eyes. He stopped.

"This is Mez Jardan, Lady Elnear's Executive Assistant," Braedee said, the words dry as sand. "Go with her. She'll brief you as much as possible on what your duties will be as Lady Elnear's aide. Afterward I'll see you again." The last part was more a threat than a promise.

I nodded and stood up, meeting the woman's eyes for the first time. I had to look way down; she barely came up to my shoulder, and she was wearing platform shoes. "I'm all yours," I said. Her expression didn't change; she still looked like she smelled something rotten.

I followed her to the ship's commons. There were long bone-colored couches hugging the wall, a round metal table with magnetic chairs locked to the floor. Private—but not too private. She sat down at the table, looking back at me.

"I already know how to eat," I said from the doorway.

"I doubt that." She folded her hands. Her voice was high-pitched, almost like a child's. "We don't have a lot of time, and you know almost nothing of the world you will be entering—"

"Earth?" I came into the room and sat down.

"No," she said. "I meant politics."

I leaned back in my seat, twisting the chair on its single leg with the motion of my foot. "There's that word again."

Her doll's face reddened. "Now listen to me, Mez . . . Cat," stumbling over it, as if there should have been more to my name. "I watched your performance back there with Braedee. It didn't impress me. You have a smart mouth, but I see no proof that you have a mind to match it. I am going to give you a lot of information, and I am forced by circumstance to deliver it verbally. I will repeat it as often as necessary until you understand everything. You may interrupt to ask me questions, but they had better be short and to the point."

I shrugged, smarting a little. "You won't have to repeat yourself. I'll get it right the first time."

Her small mouth twisted down.

"Try me." I leaned forward.

She took a deep breath. "All right, then. Some background, to begin with . . ." She told me what Braedee had already told me about Lady Elnear and how she'd married into the taMings. "A premarital noninterference agreement was signed, but since the Gentleman's death the taMings have . . . taken a greater interest in ChemEnGen's policymaking. . . ." Her voice soured; she wanted to say more. But she knew whose ship we were on, just as much as I did. Combines had long memories. "The Lady is under constant Centauri Security protection at all times since the . . . the incidents." Her hands, which had been lying quietly on the table, curled around each other, protecting, strangling. Suddenly I was sure of one thing: Mez Jardan's loyalty to her boss was as total as her hatred of Centauri. With an effort that cost her, she controlled her hands and laid them quietly one on top of the other on the table surface again. She glanced up at me. "Well?"

I began to repeat everything she'd told me, word for word.

Her eyes widened, for a heartbeat, before the tight, furrowed frown came back. "Are you hotwired?"

I touched my head. "It comes with the wetware. Package

deal." She looked blank. "I was born that way. Most telepaths can do it, if they want to bother." I'd bothered because it helped me learn. I remembered things perfectly. It was forgetting that was hard to do.

I felt more than saw her withdraw, as if every separate cell of her body wanted to crawl away from me.

"Psion," I said, and she flinched. *"Telepath.* Better get used to it."

"We didn't ask for you," she snapped. "You were Centauri's idea. The last thing that Elnear needs is a taMing mindreader to spy on her."

She'd said "Elnear." Not "the Lady." She must be more than a top aide; maybe a personal friend. "She send you to check me out?" I asked.

"In part." She glanced away. "We're forced to accept you, in any case. The least I can do is try to make you presentable." Emphasis on *try.* "Not even all of the taMing family will know that you are a psion, when you arrive. They think that I am away simply to find her a new personal aide. Her previous aide was poisoned." The frown looked almost like pain now.

"How?" I asked.

"A piece of sillaby, intended for Elnear, which Elnear had given away because she doesn't like sillaby. Clara nearly died. Her health is still not good. . . ."

"Poison candy? Pretty crude," I said. Maybe they'd counted on surprise. "Who do *you* think would want to kill her?"

"I don't know." She shook her head, looked down again. "I just don't know. Braedee comes up with new possibilities every day, and all of them are *possible.* . . . I've been with her for twenty-five years, and nothing like this has ever happened before."

"You sound like it's a big surprise. I thought the combines spent half their budgets trying to screw each other." I'd done a lot of reading, after Jule had taught me how, and a lot of accessing once I'd joined the university . . . trying to figure out how the Federation worked, and how I'd come to be who I was, and where I was in it. Facts and figures can tell you a lot, but they can't tell you that.

Her face eased. "It is a fact of life in her position, yes. . . ." Her gaze left me again. "But Elnear is not like that. She believes in the perfectability of humanity. She works only for the greater good—"

"That's enough to make some people want to kill you, right there."

Her eyes snapped back to my face. "Listen to me, you deviant. If you ever say anything like that in front of her, I'll have you—"

"Hey," I said, cutting her off before she could finish it. "Okay, Mez Jardan, you're one tough bitch, and your boss is a goddamn saint. Just tell me what I have to do, and get it over with."

She smoothed her hands again. "As I was about to say . . . Lady Elnear considers her true work to be her involvement with the Federation Transport Authority's independent Drug Enforcement Arm—"

A nark. A combine vip, a saint, and a nark . . . everything I heard about Lady Elnear made me feel less like I ever wanted to meet her, let alone save her from death. . . . I didn't say anything.

"She has been so dedicated in her work for the Arm, and such an effective media representative, that the FTA is considering her for the current opening on the Security Council."

I whistled softly. Braedee hadn't mentioned that. That was something like going from being a saint to being a god. There were only twelve human beings on the Security Council, and they made all the FTA's policy. And the FTA regulated all interstellar commerce.

"As you can see, you will be exposed to levels of society and government about whose rules you know almost nothing. You may allow people to believe that you are acting as a kind of physical bodyguard as well as in the capacity of an aide, to help explain your lack of the—usual requirements for the position. But under no circumstances will you tell anyone that you are a psion."

"Why?"

"That should be obvious. If you're to be of any use at all in helping discover who is trying to kill the Lady, then your ability has to be kept secret."

"That's not going to be so easy." I pointed at my eyes, the long slit pupils. A lot of people knew what that meant.

"Braedee will take care of that," she said.

I smiled, more like a nervous tic. "He's going to give me his?" They were even stranger looking than mine. I wondered if he left them on the table at night when he slept. "He's cybered, right?"

"Of course he is. Do you think he could be Security Chief for a combine without augmentation?"

"He looks pretty normal. I've seen some grotesques—"

"Only a fool would advertise exactly what he can do."

I thought about that. "Depends on what you're into, I guess."

"We're not dealing with street gang pathology," she said. I wasn't so sure, but I didn't say anything. I knew the combines didn't allow most of their employees more than an occasional memory plug-in, besides what they needed to do their specific jobs. The higher you were in the network, the more augmentation you were allowed. If it was really good, it didn't have to show; but if you had that kind of power, why not flaunt it? She said, "Most combines discourage flamboyant displays of personal engineering. Most of humanity still finds aberrance threatening."

"Yeah." That made perfect sense. "I've noticed." I touched my head.

As if she hadn't heard that, she reached into the soft leather bag she carried and pulled out a handful of holos. She tossed them out onto the tabletop in front of me. "These are some of the people you will have to recognize and deal with." I couldn't believe she didn't have some better way of giving me information. Maybe Braedee was making it hard for her. I had the feeling she hadn't been exactly welcome on this trip.

I picked up a holo, stared at it. "Family portraits." Not even a question. It was a picture of a middle-aged man, but the resemblance to Jule was so striking that a cold finger ran up my spine. I shuffled through the rest of them, holding the membranes up to the light, looking at profiles and full faces as they stared, yawned, smiled or frowned through a moment of their existence, over and over, trapped in a kink of time. Too many of them could almost have been Jule's twin.

Jardan named them, one by one, as I picked up the pictures. She didn't really have to tell me which were the outsiders who'd married in.

For the first time I saw Jule's father, a grandfather, a great-grandmother, a cousin . . . a brother. I didn't even know she had a brother. He looked just like her too. Holding images of her face over and over again, barely changing, began to make my fingers tingle as if mice were crawling over my hands. "Why do they all look like that? They all look just like her—"

"Like who?"

"Jule."

She looked at me blankly for a minute, before she remembered. "Oh. Yes," she said, as if she was disposing of an unpleasant reminder. "As you may have gathered, Centauri Transport is something of an anomaly: they are still controlled by the heirs of their founder. After more than three hundred years, that is a rare accomplishment."

"So why do they look like clones? They're not marrying each other—" I tossed the holo back onto the pile.

"They control the transfer of their genetic material very strictly. Only a minimal amount of outside material is introduced into each new generation. They select for the psychological traits that have given them success in the past—and, obviously, for physical resemblance. It's part of the control factor . . . part of their mystique, if you will."

Genetic incest. I thought about Jule—a psion, an empath and teleport born into that family of perfect mirror images reflecting back through centuries. A mistake. A mistake that had almost driven her insane. I wondered how it could have happened. I glanced at the pile of pictures again. "You have one of Jule's mother?" Jule looked like her father. I didn't know much about her family life, but nothing I'd heard about her father was good. I couldn't help wondering what her mother was like.

"Lady Sansu is dead."

I let the holo I was holding drop. I looked down at the pile again, realizing suddenly who else was missing. "Where's Elnear?"

" 'The Lady'," Jardan said. "You will refer to her as 'Lady Elnear.' Or 'ma'am.' "

I grimaced. "So where's 'The Lady's' picture?"

"You've never seen her?"

I shook my head, wondering if she was supposed to be a threedy star too.

She took one more holo out—out of her jacket, this time—and handed it to me, with all the careful respect that had been missing from the way she'd given me the rest.

I took it between my thumb and finger, holding it up. "That's her?" I said, surprised into asking it.

"What do you mean by that?"

"Nothing. Except . . ." Lady Elnear didn't look at all like a taMing, which was a relief. But she was . . . ordinary. A woman who looked like she was past fifty, with a long face and too many teeth, colorless hair, a body that was doughy and soft. Her clothes fit like they didn't belong to her. I looked up at Jardan, saw the resentment in her eyes, and almost couldn't say it. "She's not—beautiful. I mean . . . hell, they can afford it, right? They can get it fixed if they don't like it, they can get all the systems running right, they can get their body clocks set back? They never have to get too fat or skinny or old. . . .''

"Lady Elnear believes that there are better uses for her time and money than indulging in personal vanity."

"Hnh." I glanced at the picture one last time. Lady Elnear looked tired and sad and horse-faced as she turned away from me, again and again. I handed the holo back.

She put it away carefully in her jacket; piled the other holos up neatly and left them between us on the tabletop, like a small wall. Then she began to tell me How to Act: the official duties, the endless lies and phony rituals of people pretending to be decent to each other while all the time they were trying to get behind each others' unprotected backs with knives. I set my brain on *record* and thought about other things . . . about getting jerked around like a puppet by fate and the combines. About seeing Earth . . . About Kissindre Perrymeade and whether she'd think my being gone was because of her. If she even noticed I was missing . . . I forgot where I was, and laughed.

"Are you listening to me?" Jardan's voice was as hard as a slap.

I looked up, blinking. I fed the last few sentences she'd spoken back to her. "Don't worry. Even if I fall asleep, I'll remember it."

Her mouth thinned. "Do you actually understand any of this? You haven't asked me a single question."

I frowned, because I hated what I was hearing, and hated being forced to listen to it . . . and hated to admit that maybe she was right. "It's like getting the instructions for a machine you've never seen. It's not going to make any sense till I get there. If I have questions, I'll ask The Lady."

"Braedee!" She got up from her seat. Braedee appeared in the doorway before she'd finished the motion.

"You're pretty good at that, too," I said sourly.

"I'm through with him," she said, meaning me. It sounded as final as if my next stop was the incinerator chute.

"On the contrary." Braedee shook his head.

Her frown deepened. "He'll never pass."

"For human?" Braedee's eyes flicked over me, probably scanning me all up and down the spectrum, straight to my bones. "He will when I'm finished with him."

"That's not what I mean."

"He'll have to. You—" He pointed at me. "Come with me." I did.

He led me to what looked like his personal lab. It wasn't impressive, cool green and antiseptic tile, a lot of strange-surfaced alloys, but nothing that would make you want to get the hell out of there. But knowing who he was, and suspecting what he could do, I knew those walls probably hid as many secrets as his skin did. "Sit down," he said. "I'm going to fix your eyes." He nodded at a stool in front of what looked like some kind of scanner.

"There's nothing wrong with my eyes," I said.

"Don't act stupid." He shoved me toward the seat. "You look like a freak."

"All I need is some eyeskins—" I hugged my elbows, looking toward the doorway.

"I just want to look at your eye structure." He sat down, waiting for me. I sat down too, slowly, and put my face against the headpiece. "Look at the rings." Nothing inside but darkness, and a set of concentric rings floating in space like a target. I watched it for a long minute, squinting my eyes. Nothing. I began to relax.

There was a sudden blow against my eyes, that wasn't light or heat or pain, but somehow all three at once. I jerked back, swearing, rubbing my face. "You shit. What did you do to me?"

"See for yourself," he said. A mirrored plate slid down over the window in front of me. I stared at myself. The long slits of my pupils were changing while I watched, shrinking into pinpoints, the green of my irises filling in like crystal growth. "A simple molecular graft. Eyefilms would leave you half-blind in dim light. Not useful. Also detectable. This isn't permanent, but you can have it made permanent."

I looked up at him, away from the perfectly ordinary human eyes staring back at me from the mirror; away from the expression on my face. "What makes you think I want to look like a human?" My voice sounded shaky again.

He ignored that. "A little cosmetic facial surgery would be better. . . ." He hesitated, watching me. "But to do it safely takes more time than we've got. You can pass, I suppose; there are enough exotics around to make you look normal."

I took a deep breath, glancing at the locked storage units along the walls. He could turn my whole face into boneless mush with some of the virals he probably had in there.

He smiled; he enjoyed keeping people off-balance. "Mez Jardan has told you everything she considers important—" Heavy on the sarcasm. No wonder she hated him. "Now I'm going to give you what you really need. You can use a standard access—?"

"Sure," I said, as if I'd been doing it all my life.

He passed a programmed headset across the table. He had everything ready and waiting, every step planned. I took the headset, carefully. They always looked like a twitch would crush them, even though you could wad one up and keep it in your pocket for days. I dropped the net over my hair, waited a second while I cleared my thoughts out. Then I pressed the trodes to my forehead, and waited for the hard rush of image to hit me. I'd had some trouble learning to use one, because my mind wanted to treat the information feed like an invasion. But once I'd learned to access it was like being a sponge. I'd spent most of a standard year submerged, doing nothing but sucking up facts.

This time there was a megadose of data about the rise of the combines and the Federation Transport Authority. Most of it repeated what I already knew about the bad blood between them, stretching back over centuries to Old Earth days. The FTA's control of telhassium, and with it, of shipping and communications, meant that they butted heads with the transport networks every time they put an embargo on some government they wanted to toe their line better. It cost Centauri Transport every time the FTA wanted to make some other combine pay. Centauri hated their guts. They were the Big Enemy, to Centauri.

But Centauri Transport had other problems, and the flow began to change color, getting more personal. Now it was intercombine warfare, shifting loyalties and alliances. Focus on Triple Gee, Centauri's prime competitor, always looking for a way to give them grief. Anything it could get away with: goods delayed until the transport contract was invalid; an explosion in a fitting yard; a trade ambassador who never arrived to negotiate a deal, who never arrived anywhere again. Images of derelict vessels with breached hulls, bloated bodies drifting; of what a vial of biotoxins did to a shipment of transplant organs—and the ship's crew. The usual kind of thing.

Focus on Lady Elnear, her work for the FTA, work that Centauri didn't like much, that a lot of combines didn't like even more. She had a rival for the opening on the Security Council, one with heavy combine support. A lot of networks would do anything to plug him into that slot in her place. Anything they could get away with. One murder was nothing. . . .

The whole transfer took less than a minute: Centauri's self-serving picture puzzle of who would want to kill Lady Elnear, in about a hundred tiny bits. It was going to take my brain a day or so to put them together so that I understood the details completely . . . but already I had the feeling there were pieces missing. I didn't ask about them—not yet.

I took off the headset, and started to lay it down.

"Keep it," Braedee said. "Replay it as often as you need to, until you know everything on it."

"I already do," I said. Most people couldn't retain that much data that fast; they'd need to replay it over and over as it settled in.

"You really remember everything?" he asked. There was curiosity as much as challenge in it. "That easily?"

It was my turn to smile, for once.

He took the headset, and didn't ask again. "You'll find more acceptable clothing in your cabin. Put it on when you get back there. And use this on your hair—" He tossed a tube of something at me. "Give it some shape. Nobody wears their hair like that."

I glanced at my reflection again, and back at him. If he had any hair at all, I couldn't tell. I raised my eyebrows.

"It's my business to know what's expected. You'll have enough trouble not violating sensibilities every time you open your mouth. Try to keep it shut."

I picked up the tube and pushed to my feet.

"Not yet," he said, waiting just long enough to make me feel awkward. He held up a thin strip of transparent plastic, covered with maybe a dozen colored dots. "We aren't finished yet. About these. . . ." The drugs.

I sat back down, suddenly feeling lightheaded. One hand caught hold of the other, squeezed it too tight, like lost children under the table's edge. Those very expensive little skin patches would give me back the Gift . . . make me whole again. Let me touch another mind, warm myself at its fire without the cost, the sickening echoes of somebody else's deathpain that blinded me every time I tried to make contact—that made me stay out in the cold and the darkness, always remembering. . . . Except the pain would still be there. Just numbed. Nothing was really free.

I was half Hydran, and I'd killed a man. If I'd been all Hydran it would have killed me too; the psychological feedback mechanism was built into Hydran brain circuitry along with the psionic abilities that made it necessary. If you could kill with a thought, there had to be something to stop you. Humans didn't have the psionic ability, or the safeguards either. That was why the Hydrans hadn't stood a chance against them. I was half human, with half the ability of a real Hydran, and half the safeguards. The feedback hadn't killed me, but it had crippled me real bad. Time was the only thing that could heal me: fresh bandages of clean memory, safe experiences grafted on like layers of new skin. There hadn't been enough of either yet.

With the right drugs acting on exactly the right areas in my brain, I could use my telepathy and not hear warning bells. But it was like I'd told Braedee: sooner or later I'd start to pay for it, doing more damage, until maybe it crippled me for good. But what kind of choice did I have? I needed the money.

And I needed to feel that fire. I felt a flush start to crawl up my face, saliva filling my mouth, my palms sweating.

"You have all the physiological responses of an addict," Braedee said. "Does it really mean that much to you?"

"Deadhead," I whispered, "you can't imagine." I reached out for the sheet of patches.

He held it back. "What about the side effects you mentioned— 'like walking on broken legs,' you said."

"That doesn't matter. I'll worry about it later. . . . I'll do whatever you want. Just give me the drugs." I stretched out my hand.

"When we arrive," he said, beginning to frown.

"*Now*. I need some time to work on it, get my control back. . . . Come on." My hand fisted.

He hesitated, staring at me, reading responses. Doubt, calculation, mockery—all of them could have been on his face, or none. I couldn't read him. Finally he put the sheet of patches down where I could reach it. I snatched it up, staring at it.

"Keep them out of sight—especially when you're using. They last for one standard Earth day. I'll have more, when you need them."

I nodded, not really listening.

"If you need targets, use Jardan and my aides. Don't tell them." He hesitated. "If you ever try to read me, I'll know it. And I'll kill you."

I looked up, then. I got to my feet again without saying anything, and left the lab. Before I'd gotten halfway back along the hall, there was a patch behind my ear.

THREE

THERE WAS SOMETHING about coming to Earth . . . it was coming home. It didn't matter that Earth had stopped being the center of the Federation centuries ago, that it was a backwater stagnant world, a living museum; that the only reason the Federation Assembly still met here was tradition. It didn't make any difference that Ardattee, where I'd spent my whole life, was the Hub and the Heart now, where everything that really mattered happened first. . . . Or that I was too Hydran to feel really human, and too human to ever really be Hydran. It went deeper than that, below the scars and the memories and time itself, catching me by surprise right in the gut.

It kept me silent and wide-eyed as we left the Centauri Transport field complex. The entire planet had been a Federal Trade District for a couple of centuries, under the direct control of the FTA; it was peppered with starports because of the tourists. But most of the heavy shipping and distribution activity still centered on a place called N'yuk, and so the major transport combines had been granted footholds there. The Federation Assembly met in N'yuk, on neutral ground, inside a sprawling plex that also held the FTA's Security Council and head-quartered all its activities. I'd spent five carefully monitored minutes of access time on Braedee's ship studying up on it.

N'yuk was on the coast of a major continent, just like Quarro, where I'd grown up, but it was centered on a handful of islands instead of a peninsula. The prime starport, and the Centauri complex, took up the largest island, Longeye. Triple Gee was based on another island called Stat. Combine embassies sprouted on the mainland like crystal growths, fantasy fortresses, for kilometers along what had once been one of the most polluted stretches on the face of the planet. Like everything else, the pollution was still there, just different. It was data pollution, now.

Braedee put me into a mod with Jardan and sent us on to the family estates, somewhere inland. "I'll be in touch," was all he said before he let me go and slipped like a fish back into his own world. And then I was alone with Jardan, and my thoughts. She didn't say anything for a long time, gazing out at the red/gold/green world flowing by below us. Somehow I'd expected it to be blue, because blue was what it was on the Federation Seal, the logo all the FTA's Corpses had worn back in Quarro's Oldcity. In the distance behind us the ocean reflected the sky, as blue as I'd always imagined, but below us the land looked like it was on fire.

Jardan wasn't impressed. Her mind was far ahead of us, already trying to deal with the hundred different scenarios of disaster and humiliation she was sure she was bringing back with her. Earth was just something you stood on, to her. . . .

I made myself stop reading her with an effort. While one part of my mind was staring slack-jawed out the window at the scenery, another separate part was always tracking her, gathering in the random images that floated on the surface of her thoughts . . . feeding on her reality. The world around me was alive again; the solid human flesh, hers and everyone else's, that had been invisible to my mind for the last three years was suddenly there again—breathing, thinking, feeling.

It was hard to remember now that for most of my life I hadn't used my Gift, hadn't even known I was a telepath. My mother was Hydran. When I was barely old enough to know what was happening, somebody had murdered her in an Oldcity alley. I'd felt her die, and survived it, but it had burned out my psi. After that I'd been alone for years, living like a deadhead, without even the memory that once I'd had someone who cared about me. I'd spent most of my time drugged into oblivion, hiding from the life I'd lost, and the living death I'd ended up with instead. Then the FTA had come along looking for psions and jerked me out of the gutter. Dr. Ardan Siebeling had put my mind back together and taught me how to use it. And Jule taMing had taught me why it mattered. And then the FTA had used us for pawns in a power game, and I'd killed a man, and died all over again. Only this time I remembered what I'd lost.

Now I had it back again. And knowing I couldn't keep it only made having it that much sweeter. I wanted to touch Jardan with my mind: Share, give . . . let her know the mystery she was blind to. Make her feel what I felt when I looked out the window at this world—the emotion too deep to put into words that didn't sound stupid. All words turned stupid and clumsy when you could share someone else's mind, and simply *know*. . . .

She looked up at me suddenly, her dark eyes sharp with *guilt/anger/suspicion*. "Are you reading my mind?"

"What? No—" I lied, picking up the red heat of her resentment without even trying. Wondering if I'd really slipped that much. But I realized then that I hadn't let her feel it, hadn't let my control slip—it was only her own deadhead's fear suddenly catching fire, afraid I was hearing what she thought of me.

"Braedee said he gave you drugs, so you could—"

"I'm not using them yet," I said, as calmly as I could. If I told her the truth I knew she'd panic, and we were alone way the hell up here in the air. God only knew what she'd try.

She glared at me, but I saw/felt her easing up, relaxing a little.

"Don't worry. I won't read everything you think anyway. I have to really concentrate on it. And I'm not that good." It was true. I wasn't much good. Not like I used to be . . . and it wasn't just that I was out of practice: the stuff Braedee had given me wasn't much good either. There were drugs on one of those customized dreamdots to block the chemical reactions I called pain and terror and grief that my memory triggered every time I used my Gift; and there were drugs to deaden the traumatized response centers that short-circuited my psi every time I even tried to get that far. But I already knew that if I pushed too hard, I still hit a wall. Even with two patches. They weren't strong enough. Braedee didn't want me as good as I could be; that made me too dangerous. If that was how it was going to be, I didn't see why he wanted me at all. Maybe fear just made him stupid, like most people.

I'd tried his mind, in spite of his warning—but carefully. He was burglarproofed, all right, for all kinds of electromagnetic snooping. Even psi energy might trip something. Maybe not; but I wasn't curious enough about him to get myself killed finding out. I looked out the window again. "I never thought I'd see Earth. I didn't think it would be like this."

"What were you expecting?" she asked, after a long minute. Her voice was almost pleasant with relief.

"Blue . . ." I stared at the lavender-blue mountains rising up ahead, looked down again at the trees. "Not all these colors."

"A world isn't all one kind of thing, you know."

I looked back at her. "I guess not," I said, thinking of Ardattee—of Oldcity, and Quarro. Mine had been.

Her face hardened over again as she met my eyes. She broke my gaze. Her glance flicked over the new me, dressed in a high-collared shirt, a loose, belted green jacket and pants. They were plain but expensive, and they fit like they'd been made just for me. Maybe they had. There was a Centauri logo on my sleeve: branded. "Why is your hair like that?" she said.

I almost reached up. "Braedee told me to fix it." I'd used the tube of gel he'd given me on it, making the curls stand up in spikes. It was something I remembered was going around Oldcity just before I left.

She sighed, more like a hiss, and murmured, "Scum." I settled deeper into my seat and didn't try to find out which of us she meant. She didn't say anything more, and neither did I.

It wasn't much more than half an hour from the time we left the Centauri fields until the mod began to lose altitude again. That meant we'd probably come three hundred klicks or so. I'd been surprised at how much open space there was, this close to the urban corridor that hugged the eastern coastline. I'd seen a handful of lone houses, and towns that didn't look anything like the few combine claves I'd seen other places. But then, Earth wasn't like other places, and the combines didn't run it. It was hard to believe that nobody wanted to live here. But most people went where the money was. Only people who already had money could survive on a world like this.

The mod drifted down into the arms of a steep-walled valley. If it was autumn up on the mountainsides, it was still summer in the valley's bottom; it looked like it was carpeted in green velvet. I could see estate houses lying along the silver road of the river that ran the length of it, each one larger and more expensive than the last. "Which one is the taMings'?" I asked, finally breaking the silence.

"All of them," she said. "The entire valley is their private estate."

I shook my head. "Is it big enough?"

"They have many others—here on Earth, on Ardattee, all through their network." She didn't even bother to glance up. Her voice was dull; her hand rose to touch the logo at her throat that wasn't Centauri's.

I grunted.

The mod landed softly in the courtyard that had been widening below us. The yard lay behind a building that looked like it had grown up out of the soil, part of the overgrown mass of trees and shrubs that surrounded it. It was all stone and wood. Small windows, their glass crosshatched into half a dozen tiny panes, watched us silently as we got out and stood together on the cracked, ancient flagstones. The long shadows of late afternoon lay across the yard, but the air was sweet and warm, without the chill I'd been expecting. Here the trees were still a fresh green; flowering vines climbed trellises and spilled over a high stone wall. A stooped old man in a baggy coat was patiently and almost soundlessly trimming a hedge with a hand-guided lightstick. He glanced up at us half-curiously, and went back to his work as Jardan nodded at him. For a moment the clenched-fist way she'd held herself ever since I'd first seen her eased. She'd come home, at last, standing in this yard.

"This place looks like it's been here forever," I said.

"For five hundred and eighteen years." She answered without thinking about it. Then she looked at me, and the fist clenched again. "This is Lady Elnear's private residence when she is on Earth, which is most of the time these days. Each family member maintains his or her own estate house, as they choose. I live here too; so will you."

With a click and a hum the mod lifted again behind us, going off obediently to some outbuilding, where it wouldn't spoil anybody's illusions. You could almost believe it was five hundred years ago, pre-space, another age. There was no trace of any security anywhere, although I knew that on the way in the mod must have cleared half a hundred snoopscans that were backed by measures which would have taken us out if we'd failed any of them. The more money and privacy you wanted, the harder a shell you needed. Some things probably hadn't changed in a lot longer than five hundred years.

Jardan started toward the house entrance, up the wide stone steps that led onto a vine-walled porch. I shouldered the bag with the few things Braedee had forced me to take, and followed her.

It was dark inside. The pupils of my eyes didn't work as well as they used to. But they worked well enough; after a minute my panic eased. I followed her down a hallway that smelled like oiled wood, up more creaking stairs, along another hall. The house was larger than I'd thought. We stopped in front of a closed door, and she glanced at me. I stood there, waiting, but the door didn't open. She pushed me aside and opened it by hand, looking at me as if I was stupid for

expecting it to open itself, like every other door I'd ever seen that
wasn't in a slum. "This will be your room."

I looked past her through the doorway. A bedroom . . . I could
see the bed. The bed, inside its forest of carven wood, was large
enough to sleep four, easy. The room itself seemed to go on forever, filled with bureaus, tables, chairs, and things I couldn't name.
Only the desk/terminal in the window alcove didn't look like it had
been there as long as the house had. The rug was dark and dense
under my boots as I moved across it, and patterned like a kaleidoscope with jewel-bright flowers. The ceiling was at least three
meters high. I put my bag down on the bed; the bed jiggled, full of
jelly. I sat down beside my bag on the smooth, cool surface of the
covers, suddenly feeling more than a little lost. Jardan was still in
the doorway. I forced a smile. "Well . . . it's cramped, but I can
stand it."

She didn't react; no sense of humor at all. She touched an inset
in the wall beside the door. "If you need anything, this gives access
to the housekeeping programs. There is also a small human service
staff."

I nodded.

"Any questions?"

I shook my head.

"Perhaps you'd like to rest—"

"No." I stood up. "Let's get it over with."

Her face pinched. "All right then . . . You may come with me
to meet the Lady."

Her doubts were screaming silently at me. They weren't any
louder than my own as I followed her out of the room; but anything
was better than staying behind alone.

Lady Elnear was sitting by herself on a sun porch. The light
streamed in through the tall windows around her, golden and green.
She was painting a picture on a lightbox: the view from the window,
half-hidden in vines. It wasn't very good. And it wasn't what I'd
expected. . . . I wondered what I had been expecting.

She turned as she heard us enter. I saw the sad, sagging face I'd
seen in the holo, the awkward body, the plain clothes. And then she
smiled, as she saw Jardan—and suddenly she was another person. She
had the most beautiful smile I'd ever seen. Like the sun, it made you
blind to everything else. "Philipa, you're back." And then she saw
me. The smile disappeared. "And this is . . . the young man. The
one Braedee sent to watch me. Jule's friend." Even her voice had an

odd quality: almost quavering, musical and uncertain all at once. It warmed just a little as she said Jule's name. She was staring at me, trying not to. "The telepath."

Because she was looking at me, I nodded. Jardan gave me a sharp poke in the side. "Yes, ma'am," I said. "Lady. I'm Cat."

"Cat—?" She raised her eyebrows, waiting for the rest of it.

"Just 'Cat.' " I shrugged, glancing at Jardan. "Ma'am."

"Oh." She smiled, but it was false this time. She knew she should offer me her hand, a peace gesture; but she couldn't quite make herself do it. Like maybe I'd give off sparks when she touched me; like being a psion might be contagious.

I put out my hand: not a peace offering. More like a dare.

She took it. Her hand was strong and warm. "I've never met a . . . Hydran before." But she had to say that.

"Half-Hydran," I said, letting go. "Half human . . ." Most people had never met a halfbreed either; because most humans would rather have a brainwipe than a cat-eyed freak for a son. Once humans had been glad to know that they weren't alone in the universe. That time was long past, now.

Her colorless cheeks reddened a little. "Please forgive me if I seem . . . awkward, and self-conscious. It isn't personal. It's just that being in the presence of a telepath is not something that I'm used to. It will take a little time. . . ." She stepped back, her hands helpless at her sides.

A lifetime probably wouldn't be enough. I only shrugged again, trying to shake loose the invisible weight that pressed down harder and harder on my shoulders.

Jardan moved away from me to Elnear's side. She whispered something I couldn't hear: she was telling Elnear that I was a cripple without drugs; that I couldn't read them at all right now.

"Yes I can," I said. "I lied to you."

Her head snapped up, her eyes cold with fury.

Elnear put a hand on her arm, gently but firmly. "Temper, Philipa," she murmured. She looked at me as if she expected an explanation.

"Centauri hired me to help protect you. Jardan's right—I can't do you any good unless I use the drugs. I figured the sooner I started doing my job, the better. If you can't handle that, it's your problem," I said, looking at both of them. "But if somebody was trying to kill me, I'd damn sure be glad of anything that made it harder to do. Ma'am." Might as well be the tough guy. It was better than being the freak.

Elnear nodded, but their faces didn't change much. Elnear led Jardan past me. Her hand was still on Jardan's arm, as if she didn't trust us that close to each other. "Come, Philipa, it's nearly dinner time. I have to dress. They've asked me to join the family at the Crystal Palace, and I can hardly refuse again. Will you keep me company?" They went on out of the room together, talking softly, as if I wasn't even there.

I stood where they'd left me. I watched them get smaller and smaller as they went down the hallway, leaving me there without a word, not even looking back. Only I was the one getting smaller and smaller, being swallowed up in the suffocating emptiness of the silent house; so that by the time they came back again, I would have disappeared. . . .

(I didn't ask for this either!)

They spun around together as my sending caught them from behind; gaped at me, with their hands pressed to their heads. For a minute, neither of them moved. Then Lady Elnear started back down the hall toward me. Jardan caught at her hand, but Elnear shook her off and kept coming. When she reached the doorway she stopped again. Her baggy sleeve slid down her arm as she caught at the white-painted wood for support. She stood there, still staring, her free hand still pressed to her head. "Come with us," she said, finally. "Of course you should come with us to dinner. You should meet the family. You are my new aide. . . ."

It took me a second to believe I'd heard it; another to make myself move. When I reached her side, she was as surprised as I was. We began to walk together. Up ahead of us the hall was empty.

"What are the terms under which Braedee hired you?" she asked, as if she hadn't even noticed that Jardan was gone. I told her. "I'd have the contracts run through a legal advisory program, before you agree to anything, if I were you," she said, her face expressionless. "One can't be too careful."

"I will." I nodded. "I know." And smiled.

She smiled too, just a little, looking straight ahead.

FOUR

THERE REALLY WAS a Crystal Palace. It looked like something carved from ice, lit up from the inside, and it stretched out along the darkening riverbank, admiring its reflection. Earth's sun had slipped down behind the western mountain, and the valley was blue with evening by the time we stood on the palace steps. It reminded me a little of the combine centers in Quarro, but it was built of glass and iron, had to be at least as old as the house where Elnear lived. She'd told me it had been transported to this valley from somewhere else on Earth, like most of the buildings here . . . anything that caught a taMing's fancy down through the centuries, and had a price. Some people collected antiques; the taMings lived in them. Looking up as we went in through layers of splintered light, I felt my senses go into overload. This was a private home. . . . This was a dream; nobody lived like this.

I followed a few steps behind Lady Elnear, not because Jardan had told me those were the rules but because I didn't know what the hell else to do except follow somebody. I felt like I was walking through a minefield. Elnear was dressed in a long, loose sack of a tunic over leggings, wearing ropes and ropes of jeweled necklaces. She didn't look elegant, but at least she looked rich. Jardan walked beside her; I knew it had taken a good half hour for Elnear to get her to come out of her room after I'd mindspoken them. Elnear hadn't mentioned what I'd done, or even warned me not to do it again. She treated me exactly like a new assistant, explaining, suggesting, pointing things out as we rode up the valley. She didn't do it because she liked me; she did it because she disliked unpleasantness. She was good at keeping the things she felt off of her face. It was all part of the games they played in her world. She had no choice, and so she pretended I was normal. Considering all the choice I had, I was grateful she was a good player.

The interior of the Crystal Palace had been one huge open space, once; I wondered what it had been used for then. The taMings had broken it up into rooms and levels, like a glass beehive. The walls, the ceilings, the floors were transparent, but polarized, so they could be made opaque in changing patterns.

"This is the original family residence that Estevan taMing had brought here after he returned to Earth. He started Centauri Transport and made his fortune out in the Centauri system." Elnear was still giving me the guided tour, reading the questions in my eyes. "My brother-in-law . . . Jule's father lives here now. After so many generations in one home, sometimes you get tired of seeing the same four walls." She glanced away; you could see the river, through half a dozen perfectly clear panels.

"Why not just move?" I asked, and felt like a fool as soon as I'd said it.

"Tradition," she said softly. "They are a very stubborn family. They don't like to let things go."

I didn't say anything, thinking about Jule. We were closing now with the hot cluster of minds that I'd picked up as we entered. Elnear had told me there'd be more taMings than usual tonight, because Centauri was having its quarterly board meeting right now. The floating butler that had led us through this maze of mirrors disappeared suddenly through the doorway in a wall opaqued to a pearl-gray.

The butler chimed as we entered the room, and then began to drift away. "Thank you," Elnear said, even though it was nothing but a machine. There were twenty or thirty people there already. Heads began to turn as the three of us stopped in the doorway. I felt Elnear clench up inside, like someone about to dive into cold water.

"Auntie! Auntie!" A shrill child's voice cut like a drill through the polite mumble of adult voices talking treaties and voting and forced merger. A little girl with long black hair pushed through the legs of the crowd and came bolting across the room. She collided with Elnear like a heat-seeking projectile, and hung on her tunic skirt, squealing with delight.

"Talitha." Elnear smiled, the smile that could change everything, stroking the dark hair as the little girl beamed up at her. "How's my favorite girl?"

"I have new shoes," Talitha said. "See?" She stuck out her foot, which was covered with something that looked like a large, hairy bug wearing a red hat.

"Lovely," Elnear said. "Just the thing! Show them to Philipa."

Talitha hopped around her, one foot still up in the air, until she saw me. She froze, staring, then buried her face in Elnear's tunic. One clear gray eye showed again after a minute, and then the other. "Talitha. This is my new aide." Elnear patted her shoulder. "His name is Cat."

She looked up at me from under her shining black bangs. "I have two cats," she said. "Their names are Blunder and Calamity. I'm four." She held up the right number of fingers.

"Nice names," I said. Suddenly I was remembering Jule again, seeing her face in Talitha's, just the way she must have looked when she was small. She'd probably never even seen Talitha. "You remind me of your cousin Jule."

A frown wrinkled up her nose. "We don't talk about Jule," she whispered, and pressed her finger against her mouth. "She's bad."

I looked at Elnear.

"No, treasure, she isn't bad," Elnear said gently, not looking at me. "She was just . . . unhappy. But now she's better."

"Daric says she's bad—"

"Talitha!" This time it was a boy's voice calling. I glanced up and saw him coming toward us. He looked about eleven, with the same shining black hair and gray, upslanting eyes. "Oh, hi, Auntie." He stopped next to her, kissed her cheek as she hugged him with her free arm. "Mother said you weren't coming tonight. I was so bored I thought I was falling into a black hole. Can we sleep at your house? I hate it here." His voice turned sullen as he looked over his shoulder at someone.

"We'll see," Elnear said. "I'll ask your mother." He grinned again, abruptly. She turned him to face me. "This is Cat. Say hello."

"Really?" He stared me up and down, his eyes wide. "That's your *name?* Wow, your hair is terminal!"

"My thought exactly," Jardan murmured.

"Will you show me how to do mine? How old are you? Are you Auntie's lover?"

"Jiro—!" Elnear's hand flew up like it wanted to clamp over his mouth; fluttered in the air, dropped to her side again. "Cat is my new aide."

"Oh well." He shrugged. "You have to fix my hair," he said, looking at me, "you promised. Come on, Talitha. Let's find Mother. You want to stay at Auntie's, don't you—?" He hauled his sister away, squawking.

"You should have boxed his ears," Jardan said, when he was safely out of range.

Elnear smoothed her skirts. "Well. It's not easy to be young here. Or old. . . ." She glanced at me, finally, almost sheepishly. "You've just met the new generation of taMing empire-builders. You may as well meet the rest."

I followed her on into the shifting dance of the crowd, into the bodies in orbit around the long table covered with food and drinks. Too many of them, too much alike. Parents and children, aunts and uncles, nephews and nieces, at least six generations of them—but none of them, even the oldest, looked any older than Elnear. Even the ones who didn't look like taMings were all too beautiful, and they all wore perfect clothes and jewels that made my head swim, and murmured things I didn't understand and thought things I didn't want to hear. . . .

And all of them were *alive,* too real, thinking, feeling . . . not just around me any more but inside me, *angry mocking tense bored smug afraid.* I'd forgotten what it was like to be open all the time; forgotten how to really control it. It was like being thrown headfirst into a mob after three years in solitary. My nerves were closing in on burnout fast.

I reached up when no one was watching and picked off the patch behind my ear, dropping it on the floor. Then all I could do was hang on until the drugged nerve centers half asleep in my mind woke up again: until the black ache that was pain without a name came crawling back; until my crippled psi response went fetal, smothering the fire of too many other minds inside me. . . . I went on, trailing Elnear through more meaningless head-on collisions like a dazed deafmute. No one seemed to notice, or care, not even her. She was only using me as a crutch; I was something to say, to people she had nothing to say to.

Until we came face to face with still another taMing, a handsome man in a silver-threaded evening coat, wearing a ruby button as big as an eye. He looked like he was in his mid-thirties, but he couldn't be: he was Jule's father.

"Gentleman Charon taMing, Cat," she said. "This is my new aide—"

"Yes," Jule's father said. I looked back at him, surprised. "I already know about him." He did know: he knew what I really was. *Jule's freak.* He was the head of Centauri's board; the one who'd had me hired.

"Just do as you're told, and don't do anything else, and you'll get along fine, boy," he said, with a smile that never touched the words.

I looked away, my hands clenching over the loose cuffs of my jacket. Somehow, somewhere, there had to be a way out of this place. . . .

"You understand me—?" When I didn't answer something brushed my shoulder, just hard enough to seem casual. His hand. But it wasn't a hand; it only looked like one, wrapped in a skin glove. It was almost pure augmentation, and he didn't just use it to direct-access. I jerked as the pressure of his grip hurt me without seeming to.

"Yes. Sir." I had a hard time getting it out. I rubbed my shoulder. "You're just like she described you. Sir."

"Who?" His glance darted at Elnear.

"Jule."

Eyes on me again. This time I didn't look down. His face darkened. But then he turned and walked away without saying anything more.

"Don't try those games with him," Jardan said to me. "You'll lose."

"What games?" I asked, because I hadn't been playing one.

"Don't try them on me, either," she snapped. Elnear only looked at me, her mind telling me something I didn't want to hear.

I turned around, bumping into the table heaped with strange food, spilling a crystal glass full of wine on my pants. I swore, and somebody frowned, and somebody else laughed. I tried to pretend it hadn't happened, wasn't happening, that I really wanted something to eat. I'd never seen so much food in my life, and none of it was anything I recognized.

I reached out for something, blindly. Behind me I heard Jardan mutter, "Pig." And the table might as well have been piled with garbage; suddenly the sight and smell of everything on it made me sick. I backed away again. At least the other guests looked like they were losing interest in eating. I told myself it would be over soon—

A butler chimed again, somewhere across the room. "At last!" Elnear murmured, as if it meant something she'd actually been looking forward to. "Dinner."

I opened my mouth; closed it again, as the crowd sucked us away.

Elnear looked at me, curious. "You look like you expect to be the main course," she whispered. "Cheer up! The food is actually quite good."

I grimaced, hoping it looked like a smile.

"Auntie—!" Jiro and Talitha were back, dragging a tall black-haired woman after them.

Jule. I almost said it out loud; stopped myself. It wasn't Jule's mind when I found it; not even her face, when I saw it clearly. This woman was more beautiful; only hers was a soft, spoiled kind of beauty, not the strong clean lines of Jule's face and body. She looked like she'd never even thought about the kind of pain Jule had always known. But still the resemblance was so strong it made my throat tighten.

"Mother says we can stay with you!" Jiro was shouting triumphantly. "It's all set!"

Charon taMing came drifting up behind them, his eyes on the woman's back, a half frown pulling his lips down.

The woman made a quick hidden gesture with her hands, asking Elnear a question. Oldcity had its handcodes too, but this wasn't one of them, and I couldn't read it.

Elnear smiled at the children, half doting, half amused. "Of course," she murmured to the woman. "You know you're always welcome, Lazuli."

"This is my mother," Talitha said, looking at me suddenly, hanging on Lazuli's arm.

Still staring at her mother, I managed to nod.

"We're going to have a baby brother!" Talitha sang. "He's going to look just like me."

I glanced at Lazuli's body without even thinking. She was wearing a clinging bodywrap that glowed like moonstones, and she sure as hell didn't look like she was expecting a baby any time soon.

Her glance followed mine downward. She smiled. "It's in vitro. No one bothers with *that* any more. . . ."

I looked away again, in a hurry. Charon taMing's eyes were on me, his frown deepening. I glanced away from him, too, not knowing whether it was even safe to look at anybody.

"I mean pregnancy, of course." Lazuli laughed, like music, and I couldn't help turning back to her.

"Not sex," Jiro said helpfully. "Mother likes sex. Do you?"

"Jiro!" she murmured, going pale when I expected to see her blush. "What am I going to do with you—?"

"Get him a girlfriend," I muttered, and Jardan jerked me away from them like I had a disease.

As I turned, I saw Charon catch hold of the boy's arm with that hand, and squeeze it hard. Jiro bit his lip, but he didn't make any sound. I looked away again.

Someone was watching us, his mouth curved up in a half-smile. Jule's brother, Daric. He'd just come in. In a crowd of rich-colored party clothes, he was the only one still wearing basic business drab. There was somebody with him, a woman—his woman, from the way he held onto her. My eyes stopped dead in their tracks when they got to her. If the way he was dressed made everyone else in the room look like tomorrow, she made them look like yesterday.

She was an exotic: she'd had things done to her body that were meant to make people look at her and see something new. Her skin was silver, gleaming in the light. Her hair was a silver-white shockwave cresting over her copper-colored eyes, spilling down her back. Even her fingernails were silver. She was wearing a holo, the abstract forms and colors flowing around her, always almost letting you see too much flesh but never doing it. . . . She moved with a kind of easy laughter playing around her like the colors, as if upstaging everyone in the room, making them murmur about her, blush, swear, gossip in hand-sign, was exactly what she wanted out of life. I wondered what she was doing here, with somebody who looked like him.

"Jeezu, ain't that a piece and a half. . . ." I said, and then realized I'd said it out loud as Lady Elnear turned back and gave me a look. I felt the tension-coil inside me wind one twist tighter; realizing suddenly that I couldn't afford to stop thinking about anything I did or even said around these people, not for one second.

"Her name is Argentyne," Elnear murmured, not having to ask what I meant. "Daric's . . . companion. She's an entertainer—a symb-player, I believe." Even in her voice there was more fascination than disapproval.

I pulled my eyes away from Argentyne, looked at Daric again. He was still watching us back, measuring our reactions with that smile on his face. He raised his eyebrows as he looked at me. I looked down, and away.

Before I had the chance to ask any dumb questions they were gone, and the table was in front of me. I sat down. Jardan flanked me on my left, Elnear on my right. There was already food steaming under a clear dome on the plate, and what looked like bread and fruit and tofu on smaller plates, like planets circling a sun. I reached out, toward something familiar.

"Don't touch that!" Jardan hissed.

I pulled my hand back. No one else was eating. They were all looking toward the head of the table, where Gentleman Teodor, the oldest active board member, was sitting. He didn't look more than fifty; he was four times that old. Watching the way he moved, the slowness, you could tell. They could set back the body's cellular clocks, but they couldn't fool time forever. Not yet, anyway. He went through some hand ritual, and everyone around me responded. Then, finally, he reached for the food, and so did everyone else.

I flipped the steam-clouded lid off my dish. I jerked back; the chair I was sitting in *skreek*ed on the floor. There was something dead on my plate. Its glazed silver eye stared up at me from a bed of different-colored lumps glistening with sauce. The sauce looked like it had rat turds in it.

"What is the matter with you?" Jardan murmured.

"It's dead." I looked at her plate. There was another dead thing on that one.

"I assume you'd prefer to eat it alive," she said, dripping venom. She picked up one of the dozen silver utensils in front of her and dug a piece of flesh out of it. She put it into her mouth and began to chew.

"You've never eaten fresh fish?" Elnear's voice made me turn back.

"Sure," I said, half frowning. This wasn't it.

"I mean freshly raised fish." She nodded at her own plate. "It tastes much better than cloned. Try it."

I looked at the fish, and the utensils laid out between my own dishes like dissecting tools. There weren't any chopsticks, so I picked up a fork.

"No," Jardan whispered. "Start from the outside." She pointed at a different fork.

I dropped the one I was holding. It clattered across my plate. I picked up another one, and dug into the fish near the tail. I ate a bite, trying not to gag.

Elnear had it right; the food was incredible. I looked up at her, wanting to tell her so, but she was already talking to someone else. I went back to my eating. When I picked up the fishhead Jardan knocked it out of my hand. I realized then that a lot of people were staring at me . . . realized that my mind had quietly gone dead while I was eating, and I hadn't noticed. Jule's brother was sitting almost across from me, still wearing that same half-smile. He was younger than Jule, which meant he couldn't be a whole lot older than I was; but somehow he looked twice his own age—or half of it. He had the same night-black hair, the same eyes . . . but if I hadn't known he was her brother, there was nothing about him that would have made me believe it.

I looked away from him, feeling my face flush again. Argentyne was next to him, and she laughed as he kissed her throat and whispered something in her ear, probably about me. She winked at me as she saw me staring at her. I looked away from her too, wishing I was dead. Trying to ignore their eyes and everyone else's, I reached out for a pitcher to refill my glass.

And then it happened. As I picked up the pitcher, something invisible took hold of it, trying to pry it out of my hands. My brain countered instinctively; my fist tightened again before a drop spilled. I pulled the pitcher toward me slowly, watching my hand every millimeter of the way. I kept my free hand tight around my glass as I refilled it, and set the pitcher back where it belonged. I raised the crystal glass to my mouth—and it happened again. The glass jerked; my hand spasmed. I almost snapped the fragile stem in half as I choked, and drops of clear red splattered onto my jacket. I gulped the wine down in three swallows, and set the glass on the table. And then I sat with my hands knotted into fists below the table edge.

Someone had used psi on me . . . someone in this room. My eyes tracked face after face along the table, but every face was the same, a mask I couldn't read. I swore under my breath. I'd thrown away that patch, figuring it was safe, that there was no one here Elnear had to worry about . . . when I should have been worrying about my own skin. These people might seem like nothing more than a bizarre family of clone-faced eccentrics, but some of the most powerful and ruthless vips in the Federation were sitting right at this table with me. They *were* Centauri Transport—and now I belonged to them. This was the peak of the pyramid that had crushed me all my life . . . and if I ever forgot it again, it could be the last mistake I ever made. Because one of them was a psion, too.

It didn't seem possible. How could a psion pass, and no one ever suspect it? Jule had been driven out of her home, driven half out of her mind, by the untrained psi she'd been born with. She'd even told me there were no others . . . that no one in the family knew why it had happened to her. But what had just happened to me wasn't my imagination, and it wasn't an accident. I'd been doing a good job of looking like a jerk without even trying. But for somebody here, that wasn't enough. They wanted the new boy completely humiliated. I wouldn't even have known it wasn't my own stupid fault . . . except that I wasn't just another deadhead. Someone with a sick sense of humor must be wondering right now why the trick hadn't worked this time. I looked at Elnear.

She glanced at me, her faded blue eyes intent. "Did you want to ask me something?"

My eyes scanned the table, flicked back to her. "Ah . . . can I have your roll? Ma'am."

She passed it to me without comment, and looked away again.

She didn't tell me there were still three courses of dinner to go.

I kept picking at my food to keep from seeming stranger than I did already. Nothing more happened. After what seemed like hours, and was, people began to leave their seats around me. As I got up from the table Jule's brother Daric was suddenly there in front of me, so close that I nearly stepped on him. I didn't, but it took an effort not to look like I was trying. Argentyne came up beside him, shimmering like a mirage.

"So this is your new aide, Elnear." He wasn't impressed. "Where did you find this one?"

"I know your sister," I said.

"Many men have known my sister. That hardly seems like the sort of experience that you'd be looking for, Elnear?" He had such a toneless voice that it took a second to realize what he'd actually said.

Before I could do anything, or Elnear had to, Jardan said, "Your father chose him. For security reasons."

"Really?" He looked at me again, still deadpan. "And what special equipment or skill qualifies you for that important duty?"

For just a second I was still thinking about kicking him in the balls. Instead, I reached out and found the nerve inside his elbow. I pressed hard. "I fight dirty," I said.

He gasped and went white. His mouth opened, but nothing came out. Argentyne looked at us with an expression I couldn't put a name to. Everybody else stopped breathing, including me, as I suddenly realized what I'd just done. I'd just hurt a taMing.

But then the color came back into Daric's face in a red rush. "Good . . ." he whispered, shaking out his hand. "That was just perfect." The look in his eyes was so strange I almost thought he meant it. He began to turn away; turned back. "You're the first interesting person Elnear has ever brought into this house." He flipped me a salute. And then he was gone again, leading Argentyne after him, with a jerky swagger that made no sense at all inside the clothes he was wearing.

I looked back at Elnear and Jardan, with my guts full of jelly.

"What in the Nine Billion Names of God do you think you're doing—" Jardan started.

Lady Elnear held up her hand. "His job," she said, sounding surprised.

And then Jiro was at her side. Lazuli trailed behind him, looking exhausted, carrying Talitha, who'd fallen asleep somewhere after the second course. We moved away through the crowd, taMings scattering and regrouping like fragments of a stellar explosion. As we walked Elnear suddenly stumbled. She would have fallen if I hadn't been following closer than I was supposed to, and reached out to catch her. She thanked me, more embarrassed than grateful; nothing important. Except that I couldn't see any reason at all for her to have stumbled like that.

When we finally reached the manor house, I went straight to my room and put on another patch. By the time it had taken, I knew that I was the only one still awake in the entire house . . . and that I probably wasn't going to sleep at all that night. My body felt like it didn't know where it was, what time it was, what year. My brain was going around like a caged rat, going back and back over everything it had seen the last day and a half, all the data Braedee had fed me, every random flicker of dream it could suck up from the surrounding rooms. And still none of it could make me forget that I was lying in the hollow silence of a room as big as a house, alone in a bed that could have slept four, staring at the darkness with a stranger's eyes . . . that I was utterly lost here, afraid to touch anything, eat anything, even say anything, because everything I knew was wrong. . . .

I pulled my knees up against my chest, pulled the covers over my head against the darkness of a world that was nothing like the darkness or the world I'd always known, and lay there trembling.

After a long time I let go of myself again; stretched out my knotted muscles, pushed back the covers. I got up and took a leak, ate some of the leftover fruit I'd stuffed into my pockets, went to the glass doors that opened onto a narrow balcony. The stars were out, their millions crowding the night sky—that dead black nothingness that was so much greater, and stronger, and more permanent than any of them.

I recognized a pattern suddenly, the constellation called Orion—recognized it in a stolen memory of Jule's. This sky looked totally unfamiliar when I matched it against my own memories. So did any night sky I ever saw, even Quarro's. Growing up in buried Oldcity, I'd never seen the stars.

As I stood there, I realized suddenly that I wasn't the only one awake in the house any more. I caught the candleflame of someone else's thoughts wandering the same night sky, invisible to my eyes but not to my mind, watching the same stars, the same black emptiness between them . . . thinking like I had that no one else ever saw them that way. I let myself weave a little deeper into the strands of unguarded thought: Doubts and longings, unnamed fears, memories of death, loss, emptiness . . . a sadness so deep that when I reached it I broke contact, because it was too painful. It was a mind I'd seen once before. One I'd never expected to hold the kind of things I'd just found there. It was Lady Elnear.

I looked down at my hands, clenched over the railing of the balcony. The fight scars on my knuckles showed silver-white in the moonlight. I remembered how even before I'd met her, I'd figured the Lady had everything anybody could want; everything I didn't have—money, power, family. But she felt lost, helpless, trapped inside the motion of things she couldn't control—surrounded by enemies and strangers. I'd never imagined that someone like her, living in a place like this, could feel that kind of helplessness . . . a helplessness as total as my own. I let go of the railing, let my hands fall back to my sides . . . touched her mind again, just enough to keep contact, not enough to intrude.

I waited until she left her window at last, drifting silently back to her bed, still thinking that she was alone. The aching awareness of her life had been made small again, bearable again, by her awareness of the night, so that she could try to sleep.

I went back to my own bed and lay down again, finally, and slept.

FIVE

ABOUT THREE SECONDS after dawn somebody came crashing into my sleep like a bolt of lightning. "Are you still *sleeping*—?" It was Jiro taMing. His voice took a sudden broken leap of about an octave in the middle of the sentence.

"Not any more." I pushed my face up out of my pillow, feeling like shit. "What do you want?"

"I want you to fix my hair like that. And that thing you did to Daric, that was really a fanged move, I want that too. Why don't you have any pajamas?"

"Jeezu." I let my head drop back into the pillow. "I'm too tired."

He jerked my arm. "You work for Centauri, you take orders from me."

I sat up, so fast that he didn't have time to move. My hand clamped around his arm, just over the elbow: "You want to know what I did to Daric—?"

His mouth fell open, and he almost fell over himself trying to pull away. I shoved him, letting him go. "Get the hell out of my room."

He scrambled backwards toward the open door, his mind a tangle of asinine awe and terror. The door slammed shut.

I lay down again, and tried to go back to sleep. But adrenaline was dumping into my veins now as I remembered where I was, and why. Finally I pushed myself up again and stumbled into the bathroom. I stood in the fresher for a long time, letting it needle my skin numb and loosen up my muscles, my brain.

I stopped to look at myself in the mirror when I stepped out. My eyes still looked like somebody else's. My hair still looked the same, standing up in soft fingers, even after I'd slept on it. I touched it; good stuff. I wondered if I'd have to shave my head to get rid of it.

I went back out into my room, still feeling a little dazed. I picked through the clothes I'd brought, hating the sight of them, the company logos and what they stood for.

"Where'd you get all those scars on your back? . . . Are you a merse? Were you in a war?"

I looked up. Jiro was in the doorway again, staring at me. "No. Yeah . . . sort of." I caught up the first shirt I could get my hands on, and jerked it over my head.

"I wish I was you," he said, dreamy eyed.

"No you don't." *Stupid little bastard.*

"Is that a tattoo—?"

"Yeah."

"Why do you have Draco's logo tattooed on your butt?"

I looked down at the blue lizard slithering up my hip, the holoed collar of feathers or flames shimmering around its head. I could never see the thing well enough to tell which it was, feathers or flames. "It's not Draco's logo."

"Yes it is, the dragon and the sunburst—"

"It's just a lizard." I saw the tube of gel Braedee had given me lying in a tangle of clothes. I picked it up and threw it at him. "Here. Put this on your hair and let it set." Hoping that would get rid of him. But instead he came on into the room. He planted himself in front of my bathroom mirror like it was his own. I finished dressing, as quickly as I could.

"Hey, this doesn't work—!" Jiro stuck his head out of the bathroom as I was starting for the door.

I stopped, looking back at him. His shoulder-length hair stood up and then flopped down again over his face, like black curtains. I bit my lip to keep from laughing. "Your hair's too long."

He pushed it up and back again, squinting. "Well, what am I supposed to do?"

I shrugged, "Cut it off," and left the room.

Everyone else was still asleep, even the servants. I went downstairs, moving as softly as I could, relieved to be alone. I wandered until I found the kitchen, which was as big as a warehouse. At least it was cleaner. I went from counter to counter, nervous but hungry, querying systems until I'd gotten what I needed from the hot and cold units. On the far side of the room there were doors opening into a small courtyard. I went outside and sat down on a wooden bench, gulping black coffee and listening to birdsong, waiting for the sun, or whatever happened next.

"I'm hungry." I felt the bright, tangled web of a child's mind behind the words; looked up as Talitha came shuffling out into the courtyard, dragging a blanket and wearing bugs on her feet.

"Ask your mother," I said, damned if I was going to be a servant for every taMing who looked at me.

"She's asleep." She stopped in front of me, pressing the blanket against her face.

"Ask your brother, he's not."

"Jiro woke me up."

I sighed. "Me too."

"He said I didn't get any dessert yesterday. . . ." Her gray eyes filled with sudden tears. "He said I didn't get any dessert because I was a bad girl, I fell asleep at the table. He ate all my desserts."

I stood up as the damp wave of her misery rolled into my brain. "Your brother's a croach. Here." Reaching into my pockets, I emptied out the candy and nuts I'd brought back from dinner last night. "I saved dessert for you last night. Eat this first," I pointed at what was left of my food.

Her eyes went wide. She scrambled up onto the bench and began to eat, still looking at me. "You're my special friend, right?"

"Right." I smiled, and touched her hair. Maybe she said that to everybody, but what the hell. I needed to hear it; it felt good. I went back into the kitchen and began to get myself some more breakfast.

Someone's surprise caught me from behind—surprise so sharp it was almost anger. I turned around and Lady Elnear was standing across the room. She wasn't expecting to see anyone, especially not me.

I felt my expression turn guilty as I saw her face, as if she'd caught me stealing food, instead of just preparing it. I forced myself to meet her eyes, to remember that I had a right to eat, at least.

"You're up very early, Mez Cat," she said. Not happy about the fact.

"So are you," I said, because I couldn't think of anything else. "Ma'am."

"I've always gotten up very early." She came slowly into the kitchen, and began to call up some tea. "I value this time alone before the day begins, before anyone else is about, to disturb me." She had her back to me, but I could feel the sharp edge of every word. "Do you always get up so early?"

"No, ma'am," I said. "I like the night. It's what I'm used to." My second breakfast slid up onto the counter in front of me. I picked it up, before I let myself look at her again. I could feel her eyes on me, questioning. "I didn't plan on getting up so early. Couldn't sleep. Guess I'm still a little timewarped. I didn't figure you'd be up this early either."

"Oh? Why not?"

Without really thinking about it, I said, "Last night, when I couldn't sleep, and you were . . ." I broke off, too late, as she suddenly knew what I meant. All the expression disappeared from her face, but her mind recoiled as if I'd seen her naked.

I set my food down again. "Maybe I'll go back to bed." Realizing with a kind of sick frustration that I'd just completely destroyed any trust that might have been starting between us yesterday. Not looking at her now, I headed for the door.

"Please be ready to go into the city with me in three hours. I'm going to the Arm today," she said, her voice resigned and cold. "I'm told you will accompany me."

"Yes, ma'am." I nodded, still without looking at her, just wanting to get out of there. As I went back along the hall I heard Talitha's voice, "Auntie look! Dessert!"

When it was time, I went back down. The Lady and Jardan were waiting together at the entrance, side by side. They looked like they were waiting for the enemy. Or for me. I felt my face settle into a frown.

A mod that was larger and more plush—and a lot more secure —than any I'd ever been in carried us back toward the coast. After a while N'yuk began to take on reality in the distance, rising above the sprawl of the surrounding urbs; a manmade mountain range of peaks and valleys, one solid block fused from the skeletons of the countless ancient corporate towers that had squatted there on the bedrock of an island between two rivers. The rivers were bridged by arcing buttresses of more structure.

The dully-gleaming mass of it swallowed us at last, down through a crevice and into its hidden nervous system. We took some kind of shuttle from the garage. It sucked us through transparent tubes toward the destination that Elnear gave it—gliding, slowing down, shifting our track; guided by some invisible master plan that shuffled the moving vehicles like someone juggling at the speed of light. I caught glimpses of storefronts, offices, restaurants. People did everything here, spent their entire lives here, all of them pulled into the gravity well of a government center a lot of people wanted to believe was as obsolete as a human's appendix. Somewhere in the middle of all this the Federation Assembly and the FTA Security Council both met, and tried to outmaneuver each other.

And somewhere else, in the real, hidden heart of city, was the brain that made it all work: the communications and data core that was one of the brightest stars in the invisible universe called the Federation Net. One perfect telhassium crystal no bigger than my thumb was able to store all the information, contain all the mindboggling manipulations of it that kept this city's systems from collapsing of their own data density. They only needed a few thousand more in order to calculate hyperspace jumps for most of the ships leaving this mainline port. Telhassium made the kind of computing power the Federation had to have cheap and easy to use . . . and as long as the FTA kept control of it, the Council would never lose its influence over how the Federation ran.

Finally we entered the government complex. The blue logo of a

slowly turning Earth, which the Federation Trade Authority had decorated with wings and claimed for its own, watched me like a shining
eye from datascreens and wallways as the shuttle car slowed for its
final stop. We exited into the velvet-covered fist of a security station.
Lady Elnear and Jardan waited patiently while my databand was dou-
blechecked, while I was bodyscanned, retina- and finger-printed,
holoed, filesearched, and registered.

The FTA didn't take any chances here; they couldn't afford to.
The vulnerability of the Council, and the massive concentration of city
around it, was enough to make a stone paranoid—and the FTA had
at least that much imagination. It was hard for me to imagine how
even a flea ever got this far without someone noticing it, somewhere
in the overlapping layers of security they must have crusting this place.
I was real glad the commendation I'd been given after the FTA had
finished with me had gone on record for the data check to spit up . . .
and that because of it my criminal record had been sealed. Now that
I had a databand I wasn't a nonperson; I was real to the Federation
Net. The only problem with not being invisible any more was that too
many people got to see you naked.

When I was clean enough to suit the security registers, and im-
printed on their system forever, they let us go back into the flow of
human traffic heading deeper into the maze. By now I was completely
lost, all over again. I didn't like the feeling. People passed us on all
sides—riding bicycles, some of them pulling buggies; in floating carts;
even on skates. We walked, because Elnear believed in exercise. I
thought about the only FTA plexes I'd ever seen the inside of: their
Corporate Security station in Oldcity, and the Contract Labor processing center where I'd started a one-way trip to hell. They both
looked like prisons. This place didn't bring back any memories; the
only thing that looked the same was the Federation Seal plastered on
everything and everyone in sight. The imitation reality around me was
as full of reflecting surfaces that turned your eyes away from the truth
as the walls of any combine's HQ.

We were passing through the fringes of the actual Assembly
nucleus. I began to notice more and more different combine colors
around us; more than I'd ever seen in one place before. But then, I'd
never been here before. Lady Elnear wore no logo at all. Jardan was
wearing the logo that wasn't Centauri's at her throat again. Finally I
asked what it was, just to break up the monotony. She glanced at me
with a kind of bleak annoyance, and said, "Why do you bother to
ask?"

I stopped where I was. "You really think all I want to do is get into your mind, or hers?" I gestured at Lady Elnear, who was walking ahead of us, talking with someone wearing an FTA insignia. I picked his name out of his thoughts, and some random bits of what he was thinking about, like Braedee had ordered me to. He'd told me to memorize everyone she talked to, and why, in case there was some clue in what happened that I wouldn't recognize. In the back of Elnear's own mind a strand of her attention was always turned toward me, making every word she said painfully self-conscious. "Don't flatter yourself."

Jardan's mouth tightened.

"I'm working *for* you—"

"You're working for Centauri."

I looked down at the logo on my jacket. "Then who the hell are you working for?"

"This is the ChemEnGen logo." I felt the heat of the defiance behind it, and remembered: Lady Elnear was a controlling stockholder, with a place on ChemEnGen's ruling board. But now Centauri controlled ChemEnGen, and Jardan's boss. And now I understood what that badge really was—a finger raised in the face of every taMing who saw her.

"That takes a lot of guts," I said, but she didn't smile. I looked away from the wall of her eyes.

Elnear stood waiting up ahead, looking back at us—listening. I wondered how much freedom she really thought she had, just because she didn't wear a logo here. *This was her real work,* Jardan had said. I rubbed the patch on my jacket as we went on.

A part of my mind was always reaching out ahead of us and behind while we walked, scanning the other minds around us. I told myself I was looking for something wrong; but I knew I was like an ex-blindman, really looking just because I could. Almost everyone I scanned was interested in seeing someone else dead, but none of them had Elnear in mind. And none of them were crazy enough even to think about trying anything here. It was hard to imagine anywhere that Elnear could be safer. But Braedee claimed that his own security had picked up someone tracking her here with a dartgun.

Eventually we reached the Drug Enforcement Arm nucleus and Elnear's office in it, deep in the FTA's sector of the plex. I looked up at the Arm's logo riding beside the FTA's above her door—the black wings of a shadow-thing reaching out and down to circle a galaxy. I wondered if that was supposed to reassure anybody. After my walk through the minds of the Federation Assembly, I felt like I'd been cleaning toilets with my brain. I let the thought tracers shrivel up and die, relieved. Two days ago I'd been ready to do anything to get back my Gift. . . . Somehow it was too easy to forget that everything had two sides.

"You're unusually subdued," Jardan said to me, as we went inside. The translucent office door began to slip shut behind us.

"I'm doing my job." I said. I followed her past a couple of curious office technicians toward Elnear's private inner office.

"Elnear!" someone called, from out in the hallway. I turned, looking back as the outer door flashed open again to let in Daric taMing. I caught a whiff of his thoughts as my mind crossed his track. I broke contact; he stank. He was part of the family. That was one mind nobody was going to force me into headfirst. I hadn't been able to scan him last night, but what I caught today matched what I'd seen then better than I would have liked. It was still hard for me to believe he was actually Jule's brother. But then, she was the one the family thought was crazy.

He pushed between me and Jardan as if we didn't exist, and went on across the room to Elnear's inner office. She stood behind the antique metal desk looking like she hoped he wasn't going to climb over it. He was violating her sanctuary, she couldn't stop him; she didn't like it. "What, Daric?"

"Vote today, Elnear. Just wanted to remind you. You will be there, of course—Centauri is counting on ChemEnGen's support, as always." He knew she wouldn't forget, knew that she'd vote their way. He just enjoyed rubbing in the salt.

"Of course," she said, and sat down, doing her best to pretend he'd already gone. "Goodbye, Daric."

"Goodbye, Elnear." He turned on his heel, all his motions still full of too much energy, the way they'd been last night. He started back through us toward the door. I moved out of his way. It was the wrong thing to do. He stopped, cocking his head at me. "Hey, new aide," he said, as if he'd just noticed me. "How's your first day on the job? Just fascinating, I'll bet."

I didn't say anything.

"Oh, come on." He folded his arms. "You can speak frankly. We're all friends."

I shrugged. "It's all right." I forgot to say "sir."

He didn't call me on it. "Only 'all right'?" he repeated, enjoying himself a lot more than I was. "Where are you from, anyway?"

"Ardattee. Quarro," I said, not meeting his eyes.

He was actually surprised. "The Hub? . . . No wonder we don't impress you. You'll have to tell me all about it—are table manners really passé there?" He was watching to see if he drew blood. It took all the control I had left, but I didn't bleed. "Well, be sure to enjoy your stay on Earth. All of human history is here for you to enjoy, stuffed and mounted . . . if my aunt ever allows you any time off for good behavior." He looked away from me, back at Elnear. "Loan him to me some evening, Elnear. My friends would kill one another to meet him. . . . Oh. Sorry. Pardon the expression." He was already moving toward the door; he was gone before anyone could ruin his fun, or his face.

I followed Jardan into the inner office. A security screen blinked on across its door. Jardan went to Elnear's side, murmuring something I didn't bother trying to hear. I sat down on the window ledge. It wasn't actually a window, but a holo that did a decent job of looking like a view of the ocean. I looked at it, sunlight winking on blue water far away. I could see why she needed one.

I looked back again at the Lady and Jardan. The air was so thick with bad feeling that it was hard to breathe. I felt like a lightning rod. I thought about all the things I wanted to say about Gentleman Daric, and tried to forget them again. Instead, I said, "What would happen if you didn't vote the way the taMings want you to . . . ma'am?" as Jardan glared at me.

Elnear sighed, looking around her for something that didn't seem to be there. "Well . . ." she said, her gaze still wandering, as if she were discussing a missing stylus, "I leave that to your imagination, Mez Cat." She meant that I could find out if I really wanted to, but she didn't feel like spelling it out just to satisfy my curiosity. She was thinking that they would sell off ChemEnGen's patents and chop its network into small separate bits, and feed the pieces one by one into the open jaws of the biosci Lack Market. . . . At least, that was how Charon had put it to her. He was the head of Centauri's ruling board, and she didn't have any reason to doubt what he said. She pushed away from the desk, her formfoam chair resettling around her as she looked up at me; there was something in her eyes that I hadn't seen there before. Suddenly I was remembering what I'd said to Braedee about blackmailers—and what he'd said to me about politics.

"Does it really matter that much to you?" I asked. "Enough to let them blackmail you?"

"Yes," she nodded, "it does." She didn't tell me why.

I glanced at Jardan. "I thought Jardan said you set up some kind of noninterference contract when you married in, Lady."

"I thought so, too." A sadness filled her that had nothing to do with any betrayals of trust. It was gone again before I could see more. "While my husband was alive, everything went well. Then after his death . . . well, you remember that I advised you to have your contracts with the taMings reviewed . . . ?"

"You mean you didn't?" I said, surprised. I got up from my seat.

"Not carefully enough, it seems. They have some of the most powerful legal advisories operating in the Federation."

I looked down. "You don't think . . . is there anybody at ChemEnGen who'd be angry enough to want you dead over that?"

Jardan stiffened. Elnear shook her head. "I'm all that stands between them and a complete loss of autonomy. I don't think so."

I nodded. "I guess everything works like that around here." I didn't expect an answer; figured I already knew it.

But she smiled faintly. "Not in this office," she said, as if somehow the FTA's symbol over her door had some kind of power to protect what she did.

"What makes you think the Arm is any better than anything else?" I waved a hand at the door and what lay outside it. "It's just what they call it—*arm*. Another way for the Security Council to use muscle on the combine vips when the Council's out to get it their way. The FTA's no better than the combines. It controls the telhassium market; it runs Contract Labor. It's all the same, just power plays. More blackmail."

"For someone who's been here less than one day, you seem to have formed some strong opinions," she said, mildly; but I felt her impatience and irritation stick me in the ribs. And as I watched her, suddenly she changed again: suddenly she wasn't a vague, empty, aging woman, but someone who belonged behind that desk. "If you are going to work for me, you had better understand how we look at things in this office." She motioned at me to sit down again. I sat.

"To begin with," she said, "let me tell you something about the society we live in. Most people believe that human beings still run it. But I think they're wrong. All these centuries we have been waiting for our machines to get too smart for us and turn us into dinosaurs. We never realized we'd already created the next step in our own evolution . . ." *The interstellar combine.* She went on, telling me her pet theories about how the Federation really operated. She claimed no single human, or even a ruling board, actually controlled the largest combines now. Instead, humans had become the combines' tools; just like the AI systems and databanks they'd developed to make the interstellar networks possible in the first place.

"You really believe that?" I said, trying not to let her hear how I really felt about the idea.

She nodded. "And I'm not alone. There are many logic-studies that conclude the same thing. No one has absolute proof—no one has ever directly communicated with a network core. But I really believe that the combines are the evolving beings of a new order; that they are the way the living universe is accommodating itself to space travel."

Human space travel. I thought about the Hydrans, the Net of psi energy they'd based their own civilization on.

"The combines are the lions and tigers of a new age," she said, "ruthless, and totally amoral." They had evolved and changed to fill the niches of the super-ecology called the Federation, and their individual styles and levels of operation were the mutations that had fitted them to their functions. Some of them had evolved toward such massive augmentation that one or two or a handful of what had been humans became an entire network. Most of them had gone the other way, using millions of separate human beings as the cells of their supersystems. The combines took care of those individual cells as well as it suited their needs—some better, some worse. But most of them expected the kind of unquestioning loyalty in return that a body would expect of its own flesh. If you betrayed them, you were dead, or as good as. And any individuals or human services that fell between the cracks of their needs were invisible, as far as they were concerned.

I glanced down at my databand. I'd been invisible for a long time; it hadn't been an easy life.

"We can't judge the combines by human standards," she said, "any more than we can expect them to treat individual human beings as if we were their equals. The FTA is the only independent system capable of interacting on an equal basis with the combines." Her eyes never left my face, even while I looked down. "Over the centuries it's taken on the job of filling those empty spaces, protecting the rights of the individual human being. The FTA maintains a safe balance— a kind of Humane Society, if you will, working for the protection of our no-longer-dominant species. And that is what we do here, and that is why I choose to work for them."

I looked up at her again. It sounded so perfectly reasoned, like a speech. . . . It was a speech, one she'd given again and again. She was good; really believable. And she really believed every word of it. Maybe it was even true, for her. But the FTA she thought she knew wasn't the one I knew. I'd survived living in the cracks; but not because of anything the FTA had ever done for me. I'd gotten the FTA's attention a few times—but what they'd done to me then had only made my life worse. "I guess I've got a lot to learn," I said, but the words were as sour as vomit in my throat.

She broke off, half-frowning. It wasn't the response she was used to getting. She looked away from me, resenting the tone of my voice, my attitude, my presence, me. "The vote is at four," she said to Jardan, looking down at her desktop again as she turned toward her access unit. "I won't review the report, since I already know what my vote will be. But I have a lot of my own work to do by then. Philipa, will you call up the Sarumo file and find out what became of that data about Triple Gee? And then I guess the usual—request, turn down, and put off. Get the correspondence processing . . . when you get to that point, come back and show Mez Cat how to do it. He might as well earn his keep." She glanced up at me again finally, lifting her eyebrows.

"Yes, ma'am," I said, almost relieved. Any kind of work at all had to be better than sitting around until my butt got numb, waiting for Braedee to tell me I was free again.

Jardan nodded, and started for the door. She stopped again as the security screen blinked off. "Will you be all right alone—like this?" She almost looked at me.

Elnear's glance followed the twitch of Jardan's head. Every time her eyes registered me a small shock ran through her, as if my face kept startling her. "I expect so," she said, a little dryly. "I'll keep him occupied somehow." She was thinking that if something sensitive came up, she'd send me out on an errand. . . .

"It won't help," I said.

"What?" She looked at me, blank-faced with surprise.

"Sending me out. You'd have to send me farther than that. If I want to know what happens here I'll know it. Look, it really doesn't matter—" I pushed on before the protest could form on her lips. "Like you said, Lady, what do I know about anything? I don't care what you do."

"Centauri does," Jardan said.

I shook my head. "All I know is that they want you to stay alive to go on doing it. All I want is my money."

Elnear sighed, and waved Jardan gone. The screen came back on as she left, shutting us in together.

"Please never do that again," Elnear said, when we were alone.

"What?"

"You know."

Listen to her thoughts, and answer them out loud. I nodded. "Sorry, Lady."

Something that was a cross between amusement and annoyance pulled at her mouth. "You know, somehow when you address me as 'Lady,' it sounds entirely different . . . rather like you were yelling at me from a street corner." She turned away again, as her phone chimed.

I waited while she talked with the shimmering face on the other end, doing something strange with her left hand on the console part of the time . . . some kind of direct neural transfer. Somehow it surprised me to realize she was augmented—but I could feel her using, her brain transferring and calling up data, storing new facts; communicating with her caller on some other, independent level even while they talked, still pretending to be only human. And these people hated psions, and called us unnatural—when they had to rip apart their bodies, rewire half their brain with custom bioware, just to get a pale imitation of what a psion was born with.

I looked away again, studying the office, staring at the clutter on her desk—an uneasy mix, like she was. A crystal vase filled with dried flowers, tape readers and strange little books, datadots inside a security seal, a handmade cup . . . old holos of Talitha and Jiro and a man who was a taMing, but not one I'd met. I realized it must be a picture of her dead husband. The access unit she was using looked like a piece of stretched black silk. Her console was totally out of my league, from what I could see of how it worked—which was nothing at all.

Across the room under a slow-moving sculpture painting there was a more normal unit, with a touchboard and trodes; probably meant for an aide, or someone like Jardan. I stood up as Elnear finished her call. "Ma'am, you mind if I use that port?" I pointed.

"What do you want to do with it?"

"You have a map of N'yuk I can access?"

She nodded, figuring that would keep me out of trouble for a while. She did something with her hand and light showed on the unit. "That one answers to 'Twinkle'," she said, and looked a little embarrassed, as if she'd never really listened to how the name sounded before.

" 'Twinkle'." I kept my face expressionless as I went to Twinkle and sat down to ask it for what I wanted. It pulled the map for me. I put on the trodes, let the data slowfeed into my memory so that I could get a clearer idea of what I was learning. It was a good map, with a lot of overlays—of the underlying substructures, of major landmarks, of where to find a place to eat, to pray, to get your teeth fixed. . . . Once it had settled in I'd be able to get around almost like a native. At least that was one kind of lost I wouldn't have to be any more.

But there was one area on the map that was still a blur when I was through . . . an area at the southern tip of the city, called the Deep End. There was a street grid, but it was incomplete, and what happened there wasn't on any reference lists. The fact that it was missing was a warning; if you went there, you were on your own. You didn't find spots like that on the map of a combine clave; but the Federal Trade Districts always had them. Free zones, safety valves, escape hatches—feeder tanks. Oldcity had been one of those. I knew what I'd find in the Deep End. I hoped I wouldn't need it.

Only about ten minutes had passed while I let my thoughts walk around inside the map grid. When I came up for air Elnear was lost in her own business, even managing to forget for ten minutes that I was in the room. I went back into the datafiles and chose a dozen other things that looked interesting or useful; mostly things that would tell me more about how a vip's aide filled up a day. I tried to get them to transfer continuously, but the best Twinkle would do was three at a time. Absorbing all the files I'd chosen took me about another twenty minutes.

Then I asked for the threedy scan, looking for something to help pass the time while my mind cooled off. Even watching threedy shows had been an education, once I'd gotten out of Oldcity. At first I'd watched the most mindless shit on the Net, all the time, the same way I'd eaten food—just because I could. But it hadn't taken me long to see that the threedy could teach me things I'd never get out of a datafile, about how people who always had enough to eat and a decent job acted around each other. I'd already learned, the hard way, how much I didn't know about that.

And coming here had given me a whole new level of ignorance and inadequacy to sink to. . . . As I thought about that my stomach began to hurt. I tried not to think about it, tried to concentrate on what

I was seeing in the air in front of me as show after show winked by. I couldn't believe the number of channels Elnear had open—all the public accesses, and five times as many pay ones with full sensory feed. Most of the subscription channels were only corporate propaganda, the combines' way of sending messages and warnings to each other without seeming to. But some of the channels were experimentals, sending incredible visions, sounds, and sensations vibrating like drug dreams through my brain.

I dropped back into public access finally, too strung out to enjoy anything that intense. Ordinary light and noise was enough. . . . "Stop," I said suddenly, freezing a talking head in the air in front of me. It was a man giving a speech; not the kind of thing I liked to watch even now unless I wanted to catch up on my sleep. But there was something different about this face—something I couldn't look away from, once I'd seen it. Something I had to see more of.

He had one of the most beautiful faces I'd ever seen. I leaned back in my seat, watching him speak, somehow forced to listen to what he was saying: ". . . And I believe that we lost something more than simply our identity as a people," he was saying, "when we left our homeworld for the stars. We lost our understanding of our uniqueness in the eyes of God. The combines have become our idea of heaven, where all our physical needs are provided for, our lives laid out for us in perfect comfort from birth until death. It has become too easy to forget that there was once a higher purpose that drove us to succeed where other beings failed—"

"Greed," I muttered, disgusted. A religion hyper, shilling for some combine, probably. Holy war. I thought I was about to change the channel, but somehow I went on listening instead; not because I liked what he was saying, but because I couldn't help liking him. It wasn't just the way he looked, but something about the way he was —the openness, the earnestness, the sincerity as he told the people accessing him to "see the humanity that bound them together, as they looked into a stranger's face . . ."

You could change the way your own face looked, and he probably had. But you couldn't buy that kind of charisma. You had to be born with it. I stared at him, fascinated, even while I felt a kind of envy twist inside me.

"Mez Cat." Jardan's voice broke in on his, making me jump. "What are you doing?" she asked, staring at the image flickering in the air in front of me.

"Nothing." I blanked the port, and shrugged.

"Sojourner Stryger," she said. "Somehow I didn't expect that he would be to your tastes."

I frowned. "Why? Is he a friend of yours?"

Her mouth pursed up. "He is the leader of the Revival Movement, and an extremely active lobbyist for humanitarian causes."

"One of those," I said. She ignored that, and told me to come with her. In the outer office she introduced me to the rest of Elnear's staff. They nodded and mumbled, looking at me with their disbelief showing. I wondered what Elnear's other aide had been like. Not like me, I guessed.

The work Jardan expected me to do was dull, but I did it. Finally Elnear left her office to go to the Assembly. Jardan and I went with her as far as the transparent-walled viewing gallery; that was as close as nonmembers ever got to the Assembly floor. The Assembly Hall looked just like it did in all the media pieces: long and high, with the ancient logo of a flaming sun circled by nine worlds, the original Federation. A lot of combines hated that logo; hated even the name of the Federation, because it suggested too much centralized control. But by now it was tradition, and they were stuck with it, just like they were stuck with the Charter that allowed the FTA to initiate its own policies, independent of them.

Tier after U-shaped tier of seats faced the curve of the Security Council's High Seat, enough to hold a thousand combine representatives. The fact that my mind was working again only heightened the reality of the Assembly members moving restlessly in the seats down below. With a bug in your ear you could actually hear what they said—the arguments, the charges and counter-charges, the options open in whichever endless resource war they were trying to settle today. Most of the data I'd accessed in Elnear's office this morning had to do with what happened here.

This vote was something strictly among the combines. The FTA's Security Council was mediating, but they weren't inputting anything . . . at least not anything we could witness. They weren't even here in the flesh. At first I wasn't sure, through the murmur of so many other minds down below. But I narrowed my focus until I was positive—they were only projections, holos, ghosts. "Why aren't they up there?" I asked Jardan.

"What are you talking about?" she said.

"The Security Council. They're holos, not the real people."

She looked at me, startled. She bit her tongue before she could ask me how I knew that; because she already knew how I knew. "For security reasons."

"Is that why they call it the Security Council?" I knew the second I asked it that I should have kept my mouth shut. *No, it wasn't.*

"No, it isn't. Spare me your sense of humor," she said, and looked away.

I looked down at the Assembly floor again. The eerie thing about it—the thing that you only realized here—was that unless you were wired for sound nothing seemed to be happening. There was nothing but silence on the chamber floor. All the debate or discussion was done subvocally, or in ways even stranger and more private. I wondered what was happening down there that never even touched us, up here in the gallery.

Jardan pointed out Elnear, sitting motionless in the middle tier, waiting to cast her predetermined vote. I wondered whether most of the 'neutral' parties down there had had their minds made up for them the way she had, by pressure from merger partners with a lot of arm. I remembered what she'd told me about the combines, and as I watched disembodied numbers begin to tally on my chair arm, the feeling inside me that something important was happening down there died. Maybe she was right—those hundreds of humans around her really were nothing but mouths, ports; the combines were tallying the outcome for them. And yet her single vote still mattered, at least to Centauri. . . . I found Daric taMing up in the first tier of seats—each tier was a little more comfortable than the last, as they got closer to the High Seat. All the combine reps had equal votes; but some were still more equal than others.

And then there was the Security Council, up there on the High Seat, independent of them all and flaunting it. The Security Council made the FTA's rules, played out its own games that were usually played against the will of some part of the Assembly. The Assembly could vote down a Security Council ruling, but it took a two-thirds majority, and with the combines always at each others' throats, it had to be a damned unpopular law to get them all united against it. The Council was the FTA's brain, and Elnear was up for one of its slots. I wondered how much more satisfying that would be than what she had now. Maybe it would just be different.

The voting was over. I stared at the numbers on the screen; blinked, realized I'd been staring at them without blinking for way too long, while my brain shuffled through the information I'd swallowed whole this morning. "Who won?" The numbers didn't mean anything, when I didn't know what they'd been voting for.

"It doesn't matter," Jardan murmured, and left her seat.

"That's cosmic," I said, and she frowned.

Elnear met us down below, and we started back through the maze of halls. Her face was longer than I'd seen it all day.

"Lady Elnear . . ." Someone called her name from behind us. I looked back, tracking through the crowd with two sets of eyes and ears. No one I knew . . . someone Elnear and Jardan did know. I watched a small, slender man coming toward us, still pushing people aside even though Elnear had stopped to wait for him. And suddenly I realized I knew him, too; he was the one I'd been watching on the threedy. Nobody else could have a face like that.

"Sojourner Stryger," Elnear said, nodding uncertainly.

"Lady Elnear." He stopped in front of us; about a dozen people materialized around him in the seconds that followed. His people. "It must be God's will that we should meet by chance this way . . ."

Chance, hell. Surprise pinched me hard. He was out of breath; he'd chased her through the crowds all the way from the Assembly Hall. I stared at him. Even in person he had the most flawless face I'd ever seen. Skin, hair, eyes—every feature so perfect that my own eyes couldn't find anything wrong with them . . . except that they were too perfect. It had to be a cosmo job; but even realizing it, my eyes kept *liking* him.

I made myself look at Elnear without listening to what he said. I felt the blow of her ordinariness hit me, breaking the spell of his face; felt the raw pain of her self-consciousness as she looked at him. She struggled past it, trying to listen and not to *look. . . .*

". . . about the upcoming debate before the media," he was saying. "I hope you will not take this in a negative way, since we'll both be speaking in support of the same viewpoint . . . but have you considered whether your principles might not be compromised? After all, if the Federation does in fact deregulate pentryptine, ChemEnGen stands to make a great deal of profit . . . they do hold the ancestral controlling patent on the entire pentatryptophine family, I believe."

Pentryptine. It was a drug he was talking about. Back in Oldcity they called it *bliss.*

Elnear blinked, moved her head. What Stryger had said wasn't the thing she'd been expecting to hear. "In fact, Sojourner, my stand is, and has always been, *against* deregulation. As you know, I will be representing the Drug Enforcement Arm in this public forum. . . ."

I wondered why she called him by his first name; until I realized it wasn't a name. It was a title, one he'd taken for himself.

He raised his perfect eyebrows as if he was surprised. But he wasn't. I kept watching him, confused, because nothing about him fit. "Well, I must have been misinformed. . . ." He tapped his forehead with his finger, looked at her almost quizzically. "But surely a person with your long dedication to individual rights can't believe that there is something wrong in allowing more widespread application of these drugs? I can cite hundreds of criminal incidents that have occurred right here in N'Yuk in the past month. . . . The pentatryptophine drugs have proved safe and harmless in suppressing overt aggression, as well as in controlling many other forms of antisocial behavior. These things should have been eradicated long ago. It has seemed to me for some time that we have the way—but not the will—to completely control criminal behavior."

Elnear lifted a hand, shook her head slightly. "Sojourner Stryger, it isn't that I disagree with you on that. Not at all. It's simply that if these drugs become widely and easily available there is such potential for their abuse. The pentryptine subfamily is also a perfectly safe and harmless way for a combine to control its population illegally, to drug them into believing their lives are wonderful, when in fact they are not. I'm afraid many combines are far too willing to take the easy way out—to take away freedom of choice, and replace it with mindless gratitude."

Stryger nodded. The agreement shining in his eyes was real this time. "Of course, precisely. That was never my intention, and of course I will emphasize that the deregulation should never be allowed to further misuse—"

Elnear shook her head again, regret showing on her face. "I'm afraid our individual warnings or precautions won't be enough to stop a flood, once someone removes the dam. I simply don't have enough faith in the power of individual will. I wish I did." Her eyes clung to his face.

I was staring at him again, too. There was a kind of golden transparency to his skin, his hair, that his simple street clothes only made brighter. He looked about thirty-five, old enough to look responsible but still look young. He was probably older than that. He carried a long wooden pole in his hand, half as thick around as my wrist, and with half its length covered with carving; the designs looked like words, but I couldn't read them.

"If everyone had your own strength of will, you would not say that, Lady Elnear.'' He smiled with honest respect. His eyes were wide and clear; his voice was like water flowing. I touched his mind again, just to be sure he was real.

He turned toward me. I realized suddenly that he'd been looking at me, too, from the corner of his eye the whole time he was talking to her. "Excuse me . . .'' he said to Elnear, breaking off like he'd only just noticed me. "Who is this?''

"My new aide.'' She sounded relieved, at the sudden change of subject, and that he'd stopped looking at her.

"Really.'' He turned those searchlight eyes on me, looking everywhere but into my own eyes. "You have a rather unusual facial type . . . do you have Hydran blood, young man?'' He met my stare at last, found what he'd expected to when he saw green eyes.

And when I saw what was in his eyes then, suddenly I hated his guts. "No.'' I started to turn away.

"Forgive me—'' His hand caught my arm, pulling me back. "I don't mean to offend you. It's just that the Hydran people have been a particular interest of mine for a long time. I'm not often wrong.'' Calling me a liar. The tip of his tongue slipped out, wetting his lips just a little.

"Get your hand off me,'' I said, very softly. "Or I'll break your fingers.''

"Cat—'' It was Jardan's hard, high voice. The warning sounded far away and almost frightened.

Stryger's hand let me go, but I couldn't shake his stare. Even as he turned back to Elnear, he was still looking at me. *Someone had set him on me*. He'd come all this way, forced this meeting, just to have a look at me. *Hydran blood*.

When he looked at Elnear again, finally, I was still what he was seeing, making him see her in a new and unexpected way. "Of course,'' he murmured, like an apology but not one, "someone in your position would hardly have a psion on her staff.''

I stared at the back of his head, through it; saw into the nest of maggots squeezed into the space where his mind ought to be. He was human, all right.

He went on speaking to Elnear about meaningless details of whatever the thing was they'd been discussing. I didn't really listen; the buzzing of his brain was too loud inside my head. He called himself a religious man. He was absolutely certain that he knew what God was, and exactly how God wanted it all to be. . . . Those people standing around him, waiting with inhuman patience and goodwill for him to finish, thought he knew, too. He kept glancing at me, as if he couldn't keep his eyes off me. My own eyes kept turning traitor, still wanting to *like* his face, even when I could see what lay behind it. I wondered if he had that effect on everybody; the thought scared the hell out of me.

Finally he finished his business. He took one last look at me and went away down the hall, his disciples trailing him on an invisible string. I stood watching him go for too long, until I had to run a few steps to catch up with Jardan and Elnear.

"What does that scumbag really want—?" I said.

They both glanced back at me, surprised, almost outraged.

"That was Sojourner Stryger," Elnear said, "of the Revival Movement. It's an extremely popular prespace-fundamentalist religion; his media appearances draw huge numbers. I would not refer to him as a . . . as you did, if I were you." She looked back at me again, letting me see her disapproval, as if I couldn't feel it. "He has done more for the dispossessed and exploited in our society than anyone I know of. He has an impressive record of speaking out in defense of human rights."

"I know that . . . ma'am. I saw him on the threedy. But what's he doing here?"

"Lobbying, probably," Jardan said bluntly. "He has also almost single-handedly made the deregulation of pentryptine a real possibility. As a result of his influence, he's under consideration for the same position on the Security Council as the Lady."

I almost stopped walking. I forced myself to keep moving, to keep up with them.

"We have our differences of opinion on some of matters," Elnear said, glancing down as if it were her fault, "but I have no doubt about his effectiveness as a reformer, or the sincerity of his beliefs. He is a deeply religious man."

"He hates psions," I said, looking at her. "How religious are you—?"

She looked away. Neither one of them said anything; they began to walk again.

I followed them. "I had a friend," I said to their backs, "who told me once, 'In the land of the blind the one-eyed man is stoned to death.' " They kept walking. "He was a psion. He's dead now."

Elnear stopped, turning back. "Mez Cat," she said finally. "Is there some point to all this?"

I shrugged. "No," I said, feeling my mouth twist down. "No point at all."

SIX

I DIDN'T REALLY need anything more than the meeting with Stryger to make my day perfect. But when we got back to the taMing estates, there was a welcoming committee waiting in the yard as the mod settled. Jiro and his mother, both of them looking grim. One look, and I knew why. He'd cut his hair.

"Elnear, a word with you—" Lazuli said, tight-lipped. Her hands were on Jiro's shoulder's like clamps. "About your aide."

I stood staring at the walls while they talked it over. Jiro looked like something with bad teeth had tried to chew his head off; he'd done it to himself. He liked it that way. His mother didn't. So he'd blamed me. "Perhaps we had better return to the Crystal Palace. . . ." Lazuli was saying, the anger in her voice gone dreary now.

"Not at all," Elnear said, her own anger still honed by her embarrassment: *She had a freak for an aide; but worse than that, he was a moron. She couldn't fire me, she couldn't excuse me, she couldn't even explain why*— "Mez Cat, you will stay away from my grand-nephew and -niece from now on. You are not even to speak to them, do you understand?"

I glanced at Jiro, staring up at me with sullen guilt from his mother's shadow. I looked back at Elnear. "Yes, ma'am." I turned away and started up the steps to the house.

"Mez Cat—" Elnear's voice.

I stopped.

"I think that you owe Lady Lazuli an apology."

I turned back, my jaw clenched so tight I thought I'd never get it open. But then I looked at Lazuli. In the blue evening light, it could have been Jule standing there, angry and unhappy and confused. . . . "I'm sorry," I said. *I'm sorry, Jule.* I went into the house.

I stayed in my room all evening, not even bothering to eat.

"Hey, Cat."

I turned back from the windows, reeled my thoughts in; saw Jiro standing in my suddenly open door. "Jeezu. Stay away from me."

"You like my hair now?" He grinned self-consciously as he edged into the room, not even sure himself whether he'd come to make fun of me or to apologize.

I leaned against the glass-paned door, staring out at the night, ignoring him to keep from strangling him.

"Everybody's real mad at you."

I looked back at him again. "Get out of here, you little croach."

"What's a croach?"

"A lying little cheat who makes other people pay for his mistakes."

"You can't talk to me like that!"

I laughed, past caring what anybody did to me now. "Tell your mother. Fire me."

"You shouldn't have told me to cut my hair. That's why I got in trouble."

I looked at him. "If you're too stupid to understand sarcasm when you hear it, that's not my fault."

He looked down. "I knew you were making fun of me. . . ." He pushed at his hair. "I don't care."

"Then get out." I started toward him, ready to help him along.

His other hand was hidden behind him. Suddenly he brought it up. There was a gun in it.

I stopped short, and stopped breathing.

"Here," he said. "I brought you this."

"Why?" I asked, my voice almost strangling.

Still looking down, he said, "I want you to like me."

"Or what? You're going to kill me?"

"No! It's just a target laser. Maybe you could use it to practice. Maybe you could show me how. . . ." He moved closer, holding it out.

I took it out of his hand and threw it across the room. "What the hell do you think I am?"

He stared at me, totally confused. "You said you were a merse—"

"A merse is somebody who eats shit for money. It isn't fun."

"Philipa said you're supposed to guard Auntie. Have you killed a lot of people?" He kept insisting, blindly, not listening.

Deep in my brain, a black empty hole opened up. I looked into it, needing to feel afraid, but not feeling anything. . . . "One," I said. "That was one too many." It sounded meaningless. I looked down at him, seeing his face again. I shoved him out the doorway into the hall. I slammed the door after him, and locked it. Then I lay down on my bed and watched my hands tremble for a while. And waited.

When the house was dark and quiet, when all its minds had their shutters closed, I used the household system to call for a mod. I slipped outside; stood in the flagstone yard with my fingers crossed. About the time I was ready to give up and start walking, I saw it come drifting silently down to me.

I wasn't sure it would take my orders, but it did. I got in and it lifted, heading for N'yuk. "I quit," I said, watching the taMings fall away behind me. I lifted my finger.

This whole thing had been an insane mistake from the start. They didn't need me, and I didn't need them. I'd go into the city; find some kind of work, it didn't matter what. Anything was better than this. I settled back in my seat. Even from here, I could see the nightglow of the distant shore.

Before long I was dropping down again, somewhere over the urbs. I didn't know where I was going to land, didn't really care. There was a lot of light below me now, arrays of changing colors—too much light. It looked like . . . Grids clicked into place in my mind, artificial memories locking on. I sat up suddenly in my seat, my hand white-knuckled on the armrest. "Shit." It was the Centauri Field Complex.

Braedee was waiting on the platform as the mod's door sprung open, his arms folded, a smile on his face. The light coming up from under him made him look inhuman. A dozen Security drones ringed the mod already, bristling with weapons. I wondered if he was planning a murder-suicide.

I climbed out, slowly, and stood in front of him.

" 'I quit'," he quoted, and gave me the finger back, unblinking.

I felt my face get hot again. "You heard it right." Trying not to feel as helpless as he wanted me to. "What do you want with me?

You know everything that goes on anyway.'' I jerked my head at the mod, disgusted.

"Not about what happens inside the FTA."

"You mean Lady Elnear really does get clear of you when she goes to the Arm?'' I asked, surprised.

No comment.

"Well, that's your problem.'' I shook my head. "You should have listened to Jardan. She was right. I'm all wrong for this, and I'm out of it—''

"I need you. You're staying until I'm through using you.''

"You can't stop me.'' But I couldn't help glancing at the mod when I said it. "I'm a free citizen—'' I held up my wrist with the databand.

The databand went dead.

My heart made a fist in my chest. I lowered my hand, touched all the right spots on the band; shook it, whacked my wrist with my free hand. Nothing woke it up. My hand knotted. "Turn it back on!"

He shook his head, still smiling.

"You can't do this to me.'' I couldn't even imagine how he'd done it. "It's illegal.''

"You are a Centauri employee. In return for that privilege, you give up some rights.''

"I haven't even signed anything—''

"But your verbal agreement is on record. The rest is a formality.''

"Goddamn it—'' I looked away, across the endless Centauri grids crawling with light and activity even in the middle of the night. The wind brought me a thousand different noises—machinery, motion, voices calling—the smell of hot metal and ozone. I stood there, lost somewhere in the middle of it, remembering what it felt like to be invisible.

"Now, tell me about what you saw today. Who you saw; everyone, everything.''

I told him, when I found my voice again. And as I talked, the feeling that I was doing something wrong grew stronger with every word. Braedee looked bored, impatient, or indifferent at everything I said, but that didn't mean that I wasn't violating a trust. Even if it meant Lady Elnear was safer that way, she was losing something. But I didn't see what I could do about it. Or why I should care.

"So you've already met Sojourner Stryger?'' Braedee interrupted suddenly. "What was your impression of him?''

I told him.

He laughed. "That's refreshing. Why are you the only person I've met who didn't find him likeable?''

"He's a freakhater."

"Ah." He nodded. "And you're a freak."

"Why don't you like him?" I asked, because he didn't.

"I think he's dangerous. He's a fanatic; he's crawling with a kind of charisma that even people with real minds seem to find irresistible . . . and he's got too many supporters."

"You mean converts?" I thought of the glazed-looking mob he'd had trailing him.

He smiled, like a death's head. "I mean combines. No individual gets the kind of attention, controls the media base he does, without help. I know what his backers want from him. But I'm not sure he still remembers. . . . What I really want to know is what they're going to get that they don't expect."

"How about the FTA? They might give him that Council slot—?"

He shrugged. "The FTA is no more interested in nonexistent purity than anyone else. Everyone on the Security Council was once someone else's pawn. Do you play chess?"

"No," I said, not even sure what it was.

"I didn't think so." He bent his head at the mod waiting behind me. "Go back to the estate. Sleep it off. Do your job."

"What about my contract?"

"You actually want to look at it?" he asked.

"You bet your ass, Corpse."

"It will be accessible on your unit in the morning. I think you'll find it in order." He sounded amused; I wondered what was so funny.

"What about my deebee?" I held my databand out again.

"You'll be alive again when I think you've earned it."

I turned away, eating my frustration; trying not to give him any more satisfaction than he'd gotten off me already. I stopped, suddenly remembering something. "Who's the other psion?"

"What?" he said.

"Besides Jule. There's another one. You didn't tell me there was a—"

"Where?" He crossed the space between us in one stride.

"The taMings . . ." I almost backed up, but there was nowhere to go. "Last night, at dinner. Somebody tried to use psi on me."

His hand closed on the front of my shirt. "Don't ever lie like that to me again. I know everything about that family. I know what's not possible."

I held his stare, until slowly his hand loosened.

"You actually believe that," he murmured. He looked down at

his own hand, moved the fingers, as if he didn't believe he'd been ready to snap my neck a second ago. "Another telepath?"

I shook my head. "A teek . . . telekinetic."

"What happened?"

"It was little things—trying to make me look stupid. Nothing obvious. Nothing anybody else would even recognize."

He frowned at the suggestion that somebody could really know things he couldn't. And then his face went expressionless; his brain had gone somewhere else. After a second he was seeing me again, and he said, "You can't tell me who it was?"

I shook my head again. "I . . . I wasn't wearing the drugs. You think this has anything to do with the Lady—?"

"No." He cut me off before I could even finish the sentence. His face changed. "You must have been mistaken."

"I wasn't."

"Forget about it. Your problem is Lady Elnear, focus on her." He'd been edging me further backward, until I didn't have any choice except to get into the mod again.

I put my hand on the mod's wing door, ducking under it. "I don't think—"

"Exactly right," he said. "Don't."

I got in, the door sealed and the mod went up, taking me back to the taMings. I was nearly there before I looked down, and realized that my databand was alive again. *Not until I'd earned it . . .*

I went back across the flagstones and into Lady Elnear's house, as quietly as I could. Right back where I'd started from; like in a nightmare. I crawled into my bed and lay there, wondering where I'd be when I woke up.

"Mez Cat . . . may I speak with you?"

The next morning it was Lazuli taMing who caught me with my pants down. I looked up, startled by her voice, because I hadn't felt anyone coming. I realized too late that I'd forgotten to put on another drug patch last night. She'd opened the door without knocking before I could even move.

Now she stood staring at me, about as surprised as I was, but with her eyes still wide open, and no trace of embarrassment on her face.

Because she didn't look away, I didn't move, staring back at her, my hands at my sides. She was wearing a long loose gown that drifted against her skin like snow, as if it was defying gravity. After a handful of heartbeats I finally reached out and caught up my shorts, pulled them on. "Ma'am?" I said, my voice a little hoarse. Now I knew where Jiro got his manners. But then, I was only an employee here. Maybe I was just another piece of furniture to her; a chair, or a bed. . . . I looked at the bed, back at her.

She blinked; suddenly she looked as awkward as I felt. "Perhaps I should come back later."

"That's all right." I shrugged, pulling on my pants. Not saying the obvious.

"I just wanted to apologize. . . ." She took a tentative step into the room.

I smiled. "I'll just remember to keep my door locked, ma'am."

She did blush now; half turned away, turned back. "No—I mean, yes, of course . . . I feel like a fool." She laughed, that same chiming laughter I remembered from last night. "I only wanted to say . . ." she met my eyes again, "Jiro told me this morning that it wasn't your fault. About his hair." She smiled helplessly, gesturing at her own hair, piled up like black silk on top of her head. "I'm sorry. I really don't know what to say. You must think we're . . . well." She shrugged. "I'm sure you've thought of a lot of names yourself."

I felt my smile ease. "Yes ma'am; a few. . . . I seem to have forgotten them, though."

I thought she'd leave then, but she stood where she was, her hands hugging her elbows, looking toward the windows. "It's very difficult. I don't know what to do with him, half the time. Especially when he's around his stepfather. He misses our home, he misses his father. . . ."

"Where did you come from?" I asked, to fill up the silence.

"Eldorado . . . it's in the Centauri system. We came to Earth because I'm on the Centauri board now."

I wondered why she was telling this to a total stranger. Maybe because in this family, that was your only choice. "What happened to his father?"

She looked back at me, clear-eyed. "I don't know. He left me three years ago. Charon and I have been married a little over a year. He said that it would be in the best interest of the company if I married him. That way I could take my cousin Jule's place . . . on the board." Her chin lifted as she saw the look that must have been on my face. "And Jiro and Talitha would be in the direct line to inherit a seat."

I closed my mouth, swallowed. She was married to Charon taMing—Jule's father. She was Jule's cousin and her stepmother. "You look a lot like her. . . ." Saying the obvious didn't make either of us feel any more comfortable. I saw Charon in my mind, the head of Centauri Transport's ruling board; saw the way he'd looked at me when I'd been looking at Lazuli. "I mean, I know Jule. She's a friend. What happened to his first wife?"

Lazuli looked away again. For a moment her eyes were as empty as I'd once seen Jule's. "She was . . . she had some ties to Triple Gee. It was supposed to be a unifying marriage. She died some years ago . . . an accident." She was trying not to think about it. There were no accidents in her world.

I remembered the baby growing in vitro in a lab somewhere, wearing designer genes. I thought about Gentleman Charon's hand; wondered what it felt like to have that touch your body. I didn't say anything.

"Jiro is away at study center most of the time. But every time he comes home, and we're all together he seems more . . . more . . . It's very . . . difficult. I'm sorry." She was seeing me again. Her hands twisted. "Now I'm boring you, after insulting you—"

"No, ma'am. At least it takes my mind off my own problems." My mouth twitched up.

She smiled too, uncertainly. "You've been very kind. Perhaps sometime you'll tell your problems to me, and give me a chance to think of someone else besides myself for a while."

I couldn't tell whether she meant that, until she reached across the space that still separated us, and touched my arm, very gently. Then she turned away, in a whisper of cloud-white, and was gone. I touched the spot where she'd touched me.

It hadn't happened while she was watching me. It hadn't happened while she was talking to me. One touch, and it had finally happened. . . . I groaned, and went on dressing. I had a hell of a time fastening my pants.

Trying not to think about Jule's stepmother touching my arm, I stuck on a fresh drug patch, and asked the desk terminal for my contract with Centauri. Braedee was as good as his word; it was waiting for me. Like a bucket of cold water. Now I knew what was funny. I stared at the document scrolling up the screen. I didn't understand half the words I saw there, and even those were broken up by strings of legal code. I made a hard copy and stuck it in my pocket, before I finally went downstairs.

Everyone else had already eaten. The octagon-shaped dining room with its long embroidered curtains and wood-paneled walls was silent and empty. Almost empty. I went to the table.

"Beat it," I said to the silver-plated drone that was trying to clear away the leftovers. I gave it a shove, and it went back into the closet.

The way these people wasted food was a crime. I drank a half-full cup of coffee that someone had poured too much sweetener into, piled up a plate with untouched spice pastries and half-eaten eggs, a piece of cold smoked fish, some fruit salad. I sat on a cushioned seat beside the table and began to eat.

Lady Elnear walked into the room, with an empty cup in her hand. She stopped.

I reached across the table and picked up the teapot, held it out to her.

Wordlessly she came across the room, and let me fill her cup. "Thank you." Her eyes were still fixed on the plate beside me. "Mez Cat," she said, with a strange gentleness, "no one is forced to eat scraps in this house. Please, there's always plenty of fresh food. . . ." She gestured vaguely toward the kitchen.

"No, ma'am," I said. "There's not."

She looked at me, not understanding.

I shrugged, and ate another spice roll. "I've never been picky about food, ma'am."

She sighed faintly, and went out of the room.

SEVEN

THAT MORNING WE didn't go into N'yuk again. Instead we met Lazuli in the hallway, and a mod took us all on up the valley. Jardan told me we were going to attend Centauri's board meeting. I didn't say anything, wondering why they even bothered to tell me, when I didn't have any choice about going. I sat next to Lazuli, because neither of the other women wanted to sit next to me. Lazuli was wearing a sexless gray-and-silver business suit now. The plainness of it made her look more like Jule, and yet it made the softness in her face that much easier to see. She stared out the window like she didn't notice that I was there. But she knew it, just like I did. Her mind kept remembering what I'd looked like naked. Feeling her remember it was like being tortured with ice and a heat pencil.

The mod set down in the courtyard of a mansion that felt older than any building I'd seen yet on the taMings' land. It was far up the valley from the other houses, almost to the end, crouched like a hermit on a rock ledge above the river. The water roared over the lip of stone there like it had a suicide urge, crashing and drowning in the pit of rocks and shadows far below.

Inside, the mansion was one gigantic work of art—arched ceilings painted with murals, framed by scrolled carvings, white marble pillars, congealed flows of stairway with golden banisters. Paintings of long-dead people in bizarre clothes covered the walls; sculpted busts of total strangers lined the entrance hall like the cut-off heads of taMing enemies. If moving through the Crystal Palace had been bad, walking here, on the way to a combine board meeting, was agony. Somebody like me hadn't been meant to walk through places like this; hadn't even been meant to know they existed.

I couldn't get up the nerve to ask whose house this was. I picked the answer out of Elnear's thoughts, feeling like a thief: The mansion belonged to Gentleman Teodor, the one who'd sat at the head of the table when we'd all eaten at the Crystal Palace. The head of the family, the oldest living taMing.

Braedee met us in one of the endless halls, and I read his smug satisfaction as he saw me, right where he wanted me. He greeted the others like this was his ground, and not theirs. While the Centauri board met, it was. He told them the way to the board room, as if they didn't already know it, and let them pass. But he blocked my path as I tried to follow, nudging me toward a doorway. "He'll be right with you, Lady Elnear," he said, as she turned back, waiting, frowning. "I have some further instructions for him."

That didn't reassure her. Maybe it wasn't supposed to. She turned and went on, still frowning.

"In here." Braedee moved into the room, making me follow him.

"What?" I said, when I was standing in front of him again. The sight of a Corpse uniform and the memory of last night made me knot up inside as I looked at him. "Jeezu, don't you have anything better to do than hassle me—"

His hand shot out and smacked me across the face. I staggered, banging into a table. Something fell and smashed on the floor.

"You are not an equal here," he said. "Don't act like one." He looked down at the pieces of broken crystal glittering like knives around my feet. He crushed a shard under his boot heel, looked up at me again. "The price of the vase will be deducted from your salary."

I rubbed my cheek, glaring at him, blinking too much.

"Two ambassadors of Triple Gee are attending the board meeting today, as are the regular Centauri associates and controlled interests. I want you to pick their brains—especially the Triple Gee representatives. I want to know their real thoughts on what they hear."

"Wait a minute," I said. I had to force the words out this time. "That's not what you hired me for. I'm not here to spook for Centauri—"

He looked at me. I flinched, even though I was trying not to. But he only said, "You are here to protect Lady Elnear. Since we still do not know who wants her dead, we have to make use of every opportunity to explore the real motives of everyone she comes in contact with. Triple Gee is our primary competition. That's all."

It sounded logical. I didn't believe it, any more than he did. I was afraid to try reading him face to face, but I could figure that much out for myself. I was protecting Lady Elnear, but he could force me to pull data about the competition too, because I didn't know enough about anything to know when I was crossing the line. I was the perfect tool. No wonder he couldn't stay away from me.

"I want to know what everyone who is not Centauri thinks, you understand—"

"Everyone? Even the Lady?"

"Particularly the Lady."

I glared at him. " 'For her own good'? "

"And yours," he said softly. He jerked his head at the doorway.

I looked down, and nodded. I stepped out of the ring of broken glass, and left the room.

I reached the boardroom at last. A security screen blinked off, showing me a hall that must have been fifty meters long, with angels dancing on its ceiling. The air was blue-silver; the light that poured in through the high, narrow windows was like light from another age. I wondered what people had done in a room this size centuries ago. Probably not what they were doing now. I looked toward the table in the center of the room. Or maybe they had: Lying, cheating, fucking each other over . . . some things never changed.

As I entered the room I heard a noise, and saw a head disappear down at the far end of the long white-and-gold table. The people nearest that end turned in their seats, rising up, reaching out. Somebody had fallen. My eyes and my mind leaped, looking for Elnear. My mind found her first.

She had one of the ornamented, high-backed chairs at the near end of the table. She was standing up, leaning forward, looking toward the noise. Jardan was sitting in one of the seats lined up in a second row just behind the board seats: the row of aides and advisors. Security guards wearing a rainbow of combine colors lined the walls of the room. A couple of them had moved forward, but none of the rest looked worried. They were just there for show. The real security here wasn't anything you could touch or see.

I sat down beside Jardan. "What happened?"

"One of the Triple Gee ambassadors," she murmured. "He seemed to miss the seat as he sat down. . . ." She was thinking people who met in rooms like this one never made mistakes like that. I heard/felt the tittering amusement of the Centauri board members all around me. Triple Gee had just lost a whole lot of face.

Jardan turned to look at me again. "I suppose Braedee was simply reminding you of your duty. . . ." she said, taking my mind off Triple Gee.

"Yeah," I muttered. I looked away along the table until I saw Lazuli, sitting next to Daric . . . her stepson. She didn't look any older than he did; I wondered how old she really was. He murmured something to her; she laughed. There were maybe thirty other people around the long table. Twenty of them were the actual Centauri board. The rest, like Elnear, represented smaller combines they'd forced alliances with because each had something they needed or wanted. I counted eleven taMings sitting around the table; just enough for a majority. Something in the way they held themselves and moved said that they never forgot that for a minute. They stood out, even at that table, and it wasn't just because they all looked alike. . . . I saw old Teodor, who'd been on the board longer than anybody else, and would be until he died . . . saw Jule's grandmother . . . a couple of aunts and uncles, great-aunts, great-uncles. Lazuli held the seat that had belonged to Jule by right. It had been filled by a proxy for years, after Jule left home.

I looked at Charon, sitting at the table's head, as far from the Triple Gee ambassadors as he could get. He gave me a look that made me feel cold inside. Braedee had told him that since they had me they might as well use me; but having me in the same room with him made him damn uncomfortable. I realized the real reason Braedee took such a personal interest in me was because I was his idea, and Charon didn't like it. Charon was Centauri, as much as any single human being could be. If I caused any trouble while I was here, I wasn't the only one who'd pay. I looked back down the table again. "Why is Triple Gee here, if they're the enemy?" I asked Jardan.

"To keep lines of communication open," she said. "They exchange ambassadors whenever a board meets. They have more in common than the same potential market for their services—"

They both hated the FTA. I nodded. "I know. . . ." I said.

She gave me a strange look. I didn't bother to answer it, and she looked away again, leaning forward to say something to Elnear.

I remembered suddenly that Braedee had said Elnear held her dead husband's board seat. That must give her two votes. "How can the Lady be on the Centauri board?" I asked, as Jardan sat back again. "She's not really a taMing."

"Because they never found her husband's body," Jardan murmured. A technicality. Everybody knew he was dead, but nobody could prove it legally. Until someone did, or she died too, she'd continue to be his proxy.

I grimaced, sorry I'd asked. I settled back as Charon called the meeting to order, remembering that it wasn't the taMings I was supposed to be watching. The two Triple Gee reps were sitting like statues at the far end of the table, rigid with surface calm, groping for the dignity they knew they'd lost for good in one second's lack of attention. The one who'd hit the floor was chewing the inside of his mouth. He was sure that somebody had done it to him on purpose, but he couldn't figure out how.

Inside both of the Triple Gee reps, *suspicion, hatred, grudging respect* mixed like oil and water, leaving a scum of envy on everything they thought, everything they heard as the meeting started. From what I could see, if Triple Gee was behind trying to assassinate Lady Elnear, neither one of them had heard about it.

I glanced at Lady Elnear's back, feeling her accessing information; feeling her own self-conscious awareness of me. She wanted to tell everyone there what I was; hated herself for not having the balls to do it. I swore under my breath, hating that bastard Braedee for making everything harder for me than it had to be. I didn't even want to think about what would happen if anybody else—or everybody else—in that room suddenly found out what I was. Most combines never used telepaths for snoopware, because they were too paranoid about getting snooped themselves—by somebody else's psion, or by their own. Triple Gee would probably declare war if they knew what I was doing. Their security would kill me on the spot anyhow, even if all they did was walk out on the meeting.

I made myself focus again, shutting my eyes, trying to look like I was just bored, and not groping a lot of unsuspecting minds in the dark. The board was reporting what had been done about handling an upsurge in communications traffic in some critical sector. The Triple Gee reps took it all in, the envy static getting louder in their brains. One of them thought about the hostile takeover move on a local competitor that Triple Gee was making in that sector of their own network. Triple Gee figured the force-merger was what it would take to compete efficiently. Centauri was going to be surprised. . . .

Until I told them about it. I realized Centauri wasn't going to discuss anything here that would actually surprise Triple Gee. It was all to test out their responses. I went on around the table, until I was back inside Elnear's mind again. She was thinking about the ironies of communication, around this table, and across the Federation. That for all the technology that let them access the way they did, there was still no simple, instantaneous communication that could reach between star systems. Board members and combine representatives and millions of daily messengers still had to travel in the flesh from all across the Federation, their ports and heads crammed with artificial memory, in order to keep the universal data Net functioning, and a combine's brain alive. Centauri had it better than most combines, because outside a single solar system communication was just another commodity, and they handled it themselves. But data was the lifeblood of an interstellar network, and if somebody ever cut off the supply, even Centauri would be braindead in a week.

I broke contact, shaking out my brain; wondering if the Lady ever thought about anything as simple as which shoes to wear. Maybe not. Maybe that was why she dressed the way she did. . . . I let my mind go on around the table again, skipping Centauri heads, reading the rest, memorizing what I found there, no matter how meaningless it was to me. As I got used to the patterns of bioware, I realized none of them wore anything that could sense me. But that didn't make me feel any easier. Playing corporate telepath was still like playing Last Chance back in Oldcity . . . a suicide game.

I sat up straighter, remembering yesterday, as Daric said something about Sojourner Stryger. The two Triple Gee ambassadors leaned

forward at the far end of the table, suddenly letting their interest show.
". . . Stryger's effectiveness quotient in the independent media is still
rising," Daric was saying, "because of the exposure he has been
achieving in regard to deregulation. As is yours, Elnear—" He grinned
across the table at her like he knew something she didn't. He probably
did. His eyes moved past her to touch on me, slid down me once. But
then they were gone again, and he was looking toward the Triple Gee
reps. "Apparently the Security Council is waiting for the outcome of
the deregulation vote before filling the open slot. Since they are, as
we all know, somewhat out of touch with life in the real world, they
appear to be using deregulation as a kind of test of wills, or a way to
see whose personality has the greater force, the most impact on public
opinion . . ." He smiled, glancing at Elnear again. Her irritation prickled behind my eyes. "A moot point in the end, as we also know—
but one which seems to have some curious ritual significance to the
FTA."

The thought of Stryger ending up on the Security Council made
me feel sick. Those stupid slads, didn't they know what he was—? I
remembered what Braedee had told me, and that didn't help.

Daric leaned forward, peering down the table at the reps again.
"Tell me, Ambassador Ndala, is Triple Gee still waffling in its feelings
about deregulation?"

"Triple Gee is not so much 'waffling,' Gentleman Daric, as it is
carefully weighing the consequences," Ndala said. "We hardly need
to point out to you how much profit Centauri stands to make on this
drug, because of its controlling interest in ChemEnGen. Those addi-
tional profits could easily be used against your competitors."

Daric shrugged. "Or . . . they could as easily make us mellow
and content to let our network go soft just a little . . . especially if
you were to support us wholeheartedly in the Assembly vote. After
all, you must keep things in perspective. *We* are not really the Enemy.
Sometimes we do lose track of that; but it's true, nonetheless."

The Triple Gee ambassador leaned back in his seat, looking straight
up the table at Charon. "Perhaps we will find something substantive
waiting for us when we return to the embassy—?" he murmured. They
were lying. They already knew they were going to vote for deregulation, even though they didn't care about the drug itself. They wanted
Stryger to win. But they were going to see what kind of compromises
they could shake Centauri down for. . . .

"Consider it done," Charon said. He glanced at me for just a
second as he said it. His word was about as safe as I felt right now.

Elnear sighed heavily in front of me. She knew as well as any of them did that even though she had the FTA behind her on the drug vote, Stryger had his backers too. She wanted deregulation to fail, for reasons that ran so deep in her that I couldn't really read them. She was even thinking that she'd be willing to withdraw from consideration for the Council, even though she wanted that slot nearly as much, if withdrawing would keep some of Stryger's backers from voting for deregulation just to get him into it. But she knew nothing was that easy, or that clean.

She thought Stryger was a good man; she thought he'd be as good a choice for the Council as she was. Maybe better. She didn't believe Stryger was really the combines' tool any more than Braedee did; but not for the same reasons. She didn't know what Stryger was; didn't believe—or probably didn't give a damn about—what I'd told her. She admired and envied his faith in God and human nature. She thought it was simply unfortunate that his belief in pentryptine as a solution to everybody's problems played into the hands of so many combine interests. . . .

I slumped down in my seat, aching, not sure if I was exhausted or just depressed. These vips had the augmentation and easy access that let them keep up with the flow of interstellar empires. But it didn't give them a clue about what went on behind another human's eyes. I didn't know if I felt disillusioned, or just relieved, to know that they were only deadheads like anybody else, when it really counted.

Finally the board meeting ended; but that wasn't the end of my duty. There was another room waiting for us, this one piled high with food and drinks under a ceiling crawling with gold and white plaster flowers. I was hungry, but I didn't touch anything this time. It wasn't worth the risk. I only watched and listened, staying by Elnear like I was supposed to. Jardan shadowed me at first, but when she saw I wasn't eating or talking, she left me alone.

I was only an aide, and if I didn't talk no one talked to me. I stood listening to the mortal gods of the Federation discuss how to get around the FTA's back, and how to get into somebody's pants; how much they needed pentryptine to stop the rioting on Belke's World . . . how much the franchise disputes had hurt production . . . what a pain in the ass the FTA had been about their labor practices. . . . Advising and bitching and gossiping, sometimes all in the same breath.

I watched a tall, blond man spit out a skagweed cud and leave it lying halfway under the table; someone else stepped in it while I watched. *Jeezu, he had worse manners than I did*—But manners didn't seem to matter, if you were rich enough; just like they didn't matter if you were poor enough. It was only the billions suspended in between, those who had something to lose, who had to know how to act. I touched the logo on my sleeve; let my hand drop.

There was a crash and then laughter and cursing somewhere behind me. I turned around fast, because just for a second I'd thought I'd felt something, psi energy. But I wasn't sure, and it was only somebody who'd spilled a plate of food. Probably nothing, probably just liquor or nerves. . . . It got on my nerves, remembering there could be a psionic practical joker in this crowd somewhere, just waiting to try me again. But maybe they'd realized why the joke hadn't worked on me. If they knew, they hadn't given me away. Maybe they had something to hide, too. Maybe that was why they only did little things, things nobody could trace. Maybe they'd leave me alone; but I doubted it. Braedee had told me to back off. But what he didn't know could still hurt me. I began to loosen up my brain, starting to scan—

"Mez Cat."

I turned. Lazuli taMing was standing beside me.

I blinked. "Ma'am?"

"You look like you're asleep on your feet."

I pulled my mind back into focus in a hurry. "No, ma'am. Just . . . uh, doing my job." *Shit. Don't say that.* "I mean—"

"It's quite all right. You've barely had time to take a breath before being thrown into all this. It must seem very alien to you."

I heard the unconscious condescension in it; felt it. But she was standing here talking to me, something nobody else would do. And besides, she was right. "Yes, ma'am. Very alien." Seeing Jule's face when I looked at her was more comfort than I'd had in a long time. It helped me remember that all this was supposed to have a point.

Charon was watching us, frowning. I touched his mind with a quick finger of thought—pulled back again, tasting *jealousy, suspicion, frustration . . . hatred*. The last one for me, the rest for his wife. I felt the twisted uncertainty in him every time he looked at her. He hadn't married her for love, only for politics; he knew she didn't love him. But when he looked at her he saw Jule too . . . his own daughter. Only perfect, this time. And it made him uneasy and uncertain, things he never wanted to be; made him feel things no man ought to feel when he remembered his daughter. There was an emotion still alive inside him that should have died long ago. . . .

I looked away from him again, my skin crawling.

"What did you say?" Lazuli asked.

I hadn't said anything. "Nothing, ma'am," I answered, not sure if I'd let something leak, or only made some sound. "Is Jiro here?" I changed the subject, because I had to get my own mind off it. I hadn't seen Jiro anywhere, but if I had to pick someone who'd use psi as a bad joke, he'd be my first choice.

She shook her head. "No. He wanted to come, to observe the meeting, but I told him he couldn't. That was his punishment for lying to me."

I almost said I thought lying was what vips learned first; but I didn't. Maybe it wasn't the lie he was being punished for, anyway. Maybe it was just for admitting the truth. I looked at Charon again, saw him begin to move toward us. "Ma'am—" I ducked my head and turned away from her.

I made my way through the crowd to Elnear. She stood in a shadowed alcove, talking to Jule's great-uncle Salvador, who looked younger than she did but was twice as old.

"Mez Cat," Elnear said, nodding to me as she noticed me. She looked tired, and felt worse. "I think it's time we were leaving. I have my own work to get back to." I felt a little heat stir in her, and a lot of relief. Relief that she could finally get free of this nest of relatives; relief that I'd been here the entire time without embarrassing her. I nodded too, more relieved than she was. Jardan came up beside me, glancing at me without frowning, for once. "Thank God," she said.

Daric taMing was walking behind her as she said it, holding a lot of liquor in a large crystal mug. He stopped, looking at us, his eyes glittering. I met his stare, because this time I knew I hadn't done anything he could shaft me for.

"So you've been a good boy today, new aide—" he said. He started on, hesitated, looking back. His mouth quirked up. "Did you know that your fly is open?"

I looked down, because everybody else did; knowing it was impossible, knowing he was wrong— He wasn't wrong. Everyone watched me fasten it.

EIGHT

I WENT WITH Lady Elnear to the Arm again the next day, and the next. Before I knew it I'd been on Earth for a week. It seemed like a lot longer. But nothing happened that hadn't before, except that I became an aide. I digested the data I'd swallowed whole the first day, and used it; and every time I used the console I swallowed more. The fact that sometimes I knew more about a job than Jardan did, and other times didn't know whether to input what she gave me or eat it, didn't go over very well at first. But by now most of the surprised looks I was getting from her were relieved. Lady Elnear could even forget that I was a freak for long enough to look at me without startling, sometimes.

One lunch hour I hired a legal program and got my contract with Centauri cleaned up and registered. Some of the other hours I spent wandering the floating paths through the streets and levels of the city near the Federation plex. The bizarre combinations of old and new, soaring curves and knife-blade edges, stone and steel and ceramoplast, glass and composite, made me feel like I was caught inside the mutating guts of some ancient, cancerous crystal being. I could see the layers of time in the layers of its structure, feel the crazyquilt of lives going on all around me in its heart, a separate reality flowing through the unoccupied spaces of its body. I got myself some new jeans, right from the source, but never got to wear them.

And nothing happened to anyone that shouldn't have, except that

I had to see more of Jule's brother Daric than I wanted to. And more of Lazuli.

I thought I knew why she and her children were staying with Elnear instead of at the Crystal Palace where they belonged. It didn't have anything to do with me. But that didn't make it easier to be around them. I avoided Jiro and his sister like I'd avoid a street gang, and for pretty much the same reasons. I stayed away from their mother as much as I could; but short of staying in my room until I starved to death, I couldn't keep away from her completely. And whenever I saw her, I had to feel her think about me. And feel myself think about her. Her face stayed with me in the nights, while I lay awake waiting for Braedee to call. I knew that mindlarking about Charon taMing's wife made about as much sense as thinking about setting myself on fire. It couldn't have made me feel any worse; or any hotter.

And every night after everyone else was asleep, Braedee's ghost materialized over the console in my room, and I reported everything I'd seen and heard. What the hell, I figured; what real difference did anything make, anyway?

By the second week, I could stumble through the Lady's office routine without driving the system and everybody around me crazy. Sometimes I could almost forget that this was anything but an honest job. . . .

"Mez Cat," Elnear said suddenly, from across the room. "Haven't you anything better to do?"

I was watching "You Are There," the Independent Daily News fax; getting a lurid sensurround of a shipping disaster. I had everything damped out except the picture; screams and the smell of burned bodies were more than I really needed. The Indy was always desperate for ratings because their coverage wasn't subsidized by combine credit; they were a strange mix of honor and sleaze, and I kind of liked them.

I shut off the image and glanced up. "Everything's in the system except the committee summary; we still don't have all the data. I'm waiting for Geza to get done right now."

"What about the reports—?"

"I dumped what you were through with, and brought up the rest of your list."

She was silent for a minute, trying to think of something else she could call me on. She couldn't think of anything. "Cat," she said finally, glancing down, "I confess that you have been a surprise, in some ways. You are actually managing to do an adequate job in this position. And frankly, considering that you were totally unqualified for it, I find that amazing.''

I smiled. She did too, and turned back to her work.

I felt her go white, suddenly, as she scanned the overnight listings on her unit. Jardan came in from the outer office, and the security screen blinked on behind her. "What is it?'' Jardan asked, answering some summons I couldn't hear. I'd figured out days ago that she was more than just Elnear's assistant, and my keeper. She knew everything that mattered; she even wore enough augmentation to hold it all. She was the only one Elnear trusted that much.

"Look at this.'' Elnear put something on the screen of my unit that lobotomized the news fax. I sat back in my chair while Jardan read over my shoulder. She looked at Elnear; jerked the headset off of me and stuck the trodes on her own forehead. All that I recognized that I could see was the name of Triple Gee. "Triple Gee is boxed out—?'' Jardan murmured, as if it was more unimaginable than even the thought of her smiling at me. "You only communicated with Suezain yesterday. How could Centauri have learned about the dispersal ruling—?''

"There's no way. I took absolute measures. . . .''

Suddenly there were two sets of eyes drilling into my skull, two minds with the same idea. I sat staring at the screen, trying not to make it three. No one asked the question; figuring there was no point. I didn't answer it, either.

Elnear got up from her seat, heavily, and pulled on her drape. "I have a face meeting with Isplanasky to go to, Philipa. Lingpo can see to this business, and Geza can cover Cat's duties. . . .'' She glanced at me, resigned. I went where she went, like it or not. Right now she didn't like it at all.

We went through the halls, on foot as usual, deep into the heart of the FTA's office plex. Elnear walked seven or eight klicks a day. I didn't mind it, but it always surprised me that she didn't either. For someone who didn't seem to care what her body looked like, she took damn good care of it.

This time we passed through a huge open space I'd never been inside of before. It was hung with banners and drifting light sculptures. Gigantic holo representations of Historic Earth shimmered in the walls, behind things inside stasis fields that looked like relics from a museum. It was a place that could only be for show, for the tourist trade that helped keep Earth alive. It startled the hell out of me after the nondescript halls and offices I'd gotten used to. But once I thought about it, I realized a place like this had to be here somewhere. The FTA claimed it represented all of humanity. It had to have a public face for humans to look at.

Elnear kept walking ahead of me; navigating the trajectories of the crowd that had come to gape or take spoon-fed tours. I tried to keep up, but my own eyes kept being pulled away, toward a huge block of jade hand-carved into an incredible miniature landscape . . . a holo on the wall of a city, before and after it had been melted down by primitive nukes . . . a perfect zero-gee crystal floating inside a sphere.

"Cat!" Elnear's voice jerked my leash. "If you want to take the tour," she said, when I reached her side, "please do it on your own time."

"I didn't know there was a tour . . . ma'am." I looked away, staring at the mosaic mural on the wall behind her.

"Well, now you do," she said, but her irritation was fading. She turned, glancing over her shoulder to see what I was looking at instead of her. "A family portrait of the human race," she said.

It was a picture of maybe thirty people, old, young, all different sexes, sizes, colors. Once I'd started to look at them, I couldn't stop until I'd looked at them all. Whoever had made that portrait over four hundred years ago had done a good job of catching their souls.

"It hung originally in the plex of the old world government that preceded the Federation," Elnear said, "to remind the people of the nation-states that met there of their common humanity . . . something which they constantly forgot, anyway." She wasn't sure whether what we had now was better or worse; but she thought that at least individual humans didn't kill each other as often, or in such big numbers.

I looked at the faces again. Some of them looked less like each other than she looked like me. But none of them were Hydran faces. None of them really looked like me. There were words embedded in the picture, in some pre-space script I couldn't read. "What does it say?"

" 'Treat others as you would like them to treat you,' " she said.

I didn't say anything. She started on and I followed her. The mural's eyes watched my back as I walked away.

I didn't know who Isplanasky was until we reached the end of our stroll; I was too busy thinking about what had happened back in her office to bother picking it out of her thoughts. I only looked up as we finally reached his doorway, in time to see the logo on the wall above it: *Natan Isplanasky. Director of Operations, Contract Labor Services.* The past put its hands around my throat. I went inside, but I didn't want to.

Isplanasky actually had a room with a view, a room at the top; which made sense, for someone at the top of the FTA's biggest and most profitable operation short of the Federation Telhassium Mines. His secured inner office was huge, and it had a view of the city's rolling peaks, tier on tier of artificial mountains.

"Elnear . . ." Isplanasky got up from what looked like a purple reclining chair with some strange design quirks. He shook off a slow-moving daze as he came toward us, and at first I thought he'd been sleeping. He'd been accessing. He was loaded with augmentation, but none of it showed. "God, what a pleasure to see your face. It's been too long. Sometimes I think I've been buried and forgotten in the Net. . . ." He shook his head again, rubbing his temples, blinking. "It was good of you to come, when a call would have done it." He was wearing black, like the Labor press gangs, but his was pretending to be a suit, not a uniform. It looked good on him. He looked about forty standards; he was heavyset but not fat, with bronze skin and long black hair caught in a clip, a thick curling beard. He moved like maybe he really didn't leave that chair for days on end.

"Natan, I will use any excuse, any time, for a chance to get together with you." Elnear flashed him that shapechanging smile, and he grinned, white teeth showing in the black beard. Just friends, no more . . . but real friends. She thought he was one hell of a guy. But then, she admired Stryger, too. "Besides, you need someone to remind you to come up for air."

"Who's this?" he asked, his voice still a little thick. He smiled at me like he actually wanted to know.

She introduced me, and he crossed the room to shake my hand, telling me how damn lucky I was to be working with one of the best in the Arm. I didn't answer; my throat felt paralyzed. My mind kept trying to find the dead black core in his own mind, that would tell me how someone could head the largest slave labor operation in the Federation and still smile at anyone like he meant it. Except I couldn't find one. . . . Frustration started to burn a hole in my concentration. I might as well still be psiblind as have the kind of gray half vision Braedee's drugs had given me.

Isplanasky gave Elnear some tea. He handed me a beer and opened one for himself like we were all having a picnic on top of the world. My bottle said "since 1420" on it; it was made of brown glass. I popped it and took a long drink of thousand-year-old beer. It was pretty good. I finished it off.

"I don't like this debate with Stryger. . . ." Isplanasky said to

Elnear. I looked up again. "The very fact that it's happening stinks of interference. Too many combines want deregulation—"

"Yes, I know." Elnear nodded, sipping at her tea. "He's quite sincere in his beliefs, but he strikes me as naive. He may make a deal with the devil simply because he believes in angels—to use his own terms."

His grin came back. "Unlike you and I, who are quaintly cynical down to our socks."

I leaned back on the couch by the window, listening to them discuss Stryger as if he was some kind of harmless crank. When I'd had a couple of free minutes on the Net, I'd called up everything I could find on him. I'd listened to him speak, I'd studied his background. He'd always been a godlover; he'd been a minister of the Universal Ecumen on Gadden. He hadn't always been a fanatic about it. Everything I could dig out on his early years said he was a decent man who pretty much lived what he preached, working to make other people's lives better.

But then he'd had some kind of religious vision—at least that was what he claimed—when he'd been braindead for a couple of minutes after a fall. And he'd started to change. After that he'd come to Earth to study pre-space religion, because his vision had told him he'd find God's Real Truth waiting for him here.

Interstellar travel had proved once and for all that Earth wasn't the center of the universe; running into the Hydrans had finally shown humans that they weren't alone in it. Human religion had done a double-take then, going through the Re-creation. What survived were kinds of religion that preached oneness with all lifeforms, and practiced what they preached by keeping a low profile. It made more sense, and it didn't compete with the combines for loyalty.

But Stryger wanted to bring back the old-style religion, the kind that said there was a real God somewhere who cared enough to play favorites, and humans were it. Which meant Hydrans weren't. I couldn't figure out when he'd started to hate Hydrans so much, or why. He was careful not to talk about it, because he wasn't stupid, and he knew that the ones he really wanted behind him weren't stupid either. They probably hated Hydrans as much as he did, but now that most surviving Hydrans were under some combines's thumb, or "relocated" in dumps like Oldcity, talking genocide wasn't easy like it had been once.

Stryger had started traveling, gathering supporters and money, playing his Human Rights themes to get attention on the Net and to spread his word from world to world. He'd been at it for a long time;

he was fifty-three. He hadn't always looked like he did now—I'd been right about that. He'd had enough plastic work done on him so that the oldest images of him were barely recognizable. He preached about the dignity and beauty of the human form, unaugmented, unchanged, the way God had meant it to be. But little by little he'd played God on himself, transforming himself into a calculated vision of human perfection.

And over the years he'd convinced both the combine vips and the Security Council that he was almost as perfect as he seemed. It couldn't be easy to play both sides as well as he did, to make two enemies hear just what they wanted to hear when you spoke the same words. You had to be damned smart and slick, but more than that you had to have the kind of belief in yourself that made other people want to believe in you. He had it; I'd felt it. And too many other people believed in him already. His Movement had a higher financial profile than a lot of combines. He could buy himself anything he wanted; he had that kind of money.

Only, he hadn't done that. He actually fed most of his profits into creating the kind of help for life's losers that he preached about. I'd seen some of the shelters he'd sponsored, in Oldcity . . . I'd used some of them.

That had stopped me cold when I found out about it. I hadn't known what to make of it, I'd wondered if maybe somehow I was wrong about him. If he'd done it for promo, he'd get more for his money just hiring hypers. But then I'd realized that money, or even fame, wasn't what he was after. He wanted real power. He wanted that slot on the Security Council, and it looked like he was using the pentryptine vote as a way to get himself there. Something was still driving him to reach higher and higher, and it wasn't something holy. I'd stared at the final image of his perfect face for a long time, wondering what the hell was really going on behind those eyes. . . .

I turned to look out at Isplanasky's view; clearing Stryger's image out of my mind. I had to shut my eyes then, as they suddenly told me how high up I was. I pressed my hands against the couch, hanging on for a second until the dizziness passed. The couch was covered with something that felt and smelled like real leather. I ran my hand over it, back and forth.

". . . if this gains him any more support we'll be in trouble," Isplanasky was saying. "The majority of the Assembly is for deregulation already. Aside from the fact that you are clearly the best candidate, Stryger is completely unprepared for the real demands of a Council position. He's not even cybered—calls it unnatural, for God's sake.''

"Yes, exactly: 'for God's sake.' " Elnear rested her head against the high back of her seat, staring at the ceiling. "He really believes God is on his side. You know, I have always tried to do what I understood to be right, in keeping with the manifold ways of God. But sometimes I can't help wondering. . . . I think about this debate night and day. I dream about it, and wake up arguing with myself.''

"I know how you feel, believe me." Isplanasky moved restlessly back to his bar. "If combines start using pentryptine on their citizens—''

"You might be out of job," I said. The FTA rented out contract laborers to whatever combine wanted extra bodies, usually to do things their citizens wouldn't do. No questions asked. It also used them in its own operations—things like the Federation Mines, where they mined their telhassium on a piece of burnt-out star called Cinder out in the Crab Colonies.

They looked at me.

"Well, that wasn't exactly my concern," Isplanasky said, still good-natured. "My concern is the same as the Lady's. I oversee Contract Labor; it involves the lives of a vast number of people, who would be more at risk from combine drug abuses than most of their population. I believe that human dignity and freedom of choice are worth fighting for; that individual rights have to be protected and maintained at any cost. I don't want to see the people under my charge treated badly and unable even to protest it.''

"You want your bondies left free to eat all the dirt some combine feels like feeding them, without drugs to make it easier?" I asked. "As long as somebody keeps paying you for ten standards of their time—''

His smile disappeared. "Not at all. I work for the FTA because Contract Labor exists as a viable, humane alternative, so that those individuals who lack regular combine citizenship have somewhere to turn. It gives them a start, a second chance; useful training. 'Contract Labor builds worlds'—" He gestured at the logo on the wall behind him.

I stared at him. He had to be the most perfect hypocrite I'd ever seen, or a pathological liar—because he meant every word of that.

"Are you all right?" he asked.

I said, "How many bondies did you have to skin to cover this couch?"

"By the Nine Billion Names of God!" he murmured. "Are you an anarchist, son, or is it just that you can't hold your liquor?"

I unfastened my databand and let it drop off. I held up my arm, letting him see the wide, smooth band of white scar tissue. He didn't know what it was. "I used to work for you," I said.

He raised his eyebrows. "You seem to have come through the experience with your skin intact." His voice was cool and dry.

I reached behind me for the tail of my shirt. Just then Elnear's desperate anger caught in my mind like a thorn. I glanced at her, saw the disbelief in her eyes. "Ma'am, I—"

"Yes, certainly, you may go." She raised a dismissing hand. "Back to my office. I'll speak with you there." It was the closest thing to a threat I'd heard from her. She'd speak; but she wouldn't listen. She murmured an apology to Isplanasky, something like, ". . . he isn't feeling well . . ."

I left the room, leaving their stares behind. The memories still followed me, because there was nowhere I could ever go where I'd be able to leave those behind.

"Well, squire—" Daric taMing's twitchy, grinning face pushed in front of me as I dragged my aching stupidity back through the halls. "Where's your Lady in white armor?"

Damn. The one person in the entire universe that I wanted to see the least. I shrugged, not even sure what he was talking about, as usual. I wondered if he spent all his days like this, wandering the halls looking for victims.

"She's supposed to be with you, I thought." He kept pushing, matching my steps. "Or vice versa. That's what you're paid for. Am I right?"

"Not today," I said, my hands making quiet fists.

" 'Sir.' "

"What?" I looked at him.

"Say 'sir.' . . . You're just not very good at this, are you? You know what Elnear says about you behind your back? 'You can dress him up, but you can't take him anywhere.' "

"I thought 'sir' was only used as a term of respect."

It took him a minute, because he didn't believe I'd said that. Then he laughed. "You know, I think I admire you, Cat. You actually don't give a damn what we think of you . . . or is it just that you're really so naive that you don't know what we could do to you?"

I felt myself go cold as I realized he meant that. I kept walking, watching my feet take one step after another. "Jule never told me she had a brother."

He sniggered. "That's hardly surprising. She always hated me, because I'm normal. She tried to kill me once, when we were children. She tried to push me off the balcony at the country house on Ardattee."

I looked up, frowning. He was still smiling at me. "Then she must have had a good reason." I looked ahead again, walking faster.

He kept up with me, hanging onto me like a dog with its teeth sunk in my leg. I wondered what he wanted—because this was building up to something, I could feel it. He hadn't run into me by accident. I wondered what his problem was; if he was on drugs, or if just being a taMing was enough to fuck him up this bad.

"What was it that attracted you to my sister, anyway? Most normal people find psions repulsive. The thought of them crawling into *your* thoughts, or stopping your heart with . . . a thought. You know. Of course, maybe you find that erotic, like necrophilia, or having someone piss on you. . . ."

I spun around, my fist coming up; not even caring that half a hundred witnesses and even more security eyes were about to see me beat the shit out of an Assembly member—

"I know what you are," he said. "You're one too."

My hand dropped to my side like dead weight. "What?" I said; and then, "Who told you? That I was a telepath—"

"It's true . . . that explains everything." His gray eyes clung to my face like a sweating hand. "You are a psion. My father actually hired a psion." He laughed again, high and strained, and smacked his forehead with his hand. "God, I don't believe it."

"Who told you?" I felt the anger that had barely stopped short of his face try to reach out for him again as I realized he'd tricked me.

"Father told me." He shrugged, as if Charon taMing talked about me like he discussed the weather. "I just couldn't believe it." I didn't believe that, either. He must have overheard something, gotten access to some private file. "After Jule left home, I was sure that if a psion ever crossed his range again, he'd have her—or him, in your case— incinerated on the spot. Braedee must be more persuasive than I thought. Or he knows more about us than I realized. . . ."

"I'm not a psion, to most people around here. Braedee wants it kept that way. I'll tell him you know." Hoping that would be enough to keep his mouth shut.

"Oh, your secret is safe with me." His face changed suddenly, started to twitch again. "Being a psion . . . doesn't it make you ashamed? Doesn't it make you want to pull your brains out? Jule wanted to. The way everyone treated her—" Something haunted his eyes then: *fear*. That it could have been him, and not his sister.

"Like you did?"

He frowned, twitching.

I went on down the hallway, and this time he didn't follow.

NINE

I WAS READY in the usual place at the usual time the next morning. I was the only one. It wasn't like Elnear or Jardan to be late. If anybody besides me hated mornings in that house, I didn't know about it. I leaned against the stairway banister with my eyes shut, waiting. The nagging ache that had started in my head yesterday afternoon was still there. It had slipped away when I inhaled some painkiller, but it came crawling back every time the medicine wore off. My stomach felt queasy, and I hadn't bothered with breakfast. I kept looking at the time, watching it get later and later, until all at once I wondered if they'd left without me. Suddenly my stomach and my head felt a whole lot worse. I spun out a searching finger of thought until it jabbed into Jardan's mind, still somewhere in the house.

I went back along the hall until I found her sitting in the sun room, sipping coffee as if there was all the time in the world. "You're late," I said.

She glanced up at me with a kind of cold spite. "No." She shook her head. "Lady Elnear is attending a board meeting of ChemEnGen this morning."

"Without me?"

"She's in her study." Jardan twitched her head in the general direction. "It isn't necessary for her to attend this meeting in person; it's merely a formality." Centauri's board held all the real power. "The rest of the day she'll be accessing, in preparation for the debate tomorrow—"

"Oh." I thought about how I could still have been upstairs asleep. "Thanks for letting me know."

"—Although after yesterday I would hardly blame her if she chose to leave you behind." She looked out the windows again.

"Maybe I had a—"

"Bound and gagged."

I swallowed what I'd been going to say. "Chew on rats," I said, and left the room.

Back upstairs I peeled off the Centauri clothes I'd been wearing and pulled on my new denims and my old shirt. Then I went down the back way and outside into the fresh air. I walked through the courtyard into the field beyond, something I'd never done before. The openness made me giddier than it usually did. I pushed myself to take one step and then another away from the high stone wall.

"Cat! Cat!"

I looked back, saw Talitha waving at me as she came around the corner of the wall, riding on the back of the biggest dog I'd ever seen. Her nanny was leading it by some kind of harness.

"Look at me!" she shouted, in a voice you could have heard on the next planet. "Do you want to ride with me? Her name is Bootsie, because she has little white boots!" The nanny hushed her, frowning.

The thing was kind of tan and white, its face half hidden in a tangle of thick hair. I backed up as her nanny jerked it to a stop beside me. If the woman had any name besides Nanny, I hadn't bothered to find it out. She always wore gray, and usually looked like she'd been sucking on something sour. She looked that way now. "Good morning," she said, sounding like she doubted it.

"You can ride with me," Talitha offered again, looking hopefully at me. "Can't he, Nanny?"

"Bootsie can't carry both of you," Nanny said flatly.

"Thanks anyway." I shook my head. "I don't like dogs."

"She's not a dog," Talitha said. "She's a pony. You don't ride on dogs."

"Oh."

"Come on, Talitha. I'm tired of walking. You've ridden long enough." Nanny jerked on the pony's lead again, starting to turn it back the way they'd come.

"No, no!" Talitha's face crumpled as she clutched at her saddle. "We didn't even go around the house! Please—"

"No."

I watched them start away, feeling the nanny's boredom and Talitha's helpless disappointment in my head like the taste of old metal. "I'll take her around for a while," I said.

Nanny wheeled the pony and its sniffling rider back again, slapped the lead rope into my hands before I could think about changing my mind. "Here," she said. "Be careful, it bites."

I grimaced.

"Bootsie never bites me," Talitha said.

Nanny headed back toward the house, taking the taste of old metal with her.

I looked at the pony; touched its mind, feeling the strange, shifting surface of an animal's thoughts, like clouds drifting across a sky. Not afraid, not angry . . . content and trusting. My hold on the rope loosened a little. In the distance I could see the Crystal Palace. Spines of light hit me in the eye as the molten sun poured over the mountain wall and turned it into a burning-glass. I could see another house, closer by, off to my left. "Whose house is that?" I asked, not really caring.

"That's Daric's house," Talitha said. I was sorry I'd asked. I looked toward my right, saw the river flowing by, wide and quiet. I started toward it, pulling on the pony's rope. At least the pony was something to hold onto as I crossed the empty field. We reached the river's edge and I stopped under a tree.

"Hey, Cat—"

I looked up, startled.

Jiro came swooping down on us in a rattle of artificial wings. The pony shied, jerking on the lead rope. Talitha squealed in fright. I caught the pony's mind inside a loop of forced calm, and settled it down fast.

Jiro landed beside us, the wings folding neatly behind him as he dropped his arms. "Did you see me? Just like a bird—" He raised one arm again, the wing fluttered.

"Jiro!" Talitha said. "You scared my pony."

"Oh." He shrugged. "I'm sorry, Tally. But isn't this really vork?

Auntie got it for me. Charon said I couldn't have one, it was too dangerous.''

I wondered if Elnear was hoping he'd break his neck, and there'd be one less taMing in the world. But even as I thought it, I knew that wasn't the reason she'd done it. She didn't hate these kids; she didn't even hate all the taMings. I wondered how she felt about the one she'd married. . . . Jiro was wearing a shock suit and a helmet; she'd bought him those, too.

"Why are you dressed like that?" he said.

"Like what?" I looked down at myself.

"Like you're zeroed." *Poor*.

I frowned. "Why do you always say the first thing that comes into your head, no matter how stupid it is?"

He stuck his lip out. "You should talk. I heard about what you said to Isplanasky."

I looked away. Talitha sat on the pony's back, singing, "I love my pony, I love my pony. . . ." over and over and over, while the pony tore at the soft green grass with its blunt teeth. The sudden fright had already disappeared from both their minds. I looked back at Jiro. "Why is it I never see any of you people talk to each other, but you always know everybody else's business?"

He just stared at me, blankly.

I shrugged, trying to shrug off my frustration. "Sometimes I get angry, because nobody around here understands anything." They were the worst kind of deadheads, thinking they knew everything when really they knew nothing, didn't even want to know. "Sometimes I say things because I can't help it."

"I do too." He looked up at me, and there was someone else trapped behind his eyes. I touched that other, hidden child with my thoughts. "Sometimes I can't help it. . . ." His throat worked.

I remembered what Lazuli had said . . . remembered that he had Charon taMing for a stepfather. I touched his shoulder lightly. "I know," I said.

He smiled, a little uncertain. "Mother said she knew you were really a good person, because Charon hates you so much."

It startled a laugh out of me. I didn't say anything for a minute, while half a dozen things cancelled each other out inside my head. "Where is your mother?"

"She's up at the Crystal Palace with Charon." His face twisted. "Auntie says 'Charon' is the name of some shipper in an ancient story, who used to transport dead bodies to Hell."

I laughed again.

"Someday I'm going to give him a dog with three heads."

"I want to see the dog with three heads!" Talitha burst out. She scrambled down out of the pony's saddle.

"I don't have it now, you flit—" Jiro said. "Where's *your* mother?"

I looked back at him, surprised. "She's dead."

His face pinched. "Where's your father?"

"I don't know."

"I don't know where my father is, either. . . ." He caught Talitha and pulled her toward him, holding her close while she squirmed. "Do you think if you wish something enough, it happens?"

I shook my head, watching the river pass like time.

"Don't let anything happen to Auntie."

I nodded.

"I want to fly." Talitha pulled at Jiro's wings.

"You're too little." He let go of her, pushing her away, as he unlatched the harness. "Here, you can try it—" He slung the wings toward me. "It has lifters, you don't really have to flap."

I looked up at the sky. My head and my stomach changed places just thinking about it. "No thanks."

He shrugged, and dumped the wings on the ground in a heap. "Okay. Let's do something else then."

I winced. "Jeezu. You're going to break that."

"Auntie'll get me another one." He was already stripping off his suit and helmet.

Talitha was wandering along the edge of the meadow, picking purple and white flowers, singing a formless song. I sat down under the tree, resting my back against the rough bark. Everything smelled good here. The pony snorted, still eating grass.

"You want to race? We could get more horses—" Jiro stood in front of me, in a bright red tunic and shorts.

"I don't know how to ride." I shrugged.

"We could race skimmers—"

"I don't know how to do that either."

I could feel annoyance growing like an itch under his skin. "We could go swimming—" He waved a hand at the river. "That's easy."

"I can't swim." I looked down, tracing lines in the dirt with my finger.

"Don't you know how to have fun—?"

I glanced up at him. He was still standing in front of me with his hands on his hips, frowning. "No. I guess not." I looked down again.

"Well *I* do." He peeled off his clothes and ran down to the river shore.

I watched him wade naked into the water and dive in, watched him swim with strong, easy motions, as if he'd been born to it, like a fish. I sat where I was, feeling the echo of his thoughts, the sensations of water and motion, like a kind of mocking laughter.

"Here." A fistful of dirt-clotted flowers shoved into my face, Talitha behind them. "These are for you. Why aren't you swimming, like Jiro?"

"I can't." I took the flowers awkwardly, dropping a couple.

She picked up the strays and pushed them into my hands. "For you. And these are for Mother, and Auntie, and my pony. . . ." She showed me the clump in her other hand, then put them carefully on the ground beside me. "Let's leave them here," she said, like she was the adult and I was the four-year-old, "and we can go down to the water like Jiro. I'll help you." She pulled open my fist and laid my flowers on the ground beside the rest, tugging at my arm while she did it.

"I suppose you can swim too," I said, getting up.

"Oh, no." She shook her head. "I'm only four. When I'm a big five-year-old, then I'll be able to swim. Maybe when you're five, you can swim too."

"Yeah. Maybe." We went down to the shore. The water was clear for about a meter out from the muddy bank. I could see smooth stones and tiny darting fish lying below its surface. After that it got deep faster, shading into brown and gray, reflecting the blue-green sky further out. Talitha waded in up to her knees, splashing and squealing, scattering fish. Slowly I pulled off my boots and rolled up my pants legs, and then I went in. It was freezing cold. The cold didn't seem to bother Talitha or Jiro. Clenching my teeth, I let her drag me after her, feeling the soft bottom squelch and shift between my toes, the edge of the deepwater current lick at me. I wasn't sure whether I liked it or not. I stopped when the cold water started slapping at my knees.

Jiro shouted and waved, Talitha giggled and splashed. Spray flew like rain. The sun felt good and hot on my back, the air was sweet, my face in the water's shimmering mirror said I was smiling . . . said that this day really belonged to me. And suddenly I felt a surge of panic that took my breath away. *Thief.*

I backed out of the water again and sat down on the bank, breathing hard, putting distance between me and something that had more to do with watching them play in the river than with the cold water touching my skin, or the muddy bottom shifting under my feet. . . . The feeling I'd had when I'd entered the taMing's castle on the cliff—that I didn't have the right to be here; or even the right to know that places like this existed.

The heat of the sun soaked into my flesh, making me sweat. After a while I unknotted my fingers, stretched out the muscles in my arms, and pulled my shirt off. The wind breathed on my sweating skin, letting the heat inside me escape. I picked through the smooth warm stones that lay in a dark mosaic all around me. I tossed them into the cold water, one by one, watching the rings they made as they fell, watching the way the rings collided, overlapped, mingled like the patterns of separate minds converging.

Talitha came back onto the shore and sat down beside me. She began to make mud cakes. After a minute Jiro burst up out of the water like some kind of monster, making her shriek, and splashed ashore to pull on his clothes. He picked up a stone and threw it, making it dance across the water like it was massless. I threw another stone and it sank.

He squatted down beside me. "What's the most fun you ever had?"

I glanced at him. Three more stones hit the water and sank, while I searched my mind for an answer that would mean something to him. The kind of games they played in Oldcity were the kind you learned the hard way. "You ever see a comet ball?"

"Sure. I've got four of them, in different colors."

My mouth twitched. "I had one once. When I was a little older than you. It was incredible. Oldcity's kind of like N'Yuk in a way, closed in, no sky—Quarro buried it when the new city spread out. Except it's dark in Oldcity, even in the daytime. Your whole world's only about ten meters high, there in the streets. . . ." I'd snatched the control box out of a storefront after a fire, but I didn't say that. I hadn't known what it was. When I'd switched it on, a huge sizzling ball of light had exploded out of the wand and gone rocketing up toward the roof of the world. "It was like trying to hold onto that—" I glanced up at the sun for a second, down again. "Like trying to reel it in on a string. . . ." It had bounced off the tangled undersides of Quarro, leaped back and forth from wall to building wall, shooting sparks, lighting up the backstreet gloom like a captive star. After a minute or so of just staring, I'd begun to realize that I could control it with the wand. I could make it do anything I wanted, leap and spiral, paint pictures on my retinas with fire. "Everyone came out into the street to watch me . . . to see it. They kept handing me food and brew, shouting, 'Keep it going!' It was the best show I'd ever seen—any of us had ever seen, maybe. I felt like kind of a hero, giving them all this free sun show. . . ." I remembered wishing it could go on forever.

It had lasted for about an hour, before someone who'd wondered why somebody like me had something like that had let the Corpses know about it. They'd busted me for stolen goods. I'd spent the next four months of nights in a meter-high detention coffin, the days cleaning urinals or down on my hands and knees scrubbing the lightblocks of Oldcity's glowing pavements with a brush, wearing a monitored stun collar locked around my throat. And that had really seemed to last forever.

It hadn't been worth it. I hadn't even been able to stomach thinking about the memory afterwards. I hadn't thought about it in years. It surprised me that I'd remembered it now; almost as much as it would have surprised me then to know that someday I'd be sitting here, five hundred light-years away, on this riverbank in the sun with a couple of rich kids.

"If that's your favorite thing, you don't look very happy about it," Jiro said. *Doubt, confusion, disappointment* flickered through his thoughts like a chain reaction.

"It was a long time ago." I shrugged, and got up. "Why is it so hot here? I thought it was almost winter." On the distant mountainside the autumn colors were burning like a fire, but all around us in the valley it was still warm and green.

"It's part of the system." Jiro scrambled to his feet while I pushed my boots on. "You know—the security and everything. It never gets real hot or real cold, everybody likes it like that. It never snows down here."

I shook my head, half smiling. If you wanted your life to be a long summer afternoon here, all you had to do was say so. . . . "What if you want snow?"

"You can go to the chalet."

I didn't bother to ask what that was.

"Let's go to Daric's house. Argentyne is there—"

"No thanks." I didn't think there was anybody in the universe who could make me want to visit Daric.

"But she's famous! Don't you want to meet her?"

That was all I needed. I shook my head, tying my shirt sleeves around my neck. "Come on, Talitha. I'll take you back." She got up, resigned, and let me set her on the pony's back again. Jiro put his wings on, looking sullen. "You're going to get it, Tally—look what you did." He pointed at her muddy clothes, glanced at me as if it was my fault. Talitha pouted. Jiro ran and leaped, rising into the air like a kite. He circled us a couple of times as we plodded back across the field. Then he headed away toward Daric's house, alone. I felt kind of sorry for him; but not sorry enough to change my mind.

I led Talitha back toward the house. Nanny got up from a garden seat like a shadow and came to take her away. She caught one look at a muddy leg. "My Lady—!" she called. Lazuli came down off of the porch into the sunlight, shielding her eyes.

"Mother! Mother!" Talitha squealed, bouncing up and down in her saddle with a grin so guiltless and wide I almost didn't regret anything.

Lazuli looked at her, and at me, and I felt her try for anger, only finding laughter. "I guess you are an anarchist, after all," she said to me. It was what Isplanasky had called me, yesterday. I winced. "Oh, come on, Nanny." Lazuli looked back at the older woman. "It's only a little bit of mud. Reality doesn't frighten us that much around here—" The irony in her voice surprised me. Even she wasn't sure how she meant it.

Nanny sighed heavily, and led Talitha, skipping and waving, into the house.

"Jiro is with Gentleman Daric, ma'am." So she wouldn't think I'd drowned him.

Lazuli turned back to me. She glanced down at the half-wilted bunch of flowers in my hand, as the pony I was somehow still holding started to eat them. I held them away from its mouth.

"Are those for me?" she asked, still half mocking, and half surprised.

"Uh . . . yeah." I put them into her hands. "From Talitha."

She took them, still looking up at me as she held them close to her face, breathing in the sweet smell. An odd disappointment tickled the back of her eyes, making her blink.

Suddenly feeling like an ass, I said, "And from me too, I guess."

"Thank you." She smiled then, tucking the flowers into the waistband of her flowered tunic. Her legs were bare, and perfect. She took the pony's lead rope from my hand, her fingers touching mine. "Let me take that. You look like you want to be rid of it. . . . You're very good with children, and it's kind of you to spend time with mine." She began to lead Bootsie away, looking at me all the while. Wanting me to follow.

I followed. "They're nice kids," I said, because I had to say
something, and because I suddenly realized it was true. *Sad kids*. But
I didn't say that. I thought about them growing up into the next generation of the Centauri controlling board.

She was silent for a while, walking beside me. "I love them so
much," she said at last, the words forced out past something in her
throat. "Sometimes I begin to lose my perspective about things when
. . . things close in on me. I don't want to turn around someday and
find that I've lost them. When I think about that, when I even try to
imagine being without them, I don't think I could bear it. . . ." She
was thinking about her first husband. "You look at me so strangely
sometimes, Cat." She looked back at me, quizzical and embarrassed.

I blinked and shook my head. "It's just that sometimes you look
so much like Jule . . . ma'am."

"Oh, Jule . . ." She glanced away, stopped. Someone came
toward us from the low stone outbuildings, and took the pony. "She's
married now, isn't she?" She looked at me again, a sudden questioning
look, like she wished she could read my mind. "To another psion?"

"Yes, ma'am." I remembered that she didn't know what I was.
When she looked at me all she saw was a human face.

"Don't call me ma'am," she said gently, "it makes me feel old.
Call me Lazuli."

I nodded, suddenly not able to say anything at all.

She smiled again, as if she knew it. "Will you walk with me a
while? It's such a beautiful day, and no one gets enough exercise
around here."

"Except Lady Elnear," I said.

She laughed. "I like the way your mind works."

I wondered what she'd think of it if she really knew, the way
Jule did. . . . "Did you know Jule very well?"

"No." She shook her head. "Barely at all. I've only heard about
her. Stories . . ." *Not good ones*. "Poor thing." She was thinking
her cousin must be happier now. With her own kind.

"She doesn't need anybody's pity," I said.

Lazuli glanced at me. "I'm sorry. You really do care about Jule,
don't you?"

I nodded, still not quite able to call her by name.

"Did you love her . . . do you?"

Irritation and sudden memory spilled into each other in my mind,
oil and water. "She's my best friend." Telling the truth. Part of it.
Once I'd looked at her and wanted her body, thinking that was all love

was. But then I'd shared her mind. Siebeling had taught me a lot of things, he'd given me my psi; but Jule had given me the real gift. She'd made me whole. She'd changed everything I knew about women, and men, and myself. And I'd finally realized that I didn't love her the same way Siebeling did . . . that to be her friend was all I really wanted from her, all I really needed.

I felt Lazuli's curiosity withdraw; but her hand still held onto my arm. And she was still too much like Jule when I looked at her . . . but not enough like her to keep me safe. We walked along the shadow of the high stone wall; private, discreet. "It takes a lot of . . . courage, to be that close to someone most people would be afraid of," she said.

I made a sound like a laugh, that wasn't. "She was more afraid of all of you. And she had more right to be."

She was silent then, wondering whether she'd really understood me, or whether I was leaving too much unsaid on purpose. My bare arm under her hand was slippery with sweat; the heat of the day seemed to breathe on us. I felt a tension rising in her that had nothing to do with the conversation. I felt it rising in me, too, as I realized what it was.

"Is something wrong?" she asked, finally.

I shook my head. "I . . . just a headache. Comes and goes. It's all right—"

But she led me to a wooden bench along the bright edge of the gardens, and made me sit down. The air was filled with the hum of insects. "Sometimes if you rub the temples, just here . . ." she murmured. I felt her fingertips against my sweating forehead, moving in slow, gentle circles. . . . Her face, her hair—too familiar—her lips almost touching mine, the smell of flowers and sunwarmed skin . . . Suddenly I couldn't look away from her eyes, because I could see all the way through to what lay behind them. "Is that better?" she murmured. She took her hands away, and that was worse.

"Yes," I mumbled.

One hand still hovered, touching the white line of the scar over my left eye. It dropped down to trace another jagged line along my ribs. "You have a fine body," she said, "but you haven't taken care of it. You should treat it more gently—it has to last for a long time."

"I know." My head wasn't the only part of it that ached now.

"When you're so young, you think that everything lasts." She looked away.

"No," I said. "I know it doesn't. Lazuli—"

"Cat!"

I jerked around on the bench, looking up. I could just see Elnear standing on the balcony of her study, staring straight down at us.

"Would you come inside please?"

I pushed to my feet, the spell broken that had stopped time, stopped thought inside me. I left Lazuli there, backing away until I could make myself turn and walk looking ahead toward the house.

I went up the steps, through the door, into the cool shadowy hall, blinking as I followed it to Elnear's study. My mind was still lost somewhere back along the path from the garden. I didn't know what Elnear was going to say to me; worse, I didn't know how I was going to answer it. "Ma'am?" I said at last, my voice hoarse, as I stopped in her doorway.

Elnear turned away from the windows. She came toward me, silhouetted by the light. At first I couldn't make out her expression. But I felt it.

"I don't know what you think you are doing here," she said, not even bothering with the usual polite pretensions. "But you are not here to insinuate yourself into the private lives of this family. I will not have you using your—telepathy," she said it like an obscenity, "to take advantage of children, or of a troubled woman who doesn't know what she wants."

I felt my face burning. "I wasn't—" I broke off, realizing that it was no use. That true or not, nothing I could say would make any difference to her. And that was the worst part of all. "I don't understand it," I said, finally.

"What don't you understand?" She kept the length of a long tabletop inlaid with stars between us, and a wall of *anger contempt fear*.

"Why Jule thought you loved her. She asked me to help you because she said you were the only one who ever loved her. That's the real reason I came here—because she asked me to. You must have hated her just as much as everyone else did."

Her mouth worked; she wanted to blame me for the pain that was suddenly there inside her, but she couldn't. She turned away, looking at something across the room. Her husband's picture. She said, her voice almost inaudible, "Jule was so helpless . . . so lost . . . she needed someone so much, someone who would love her unconditionally. . . ." She looked back at me, and suddenly in her mind there was the unwanted image of how I'd looked that first day, as she'd left me standing there alone in the sunroom. "Jule was different."

I turned, moving too fast because I wanted to get away from her so much. My shirt caught on the outstretched arm of a sculpture standing by the doorway. I heard cloth rip as it jerked me up short; the loose-knotted sleeves came undone around my neck, and my shirt dropped to the carpet. I leaned down, grabbed it up, swearing. It was torn right across the front.

"Cat." Elnear's voice caught at me like the sculpture's arm.

I straightened up, the shirt wadded between my fists, facing away from her.

"How . . . who did that to your back?"

"Nobody." I took a step.

"Cat."

"Ask Isplanasky." I turned to face her again. "I got out of Contract Labor with my skin intact, right? So there's nothing wrong with my back." I threw my ruined shirt over my shoulders, tied it in a knot again, covering my scars.

"That happened to you while you worked for Contract Labor?" Not really a question. "I have heard that some of the combines treat their laborers badly," she said, awkwardly. "The FTA tries to maintain—"

"The FTA did this to me." I remembered how it had felt as the charged prod laid a line of liquid fire across my naked back, and another, and another. "At the Federation Mines, out in the Crab Colonies . . . If it hadn't been for Jule paying off my contract, I wouldn't be standing here right now. Forty-five percent of the bondies there don't live long enough to last out their time. But you probably never access that kind of information."

She looked at me for what seemed like hours, bracing herself by her hand on the back of a chair . . . looked at me and thought about my words, and looked, and thought . . . like someone looking at a square with five sides. At last she said, "I understand now why you said what you did yesterday. But I don't understand how it could happen. Natan would never allow—"

"You said it yourself. Humans don't run the FTA; it runs itself. Isplanasky doesn't run the Federation Mines—he doesn't even run Contract Labor, any more than I do."

She'd said it, but she hadn't heard what she was saying. "But the whole reason the FTA exists is to protect the welfare of . . . of the dispossessed," she said. "Not to create more suffering. Why should it exploit with one hand as it stops exploitation with the other?" There was no echo of recognition in her mind; she was so deep inside her own vision of her work that she couldn't see anything else.

"Do you eat meat?" I said.

She looked at me blankly. "Yes, I do."

"But you consider yourself a moral person, right? You love animals, you have them for pets, you'd never kick a dog in the street. How do you justify eating meat?"

"I . . ." Her face reddened. "I have to eat to survive."

"Jule never eats meat."

She looked away, her fingers stretching open at her sides. I wondered which of us was more surprised by this conversation.

"Okay," I said, "so maybe the FTA even considers itself a moral being. You called it a Humane Society for humans. But it's got to eat. And eating meat is easier."

One hand rose to her head, ruffling her hair. "Your point, Cat," she murmured, finally. "A point well taken. I will speak with Natan about it, when I get the chance."

"You really think that'll make any difference?"

She frowned slightly; the frown faded. "Individuals have been known to change their minds. Even on such a scale. But they need input, information. Just as you said."

"Is that why you're doing this debate?" I'd wondered why she bothered, if she didn't think that what individual humans wanted or believed made any difference any more. Maybe it explained why she wanted to be on the Security Council too; maybe her reasons really went deeper than just wanting power, or to escape from the taMings. "You really think there are some ways you can still matter?"

"I suppose I do." She nodded, but she wasn't sure of anything now, not even of why she really wanted that Council slot. She moved back toward the windows, the bright heat of anger gone out of her, her movements slow and almost aimless. She wanted me to go away. It was what I wanted, too, but somehow I couldn't. I couldn't let go of that invisible line between us that neither of us knew how to snap.

She stared down at the gardens, outlined by the light. Lazuli was gone; gone from sight, but not from her thoughts. "How is Jule?" she asked at last. "What is her life like now, with Dr. Siebeling? Is she finally, truly happy?"

"As happy as anybody ever is, I guess." I crossed the room until I stood beside her on the balcony. But not too close. "She and Siebeling have a little place upside in Quarro. She's got it full of stray animals . . . she can't leave anything alone that needs help. Doc just steps over them, and smiles." I'd been her first stray. After he'd learned to live with me, he hadn't minded the rest. "Siebeling's good for her.

She's good for him. They have a place in Oldcity were they help other psions to pull their lives back together, like they did for themselves . . . and for me.''

"I'm so glad.'' She was. I felt her thoughts begin to find a center, an anchor, in the image of Jule smiling, helping others to smile. Maybe there was still hope after all, even for herself. . . . She glanced back at me, her eyes questioning.

"Have you ever been to Quarro, ma'am?'' Asking it before she could ask a question nobody really wanted answered right now.

"Yes, many times. I keep a house in Quarro.''

"You ever go to the Hanging Gardens there?'' It gave me a chance to look away from her, out at these gardens again. When I'd first seen the Hanging Gardens, when I was sixteen or seventeen, I couldn't believe that what I saw was natural, barely even believed it was real. I remembered the colors had been too bright, the forms too incredible, the rich sweet perfume of the flowers too intense. The Gardens rimmed the access well that was the only way in or out of Oldcity. They'd been right over my head all my life, always just out of reach.

"It's a beautiful place,'' Elnear said. "Some of the most exquisite gardens I've ever seen.''

"It's beautiful here, too. Sometimes it reminds me of . . . of Quarro.'' I couldn't quite make myself say "home.''

"Does it?'' She looked surprised, looked out at her own gardens again. "I guess you have to be a stranger to a place to really see its beauty.''

"Did you ever look over the edge when you were there at the Gardens?''

"Over the edge?'' she asked, trying to imagine what I was talking about.

"Into the Tank. Into Oldcity.''

She shook her head. "No.''

"You have to live in a place to really know its ugliness.''

"Yes.'' Suddenly she wasn't seeing the gardens any more. Sorrow settled over her, graying her mind, sloping her shoulders, until I was sorry I'd said it. "I must get back to my work.'' She meant getting ready to face Stryger in the debate, to defend her belief in the FTA's incorruptibility (she glanced at me as she turned away from the window), to take another step toward a slot on the Security Council, and away from here, the taMings, Centauri—this trap that her world had become. "If you'll excuse me . . .''

"Ma'am—'' I said. She turned back. "I hate Centauri nearly as

much as you do. I . . .'' as she looked at me, ''I just wanted you to
know that. Braedee won't hear anything from me again that you don't
clear first.''

Suddenly she was remembering what I'd said about the real reason
why I'd come here to work for her; suddenly she was really hearing
it. She looked down, moving random objects randomly on her desk:
a statue of a child, a glass ball with a fragile puffball flower suspended
impossibly inside it. . . . For just a second I stared at it, because the
ball looked so much like something I'd had once: a Hydran thing, full
of hidden secrets, that had felt warm and almost alive when I held it
in my hands. . . . But that was gone; this was only a cold ball made
of glass, with an image inside it that never changed. Like a memory.
She looked up again, and caught me still staring. I turned away from
the look in her eyes and went out of the room without saying anything
more.

TEN

SOME DWEEB ONCE said to me, ''Cheer up. Things could always be
worse.'' He was right about that much.

The face debate on drug deregulation was set for late afternoon
the next day. I got to the place where it was going to happen about
midday, before Elnear and Jardan, working with Braedee's Security
crew this time. I'd had to argue Braedee into letting me come. I wasn't
sure whether it was the news that Daric knew about me, or the trouble
I'd caused in Isplanasky's office, or just his own fear of psions that
made him try to tell me that before Elnear got there I didn't matter.

He finally gave in, the way someone would stop chasing a fly because it wasn't important enough to waste time on.

The floating Independent News studio had been set up inside a historic landmark deep in the heart of N'Yuk. It was a thick-walled building made of gray stone that had been a godshouse before the Re-creation. Since the Indy couldn't count on an interplanetary freighter to crash-land during the debate, they'd wanted to give the viewers something to look at besides heads if their attention wandered. When I walked in, it was like walking into a kaleidoscope. The tall, arching windows along the side walls were made of thousands of bits of colored glass fused together, pictures of paradise painted from fragments of pure light. The Indy production crew had backlit them all for perfect effect, and rainbows of color bled into the stagnant air above the stage.

It had been Stryger's idea to have this debate; but the Indy News had made it a reality. They'd even gotten an exclusive lock on it. They were plugging a lot of other vips into the same circuits with Stryger, so that curious citizens all over the Federation could get close to them in a way they didn't get to very often—while they were simply speaking their minds, not sending hidden messages through channels that only they could access. With all the publicity support Stryger had gotten, the ratings for this event would probably be astronomical. Everybody involved with it hoped they would be. The thousands of channels that wove the Net's million separate corporate systems into something like a coherent whole were mostly there to keep their citizens amused; but they were also a way that combines too paranoid to communicate directly could send out messages under a white flag to each other, and to the rest of the galaxy.

Shander Mandragora was moderating the debate. Mandragora was the Indy's most popular fax hyper; even I knew who he was. He covered anything important the Federation Assembly did, and what they did was always important to somebody. Other hypers, from more combine networks than anybody knew existed, had been crawling all over the floating studio where the debate was set since before dawn that morning. Most of them were bitching about the Indy's calculated generosity in letting them help it spread its logo all over their private systems.

The media techs were easy to spot—their attitude was *if you got it, flaunt it*. They wore their cyber equipment openly as they swaggered past; third eyes and hand-cameras, all their senses wired to record. Like street gangs, they liked the idea of standing out from the crowd. It gave them a special power, like psi . . . but it was one the combines wanted and needed, so it made them different, but it didn't make them freaks. I felt a kind of jealousy as I watched them, the easy arrogance their portable territory gave them.

After a while the debaters themselves finally began to arrive. Besides Stryger and Elnear, the main draws in this particular info-tainment, there was Isplanasky repping the FTA, three Assembly members fronting various combine blocs, and a couple of Corporate Security Chiefs. Stryger came in first with his band of ass-kissing disciples, carrying his walking stick in his hand. *Sojourner* meant *seeker*. He always carried the staff, as a kind of symbol of his journey. The wash of colored light from the windows only made him look more beautiful. There was no doubt in his mind that he was going to make this day his. He was in his element; I wondered if somehow he'd had something to do with them choosing this place for the debate.

He spotted me in the crowd, almost as if he could feel me staring at him, feel my hatred, or my fascination. . . . He saw me, and suddenly his confidence screamed, rattling through my skull.

I stood there watching while he stopped his forward momentum, lifting his staff to stop the momentum of everyone around him as he saw me. They swirled to a halt in a kind of confused slow motion while he looked into my eyes and thought, *(I know you're listening. . . .)* The words were fuzzy and shapeless, formed by a mind without any sensitivity to the Gift, but clear enough. He raised his staff to me in a kind of benediction, and smiled, as if he knew some secret that only we two shared. *(Bless you, boy, you are the answer to all my prayers.)* He smiled, a smile so sweet it should have been a lover's, a smile that leered at me like a slashed throat. I wanted to use my psi on him, to find out what he meant by that—to see his smug face crack, to feel his *loathing, disgust, raw hatred*—anything but what I felt inside him now. But his confidence was real, and it turned my concentration to random noise. At last he looked away from me and went on, setting me free to slink off like a coward and lose myself in the crowd of techs.

Elnear came in with Jardan a few minutes later, and the media imageshapers crawled all over her like bugs, like they'd done with the rest. Only Stryger had his own personal image crew. I sat in a corner close by Elnear, trying to make myself invisible while I kept track of the swarms of hypers buzzing around her. She was wearing a body-guard, like all the speakers, but I did my job anyway. Now and then Jardan sent me to fetch something or someone, her voice like a barbed whip; waiting for me to do something half-assed again. Isplanasky

stopped by for some kind of last minute exchange, and glanced at me
like he expected me to explode. But as he passed me on his way out
he said, "I want to see you later." At least it didn't sound like a
threat.

Finally every piece was pushed into place. I settled onto one of
the hard historical benches beside Jardan, herded together by Security
with all the other aides and hangers-on and hypers. Up on the stage
the speakers seemed to float above the curving band of light that was
their mutual podium, flowing into the sea of light behind them. I
wondered how anyone would be able to concentrate on anything but
that light. The words had better be good.

They were good. I leaned back, listening to one speaker after
another, the talking heads that gave human faces to the beliefs and
policies of faceless economic networks. These people had been chosen
because they knew how to come across well—and because, whatever
they were saying about the deregulation of pentryptine, that it was a
disaster or a blessing or didn't really matter in the Great Motion of
Time, they believed it. They were all augmented, and they were plugged
into Mandragora, letting him monitor their sincerity electronically.
The viewers could readout for themselves exactly how much to trust
what they saw and heard. Even Isplanasky came across clean and
sincere in everything he said.

But in the end it all came down to Elnear and Stryger, the unspoken
rivalry between them, the opening on the Security Council that they
both wanted. Nobody was saying anything about it, not yet anyway,
but everyone knew: all the hypers waiting with their questions and
their prefab points of view, the Federation Assembly members, the
Security Council itself. They'd all be weighing the impression the
speakers made, their impact on the audience . . . the leverage they
could get on the Assembly, which would prove their strength when
the votes on deregulation were counted. Deregulation was still being
data-modeled by an Assembly special committee. But Elnear—and
everyone else—knew that the committee would approve it in the next
few days. And the way things stood the measure was almost as sure
to pass on the Assembly floor.

Isplanasky finished his speech and Mandragora gave the audience
to Elnear at last. She looked out over the crowd, her eyes searching
their faces as if she was looking for someone; but there was too much
light. She looked at Mandragora again. "I had a very unusual conversation yesterday," she said. "With someone who asked me why I
was participating in this debate, when I had told him that I thought

individual human beings no longer had control of the Federation's fate, that our lives were ruled by the whims of interstellar commerce. . . .''

I leaned forward in sudden surprise. Jardan glanced over at me, irritated.

"I told him that I would be here today because I believed that even something on the scale of the Federation Assembly or a multi-world combine could still be influenced, if the evidence had enough weight, enough public opinion behind it pushing. I know that there are enough individual citizens inputting us here to influence the courses chosen by even such gigantic systems. You have the access right in your hands to register your opinion on the open Net. I want you to do that, whatever your decision is, so that you can see the power you still have, if you choose to use it.

"Because yesterday this person asked me some other questions, hard questions about the things I believed in. The Federation he knows is a very different place from the one I know. It made me realize how easy it is to dismiss a problem that doesn't seem to touch you directly—how deceptive, how dangerous. He also said to me that 'you have to know a place to really see its ugliness.' . . . Well, I know the biochem business.''

I listened as she went on speaking, telling them her vision of what letting these chemicals loose could do to the individual human identities of the billions of people receiving her, and how easily it could be done. Telling everyone that she was on the board of a drug combine that held the major patents on those drugs. That it would make profits off of them that would bloat ChemEnGen (and Centauri, although she didn't mention it by name). Telling the Federation that she still couldn't accept the promises that had been made about safety, because she knew too well how much promises were worth. . . . The words weren't that different from the ones Isplanasky had spoken; but there was a heat behind them that seared them into your brain. As if this wasn't just a matter of ideology, but something she felt as responsible for as her own life. As if those invisible billions were her own family, her children. . . .

Jardan sat silently beside me, her eyes on Elnear, her face shining with pride and reflected light. All the speakers had been good, but Elnear was genuine, original—the best.

But she wasn't the last. I looked at Stryger as Mandragora introduced him, and all the eyes in the room, real or recording, began to focus on him. He was the only one who seemed to belong here. His face was as translucent and glowing as the air, radiating the intensity of his own belief, in himself, in the divine power he thought was speaking through him. If this place hadn't been chosen just to suit him, it might as well have been. He began to speak: strong but easy words, nothing about God or damnation; letting the listeners know he wasn't a fanatic, or a combine vip, but just a concerned Everybody.

I tried not to listen to what he was saying or to look at him, and yet my glance kept falling out of the air, away from the windows, back to his face again. Partly because I couldn't help hating him; and partly because, like the last time, I just couldn't look away. Maybe absolute confidence gave you that kind of gravitational pull, or maybe it was just the fanatic's intensity he'd been born with. But I kept watching, kept listening, as his speech slowly sucked a billion minds into the "dark underside of life" that he claimed to understand, like he really knew anything about it. . . . *About killing to stay alive, about stealing to keep from starving, about making ten credits the hard way, and using it to buy enough drugs to help you forget what you'd just done to earn it.* . . . Talking about how *his* drugs could "let the light" into the minds and lives of all those deeves and pervs and psions (and there was no change in his voice, as if he didn't really hate psions any more than murderers or rapists)—those trouble-makers who still kept crawling out of the cracks to violate humanity, kept it from running like a perfect machine, when we had the means within our grasp to change all that forever—His voice was ringing now, his eyes were smoking, but I could feel him still in perfect control of the rising spiral.

And there was nothing at all on the readout below him, nothing that would prove to anyone watching whether he meant every word of it or not. *He wasn't cybered,* Isplanasky had said. He had no way to tie into the Indy's system. But somehow, instead of making him seem like he had something to hide, it only made him seem to be above all that, so goddamn pure that he didn't need to prove his sincerity to anyone.

". . . Lady Elnear is concerned that deregulating the production of these drugs might lead to their misuse. . . ."

I looked up again, as I heard him mention Elnear.

". . . But I believe that it would be taking them *out* of the hands of those people who already misuse and abuse them . . . the criminals who now produce and illegally sell tiny quantities of these drugs for astronomical prices on the Lack Market. To defend the laws that force these drugs into the hands of those very criminals who are now the only ones who profit from them financially is hardly in anyone's best interest. They are the ones who could profit the most morally if the drugs were used as they were meant to be used.

"To suggest, as Lady Elnear has, that using these drugs for the purpose God intended is evil can only be called misguided. To say that the combine networks that provide for all our needs are worse than the criminals that exploit us is irresponsible. I have always believed that Lady Elnear was sincere in her unflinching crusade to create a more humane society—

"But now I must question you, Lady." He turned to face her, violating the structure of the debate, which was supposed to leave Mandragora in charge of asking the questions. "Are you not in fact protecting the deviants in our society, protecting those degenerates you claim to detest as much as I do?"

Elnear looked at him, startled, caught off-guard. "Of course not. I'm sure you know that that was not my point at all—"

"It has come to my attention, Lady Elnear, that you actually have a psion, a Hydran halfbreed, a telepath, employed on your personal staff. Isn't that true?"

Elnear flushed; for a second her gaze left Stryger's face, flashed out over the watchers. The readouts jumped and changed colors below her. "Well . . . yes, I do . . . but—" Beside me Jardan murmured a curse. I felt her sudden useless fury as she looked at me.

"What possible reason could you have for employing a member of a group known for its instability and criminality, its destructive effect on society? I hardly need to remind anyone here of what would have happened to the Federation if the psionic renegade called Quicksilver had successfully seized control of the Federation Mines, only three years ago—"

"I don't believe in holding an entire group responsible for the actions of a few of its members," Elnear said. She recovered fast. "There is a long history of persecution of psions—both Hydran and human—by the Federation. I have always tried to judge individuals on their own abilities."

"This individual, who serves as your personal aide, has a criminal record. Were you aware that he was one of the psions who conspired with the terrorist Quicksilver to hold the Federation's telhassium supply for ransom?"

Elnear broke off again, her mouth still halfway open for speech. "No, I wasn't aware. . . ."

"His record also includes assault, theft, and drug abuse . . . an all too typical record. . . ."

I swore softly. *How the hell did he find out?* It wasn't in the public records. And he was making me out to be a traitor, and that was a goddamn lie. I wanted to shout it out to Elnear, to the whole Federation—

Jardan caught my arm as I started to get up, jerking me around. "Move!" she hissed at me. I felt her rage transfer through her hand and up my arm, into my head. "Before you do any more damage."

"But it's a lie—"

"Shut up, you fool." She dragged me toward the closest exit, her mind a nightmare of what would happen if those hypers gathered like a pack of dogs around us got hold of me.

"It's hard for me to believe that with the security access available to you, you wouldn't have known about such a thing," Stryger was baying. "How you could possibly consider such a person suitable to work for you, unless there was some other reason. . . ."

I didn't give Jardan any more argument; I just followed, as fast as I could, keeping my head down until we reached the door. The door read our IDs and released, letting us out without any trouble.

"There were unusual circumstances. . . ." I heard Elnear protesting, felt her rising desperation drowned in my mind by the rising excitement of the crowd. And then the door sealed shut behind us, cutting off her voice, and that was the last I heard.

The cold, sheer-walled tunnel of street was silent and empty, except for the floating banks of lights high above us. Security had cleared everything for levels around before the debate started. As we stopped outside Jardan turned suddenly, before I even had time to react, and hit me.

"Damn it, Jardan—" I gasped.

"God damn you!" I saw the furious tears backing up in her eyes. She said, "The worst part is that Stryger is right about psions!"

"Wait a minute—" Pain began to throb behind my own eyes, frustration trying to beat its way out.

A mod dropped down from somewhere, answering her summons. ChemEnGen's logo was on its side. She climbed into it; tried to slam the door on me. I forced it open again. She let me in, but only because she remembered how much worse it would be for Elnear if she left me there for the hypers to find. She sat back in her seat, pressing into the formfoam. The mod began to drone, "Destination please, destination please, destination please," until she finally gave it orders.

"Damn it," I said. "It's Stryger, not me!"

She looked back at me, wiping fiercely at her face. "If you didn't exist, there was nothing he could have done to her—nothing. That was true, what he said about you. Wasn't it—?'' Her hand tightened into a fist.

"No! He twisted it around. I'm not a traitor.''

"You don't have a criminal record?''

"Yeah, but. . . .'' *But nobody was supposed to know that. . . . It wasn't my fault. . . .* I shook my head. It didn't matter. I'd lost Elnear the debate, and maybe the vote, and the Council . . . her freedom, the freedom of every psion. By being a psion. The answer to Stryger's prayers.

I shut my eyes, put my hands over my ears, bit my lip, stopped breathing. . . . To keep my brain from screaming out loud. The pain circled my head like a knotted cord, tightening . . . eased off as I slowly got myself under control again. After a few more deep breaths, I opened my eyes.

Jardan was rigid in her seat, staring at me like she thought she was trapped with a lunatic. I lowered my hands, wove my fingers together in the space between my knees to steady them. She looked away from me finally, wishing we were already at our destination, wishing I'd disappear.

The mod went on silently through the hollow streets, the endless muted silvers and grays, blue-greens and golds, the steel and composite caverns. We flowed through the arteries and veins of a fossilized insect sealed in high-tech amber, heading toward some destination I didn't have any control over. We'd been supposed to go back to the FTA plex after the debate; but that wasn't really an option, now. I wondered how much longer the questions would go on behind us, how long Elnear would have to face them down. I began to sweat just thinking about having those bloodsucking hypers after my throat. I wondered where we were going, where Jardan thought she could hide me from them.

At last we funneled into one of the arching legs that straddled the river on the western edge of the city. The inner skin of the tube was fleshed with more city, with offices and townhouses. The mod homed in on one of them, tracking its electronic scent like a hound until we were setting down on a terrace somewhere high above the river. A taMing townhouse. I remembered that there was going to be a reception here tonight, for Elnear, after the debate. More like a funeral, now. Until now, Elnear's biggest worry about tonight had been that parties wasted her time.

I couldn't look down along the glass-smooth, green/black building front as we crossed the black mirror of the polished terrace. Looking up along its curve was nearly as bad. I followed Jardan in through the high, lacquered doors, into a dark entry hall. Clatter and conversation reached us from a distance; I could feel the electricity of minds overloading with last-minute preparation for tonight. But here, just inside the entrance, it was still quiet, and we were still alone.

Jardan turned on me, hard-eyed. Her hand gripped my arm until it spasmed. "Follow me. Say *nothing*." She led me through the townhouse, avoiding everyone as she took me up in a lift three or four levels. She left me in a cramped, stuffy room that passed for a study, even though I knew by the dead smell of the air that no one ever used it. "Keep the door locked. Speak to no one, until the Lady has spoken to you. Do you understand me?"

I nodded, and she left me there alone. I stood in the middle of the room, without even the strength to move, staring around me. The room was high and narrow, like everything about this place. At its end there was a high, narrow window. Outside the early evening light was slanting across the river; shadows were filling in the valleys of the city's carapace. The space around me was filled with a fungal growth of pale, diseased-looking furniture.

I hated the thought of touching anything, afraid it might crumble away like rotting wood, but after a while I got tired of standing. I went toward the window, sat down on the quivering edge of a shelfseat. I couldn't hear any sounds now. I stared out at the view of the sheer, shining city wall, the gray-blue river waters rolling by below. A few hours ago it would have seemed beautiful to me; but suddenly nothing looked like it had before.

I sat and thought about the time when the most important thing in my life had been whether I could scrounge enough food to make it through another week; when all I'd cared about was slipping enough stolen goods to a freedrop to make what I owed to the dealerman; when a tough problem was finding a warm place to sleep at night. When everything was simple: Life, or death. . . . I slumped forward, letting my aching head rest in my hands. *When I hadn't understood why somebody only had to look at me to hate me.*

I stayed like that, waiting, while the sky slowly changed beyond the windows and the world blued over . . . until the day was teetering on the edge of night. Then at last I heard the soft sucking sound as the door opened, and Elnear came into the room.

ELEVEN

I HEARD THE mingled voices of people passing in the hall behind Elnear; all sound stopped as she closed the door. I got up, while light oozed out of hidden crannies in the walls. Elnear stood where she was, her body rigid. The anger and betrayal she felt as she faced me at last forced its way in through all my senses. There was nothing soft or weak about her now . . . like understanding, or sympathy, or even pity. I could forget about those. Finally she said, "I hope that Centauri is satisfied. Your presence in my life turned today's debate into a disaster—an exercise in futility. We will certainly lose the upcoming vote on deregulation now." Which meant she'd lose the Security Council slot too; she didn't even need to mention that. "Because of you." Or that either, but she did.

I looked away at the deepening indigo of the sky, back at her. We were both too visible, there was no hiding place, standing here inside this lens of light. I didn't answer, looking at the floor now.

"You're usually quicker on your feet." There was a tone in her voice I'd never heard before. "Aren't you going to argue with me? At least you usually argue with me. A good saboteur always tries to cover his work, I thought. But then, I suppose your real job is done. And I thought you were only sent here to spy on me."

I looked up. "That ain't—*isn't* what I'm here for, goddamn it. It's not my fault Stryger hates psions. I didn't tell him to nail me!"

"You could at least have told me," she said, her voice cold, "that you were a criminal."

"I'm not—" I shook my head. "Stryger twisted everything around. I was pardoned. I'm clean. My record was sealed, buried, nobody can access it any more. I don't even know how he found out—"

"Anyone can find out anything, with the right contacts. And he certainly has them." She threw the wrap she was carrying down onto the couch. She began to move restlessly back and forth, glancing at me as she moved. "The worst part of the entire ordeal was being accused of conspiring with criminals—as if by attempting to keep these drugs restricted, I want to afflict all of humanity with a plague of degenerates and sociopaths!" Her open hand came down on a tabletop, hard. "I had to agree with him, grant him his point, or look like a liar as well as a hypocrite . . . because of course I agree that criminal behavior and deviancy should be controlled—"

"You mean, like psions? Isn't it enough they can't get hired for most kinds of work? Ain't it enough they get drugwiped if they ever get caught using their psi to commit a crime? Stryger wants them drugwiped the minute they're born. That's why he wants pentyptine deregulated. That's why he wants to be on the Security Council. So then he can have 'em all put in relocation dumps, and then he can make it illegal for them to breathe—" My voice broke. It had already happened to the Hydrans . . . it had happened to my mother. Now Stryger wanted to make it happen to anybody with a single psi gene drowned in their chromosome pool. I knew what he wanted . . . I *knew*. I pulled my voice back together. "You said up there that psions deserved to be judged like everybody else, one on one. I almost thought you believed it. You could've pushed harder, you could've fought him—"

Except that after what he'd said, calling me a criminal and a traitor, she hadn't wanted to. *Stryger was right*. The same thought, the same betrayal and disgust as I'd seen in Jardan's mind. "You brought this on yourself."

"Half of what he said about me was lies. You believed him, without even makin' him prove it. Yesterday, I thought you. . . ." My empty hands made fists. "Why?"

"Because what he said about psions is true," she snapped. "Psions are mentally unstable, sociopaths—harming themselves as well as the people around them." Thinking of Jule, thinking of me . . . the only psions she'd ever seen. But she knew the stereotype: psions were all floaters, freaks, head cases. We'd only proved the point. "Perhaps they would be better off if their . . . powers were under some kind of control. . . ." Now she was the one who wouldn't meet my eyes. Some part of her knew even as she said it that it wasn't right, or just; that it denied everything she had always thought she believed. But she couldn't help herself . . . and her guilt only gave her resentment more strength.

"That's what Jule and Siebeling are trying to do," I said; trying not to reach out to her mind, not to try to *make* her see. Knowing that that would be the worst thing I could do. "To teach psions how to control their own Gift. Like Siebeling did with me, and Jule. That's how to stop them from getting into trouble. They're not animals—"

"If all psions were in complete control of their abilities, they would only be tempted to use them against others. Power is the strongest drug of all. You worked for that terrorist Quicksilver." Parroting Stryger again, the memory burning in her eyes. "He would have crippled the FTA, and torn the entire Federation apart if he hadn't been stopped—"

"How do you think the FTA stopped him?"

She didn't answer. She didn't know.

"They used psions! Siebeling, Jule, me, a bunch of others. That's when I met her. That's what I was doing out there on Cinder, at the mines. Ask Jule—" She didn't even know that. All she knew, all any of them still remembered, was that a psion terrorist had nearly brought down the Federation single-handed.

"Quicksilver didn't do it alone," I said. "He wasn't some kind of crazy god. He had plenty of combines backing him. Just like Stryger. But we still stopped him—Jule, and Siebeling, and me." I held up my fist. "I killed Quicksilver myself. I felt him die inside me, and that's why I can't use my psi any more unless I'm so drugged up I can't remember his pain." I felt tears spill out of my eyes, so suddenly that I didn't have a chance of stopping them. They burned my face like acid, like they hadn't done in years, not since the moment after the killing when I'd realized what I'd done, to him, to myself. When I'd looked into my own mind and seen the nothing hole I'd made of somebody else with my telepathy and a gun: a wound bleeding hate and terror, a wound that would never heal. When I'd realized that I'd destroyed the Gift that had become my life. That I was back where I'd started, blind and alone and going nowhere. . . . I wiped at my face with my hand, choking on sobs . . . feeling nothing.

Elnear was staring at me with a kind of horrified fascination, like someone watching a burnout scream curses on an Oldcity street-corner. If she'd had any doubts about whether freaks were all crazy, I'd just proved it was true. . . . She was backing toward the door. "I think," she murmured, feeling for the plate on the wall, "that your work for the taMings is probably finished. You have certainly done enough already." The anger and frustration were back in her voice; the door flicked open. "Under no circumstances are you to attend the party downstairs. My own Security people are here tonight. They will see that you are removed if you show yourself there."

She left the room. The door sealed shut behind her, and I was alone again. I sat down, facing out on the view of coming night, blind with tears. Pain like knives stabbed into the back of my eyes. I got up again and stumbled across the room, found the trash can I'd seen beside the desk and vomited into it. After that my head felt a little better; but the trembling in my hands went on for a long while.

I lay back on the couch, feeling the skin on my face tighten as the tears dried, wondering what in hell was happening to me. Maybe I was sick, maybe I was tired . . . *maybe it was starting. Symptoms:* My mind eating away at my body because the drugs kept it from eating away at itself. It was sending me a warning, telling me to *stop, for God's sake—* I touched the patch behind my ear. I'd just been fired, hadn't I? My cover was gone, what was the point in wearing a patch any more, walking on broken legs. . . .

I tried to make my fingers peel off the patch. *What about Elnear?* Somebody was still trying to kill her; that hadn't changed. "Fuck her—" I said. But that didn't do anything except make me feel lousier. I'd ruined her life. What did I expect her to do, thank me? Besides, it was Braedee who'd hired me, and he hadn't fired me yet. Maybe I should wait. I needed the money. I needed. . . .

I pulled my knees up, rested my head on a crust of pillows, feeling my anger slowly melt down into a puddle of envy. I listened with my mind to the rising murmur of mental noise, guests arriving, filling the levels of the townhouse below me.

Elnear had said she hated parties, they were a waste of time. She was probably going to hate this one more than usual. But I'd felt her, somewhere in the back of her mind, remembering a time when she'd loved the music and the dancing, the company of the best of the best . . . when she'd been giddy with wine and laughter; when every word had sparkled like diamonds, when every sensation was a perfect counterpoint playing on all her senses at once; when she'd been in love. . . .

I couldn't help wondering what that would feel like, to have everything you ever wanted, even happiness. It hadn't lasted for her —but what ever did? I'd thought at least I'd get to taste it for one night— But now any memories I'd have of tonight would have to be stolen ones.

I let my psi slide into the white water of those hundreds of minds, all of them together but forever alone, even in a place like this. I collided with random bits of image and emotion, collecting them: *someone else's eyes falling on a beautiful woman wearing a gown of jewels, the sudden taste of fresh kiskfruit rind dripping with chocolate, the smell of roses and imported incense. Pulsing music, pungent disgust, hot hunger as someone's blood-red nails traced a slow line down someone's/my backbone*. It was all so easy, they were all so blind. . . . I lost myself inside their pleasure, sinking deeper into fantasies, letting myself be rich and famous, fire and ice . . . *a psion*.

I sat up on the couch, jerked out of my peepshow dreams as my mind wandered in through the wrong open door. But I'd been loose and careless, not trying to guard my own thoughts, knowing none of those deadheads would ever know the difference. Except this one wasn't a deadhead. It had been a man—that was all I knew for sure before he knew, and cut me off in sudden panic. I lunged after him, let my mind fall like a net over the sea of stars-in-darkness that was the party down below. But he was gone, losing himself in the void that kept those stars separate forever. He wasn't very good—but neither was I, and one thing he knew how to do was hide.

I gave up the hunt after a while, leaning back as I sank into playing voyeur again. I was better at that, and Braedee didn't want me digging up family secrets anyway. . . . *The odor of warm flesh and perfume; the electric shock of sudden humiliation; braying laughter; synth music*. . . .

The door opened.

I sat up fast; afraid it was Elnear who'd come back and caught me jerking off my brain. But it was Daric instead. He spasmed with surprise, as if the last thing in the world he'd expected to see here was another human being . . . or me. He laughed; it cut off like a stick snapping. "Well, hello." He came on into the room, every movement full of angular momentum. "So this is where she's exiled you to. . . . The Cat's out of the bag, so I hear." He raised his eyebrows, smirking at some joke I didn't get. "Now everybody knows your secret. You won't be safe anywhere. You're a marked man, to the hypers . . . you're famous. Poor Auntie's ready to make violin strings out of your guts."

I sat forward, pressing the heels of my hands into my eyes as my head started to throb again.

"I don't mean to intrude. I can tell you must be having a marvelous time, hiding out up here all alone while the party of the century goes on without you, just out of reach downstairs." I heard him pass close by me as he crossed the room. "Hasn't she even brought you up a cup of lukewarm tea and a handful of crumbs? Thoughtless—but then, she's having such a *wonderful* time, herself. . . ."

"Jeezu!" I said. "You're really an asshole." I raised my head.

He turned back, staring at me, but not really seeing me. "You're right. . . ." There was surprise on his face now, like he was seeing himself for the first time in a mirror. "You're very perceptive about human nature. But then I suppose all telepaths are." His mouth slid into another mocking smile.

I swore and stood up, sick of being one of his sick jokes. I started for the door, not knowing where I was going, but only that I had to get away from this.

"Cat, wait—"

I stopped, turned around.

He was wearing the best imitation of a real face that I'd ever seen on him. He bent his head to one side. "Listen, I am sorry. I have made an ass of myself. You're absolutely right. And absolutely honest, which is more than I can say for anyone else around here, including myself." He lifted his hands in a shrug. "Don't go. How about a truce? I won't make fun of you, if you promise not to tell the truth."

I felt my face tighten, waiting for the next slap. I didn't say anything.

But he only turned back to what he was doing, which was putting his hand through what looked like a solid sculpture hanging on the wall. His arm disappeared up to his elbow, came out again holding a small ceramic box. He set the box down on the desk. "My drugs," he said. He pulled it open with a kid's guilty grin; showing off, waiting for my reaction. When I still didn't say anything, he took out plastic sheets covered with colored dots and began to peel them off one at a time. He decorated his forehead with blues and greens; stuck on a double line of golds and reds around his throat inside the open collar of his neat gray tunic; shoved a purple one down the front of his pants. "Ahh, that's better."

"I hope you know what the hell you're doing," I said finally. "Because I'm not going to scrape you off the floor when you over-dose."

He snorted. "Of course I do. . . . How about you? I hear you're an experienced drug abuser from way back. Help yourself." He waved me toward the half-empty sheets.

I shook my head. "I don't use, any more." There was a time when I'd tried anything anybody'd sell me, trying to find the one that could fill the empty place where something nameless had been torn loose inside me; the one that could take away the pain of living through another day on the streets. I was lucky I was still alive. I didn't need drugs, any more. . . . Suddenly my hand wanted to reach up behind my ear, to feel the patch, to rip it off. Or maybe to make sure it was still in place. I kept my arm down at my side.

Daric looked at me, half puzzled, half frowning. I tried to make myself find out what was going on in his mind. I got the usual stench of mockery and black humor; under it the electric song of barely controlled tension, aimless strands of disgust and loathing. . . . His mind was like a jungle, the drugs filling it in with impenetrable vines of random sensation as they opened up all his senses. I couldn't get any further, pushing against the limits of my crippled psi.

Daric sighed, a smile of pure pleasure stretching his face out like a piece of plastic. "*Much* better." He looked like someone who'd just had a knife blade moved away from his throat; I could almost *feel* him relaxing. No wonder he liked drugs. I watched him shove the box back through the sculpture into its hiding place. "I have no intention of staying around here for more of the overdressed dog and pony show downstairs. Trust me, you're really not missing a thing. A vicious, meaningless, and ultimately boring game of Beasts and Victims, that's all it is. I'm having my own private party, down at Purgatory. Argentyne has created a new work, just for tonight. I'm going there now. All my favorite people are going to be there. . . . Do you want to come?" His eyes brightened with sudden eagerness. "Come with me. You'll be a sensation!"

I blinked, stared, not really believing I'd heard him ask. I shook my head. "I can't."

He raised his eyebrows. "Why not? Are you afraid the hypers will eat you alive? No one will even know we're gone. You'll be safe."

I thought about it, hit with a sudden rush of excitement as I imagined getting free of this prison, feeling alive and real, for even one night—"I . . . I'm supposed to stay here. I've got to do my job. Braedee—"

"*Braedee?*" He laughed. "Do you really think Braedee cares

what you do now? Do you really think Elnear does? . . . Do you actually believe someone is going to murder her in the middle of this crowd? Besides, everyone here has been scanned right down to their entrails for weapons.'' He strolled toward me, reached out to jog my arm. ''They don't *need* you,'' he said gently. ''Don't take yourself so seriously. No one else does.''

I jerked away from his hand.

He shrugged. Irritation showed in his eyes, was gone again. ''Do what you like. Sit here and sulk. Pretend you matter.'' He turned away, starting for the door. ''You had your chance. . . .''

''All right. I'll come.''

He turned back, grinning. ''I promise you a night you'll never forget. . . . You sure you don't want any drugs?''

''No thanks,'' I said. *I've got all I need*.

TWELVE

I FOLLOWED DARIC out of the room, through a maze of empty back hallways, down a lift that only servants used . . . slipping past doorways that opened onto a wall of light/noise/motion, into darkness/silence again. I could feel him still grinning up ahead of me, lighting up my brain with his pleasure buzz, counterpointing the dry empty throbbing in my own head. We came out at last in some kind of subbasement garage, where half a dozen private mods sat waiting for people who needed a quick escape.

As we stepped out of the lift into the shadowed underworld, someone materialized from behind a pillar. I swore, jerking up short.

But Daric only laughed, and pulled me forward. "Jiro!" he called. "Good boy, you escaped them. Look who I've found to join us."

Jiro stepped out into the light. His hair was still wild, and half his face was streaked with blood-colored paint. He was wearing a brocade jacket with one sleeve missing, over a torn shirt over a striped ankle-length tunic. It took me a minute to realize he hadn't been in some kind of accident. His ear-to-ear smile fell away as he saw me. The static of his excitement faded, broken by the sudden blankness of uncertainty, sharp pangs of doubt and curiosity. *He knew,* just like everybody else did now. "Cat. . . ." His shoulders twitched. "Are you . . . I mean, are you really a freak? Are you . . . you know . . . reading my mind all the time?" His eyes were bright and dark, the whites showing.

"He knows our every secret, don't you, Cat?" Daric murmured.

"No," I said, as evenly as I could. "I'm not a freak. I'm a psion. And no," I said again, ignoring Daric's laugh, "I'm not reading your mind all the time. You're not that interesting." Jiro frowned. Daric's laughter goaded me out into the open space. Jiro skittered backwards as I passed him, came forward again, almost treading on my heels as he tried to prove something to himself. Somehow the space inside the mod seemed cramped, like there were two of me sitting side by side.

The mod delivered us right to the door of Purgatory, Argentyne's private club; what I saw of the Deep End around it made me damn glad of that. We climbed out into the glare of a hundred different hologos dancing in the darkness overhead, stepped over a burnout sprawled in the gutter. Jiro coughed from the stink of a garbage fire somewhere down the block. A gang of street slugs done in gold teeth and threedy paint gave us the eye as they pounded past. The one thing I hadn't been expecting to see was the way the city's sealed dome arced down into the bay, creating more breathing space, reclaiming the bottom of the sea. Argentyne's club was just offshore—the black wall of water rose halfway up the dome here, drowning the stars in half the night's sky.

I don't know what I'd thought a place run by Daric taMing's lover would look like. On the outside it didn't look like much: An ancient cement-block warehouse, with the word "Purgatory" holoed in red crawling endlessly over its face like a blind worm. Daric strode across the dirt-blackened bricks of the pavement as if he owned this part of town, and went down the shallow stairwell to the club's entrance. He touched something on the rusted iron door that sent out a silent call. I followed after him, staying close to Jiro, who was sparking with his own nervous energy. He was so high on excitement that I almost thought he'd been taking drugs; but his mind was clear when I checked him. At least Daric hadn't made his stepbrother the same offer he'd made me. I knew Jiro liked Argentyne, but I was surprised Daric would bring a kid like him to the Deep End. Argentyne was a symbplayer; like magicians, they worked your head best if they did it live. But Jiro had said she was famous. She must do gigs in bigger and better places than this.

The graffiti-covered door cracked open, swung wide as whoever was behind it recognized Daric. Cinnamon smoke and screaming laughter reached out and dragged us inside.

"Welcome to Purgatory!" A face, or a mask, pushed into mine—I couldn't tell which from the leering smile. Young or old, male or female . . . somewhere inside all that I found a man's mind, or thought I did. "Not quite heaven, not quite hell. . . ." His breath stank from skagweed. His hand grabbed my wrist, inside a swirl of translucent glitter cloth, yellows and golds, and he hauled me forward, shooing Jiro ahead down the hallway. "Your first time, pretty?" I wasn't sure if he was talking to me, or Jiro, or both of us. If Argentyne wanted to keep out anybody who didn't have a sense of humor, she was doing a good job.

We half stumbled, half slid down a dark ramp. It dumped us out into the middle of a madhouse. I stopped, staring. Daric was already wading through the crowd, shouting and waving his arms; the crowd parted around him like a sentient sea, and voices called his name.

I stood at the bottom of the ramp, weaving my mind into a fist in self-defense as Jiro plunged out into the shifting mass of bodies after Daric. Still just trying to take it all in—the vast, scarred womb that was the club's interior, the glaring, pounding music that filled it like an invisible force, trying to split open its walls . . . the people. They looked like they'd been bodysnatched and dropped down here from every age, every world, every imaginable level of human life. They wore lace and brocade, leather and rags, grafts, jewels, chains and batteries, plastic, hair, skins and bones. I felt like a mark, still wearing combine colors. Daric's ultraconservative suit looked so wrong that it actually made him seem to belong here. Some of the guests hugged him, kissed him, groped him. I began to spot a few that weren't natives—bored vips escaping like he was from their own respectability, trying too hard to seem like they fit in. I could spot that kind in my sleep.

Behind me, flanking the entrance, there were two bouncers—huge grotesques who'd had themselves built into shells of augmented alloy that made them damn near indestructible. Near the wall on my left three more or less naked men were wrestling in a pool of green jelly, splattering the shrieking onlookers with slime. Four gilled, sexless exotics did an underwater ballet inside a clear bubble of glass drifting past overhead. One of them put a hand against the glass, gazing down at me. Slowly I reached up, stretching to meet it; the hand twitched away as I touched the glass. Its owner was gone in a swirl of silent laughter. A pair of chained-up black dogs yelped and snapped at me as I edged past them and out into the room. The strange danced with strangers, shaking and flailing like they'd been set on fire, or sprawled exhausted on jewel-colored cushions by low tables covered with food and drinks. There was nothing here I hadn't seen before, but I'd never seen it all in one place. . . . There were clubs in Oldcity more bizarre than this, but I'd never had the credit line to get past their doors.

There was a stage at the far end of the room. It was empty now, the only spot in the place where nothing was going on. Musicians were performing all around the club; each one singing, playing something different, lost in some separate auditory hallucination. And yet somehow it was all one sound; half a dozen kinds of synths playing half a dozen kinds of songs fusing into one perfect web of music, the changing rhythms meshing like gears . . . Argentyne's symb. I'd never heard one this good. But I didn't see Argentyne anywhere; there was no lightsong happening yet either. She must be the spirit, the one who did the visuals, who made it all work.

I waded on through the dance, my body twitching to passing rhythms, my vision changing color as I passed through bands of amplified light, searching for Daric and Jiro. My eyes did a double take as my sight suddenly turned black-and-white. All the color was missing from the far corner of the room. I looked down at myself, back at the people around me; we were all still in living color. I reached the split in reality, stepped across it. I turned black-and-white, like everyone and everything around me. I stepped back again, not ready to go colorblind.

Someone pushed a drink into my hand. It was Daric, from out of nowhere, with a couple of female exotics hanging on him. "Come on, Cat. Do something. I promised everyone you'd be interesting—"

I took the drink. It was blue and steaming. I tapped Daric's thoughts just long enough to be sure it wasn't loaded. It was safe enough. I took a sip. "Where's Jiro? He shouldn't be left alone here. He shouldn't be here at all." One of the women blew kisses at me with tattooed green lips.

Daric laughed. "My God, you sound like Auntie! I thought you were supposed to be some kind of wild boy; I thought this was your element. Don't get stiff on me—"

"*I'll* get him stiff. . . ." One of the women oozed away from him, toward me. I backed up, and behind me someone else's hand slid down over my ass. I jerked forward again. The woman with a single horn growing out of her forehead threw her arms around me. There was something long and shapeless squirming in her hand, something grayish-pink and wrinkled. "This is a suckworm," she whispered. "Guess what it does. . . ." She pushed it at me, trying to slip it into my clothes.

I let my disgust slam into her brain without control, without warning. She squealed and fell back. Daric didn't bother to catch her, and she sat down hard on the floor, blinking, dazed. "Well, fuck you," she said, to nobody in particular. She picked up the worm and crawled away through a forest of legs. The crowd around Daric murmured, and I heard a ripple of applause.

"What did I tell you?" Daric said to them. "Mental powers!"

I turned back to him. "I used to live off divers like you—night trippers with fat credit, pretending they were something they weren't. You think this is all a big joke. You're wrong. I don't want Jiro hurt. Where is he?"

Daric winced. "You're telling me the truth again. That's against the rules—" He raised his hands as my own hand made a fist. "He's safe! He's backstage with Argentyne. She'll watch over him like a nanny, he's in perfect ecstasy. Relax." He shrugged, still amused. The crowd of hangers-on around him kept changing, like a kaleidoscope, leather and lace, flesh and fur. "Meet your fans, Cat. It's such perfect timing. . . . Today you became notorious, a media star. Tonight you can celebrate it, among people who really understand what it means to be unique, a freak—"

I grimaced, taking another gulp of my drink as he dragged me through the crowd to a table next to the stage. "My personal table, my guest of honor." He caught my shoulders, chivvying me around. "You'll have a perfect view of Argentyne's performance from here. Sit down—" He pushed me down onto a pillow in the sea of colored cushions, keeping an arm around my shoulders. His face was flushed, his eyes were too bright; he looked like a man with a fever. *Excitement, eagerness, pride*—I was his prize catch, a moment's inspired impulse, proof to the inhabitants of the Deep End that he was as twisted as they were inside his silver-gray straitjacket. He lived his double life with a vengeance that was hard to believe. Flaunting Argentyne at the family estates was only the surface membrane of his secret self, a hint to his family that if they dared to push through it they'd find a lot more secrets than they were ready for. He played the perfect combine vip by day, but it was only a role, just like the jaded deeve he played here by night. I wondered what the real Daric was, or where, or whether there was anything at all behind the masks.

The seats around me at the table filled up before I had time to set down my drink, and the questions started flowing. "Is it true that psions—" "—tell me what—" "Read *my* mind!" "What's your Prime?" "How does it *feel* . . . ?"

I let the hungry curiosity seep into my brain, the eager titillation as they waited for me to rape their minds with a thought. . . . *Even fear could be a pleasure—a new kind of drug*.

As the drink loosened me up I started to let myself believe that nobody around me hated my guts, or wanted to get away from me, or was actually laughing at me inside. At least I knew what kind of people these were; at least here I didn't have to worry about everything I did, everything I said, even the way I said it. . . . I felt myself relaxing for the first time in days. I answered their questions, out loud at first, until I saw that that wasn't what they wanted. Then I answered them with my mind—slowly, gently, so that nobody panicked. They giggled and held their heads like children. Daric smiled with anticipation, not asking any questions of his own.

"Read *my* mind—" the woman with scales glittering on her skin whispered again beside me. She licked her lips with a slitted tongue.

(I don't need to.) I grinned, and so did she. I finished off my drink, and there were two more in front of me before I could even ask. I took a meat-filled bun from one of the platters heaped with food in the center of the table, bit into it, still grinning. Across the table from me a bald, thick-necked slug in patchwork leather was stuffing food into his mouth as fast as he could, choking it down, hardly bothering to breathe. He'd cleared off half the platter closest to him already. I watched him eat for a minute longer; realized I was forgetting to chew the food in my own mouth. I glanced away, at a couple a few cushions past him. They could have been male or female or both, and they were slowly peeling away each others' clothes, like somebody peeling the layers of an onion. Somebody else began to give me a back rub while I watched, kneading my neck and shoulders, pressing their thumbs into the hollows along my spine. It felt good, and I let the hands strip off my jacket without even looking around.

I answered more questions as the crowd around me changed again. I drank more drinks, ate more food from the tray that never seemed to get completely empty, while everything began to feel better and better. I'd had dreams about this: about being at the center of a diver's private fantasy, as an equal. . . . I felt myself letting go, an almost physical thing, as if my bones were melting and my body was moving away in seven different directions at once. My mind began to drift, floating in a warm, hazy sea of acceptance, where the only tension was sexual, and there was no fear at all.

After a while Jiro came dancing out from behind the stage. He jumped down into the cushions beside us, panting, his face flushed with excitement, and wriggled like a puppy into a spot beside Daric. As he settled in, the music that had been all around us until I didn't even hear it any more changed, in a way that made everyone stop everything and look toward the stage. Reality shrugged, and suddenly the stage wasn't empty any more. Shimmering above it now was a gleaming black filament like the web of some mutant bloodspider. There were human victims, half a dozen men or what looked like them, dangling in the wires, with blood or something like it dripping from their wounds. The air smelled like ozone. I shut my eyes and looked at them with my mind, and they were the musicians who'd been playing all around us. They were still playing, still hooked into the symb net. Their writhing agony was a freeform dance, tied to the heartbeat of their music.

I heard Jiro suck in his breath, half frowning as he tried to guess whether what he saw was real. Knowing it couldn't be, but still not sure—

"It's just an act," I said. He nodded, frowned a little deeper, pushing his hair back from his eyes. "I know that." He hunched his shoulders and looked away at the stage again as lightning played down the web.

Argentyne was there, suddenly, drifting down through the web like some pitiless goddess of death, her hair a shockwave of silver white. Black leather cupped her like the petals of a nightflower; black silk fringe slid over bare flesh like the groping hands of her victims, reaching out for mercy as she passed. As her feet hit the floor she began to sing, swiveling out of the web and along the tongue of stage

in spike-heeled killer shoes, stretching her silvered arms to embrace
the crowd. Watching her strut it was hard to take my eyes off her;
almost impossible to separate her from the beat that drove her motion
in through every pore of my body, or her voice from the reverberating
air. I couldn't make out the words she was singing, even as they etched
themselves across my brain, like acid eating its way into glass . . .
*a song about men and women, a song of war, in and out of the
flesh . . .*

And as she sang and as she moved her flesh began to heave and
buckle, as if something monstrous inside her was trying to force its
way out. With the music screaming, her perfect flesh tore open like
rubber. Glistening limbs flailed, pushed, burst free, her mutilated body
fell away, withering like a cocoon. . . .

    *. . . about getting inside each others' skins, would it really be
so different? . . .*

A silver-haired man, the sheen of sweat on the silver flesh laid
bare above his tight black leather pants, heavy codpiece, thigh-high
armored boots. Armed to the teeth, he raised a metal-studded fist to
the crowd, and his voice was Argentyne's, and no one else's but his
own. . . .

    . . . Would it really still be war?

And he turned, and Argentyne was waiting there behind him.
Alone, defenseless, she held up her hand, as if she could stop his
slow, hungry advance on her by nothing but willpower. . . .

And the gun dropped from his hands as his chest began to heave
and tear, showing velvet as red as blood; as his face contorted and the
music screamed while a hand struggled out through his mouth . . . as
his body exploded like porcelain dropped from a height.

A silver-haired woman in a red velvet gown emerged like a snake,
shedding the man's skin, shuddering free of it as it sloughed to the
floor, kicking it away. I watched Argentyne walk toward Argentyne,
undulating like the sea. As they passed each other like figures in a
mirror, the two women lifted their hands, blowing kisses, while Argentyne segued into the final verse of her song. . . .

    *. . . if you were a woman, and I was a man . . . inside the other
side of life tonight . . .*

The crowd howled, its voice strobing inside sound like a sun gone
nova . . . as Argentyne appeared and disappeared, moving through
curtains of synthesized reality, shouting and applause . . . to settle,
as the music rolled away and the visions faded, into the space that had
somehow opened for her between Daric and me.

I stared at her, hardly believing she was actually right beside me. She looked back at me, blinking with a kind of startled recognition as she realized she'd seen me before. As she realized now, like everyone else did, what I really was.

"Argentyne . . . magnificent . . ." Daric murmured. He put his arms around her, kissing her lips, her throat, her breasts . . . laying claim to her and all that she was, all that she'd just created, in a way that nobody who saw them could fail to understand. She didn't resist him, dissolving against his body, turning the kiss into an extension of what she'd done on the stage, still radiating the white heat of her performance energy. What drove into my dazzled brain then surprised me as much as anything I'd just seen on the stage: she actually wanted him, wanted to feel his lips against her skin, and it was her own pleasure that let the contact continue long after it could have ended.

I watched them, like everybody else was watching them, with the heat of Argentyne's energy still burning inside me, mutating, shifting, getting hotter; Daric's arousal, my own. . . . Slowly realizing that there was a whole hidden layer of sensation that only I could share, out of everyone in that room who saw them. I shared it, hungry, greedy, not able to stop myself . . . knowing all the while that they knew I knew, and wanted me to know, and liked it that way. . . .

They broke apart at last, to more whistles and howls. Jiro sat gaping, caught somewhere between awe and panic. Daric looked straight at me, grinning, still with one arm holding Argentyne close. He said, "How did you like the show?" He didn't mean just the one on stage.

I grinned too, leaning back in the soft embrace of the pillows. I could sense the entire room now, as I let my focus dissolve: the flow, the heat, the pressure, the wild energies . . . feel it all funnel back along the lines of contact until my mind felt like a star. I let out a little of that raw fissioning fire, feeding it into him, into Argentyne, into every mind around me at the table; letting them feel exactly how much I enjoyed it. There were gasps and giggles, aftershocks of stunned disbelief, and then everyone's eyes were on me again. They all wanted more—The slug across the table even stopped eating for long enough to look up at me. I opened myself to them, feeling the contact ebb and flow as I dropped the circuit breakers in my mind. A strangled laugh escaped from Daric. I felt his craving for the forbidden touch . . . the terror that squeezed it, compressed it until it became a kind of lust. . . .

I broke contact with him as I suddenly remembered Jiro. Jiro was staring at me too, his throat working. He was even more terrified of what I'd just done than Daric was, but he was trying desperately to look like he'd enjoyed it, to look like everybody else.

I wanted to say something to him, but then Argentyne leaned away from Daric, toward me, looking directly into my eyes with all her attention; really seeing me for the first time. "That was incredible," she murmured. She laughed, shaking out the silver mane of her hair. I felt her enjoy the feel of it down her back, felt her titillated by the sensation of thoughts turned inside out; felt her wanting to feel another mind run its fingers through her own again. I brushed her mind with an image, and she shivered. "I'm ruined. . . ." she said, her voice caressing me like warm fingers. "You're like silk. Accessing is going to feel like sandpaper in my brain for the rest of my life. You've ruined me with one touch. . . ." Her hand reached out this time, brushing my cheek. She was only half serious, but Daric's grip on her tightened, pulling her away. She glanced at him, more amused than annoyed, pulling her spike-heeled feet in closer to her on the cushions. "You brought him here, love. Let us enjoy him. We don't see nearly as many psions here on Earth as you worldjumpers do."

"Why not?" I asked, half realizing that down here where nothing was a surprise, telepaths shouldn't be as interesting as I seemed to be to them.

"This is Earth," Daric said, his smile twitching with spite. "Psions are . . . well, abnormal." He shrugged. "They're discouraged from settling here. They might pollute the stock." His eyes moved, not meeting mine, as his own paranoia suddenly set in again.

My anger shot out past my control, spilled over into the open lines of my mind and hit him. The people gathered around the table jerked and gasped . . . laughed, nervously. Daric wiped at his eyes, shook his head—looked at me again. Eager again, in a way that should have made me want to get away from him. But the warm feedback of everyone else's acceptance melted my anger, dissolved my resentment. I couldn't hold onto my thoughts, any more than I seemed to be able to keep them to myself . . . and somehow I didn't even care that something was going wrong.

"Have you ever plugged in?" Argentyne asked, leaning toward me again, her copper-colored eyes intent. "Have you ever worked a symb circuit? Would you like to try?" Do what she did—the music, the images, creating a mass hallucination out of the artist's imagination. I shook my head. "God's teeth," she said, "you'd be astounding— you could make people *live* what they see and hear. The ultimate."

"That's socketwork. It's illegal," I said, the words flat, "for psions." Even I knew that. "If they catch you, they drugwipe you."

"If I could create that kind of effect, even once," she said, "it would be worth it."

"It's not your brain."

She shrugged, and the petals of black leather she'd been wearing were suddenly watercolor silk. I blinked, wondered what she was really wearing. . . . The image I was trying not to form inside my head formed anyway, and leaked. More tittering laughter. Argentyne smiled. "Fairly accurate," she said.

Daric's frown came back, but he only kissed the back of her neck, and said. "Argentyne, Jiro would like to dance with you, but he doesn't know how to ask."

She turned away, looking toward Jiro. "Delighted." She pushed to her feet in a wash of liquid color, and took Jiro's hand. Jiro scrambled up, speechless, and followed her away toward the dance floor. I watched her go, watching her tight dancer's muscles flow beneath the silk until she disappeared into the crowd. I left a strand of thought tied to her mind even after I lost sight of her.

As I looked back, across the table from me the Eater stuck his finger down his throat, and puked into the bucket waiting beside him on the floor. When he was finished he began to eat again. More bodies slid into the empty spaces beside Daric, like sand funneling into a pit. I turned to look at the grotesque who was shoving in beside me. The wall of his chest had been replaced with a transparent synthetic. Blood pulsed though veins, wet purple and gray organs churned, muscles slid and contracted. He stared back at me, just as curious.

Something warm and wet circled my ear, probed inside it. I jerked around, startled. The woman with the long, slitted tongue was back, kneeling behind me. The tongue that had just been in my ear licked her lips again, left them wet and glistening, as her hands slid down across my shoulders, massaging my chest. Her eyes were a golden yellow; her pupils were long slits, like mine should have been. But hers had been engineered to look that way, the way mine had been engineered to look human.

The thin film of scales on her skin caught the light, gleaming like a sheen of sweat. I reached up, touching her face. The scales felt warm and dry, softer than I'd imagined. Her lips were very soft, opening as I rose up on my knees to kiss them. Her tongue slid into my mouth, as casually as if it belonged there; stayed there, investigating every corner, while our kiss went on and on, and a hot throbbing pressure grew between my legs. I heard a whimper, a stifled groan, from somewhere around the table.

I tried to break off the kiss, looking back at Daric. I caught an unfocused flash of his knowing smile, someone else behind him, arms circling his waist . . . And then the woman's hands were drawing me back and around and down into the cushions beside her. Long deft fingers slid down the seal on my shirt, pulled it open, raked my skin with sharp nails and left me burning. I reached up, cupping her breasts with my hands through the gaps in her slitted ivory gown. She squirmed and sighed, with my pleasure and hers, lowering herself until my lips could reach her. I covered one of her nipples with my mouth.

Sounds and movement were all around me now, as the others at the table began to melt and flow together in my heat, their heat radiating back along the sizzling filaments of contact into my brain, until it was all one molten sea, and I was sinking into it, ". . . don't . . . stop . . ." Begging to drown.

Someone else's hands seemed to be pulling at me, hands everywhere, peeling off my shirt, sliding over my skin . . . unfastening my pants, setting the hard rod of my erection free, to giggles and moans of delight. The scaled woman's tongue was back inside my mouth now, going deeper. Something sweet and sticky was trickling from a pitcher onto my belly . . . someone was licking it off. . . .

Daric was beside me, smiling, his breath coming in shallow gasps as he lifted my hand. He sucked on my fingers, one by one—sank his teeth into the flesh between my thumb and forefinger until he tasted my blood. I screamed and jerked, screams echoing around me as he gasped and let go, falling back with my pain inside his head. He crawled forward again and dumped a freezing cold drink onto my naked skin. Gasped with my pain again, and laughed—

I struggled to sit up but the hands weighed me down, the mouths, the bodies . . . soothing, stroking, caressing, probing. Until my bones were rubber and my mind flowed into the drowning pool again, helplessly willing.

Something warm and shapeless flopped onto my chest. I lifted my head, saw the suckworm lying there in an oozing pool of syrup. Panting, I watched it squirm along my belly to the music of their laughter . . . waiting for it, helpless with their hunger, burning with their need, screaming inside. Their hands held me down with silken cords of muscle and flesh, as they drank in the sweet juice of my yearning, the vinegar of my disgust. . . .

"Jeezu!" Argentyne's face swam into sight above me. "What the hell are you doing—?" Staring down at us, her eyes widening enough to take it all in. I had a sudden strobe flash of what it looked like from where she stood, driven into my brain by the force of her *incredulity disgust *arousal* anger *arousal* disbelief *arousal* disgust—*

I tried to struggle, tried to hold onto her anger, to push free of the soft, yielding heaviness that was suffocating my will like a pillow of flesh . . . couldn't.

"Argentyne, come on—" Daric crawled on his knees to her, his own clothes hanging open. He reached out for her, pulling himself up her body. "Come and *feel* the real thing. . . ."

Argentyne punched him hard in the gut, doubling him over. She began to turn away, and I grimaced as I saw Jiro's face behind her. She blinded Jiro with a sudden slap. "*You* keep your face out of this! Stay there." She turned back, stepping over Daric's head, shoving half naked bodies out of her way as she leaned down and picked the worm off of my belly. She hurled it away. "This is my club, I put on the floor shows here. Get your clothes on and get out, you shit-eaters." She kicked a few more bodies; their pain went off in my head like explosives in a sea of mud. I groaned and rolled over as everything imploded; burying my hard-on in the pillows.

"*You—*" Her hand caught my shoulder, wrenching me back into the light again. "Put your fucking pants on, you mindraper. Take your freakshow someplace else."

I struggled with my pants, struggled with my brain, my thoughts still running out of me like diarrhea. "I can't. . . ."

"Like hell." She fastened my pants for me, making me gasp; picked up my shirt and threw it in my face.

I couldn't sit up. I managed to get over onto my hands and knees. All I could feel now was *her,* no room left in my mind for any thought, any choice, any decision of my own. "I can't . . . help it," shaking my head. It didn't do any good.

She was standing over me, staring down at my back. I felt her eyes catch on something, felt the giddy change of direction as she leaned over to pick it off my neck like a flea. A patch.

"No, wait—" I put up my hand, but the patch behind my ear was still there. I sat back, making my eyes focus on her while she studied the patch on her fingertip. Her face twisted. She flicked it away. *A dose of easy.* It took away your inhibitions and your self-control; made it easy to do anything. . . . I felt the anger drain out of her/me. Not wanting it to go; wanting to be able to feel my own. "All right," she said gently, "I guess the boy can't help it, after all." She reached down, helping me to my feet. "You understand what happened?" she asked me. "Somebody drugged you." I nodded. "I think you're going to be ready to kick some ass in a few minutes," she said. "Or you should be."

She let go of me and turned away. Daric was on his feet now too, grimacing. Her knee came up, stopped just short of his crotch. "No," she said, her voice spiked with spite. "You'd enjoy it too much. You turd. You drugged him, didn't you? And set him up for this gangbang—" Her arm swept the circle of chagrined partiers still fumbling their clothes on.

He shrugged, making odd faces, like a kid caught cheating at Square/Cubes.

I pulled my shirt on with stiff, clumsy fingers. I couldn't see my jacket anywhere. I kept my eyes on the floor, because there were so many other eyes looking at me that wouldn't go away, so many minds. . . .

"Come on," Argentyne said to me. The odd gentleness was back in her voice. She took my arm again, making me move forward. I saw Jiro then; he hadn't kept his back turned for long. I couldn't make sense out of what flashed into his mind as he looked at me. Maybe he couldn't, either. I looked down again. Argentyne caught his arm with her other hand, steering us both toward the entrance. "Daric!"

He followed us through the crowd, across the dance floor, toward the door. He moved slowly but inevitably, as if she held him too, dragging him along on an invisible chain of will.

My head began to clear out just a little as we left the club. Putting the physical barrier of the walls between me and the eyes and the minds made it easier. I took in long swallows of cold night air, tasting smoke and dankness. The mod that had brought us here came down from wherever it had been waiting overhead, homing in on Daric. It settled onto the street, scattering the ground traffic. The doors popped. I stood staring at it, starting to shiver inside my thin, syrup-soaked shirt. Trying to decide what to do . . . trying not to wait until somebody else told me.

Argentyne turned away as Daric came out into the street and the gatekeeper slammed the door behind him. She was back in leather again, this time head to foot, solid and heavy like a trooper. I couldn't help wondering again what I'd actually feel, if I touched her . . . see, if I touched her mind. . . . Desperately I tied up my thoughts, and this time it held. Relief hit me so hard it felt like an electric shock as I realized I was getting some kind of control over the psi again . . . relief, and disbelief. And then the betrayal and the fury, riding each others' backs as I turned toward Daric.

But Argentyne was there first, the mask of control she'd worn inside the club gone, the anger naked on her face. "You bastard," she said, and the words trembled. "You scumbag, how could you pull a piece of shit like that in my place? How could you do it to me? How could you do it to him—" waving a hand at Jiro, "—or him?" Pointing at me. Jiro stood as silent as stone behind me. People swirled past and around us, making a religion of disinterest. "What makes you *do* these lousy—" She broke off. There were tears in her eyes. "Why do I let you do it to *me.* . . ." Her hands jerked, as if they wanted to beat on him. And trapped behind the transparent window of her anger there was the kind of pain that only grew out of one emotion. . . .

Daric stood without resisting, his mind full of the same twisted pain, letting her bury him in garbage, *hating/loving it/her/himself.* . . . "I'm sorry," he said at last, when she'd run out of things to call him, and the energy to spit out the words. "I'm sorry. . . ." He said it again, as humbly as if she was the taMing, and he was no better than the burnout still face-down in the gutter behind us.

"Go home. Go back where you belong." She waved him gone, turning her back on him. "Stop fucking up my life. . . ." without even the strength left to sound like she meant it. She was facing me again. She pushed her hair back from her eyes, studying me until I had trouble meeting her stare. "You okay?" she said, finally. She was worried about me filing a complaint . . . she was worried about me.

I felt the corners of my mouth twitch, like a spasm. "My brains aren't hanging out any more. . . . So, yeah." I shrugged, nodded. "Sex never killed me before. I guess I'll live."

She half smiled. "Forthright," she said. "You seem to know this territory by heart." She touched my chest, let her hand drop. "Will you get these lost babes back where they belong? Since you're the only one who really knows where that is." She glanced at Daric, Jiro.

I nodded; felt a smile of my own start, in spite of myself.

She began to turn away. But it was only her body turning. Her mind stayed behind. . . . And then suddenly she was facing me again, and her arms were reaching out to pull me against her. She kissed me, long and hard, her nails digging into my back. She let me go and pushed away; stood looking at me again, her open lips smiling, her eyes hot. "Now you know why I had to throw you out of there." She nodded toward the club, and took a deep breath. "If that helps, remember it."

She went to Jiro, kneeled down beside him, gave him a hug. He stayed rigid and silent in her arms. "Oh, baby," she said, looking away. "Sometimes life's a bitter drug. If you have to take it, it's better if you get it from somebody who cares about you. . . . You dance great. Go on, now." She nudged him toward the mod. He got in, as numbly obedient as I'd been ten minutes before.

She passed me again, grazing my thigh with a warm hip; passed Daric, who was looking at her, at me. "It's your fault," she said to him. His eyes followed her like a dog. The door to Purgatory swung open as she started down the steps, and slammed shut again behind her.

I waited while Daric's eyes tracked back to me. I was ready to smash his face if there'd been anything behind them that even reminded me of laughter. But his mind was the color of the streets, of need and anger and desperation. I turned my back on him too, and got into the mod.

After a long minute he climbed in, and ordered the mod to take us back uptown. Jiro sat squeezed down into a corner, as far from either of us as he could get. I stared at my feet, not wanting to watch as the mod lifted from the ground. My hand hurt. I looked at it. In the dim light of the street below I could see the black stain of drying blood where Daric's teeth had gone through my flesh. I focused my mind on stopping the pain, to keep from thinking about how it had gotten that way.

Daric was looking at the wound too when I glanced up at him, the way a starving man would look at a half-eaten piece of meat. Only it wasn't causing pain that he still wanted. It was feeling it. . . . In the moment after Argentyne had left him, there'd been something I could relate to going on inside his brain. It was gone now. "You got any diseases I ought to know about?"

His mouth twisted. His eyes were empty as he looked away, out the window.

I sighed, letting my head fall back against the seat.

"Why did she kiss you like that?" Jiro asked me. His voice was tiny, accusing.

Me, like she meant it. *Me,* not Daric. *Me,* not him . . . I only shook my head. "Ask Daric." I lifted my aching hand, pointed it at his stepbrother.

He didn't ask. He only squeezed deeper into his corner, trying to get away from the ugliness and confusion in his own head, the images that looking at us only made clearer. And Daric didn't answer. If he had any regrets about what he'd done to either of us, they hadn't occurred to him yet.

I started to reach out to Jiro with my mind, knowing that he needed help, and that no words could help him. But even as I did, I knew I wasn't up to it. That if I tried to help him now, he'd know it. I pulled back into my own disgust and exhaustion, and left him alone. And suddenly I remembered where we were going to be again in another few minutes. I tried not to wonder who was going to end up getting blamed for everything when we got there.

THIRTEEN

I FOLLOWED DARIC back through the halls of the townhouse, feeling like someone who couldn't wake up from a bad dream. Elnear's party was still going on, but by now it had shrunk to just one room. Daric ducked in through the first doorway that opened onto light and noise, leaving me behind with Jiro as he lost himself in the crowd. I stared after him, not sure whether relief or envy was winning out in me as I watched him slide back into his other skin with smiling ease. Jiro stood shuffling his feet, not wanting to be left standing beside me, but filled with sudden panic as he thought about facing his family . . . his stepfather.

"Go on in," I said softly. I reached out, put my arm around him. "You didn't do anything wrong." *You didn't—* Repeating the same thing to myself, for the hundredth time.

He didn't believe it, any more than I did. He jerked away from my hand and ran into the crowded room without looking back. I stayed where I was, suddenly more afraid of going in than he was, as I remembered what had happened this afternoon. To me it seemed like about a million years ago, by now; but it probably didn't seem that long to the people in there. I let my mind search the crowd, searching for hypers, or for Elnear. Somehow I had the feeling she'd still be there. She might be a lot of things, but she wasn't a coward. I wondered what her evening had been like while I was gone; if it had really been as bad as mine, and what that would mean when she saw me again.

My eyes followed my thoughts restlessly, taking in the scene. The shifting mass of bodies stunned me with its normalness. There were a few exotics, wearing feathers for hair or calico skin, but it could have been makeup, costuming, for all I could tell. There was nobody who looked like they'd be caught dead wearing their guts out in the open. But I could have passed for human. . . . I could have been in there, having a painless good time, having the best night of my stupid life. I *should* have been there—

I wondered what I would have had to say to anybody if I had. . . . Probably just the wrong thing. I sagged back against the wall again, safe, out of sight, and suddenly too tired to move. Those were the elite of this world and dozens of others, in there—the richest, the most powerful, the most successful. They didn't need to wear their specialness on the outside, forcing the world to blink when it looked at them, to notice them, to acknowledge they were alive. Their only problem was convincing each other that they were still human, when half their head was full of bioware . . . when half of their souls were dead. . . .

Or all of their brain. My own brain stumbled as it hit a mind as empty as a broken eggshell. My sight homed in, and I stared at him: A perfectly normal-looking total stranger, wandering through the crowd with a drink in one hand. He moved through the same aimless circulation patterns as anybody else, making programmed responses when they needed to be made, circling. . . . *Why?* I pushed deeper into the blankness where a mind should have been. I didn't have to be careful; he couldn't feel me. The organ was intact, the wrinkled gray container of flesh that should have held all the complicated magic that made him a sentient being. But it wasn't anything now except a piece of meat. Something was in there, keeping his vital signs up, making him respond. . . . *Programmed*. That was it. What was imitating a mind was nothing but somebody's biosoft.

I felt my stomach turn over. *Elnear*. Where the hell was she? Suddenly I was sure she was still in the room, that he was waiting for the crowd to thin out a little more, for some perfect moment—I found her, standing on the far side of the room, carrying on a conversation she didn't care about with a person she didn't know. Her arms were folded, her large-knuckled hands clutching her elbows; but otherwise you couldn't tell that she was enjoying this about as much as standing on a bed of broken glass.

I started into the room, keeping a fix on her mind as I pushed my way toward her. It was like working the night crowds back in Old-city. . . . Some half-buried itch couldn't help signaling me that I could steal half the people in this room blind, and they'd never know what happened—

Two sets of hands suddenly locked over my arms. A man and a woman I'd never seen before, with bland, too-perfect faces, were smiling at me. "How good to see you." "So glad you could come . . ." The pressure on my arms suddenly increased until if I didn't stop moving something would snap. I stopped. Looking at them, groping . . . *They were Corpses*. Guilt smacked me with an open hand. But then I realized they were Elnear's Security people, the ones she'd warned me about. They knew I'd know what they were, that I'd hear the message behind the meaningless words.

"Listen," I said, "I have to tell—"

"—Look at his hand, Adson, poor fellow, whatever did you do to yourself come on sweetheart we'll fix it right up . . ." *(Don't make a scene, you little bastard, just come on—)* They turned me around in my tracks and started me back toward the door.

Suddenly I saw Lazuli. She saw me too: I got a sudden flash of how I looked from across the room, my coat gone, my shirt fastened crooked and hanging out of my pants.

I opened my mouth. "Where's—" The pressure on my arms got so bad, so fast, that I had to clench my teeth to keep from crying out. (Take me to Braedee or the whole room hears this, Corpse!) Their hands loosened as if I was red-hot. "I need to see him," I said to them, trying to keep my voice down as Lazuli came toward us. "It's important. It's about Lady Elnear."

Lazuli was searching the crowd, frowning with concern, but it wasn't about me. "Cat, have you seen Jiro?" she said. "I haven't seen him since—"

"We'll take you to Braedee," the man muttered, his voice grating, urging me forward again. "Come on."

"Jiro's all right," I called back over my shoulder. "I'll explain later." Not knowing how, or when, or what in hell I was going to tell her.

Braedee was waiting for us, out in the darkened hallway beyond the door.

"Braedee, you've got to—"

"What now?" His mouth pulled up in the usual sardonic smile. "First you want to quit, and now they have to drag you away from the Lady?"

The two ChemEnGen Corpses on either side of me were watching him the way you'd watch a snake. "Lady Elnear's orders were to keep him away from her tonight," the woman said grimly.

"No one told me that." Braedee's eyes never seemed to move from their faces, but suddenly he was looking at me. "Who did that to your hand?"

"I bit myself, eating. Shut up and listen to me, damn you. There's somebody in that room who doesn't belong there. He's brain-dead—"

Braedee's laughter rattled up and down the hall. "Almost everybody in that room is brain-dead. It's hardly a secret."

"I mean literally, goddamn it! He's a total burnout running on somebody else's 'ware. There's nobody *in* there." I brushed my head with my hand. "I think maybe he's after the Lady."

Braedee's head twitched, as if he was about to reject the whole idea. But then he said, "Show him to me."

Elnear's Security people went rigid, as if they were ready to use their own bodies to stop us. "He's not going back in there. We have orders—"

"He works for me," Braedee said. "And you don't. This is my system, and it covers everyone on these grounds equally." Suddenly there were two more Corpses, wearing Centauri colors, standing in the hall shadows behind him. "You are in my way."

My arms were free. The two Chem Corpses didn't move as I turned around. I didn't wait for Braedee to step on my heels before I was on my way back down the hall. I stood in the doorway, scanning with my mind—found Elnear, a lot closer to us now. She was standing with Daric and Lazuli. I veered away, not wanting to know what he was telling them, trying to keep my concentration whole.

"There." I pointed. The burnout was across the room but angling toward her, still smiling, still empty. My mind cringed. "Get him out of here. Stop him. He's trouble—"

Braedee watched the stranger, with God-knew-what going on in the systems behind his eyes. "He's a legitimate guest. There is absolutely nothing that could injure anyone concealed anywhere on or inside his body. He's drinking something harmless." He glanced at me. "You've had too much to drink. For God's sake, tuck in your shirt." He began to turn away.

"Braedee—" I caught his arm.

He jerked free. "Don't ever do that again," he murmured, smoothing his sleeve. And then he was walking away.

I swore, and went back into the room, going after Elnear.

Daric saw me coming, this time, and nudged her arm. She didn't see him smile as she turned away, searching the crowd for my face. Lazuli looked up with her. I felt Elnear subvocalize a call to her Security people as she spotted me wading toward her. Her frown deepened as they didn't appear.

"Lady—" I gasped it out as I got close enough for her to hear without me having to shout it. "Please, ma'am—" Not daring to touch her mind, knowing how she'd react. I saw the walking vegetable stop, a few meters behind her, and smile his empty smile at me. He looked back at her, taking an awkward gulp of his drink.

She was calling Jardan now, as she realized the guards weren't coming. Something that wasn't quite frustration and wasn't quite panic began to wind like a spring inside her. She took in my syrup-stained clothes in one quick glance, hating the sight of me. "Mez Cat—" Her voice was perfectly calm, and cold. "What are you doing here?"

"Ma'am, I think you're in danger. There's not time to explain. Please, will you please just come with me?" I reached out for her hand.

"Where is my Security?" She stiffened, her hands clenching at her sides. "What are you doing here?"

"Probably wants to tell you all about his evening in Purgatory." Daric leered. "I was just telling them what a good sport you were."

I felt my face flush. "Shut up, you slad." Lazuli was frown-

ing now. Heads were turning; I half heard the whispers starting.
"Lady, I'll explain anything you want if you just come with me."
I caught her arm, tugging her forward. "No trouble, I swear—" I
saw Jardan push past the burnout, coming toward us. He almost spilled
his drink; finished it in a desperate gulp, his eyes riveted on us. The
drink. He started forward as he saw us begin to move. . . . *The
drink.*

$$\left(\begin{array}{l} \text{Get down!} \\ \text{Oh, shit—} \end{array} \right)$$

I shoved her, knocking her into Daric and Lazuli, knocking all
of them flat. I landed on top of them in a tangle of hard elbows and
knees, just as the stranger exploded.

The shock of the blast punched into my eardrums like an icepick.
More bodies crashed down on top of me, crushing the air out of my
lungs. I lay there for a long time, trying to breathe, trying to tell
whether the pain I felt everywhere was inside me or outside; if any of
the groans and screams were mine, if the wetness dripping into my
eye was really my own blood. Everything was in slow motion: sounds,
movement, all sensation with it, as if I'd been hit by a tidal wave and
drowned. . . .

Someone was picking bodies off of me. Someone was hauling
me up like a body. I blinked my eyes clear. There were uniforms
everywhere, Centauri logos, blood. A hand slid down my shoulder: it
wasn't attached to anything. I watched it drop to the floor, lie there
in a red puddle. I saw Lazuli, heard her screaming, over and over;
saw Daric, silent and dazed, and Elnear, her eyes closed. . . . My
head was so full of shock and pain and horror that I couldn't hold it
all.

Suddenly Braedee was in front of me, blocking out my vision,
his hand lifting my chin. "Can you hear me?"

"No," I mumbled, scratching at my ear. I was ready to start
screaming too, as I tried to find the strength to close down my mind,
shut out the terrible noise. . . .

He leaned close to my face. "Damn it, boy! How did you
know—?"

I swore, shaking my head. "Told you. I told you. . . ." It was
all the answer I could get out. And all the answer he deserved.

FOURTEEN

THE HUMAN BOMB had killed three people. Elnear wasn't one of them. He messed up a whole lot of fancy clothes; about twenty more people were transferred to the med center. I was one of them, although cleaning me up was the worst part of what they had to do to me there. They scanned me and picked some bone shrapnel out of my shoulder, then let me go. I was bruised and half-deaf, but otherwise there was nothing wrong with me that wouldn't be wrong with anyone who'd just had somebody else's guts scraped off of him.

I finally let my eyes clear when they told me I could leave the examining room. I put on the clean clothes that had appeared out of nowhere, and walked out through the doorway; bumped into the jamb, and stopped.

I knew that I was in a hospital, and that it had to be a good one, considering the clientele. But it could have been a suite in the best hotel in N'yuk that I'd walked into: a cool green room that was all softness and peace, thick rugs on the floor, hidden lighting, music that was almost subliminal; no cold antiseptic halls, no ceramics, no noise: no evidence that anybody ever felt pain, or needed help. It stank of total unreality. But it couldn't keep the handful of people sitting together on the modular couch from looking like survivors huddled together in a lifeboat. None of them were wearing what they'd worn an hour ago.

I saw Lazuli, sitting with her arms around Jiro, her face too white and calm, as if she was tranked on the same sedatives they'd tried to give me. I'd had enough drugs for one night. Daric sat across from her, sitting on the edge of his seat like he had a stick up his ass. His mouth pinched as he saw me, but this time he kept it shut. Everyone sitting in the circle was a taMing. There were two others that I recognized; one of them was Charon. There were no outsiders—except me.

And Braedee. He was standing in the center of the ring of faces; asking questions, probably. Or maybe answering them. I couldn't hear what he was saying. I wouldn't let myself feel what they were feeling; not yet. I was still too close to the edge. I'd managed to build the mental shield, strand by strand, that put silence between me and the agony all around me. I was afraid to let it down again.

I stood where I was, half wondering whether I wasn't here by mistake, as more heads began to turn. But Braedee gestured me toward them, said something impatient-sounding that I couldn't make out. I went over and sat down in the circle of taMings, feeling all their eyes fixed on me. They all had to know who and what I was now; but I still wasn't sure what that meant. I looked up at them, down again, wetting my lips.

"Thank you," Lazuli said quietly.

I glanced at her. She smiled, ruffling Jiro's spikey hair with her fingers. He pressed closer to her shoulder as he stared at me, his eyes dark. Other faces smiled, other voices echoed her thanks around the circle. Charon taMing didn't say anything, and there was no crack in the cold wall of his face.

I glanced at Daric. His face was frozen too, a warped mirror of his father's. "You're welcome," I said, still meeting his stare. His gaze broke suddenly and he looked away. I almost thought he was ashamed, but maybe it was my imagination.

"Where's Elnear?" I realized suddenly that I'd forgotten to say "the Lady." But for once no one frowned. Maybe saving her life had given me the right to forget, for once. "Is she all right?"

Braedee sat down on the couch an arm's length away from me. He nodded. "Thanks to your . . . loyalty." The catch was back in his voice, the way I'd heard it the first time I'd seen him; as if he hated having to say it. His finger traced the curve of his brow around the edge of his eye. It was the closest to a case of nerves I'd ever seen in him.

I wondered if he'd rather have seen more people die than be proved wrong by me. I wondered what he'd told the taMings—if he'd told them how he hadn't listened to me. I didn't say anything.

"She's with Philipa," Lazuli said.

I looked up, suddenly remembering that Jardan had been passing the stranger just as he finished his drink.

Lazuli nodded, reading the question in my eyes. "She was . . . badly injured." She took a breath, getting her voice under control. "They say . . . that they don't know. . . ." Her voice trailed. She blinked, like something hurt behind her eyes.

I grimaced. I glanced at Braedee again. His lips thinned. "Can I speak to her? Elnear—Lady Elnear, I mean. I need to tell her . . . something."

Braedee frowned, and Charon taMing said, "I have questions about what happened tonight that I want you to answer before you go anywhere." His voice was as cold as his eyes.

I shook my head, looking at him. "Not tonight," I said, and I didn't look down. I stood up, slowly because I was getting stiff. "I'm too goddamn tired. I just want to see the Lady, and then I want to sleep. Ask me tomorrow."

He stiffened. I saw real emotion on his face for the first time. It looked like disbelief. Before he could say anything, Lazuli said, "Of course, Cat. I'll take you to her. And then . . ." she glanced at Charon, back at me, "perhaps you would be kind enough to see us home to the estates?" She got to her feet, nudging Jiro up.

I blinked, feeling a sudden warmth creep up my face. "Yes, ma'am."

"Lazuli." Charon reached out, catching hold of her arm. "We are staying at the townhouse tonight."

She went even paler, but then her color came back in a rush. "No," she said. "You can pretend it didn't happen if you want to. Not me. Not Jiro." She jerked her hand free, and crossed to my side. Jiro followed her, glancing nervously over his shoulder.

Charon half rose from his seat; settled back again under the weight of too many watching eyes. "Very well. I will see you tomorrow, then." His own gaze flicked from her to me, back again.

Lazuli lifted her head, still defiant. Her hand slipped around my arm. I saw Charon's eyes fix on it, and wished she hadn't done that. But there was nothing I could do about it now except follow her out of the room.

Elnear was sitting alone in another room that hardly looked like a hospital waiting room. But it was, and she was waiting, her face heavy with grief and shock and exhaustion . . . all the things I wouldn't let myself read in her mind. Behind her was a wide stretch of dark glass. At first I thought it was a mirror. It wasn't. It looked down into

a surgery. She could watch, if she needed to; but right now this was
as close to Philipa as she could get.

"Elnear—" Lazuli said softly, as she started across the room.

Elnear looked up at us, the dazed suffering fading from her eyes.
She rose to her feet, a little unsteady, and held out her arms to Lazuli
and Jiro. She held them close, before she pulled them down beside
her.

I hung back, feeling like an intruder, as her eyes found me again.
They were red-rimmed, but there were no tears in them now. They
were a clear, steady blue as she looked at me without saying anything,
looked at me until I began to wish I hadn't come. And then she lifted
her hand from her lap, holding it out to me.

I crossed the room, stopped in front of her, uncertain. Slowly I
took her hand, and she put her other hand on top of mine, making me
sit down beside her on the cushioned seat. "I feel . . ." she said at
last, and broke off, as if for once she was having trouble finding the
right words. "I feel as if I owe you such a debt that to thank you, or
even to apologize to you, can only be so meaningless that it would be
insulting. . . ." She looked down at my hand, up at my face again.
"But thank you for what you did. Thank God you are all right. And
I am so terribly sorry, Cat. . . ."

I looked away, choking on the crazy laughter that suddenly filled
me up. I tried to stop it, but it burst out of my throat anyway, in a
strangled bark that sounded more like a pain cry. I pressed my hand
over my mouth, taking a deep breath, and another, until I was sure I
could keep a straight face when I looked back at her again.

They were all looking at me, but no one looked like I'd done
anything strange. Maybe after what had happened to us all, anything
we did seemed normal. I glanced up at the window behind me, careful
not to focus because I might see what was happening on the other side
of it. "I'm sorry too, ma'am. About . . ." I nodded my head at the
window, "Philipa." It sounded about as meaningless and empty as
what she'd just said to me. But even that was almost a relief, somehow.

She nodded, her eyes dimming again as she remembered what
was being done in there.

"They have the best of everything here, Elnear," Lazuli said,
touching her shoulder. "There's almost nothing they can't do. And
they'll do whatever is necessary for her."

"Yes, I know." Elnear sighed. Her hands were back in her own
lap again, clenched together.

"Won't you come back to the estates with us?"

She shook her head. "No. I'll be fine here. I'm not going anywhere until I'm sure that . . . that everything will be all right."

Lazuli nodded, getting slowly to her feet. She glanced at me as
Jiro stood up beside her. I stood up too, waited until they were halfway
toward the door. I looked at Elnear. "Ma'am . . . I told you the truth
before. I've never lied to you about anything. And the other things
Stryger claimed, about things I did back in Oldcity—I did them to
stay alive. That's all." I turned away and followed Lazuli out of the
room. Not knowing, not really caring, whether the words meant any
more to her now than they had before, or whether she'd even remember
that I said them. At least I'd know I said them.

As I followed Lazuli and Jiro back through the med center's halls,
I began to realize that everyone I saw wore either a Centauri logo, or
a Centauri security clearance. "Do you own this hospital too?" I said
finally.

Lazuli hadn't said anything, or even looked at me, while we
walked. Now she glanced at me, distracted by my voice—glad of the
distraction. "It must look that way." She laughed, a little too sharply,
still teetering on the brink of something darker. "Centauri contributed
a great deal to the construction of this wing. In return, we retain certain
facilities on long term lease for our private use."

"The taMing Wing?" I said, and laughed.

A little color came into her cheeks, a smile touched her lips. "A
number of the larger combines do the same thing. It's more . . .
secure. . . ." She glanced away, her words fading. She slowed her
footsteps until she was walking beside me. She held Jiro's hand tightly
in hers, and he didn't complain.

We took the lift up to the garage level. A few more steps across
a silent space to a mod and I could let my whole body drop into
autopilot. The day would finally be finished with me.

The doors slipped open. The first thing I saw was Daric. He was
surrounded. A dozen hypers were swarming over him like flies on
garbage.

"Jeezu!" I whispered. "Who let them in here?"

"It's a public access—" Lazuli looked left and right, her face
pinching as she searched for a way around them.

"Get away from me. I don't know anything about it!" Daric
waved his hands, twitching with irritation. "Ask him." He turned,
pointing at us, at me. "He's the one you want to talk to. There's your
hero—" He ducked through the gauntlet and ran, as the hypers turned
to see what he meant.

And then they were all over us, trapping us against the wall, shoving hands that were cameras and spotlights, and faces with three eyes into my face—

Suddenly the nearest hypers were stumbling back like something had sprayed them with bug killer; suddenly their echoing voices sounded like they were coming at us from the other side of a wall. We were shielded. "Cat," Lazuli murmured, "you don't have to speak to them now. We're still inside Centauri's security system."

I'd covered my face with my arm, ready to cut and run like Daric had if I needed to. But then I began to hear what the hypers were trying to ask me. It wasn't about this afternoon . . . it was about tonight.

Slowly I lowered my arm. Shander Mandragora himself was planted right in front of me; I could see him subvocalizing to his audience.

"It's all right," I said to Lazuli. "Let it down. I want to talk to them." The sudden rush of adrenaline that had hit me when I saw the hypers was making me feel brave and alert. She didn't look happy, but suddenly the voices were rattling in our ears again as the hypers surged forward.

". . . Lady Elnear Lyron/taMing's controversial young psion aide," Shander Mandragora said, suddenly coming on audio as he elbowed somebody out of his way. "You're quite a hero." He smiled at me, cool, confident, and looking earnest as hell. He was wearing padded body armor. So were the rest of the hypers. I wondered if it was to protect them from each other, or from their victims. "Tell us how you managed to save the Lady and several other members of the taMing family from a human time bomb." He was gazing right into my eyes, and his own eyes were the color of sapphires. He was standing so close to me that we were almost touching, and he looked just as good as he did on the threedy—lean, square-jawed, tough. I remembered having a dream about being him once, while I was asleep on a moldy mat in the back room of an abandoned building. "Did you use your mind?"

I felt the crazy laughter try to get loose inside me again. I swallowed it, along with half a dozen wiseass answers. I couldn't help staring at the camera lens in the middle of his forehead. It looked like a paste-on jewel, the same color as his eyes; but once you knew that it wasn't, it was hard to look away from. Kind of like the muzzle of a gun. "Well, I . . ." My throat suddenly went dry with the fear of saying the wrong thing, and I had to swallow again. "Yeah. I used my . . . my Gift." Trying not to sound like I was embarrassed to admit it. "I picked up on a party guest who'd had something done to his head. He wasn't . . . human any more, he was a machine. I knew I had to warn the Lady. I was almost too late."

"What made you read the guests' minds tonight?" Mandragora asked, blinking as if he suddenly wondered what I was doing now. "Are you always 'on'?"

"No." I shook my head, tried to smile away the look on his face. "It's hard work. I was just doing my job. Checking out the crowd to make sure they were all right. It's part of what I was hired to do."

"You mean you were hired by Lady Elnear as a personal spy—" Someone's open hand flashed in front of Mandragora's face; a camera eye stared at me from its palm. Some combine logo I didn't recognize was tattooed above it.

"No—" I bit off the curse that wanted to follow, wondering if the hand belonged to Stryger's media base.

"To spy for Centauri—?" This hyper had on Triple Gee colors.

"I was hired to protect her! Because somebody's been trying to kill her. Like they almost did tonight."

"Why didn't the Lady Elnear tell us about that in her rebuttal—?" Shander Mandragora was back in my face again, and somebody was groaning in the background.

I shrugged, feeling my frown get deeper. "Maybe she didn't feel like discussing it with the whole galaxy."

"Lady Elnear—" Lazuli said, very loudly, very clearly, "didn't want the people watching to feel that she was using a personal problem to gain their support. She felt that her arguments had to be strong enough to stand on their own."

I smiled, grateful, as the cameras, and the heat, turned away from me toward her.

"Lady Lazuli taMing," Mandragora said, acknowledging and identifying her from an augmented memory bank. "Another survivor of tonight's tragedy. Do you have any idea who would want to kill Lady Elnear?"

"No." Lazuli shook her head. "No idea at all." I felt her falter behind the skin-deep mask of a board member's arrogance.

"How is Lady Elnear? Why hasn't she come out yet?" someone shouted. Mandragora was losing ground.

"She's fine, perfectly fine!" Lazuli had to raise her voice again to make them listen. "A personal friend was seriously injured. The Lady is waiting for news about her condition."

"Why didn't you save everybody?" Somebody else jarred me back against the wall. "Why didn't you bring in Security?"

Whose logo was it? I couldn't even see. "I did—didn't have time." Not sure why I was covering for Braedee.

"Why didn't you stop him yourself? Why did you let those other people die? You could have stopped him with your mind."

"It doesn't work like that. I'm just a telepath, that's all. Not even a very good one. I'm not God. I'm not a Corpse, either."

"But you are a criminal. Why did Lady Elnear hire a traitor who worked for a psion terrorist? Why are you free? Sojourner Stryger called you—"

"I know what he called me." I shoved the camera away, and three more replaced it. "He's a liar!" I twisted until I could see Shander Mandragora and he could see me. "You let Stryger smear the Lady today!" I yelled. He'd done it . . . he could fix it. "Jeezu, I don't believe this—I didn't work for Quicksilver. I killed him! Doesn't anybody here know that? How the hell can you know all about me and not know that?"

"Do you mean you were a part of his terrorist group, and you betrayed him to the FTA?" he called. *The stupid bastard.*

"I killed him in self-defense, goddamn it! And to save my friends, and to save your stinking telhassium. I wasn't a traitor, I worked for the FTA. You've got a head full of history, why the hell don't you use it? We were fucking psion heroes. For about as long as it took to say our names . . . just like tonight. But I missed it all, because I had a nervous breakdown after I killed him. That's what it means to be a telepath, and kill somebody. . . ." I had to stop, taking a deep breath in the sudden silence. "And I guess it still doesn't mean shit to be a psion and a hero."

By the time the questions started again, it was too late. I was halfway to the waiting mod. Lazuli and Jiro followed behind me.

The mod sealed us in, out of reach, and took us away at Lazuli's order. As we left the garage, its too-normal voice said, "Lady Lazuli, I have detected five intrusive listening devices in the clothing of the passengers."

"Deactivate them," she said, her voice still perfectly calm. I almost thought I felt the scramble burst that burned them out. Lazuli waited until the voice reported, "Clear." Then she slumped back into the formfoam of the seat, and covered her face with her hands. After a moment her hands slid down again, dropped limply into her lap.

"They bugged us?" I said, incredulous.

She nodded. I saw tears shining on her face in the brief light of a passing streetlamp. Jiro looked up at her, and his mouth began to tremble as he saw his mother crying. Suddenly tears were running down his cheeks. He hid his face against her as he cried.

I swallowed hard, keeping my mind clenched, afraid that in a minute it was going to be three of us. "I'm sorry," I murmured, only realizing now how much it had cost her to show the hypers that proud, cool face; to protect me, and Elnear, the way she had. "I didn't know they'd . . ." My hands made fists; let go again, too tired to hold onto the anger. My whole body ached, my nerves felt raw. I wished I'd taken everything they'd offered me at the med center.

"It's all right," she lied. "I'm quite used to them." She sat up straighter, wiped at her eyes. "It was just the final . . . the last thing, that was too much. They had no right to do that to you, to Elnear through you . . . no right!" She blew her nose. "But it's all they know how to do—"

"I knew the combine hypers were all liars," I said, rolling the sour words on my tongue. "I just didn't know the Indy's hypers were all shitheads."

Her mouth twitched, and Jiro lifted his face from her shoulder to stare at me, as if hearing someone talk to his mother that way was more than he could believe.

"'Scuse me, ma'am." I looked out the window at the one large moon rising, the dark world down below; for a heartbeat remembering somewhere else.

"Don't apologize," she said. "I find it refreshing." She frowned then, thinking about something else. "Our own media people should have been on this, and given them the true story by now. I don't understand why they didn't seem to know the truth."

I glanced back at her, realizing that she knew what everyone else knew about me, now—the truth, and even the lies—but it hadn't seemed to make any difference to her. "Ma'am," not using her name, because Jiro was still looking at me that way, "did Braedee say anything at the hospital tonight about the—about what Stryger claimed I did?"

She shook her head.

"Nobody asked him?"

"Great-uncle Hwang did," Jiro volunteered. "Charon said forget it. He said it didn't matter, it just made everything perfect."

"Perfect?" I frowned, wondering what in hell he'd meant by that. I was too tired to try to figure it out. "I'm not a traitor," I said.

Lazuli looked at me, her face calm in the wash of moonlight. "I never thought you were."

"Why not?"

She glanced down suddenly, and shrugged. "You don't act like one."

That didn't make any sense either, but I didn't push it. Instead I asked, "What did Daric tell you and the Lady?"

She looked surprised, as if I'd asked something totally pointless. "He said he took you and Jiro to hear Argentyne perform. He said that you seemed to enjoy the show more than Jiro did. . . . I asked him not to take Jiro anywhere again without telling me first." Her arm curved around him protectively.

I glanced at Jiro, glad we were all in darkness just then.

"I'm never going anywhere with Daric again," Jiro said, his voice hard with anger and betrayal. His eyes kept touching me and jerking away, coming back to my face again.

"Why?" Lazuli asked.

"He's a croach," Jiro said.

Her fingers moved in a short, silent question. He shook his head. She looked back at me again. My stomach tightened as I waited for her to ask me what had really happened. But she didn't ask. Nobody said anything more.

When we finally reached the estates, I helped Lazuli steer Jiro to his room. I waited while she put him to bed, letting the doorway hold me up, too exhausted to bother moving. But as she waved the lights down and came out into the hall, I heard Jiro call my name. I glanced at her, and she nodded. I went into the room.

"Cat . . . ?" Jiro said, his voice thick with sleep.

"Yeah, I'm here." As my eyes adjusted, I could see his face clearly in the dim wash of light from the hall. He couldn't see mine.

"You probably think I'm real stupid, don't you?" he said.

"No." I half smiled. "Just real lucky. I guess nobody's luck lasts forever."

"You saved Aunt Elnear, just like you promised. And you saved my mother too—" His voice blurred with feeling, his eyes got wet again. "I'll give you anything you want. I have stuff like you've never seen—"

I didn't say anything. I turned away, starting back across the room.

"Cat—?"

I stopped.

"I was scared of you tonight. I hated you, too."

"I know."

"I don't any more."

I did smile, this time. "That's all I want."

Out in the hall Lazuli looked at me, curious.

"He just wanted to say thanks."

She nodded, hesitated . . . reached out and put her hand on my arm. "Cat . . ."

"You already have. Good night, ma'am." I went back along the hall, before it was too late. I stumbled up the stairs to my own room and fell into bed, hardly stopping long enough to peel off my clothes.

I couldn't sleep. I lay there, feeling the seconds pass like water dripping; feeling every centimeter of my spreadeagled body twitch and crawl and shiver like a plucked string. Closing my eyes only made me see things I'd never wanted to see in the first place. Opening them again, in the empty bed in the empty room, only reminded me of how alone I was.

And then my door opened softly, and someone stepped inside. Caught in the random moonlight, her pale gown moving around her . . . *Jule*. A tiny spark of light caught fire in the palm of her hand, guiding her across the uncertain darkness to me.

"Lazuli . . ." I pushed myself up, feeling the covers slide down over the sudoskin bandaging my shoulder. *You shouldn't be here don't do this to me I want you.* . . . Afraid to speak, because I didn't know what would come out of my mouth first.

She set the lamp chip on the table beside the bed, stood gazing down at me. Her night-black hair fell free over her shoulders, her skin was like amber in the lampglow. She reached up, began to unfasten the pearls that buttoned the neckline of her restless gown.

"Wait—" I whispered, my throat tight.

Her fingers froze; her eyes clung to me.

"What about—Charon." I looked down, not sure who I was more afraid for, her or me. "If anybody finds out—"

Her eyes filled with sudden tears. "Please . . ." she said, and her voice trembled. "Please don't make me beg you. I need someone. I don't want to be alone tonight. . . ."

I raised my hand; she caught it, kissed it, settling onto the bed. Dizzy with disbelief, I let go the clenched fist that my mind had been since the explosion, letting it fill with her thoughts, her emotions. *She'd almost died tonight. . . . But she was alive, so alive that every nerve in her body sang with need.* Nothing mattered tonight, not Charon, not tomorrow, not who she was or even what I was. She needed to feel loved, and that was all she knew. She wanted me to love her, *me and no one else,* because she'd known when I looked at her how much I wanted it too. . . .

I pulled her down beside me with unsteady hands, feeling her hair brush my cheek as I found her mouth and kissed it. I broke away again, not able to meet her eyes. Burning with the hunger in my blood . . . not knowing what to do next. I'd been naked in bed with strangers before, for nearly half a lifetime; but all there had ever been between us was money. Nameless, faceless, we'd done what we had to do, with no real emotion and no expectations. I'd never had a woman like this—this beautiful, this untouchable—not in my wildest fantasies. One who really wanted *me.* . . . One who had a right to expect things that maybe I didn't know how to give. The fear that I didn't know how to be what she wanted suddenly seemed like the worst fear I'd ever known.

But she took my hand as gently as if she thought I was a virgin, and laid it on her breast. I fumbled with the buttons of her gown, awkward and uncertain as I finished what she'd started. The gown seemed to melt away under my clumsy fingers like it had a life of its own, the silken cloth becoming her flesh, warm and yielding. I shuddered with the electric shock of our contact as she pressed herself against my thighs; rolled onto her, holding her there under me, her softness beneath my sudden painful hardness. It was too easy to go on then, after all that had happened tonight . . . too easy.

She clung to me, her mouth open, hungry for my kisses. Her lips were like flowers after the rain, I could have kissed them forever, lost inside the wet, warm contact, feeling her pleasure . . . *she had always wanted to be kissed this way, kissed and kissed endlessly* . . . feeding my own. Her hands explored me in slow, grazing circles, the white scars on my back, the smooth brown of my sides, my thighs. I slid off of her, my own restless hands covering her breasts, curving down along the gentle hills of her belly, into the warm, waiting valley between her legs.

She moaned softly, her hips moving to meet my touch, guiding me deeper into her hidden places. I felt the murmur of her mind, as open and yearning as her body. I followed its whispering voice down, deeper and deeper, until I knew every sweet ache, every burning, dazzled second of her arousal. I'd never made love to a woman while I'd had my Gift—never known what it could do, how it doubled every ecstasy, her pleasure woven into mine until every place I touched her body brought heat as dizzying as her touch against my own. Suddenly I wasn't afraid any more that I couldn't give her what she wanted. Because I knew what she wanted. . . .

My mouth left hers, traveling down over her throat, her shoulders, her breasts . . . following her lead, granting her every unspoken wish with growing urgency. Her breath came in shallow sobs, she whimpered, and then began to tremble, as the realization grew in her mind of what was being done to her. *Wonder, joy, frantic longing, rising panic*—

The hands that had clung to me, caressed me, urged me, suddenly were trying to push me away. Gasping for breath I let her go, backing off, putting space between us for the length of heartbeats it took for the heat of her unfinished desire to burn away her fear. And then I began again. This time I took more care, not answering every need, or not too soon; drawing it out, letting her feel that there were still secret places that she could keep hidden, if only in her mind. Soothing, lingering, exploring, until my mouth reached the place where she had ached for someone's mouth to be—

And the rising wave of her pleasure reached its crest and broke over her, over me, through every synapse of my body, until it was all I could do to hold myself under control. I swung my hips over her again, down into the waiting space between her open thighs. I slid into her, deep into the final place that now at last she was ready to share. I began to move, feeling myself, feeling myself inside her, stunned with sensation. Her hips rose to meet my thrusts, while the tide rose inside me this time, rising and rising toward that impossible crest, and exploding over me, out of me, back along the filaments of contact I had woven and into her unprotected mind. I felt her come again, her climax recoiling through my own like a riptide, fusing us into one. I covered her mouth with mine to drown out her cry, and she kissed me and I kissed her, echoing echoing echoing, until there was nothing left of us but warm ashes.

She held me inside the circle of her arms, I held her inside mine, and there were tears on my face, but I didn't know whose they were. Still clinging to each other while the darkness slowly faded into dawn, we slept.

FIFTEEN

WHEN I WOKE UP again it was the middle of the morning, and my mind was still half in a dream. I sighed, reaching out into the warm band of sunlight to touch warm skin, reaching out with my mind. The bed was empty. My mind touched the mind of a total stranger.

I pushed myself up, confused—jerked back as my eyes registered the pair of uniformed legs standing beside the bed. The Corpse looked down at me, expressionless, and said, "The Chief and Gentleman Charon want to talk to you about last night."

Lazuli— I bit my tongue to keep from blurting out the question before I found the answer. *No.* She was nowhere in sight, nowhere in his mind. It was about the explosion, that was all. If the Corpse wondered why I looked so guilty, or why I looked so relieved, he didn't let it bother him. A one-track mind had its points. "Sure. Just give me a minute."

While I pulled on some clothes I wondered about why they'd sent a body to deliver the message, instead of calling me. Maybe they were that paranoid about security, after last night. Or maybe they just wanted me paranoid.

As I passed the bathroom mirror, a sudden flash of green caught my eye. I stopped, looking at myself, turning my head—saw the light wink again. My ear. I reached up, touching it, with a slow smile starting. There was an earring in my ear, one I'd never seen before. Green glass, catching the light when I moved, like a cat's eye. I knew

I hadn't put it there . . . I figured I knew who had. I stuck a drug patch behind my ear, and went out of the room.

The first thing the Corpse did when I came downstairs was make me take the patch off. Braedee's orders. It took about half an hour for the effects to wear off. By the time we reached the city, he wanted me deaf and dumb. The Corpse threw the patch away. I didn't bother to tell him about the second patch I'd stuck on behind my other ear.

He took me back into N'Yuk, to the taMing townhouse. You'd never have known there'd been three murders and a lot of blood there the night before. I followed the Corpse through the room where it had all happened, and everything in it was immaculate—walls, carpets, furniture. Some of the furniture looked different than I remembered, but otherwise it fit the room perfectly. It made my skin crawl.

Braedee and Charon taMing were waiting for me in the room beyond, a space like a cell, which didn't make me feel much better. As I walked through the doorway I felt something not-human whisper across my brain and fade again. Then I understood. It was a whiteroom—so thick with security that my psi actually registered it. I stopped, uncertain, as Braedee stood up from the couch. Charon stayed where he was, deep in its folds, staring at me. I made myself look right at him, my face as stupidly expressionless as I could manage. Trying not to look like I'd just slept with someone's wife was something I didn't have a whole lot of practice at.

"Why are you looking at me like that?" he snapped.

"Nothing, sir." I glanced away from him, at Braedee, at the door.

"Sit down," Braedee said, and pointed at a chair.

I followed his hand, glad to have somewhere else to look. But my mind was still focused on Charon, just as paranoid as he wanted it to be, for all the wrong reasons. But not deaf, or dumb. Inside the forest of his augmentation, I felt him daring me to sit in that chair. Somehow I managed not to turn back and stare at him. I kept looking at the chair, the one Braedee had pointed out. Soft, humpbacked, blue-gray—there was nothing unusual about it. But whoever sat in it was going to get one hell of a shock, right where it hurt him most.

My own disbelief made me freeze. Why—? A trap. If my psi was really shut down the way he wanted it to be, then I'd go to the chair and sit in it, and he'd get to watch me jump. But if I could read him, I'd know—

Braedee was looking at me again. I clamped down hard on my body functions, hoping I could keep the readings normal enough to suit him. Forcing myself to stay calm, forcing myself to move, I crossed the room. Without taking a deep breath, I sat down in the chair.

They weren't bluffing. I leaped up again with a curse, as the current sank its teeth into my ass. "What the hell—?" I yelled, as if I didn't know. I didn't have to fake the anger that came with it. "Is that supposed to be some kind of fucking joke?" I looked at Braedee and shook out my smarting hands.

Braedee stood where he was, his arms clasped behind him. He didn't move to do anything, which had to mean I'd passed his test. Charon settled back into the couch, his body going loose as the suspicion flowed out of him; satisfied, because Braedee was.

"Not a joke, I assure you," Braedee said mildly. "A test."

"Of what?" I remembered to ask, still frowning.

"Of whether you were reading us."

"Shit," I said. "Maybe that's where your brains are," rubbing my butt, "but mine are up here." I jerked my head at him. "Whose chair is that—Daric's?"

His mouth twitched. "Sit down . . . I promise you, it won't happen again."

"You sit in it," I said. He was telling the truth, but I didn't feel much like sitting down, anyway.

He shrugged, and sat down in the chair. Nothing happened to him.

"Why do I have to play deadhead for you, anyhow?" I asked.

"The Gentleman prefers it that way," Braedee said, and glanced at Charon.

I turned to look at him again. It was easier, this time. "I thought you were paying to keep me switched on." I wondered if it was just his disgust at the thought of being touched by my mind, or if he really had something to hide. By the time I got out of this room, I was going to know which it was.

His anger was like a wave of heat. "I'm paying you to do what you're told," he said. "We will ask the questions. You answer them—civilly." He shot a dark look at Braedee, one that said he thought Braedee was letting me get away with too much, letting me mouth off without stepping on me. I remembered what Braedee had done to me before the board meeting. He hadn't let me get away with it then. But then I hadn't known something that could ruin his career. He'd finally stepped off the edge.

I said, "Yes, sir," anyway, because Charon was making a fist of his cybered hand. I didn't have to read his mind to know what he'd

like to do with it. Knowing what he owed me for saving his family
and Elnear last night hadn't changed how he felt about psions, except
maybe to make him more bitter. I went to the couch and sat on it,
because it was the only place left to sit down. I kept as much space
between him and me as I could. Its soft folds were filled with something
that shifted out of my way like water. I tried not to flounder. "What
do you want to know? Sir."

"You read the mind of that assassin last night," he said. I nodded,
even though it wasn't a question. "And you saw something that gave
him away to you, something that didn't register on any of our security
scans. What was it?"

I glanced at Braedee. He hadn't told them. He was looking back
at me, looking a little grim, but that was all. I slipped in through the
hissing grids of his implants, waded too-clear streams of biosoft, treading as lightly as I could: He knew I hadn't told anybody what he'd
done—or hadn't done—last night. He was counting on me to cover
for him again, even though he wasn't sure why I'd done it, any more
than I was. . . . He figured I must want something from him.

I realized he was right. I just had to figure out what it was.
"Somebody had stripped his brains. He'd been reprogrammed to act
human, but he wasn't. He was just a . . . a bioware death machine."
The memory of what had been done to him made my jaw clench until
my teeth hurt. "Who was he?" *The poor bastard.*

"A midlevel official of Centauri." Charon waved his hand, pushing the dead man aside like yesterday's weather report. "No one
important." I looked at him, looked away again. "What is important,"
he said, his voice dropping until it was barely audible, "is who did it
to him." Now his face showed something. Now he was *angry, frustrated, sick with rage, aching for revenge.* They'd analyzed every
dripping millimeter of the human bomb's remains, without finding a
clue. But he had to know—not because whoever had done it had
destroyed one life, or four, in a way that would make a hit man retch.
How they'd done it, what they'd done, didn't matter to him half as
much as the fact that they'd done it to Centauri . . . to him.

"I don't know who did it," I said, too softly.

He leaned toward me, his eyes hot and hard. "You have to know.
You saw inside his mind. Who wired him? Who sent him here?"

I shook my head. "I told you, I don't know! Whoever did it was
good—they didn't leave any fingerprints."

"Is he telling the truth?" Charon said to Braedee. Braedee nodded.

I frowned. "He didn't even know who he was looking for. They'd set him up so that when his eyes registered the right visual cue, he'd drink that drink. He didn't know anything until he saw it—'' Her. Elnear. I saw him in my mind, trying so damn hard to swallow that drink down before she got away from him. If only Jardan had really made him spill it. If only I'd understood what it meant, before it was too late. . . .

"You knew about the drink?" he asked, his voice jerking my attention back.

I nodded. "I knew—but it was too late. It was the way he *had* to drink it. . . ." I glanced at Braedee again. "I just didn't figure it out until there wasn't time to stop him. All there was time for was hitting the floor. What the hell was in it?" *You said it was harmless.* The words almost got out of me.

"A glass of wine with a few random molecules of ceboric in it," Braedee said, thin-lipped. "It appeared perfectly innocuous—and it was, until it catalyzed the LDA they'd planted in his stomach. Then it blew him up."

"I know. I saw that part." I looked down, swallowing.

"Then there's nothing—absolutely nothing else you can tell us about who set up this attack?" Charon said.

I hesitated, searching my memory for something I might have forgotten, or refused to remember because it was too ugly. . . . Finally I shook my head. "No sir. I told you everything. There just wasn't anything *in* there to see."

Charon swore, turning back to Braedee. "Now what? This is critical, goddamnit. I want answers. You said nothing could go wrong—and everything has. You slipped, Braedee, you nearly cost Centauri Elnear. She's no good to us dead—" He stood up, looking like he had something down his shirt, gnawing at his flesh.

Braedee glanced at me, frowning, as if he was afraid I was hearing too much. . . . *Too much about what?* He looked back at Charon, his face under control again, as he said, "The psion served his intended purpose, sir." Every word carried a weight on it. Iron. *Irony.* It took me an extra beat to realize that he was talking about me. "He filled a breach in our security, just as I said he would; one that could not have been filled any other way. Because of that Lady Elnear is still secure." Not *alive;* secure. "Your stepson and your wife, as well." Taking the credit as calmly as if it belonged to him. "The attack was almost undetectable. Not many of our competitors have the capability for something like that, even if they have the intent."

"What about Triple Gee?"

"Their ambassadors didn't know anything about it," I said.

"That doesn't prove anything," Braedee murmured. "But the way it happened was too imaginative for Triple Gee's Security."

"Anybody can hire a specialist," I said. "There's plenty of arm in the Lack Market, who'll kill anybody for you, any way you want it done. That doesn't take much imagination." Something that didn't make sense bumped up against the back of my eyes as I said it. The other attacks on Elnear had been so crude they were almost a joke. Nothing at all like this one.

"That's impossible," Charon said coldly. "No combine's board would consider that."

I laughed; stopped laughing as they looked at me. They actually meant that. They had their own armies, spies, assassins. They thought they didn't need outsiders. "You mean it's more fun if you do it yourself?" The stares got blacker. "Look, this attack doesn't match the others at all. Maybe they gave up and turned it over to somebody who knew what the hell they were doing."

They looked at each other. The subvocal exchange between them said they knew I was wrong. *They knew. How could they be so sure?* I sank a quiet hook deeper into Charon's brain.

"What about the Lack Market?" Charon murmured, his eyes still on Braedee. "Could there be any possible tie-in—?"

"Hardly," Braedee said. He was back in the control seat again. I'd covered his ass, he didn't have to worry about Charon any more; just me. "It's in their interest to keep the drug restricted, and that's what Elnear wants too."

Charon nodded, thinking Elnear wasn't exactly the sort to get into trouble over secret gaming debts. But then he was back to wondering who was taking advantage of this, and why—? Panic alarms were going off inside him. He had no idea who it could be, he only knew this attack had nothing to do with the things that had happened before. I pushed deeper: *There was no doubt in his mind—*

Braedee's head swiveled around; he gave me a strange look. "What's the matter with you?" he said.

"Me?" I blinked, pulling back fast.

He looked pained. "I'm not talking to myself."

"I'm . . . just trying to think." They acted like they were thinking about this for the first time. Like they'd never really considered any of this before. . . .

"Do it without your mouth hanging open." He looked back at Charon. "What about him?" *Me*.

Charon frowned at me. "He's told us all he knows, obviously. Send him away." He was looking straight at me, but still talking about me as if I couldn't understand a direct command.

"I don't mean that," Braedee said. "I'm talking about keeping him on."

Charon's head jerked back toward him. His mouth tightened, as he barely stopped a refusal. "Are you serious?" Half sarcasm, half incredulity.

"After what he did last night, yes, sir. We still need him. . . . His function has simply changed."

"He fed the hypers last night, for God's sake! Did you access the Morning Report—?"

I sucked in a breath, imagining what kind of cretin they must have made me look like. "I only wanted to help the Lady, sir. After the way Stryger lied about me, I thought if I could make them understand the truth. . . ."

"You wanted to help!" His hand jumped, fisted. I sank back into the corner of the couch, as his sudden fresh anger slammed into my unguarded thoughts. He'd seen the 'cast, and he thought I *had* helped her. And that was the last thing he'd wanted. He wanted her alive . . . but discredited, demoralized, a failure—under his thumb. "You misbegotten guttersnipe." His hand loosened, and he pushed to his feet.

"All the more reason to keep him here, at least until the vote," Braedee said. "It would look bad."

I stopped listening as sick realization filled me up. They hadn't planned to keep me on until they found out who was trying to kill Elnear . . . because nobody was trying to kill Elnear. They'd staged the attacks themselves—Centauri, Braedee, under the direction of the board; of Charon. Just enough to throw her off-balance, to frighten her, to make her dependent on them and their Security. Just enough so they could force her to accept me. They'd lied to her, they'd lied to me—they'd been using me all along, to spy on her, just like she'd figured.

But more than that—they knew that Stryger hated psions. So they'd set me up as a target, and let him knock me down. So that they could make sure Elnear would be humiliated and lose the debate, and the vote, and the seat—

Except that somebody had found out about the phony attacks on her, and tried to use them to cover up a separate attack, not knowing that the others had all been faked. So now Centauri really did have an attempted assassination on its hands.

"Do what you want with him, then," Charon was saying. He started for the door. "Just get results. And control him—keep him away from me."

He had to pass by me one last time to get to the door. He glanced down at me, as if something had caught his eye; stopped. "Where did you get that earring?"

I shook my head, still dazed. I raised my hand to my ear; felt the slick, cold surface of the cut glass under my fingertip. Froze. "I— uh—got it from a street vendor."

He grunted, and went on out. The door sealed behind him, leaving me alone with Braedee.

"All right," Braedee said. "What do you want?"

"What?" I couldn't remember what he was talking about. I rubbed my eyes, feeling the pressure/pain build behind them.

"You know what I'm talking about." He moved two steps one way, two steps back, his hands locked behind him. His eyes were on me all the time. "To keep quiet about last night."

I laughed. It didn't sound real. "Oh. That."

He stopped moving. "What the hell's the matter with you?" He was half afraid that I was just plain crazy.

I looked up at him again. "You used me," I said. "You bastard, you were using me all the time—you and the taMings. There was no plot against the Lady, not before last night! You set her up, so you could use me to fuck her over."

He stared at me.

" 'How do I know all that'?" Taking the words right out of his mind. "How do you think I know, deadhead?"

His face went white with fear, and fury. He looked at the chair we'd both sat in.

"It didn't work, Braedee."

His black eyes snapped back to me. "You were reading us all along. You sat down anyway. Why?"

"Come on," I said. "Wouldn't you have done it, if you were me?"

He looked at the chair again. "I didn't think it was possible." For me to have fooled his lie detectors. For him to have been so wrong.

He'd really believed I was that much of a coward. That stupid. A punk kid, another screwed-up freak. No threat, no problem. "Surprise," I said.

And then I watched his hand reach for the gun hidden under the smooth line of his uniform jacket. . . . For a minute he really didn't know whether he was going to let me live or kill me—

I sat there while he decided, feeling my palms go clammy with sweat as I suddenly wondered if I'd misread him even worse than he'd misread me.

His hand came out of his coat again, at last. He needed me. . . . He was still frowning, thinking I knew everything he thought; but I watched his body ease out of its systems alert. He lifted his shoulders, in something that almost looked like a shrug. "So you know it all, now. I'll repeat my question—what do you want?"

I sighed. "How about an apology?" I said, just to see if I'd get one. I didn't. "You want me to work for you—for real, this time. Lady Elnear's no good to you dead, and you really think I can do something to help you keep her alive. That's what you were telling Charon. Right?" He nodded, barely. "That's what I want, too."

He looked surprised. "Why?"

My mouth twisted. "You want to hear something else I've learned since I came here? The only real difference between a combine vip like Charon and a streetrat like me is how many people believe the lies we tell. . . . I don't enjoy feeling like your whore. And that's what I'll feel like if I leave now. I want to finish this job, now that it means something."

His eyes narrowed. "I suppose that's reasonable." He didn't know what to believe about me any more, and it bothered him.

"But it'll cost you."

He smiled, relieved. He could relate to that. "That's what I thought. Centauri will double the amount of your contracts."

"All of it—for the Center, too."

"Of course." He nodded.

"Do it now."

He glanced away from me for a long second, and back. "It's done."

"I'll check it when I get home." The formless couch was beginning to give me a sensory deprivation attack. I stood up, shaking it off. "What happened to Elnear's Security people?" They'd been witnesses—the only witnesses—to my warning him about the bomb.

"Don't ask questions you don't really want answered." He folded his arms; watching my expression. "You think you've figured out how to play this game, don't you? Just because you hold the key pieces, right now.'' He shook his head slowly. ''Believe me, boy, you've had beginner's luck. Don't push it.'' Meaning that I'd been stupid not to spill what I knew about him when I had the chance. Because if he hadn't decided right then that he needed me, there would have been one more fatality after that explosion.

I rubbed my hands on my pants legs. Then I said, ''There's one more thing I want.''

He raised his eyebrows. ''What is it?''

''I need stronger drugs.''

''No.'' His mind closed like a door.

''I'm still half-crippled, Braedee. What you got me isn't good enough. I can't do what I need to do, if you really want my help.'' My hands flexed. ''And I'm starting to get . . . symptoms.''

''I can't get you anything stronger. The board wouldn't permit it. I had a hell of a time even getting you this far.''

''You can do it if you want to. If Lady Elnear winds up dead, Centauri loses ChemEnGen. And you lose, too. . . . That's heavier on the scale than what Gentleman Charon thinks of psions.''

''I can't do it.''

''You owe me. Get me the drugs.''

''I can't.'' He shook his head. ''You underestimate how difficult it is for me to get what you need. That's not some streetcorner dreamdot you're asking for. Charon monitors everything that's done concerning you. . . . You also underestimate how much he resents your presence here.''

I made a face, my hands tightening again.

''I'll give you this,'' he said finally. ''I'll give you space. If you can get what you want somewhere else, I won't stop you.''

I nodded, surprised.

''Lady Elnear is still at the hospital. She is expecting you to join her there. I don't have to tell you to keep your mouth shut about what you know. Do I—?''

I hesitated. ''I guess not.''

He nodded at the door. Somehow it had opened again while my back was turned.

I started for it, happy to be going out.

''One more thing.''

I stopped. ''What?''

''That earring. I wouldn't wear it again, if I were you. Particularly not around Charon.''

My hand went to my ear, covering it, protecting it. "Why not?"
Not quite able to keep all the tension out of my voice. "It's only a
piece of glass."

His lips pulled up. "It's an emerald, you fool."

I stared at him, still touching my ear. "What—?"

He'd scanned its density just by looking at me. He looked at me
now, and shook his head again. "You're lying about where you got
it, too. It carries a taMing registry code; it belongs to Lady Lazuli."

My hand dropped to my side. I turned and went out the door. I
felt his eyes following my back as I crossed the endless, lifeless room
beyond.

SIXTEEN

ELNEAR WAS WAITING in still another private lounge when I got to the
med center. She looked like a different woman from the one we'd left
there last night. *Philipa was going to live.* It was all over her face,
her mind. "How is she?" I asked the question anyway, so that she
could tell me herself.

"She's going to be fine. Everything is going to be fine." She
stood up, smiling that smile that made you feel like you'd just stepped
into sunlight. Actually smiling it at me. After spending time with
Braedee and Charon, getting that smile was like winning a prize. Right
then I probably would have jumped out a window if she'd asked me
to. The smile faded again, as she said, "Someone said that you were
injured—"

I touched my shoulder; hardly even felt any soreness. Surprised
by that, too. "Nothing much," I said softly, remembering to answer

her, ''ma'am. Glad to hear the good news.'' Not as glad as she was, but close, for her sake. ''Have you seen her?''

Elnear shook her head. ''No. She's still in the intensive unit; she'll be there until the reconstructive work is finished. It will be several weeks, they say.'' Her voice got a little weak. ''She's suspended, of course, so she wouldn't know that I was there. . . .'' But still she wished she could be. ''At least she'll have only peace, no memory of—of this pain.''

''She's lucky to have friends like you.'' Saying it because I couldn't help remembering what happened to people who didn't have friends like her. Loyal . . . and rich. I touched my shoulder again, looking away at the flow-mural wavering aimlessly over the far wall.

She glanced at me, curious, but she only asked, ''Have you talked with Braedee?''

I nodded. I sat down on the long sofa next to her, suddenly feeling tired.

''I seem to have misjudged Centauri, for once. It seems he was right all along about how much I needed you.''

I kept my face empty. ''Yes, ma'am. I guess so.''

''Are you still thinking about yesterday?'' she said, trying to read my expression. ''About Stryger? About all the—injustice?''

I was thinking about today. But I nodded, because hearing her say Stryger's name suddenly made me remember yesterday. I looked back at her, as the final thing she'd said registered. *Injustice*.

''Yes,'' she said, answering what was clear enough on my face now. ''I've seen the Morning Report.''

I laughed once. ''I slept through it.'' The Indy's Morning Report—that was what Charon had been talking about. ''It must have been good.'' Or at least not as bad as I'd figured. ''I seem to be the only person in the galaxy who missed it.''

''I hope so.'' She smiled again, but this time it was full of steel. ''I hope everyone sees it. Do you want to see it now? I can call it up.''

I nodded, and the mural that no one had been watching suddenly disappeared from the wall across the room. A new image came on-screen, jumping out at us as it went threedy. Sound came with it in a blare that made me wince. Shander Mandragora was suddenly in the room, somehow looking me right in the eye while he repeated yesterday's news. The only way I could tell he wasn't actually there was by the empty place where his mind should have been. But then, after what I'd seen last night, that probably didn't prove anything. I waited for some lurid full-feed of the bombing; feeling my eyes try to look away. But instead the report was on the debate between Elnear and Stryger. Images from it opened out behind Mandragora as if he could project his own memories; he could, in a way. I watched Stryger tell his lies about me again. I started to frown, wondering why Elnear wanted to make me look at this.

And then suddenly it was me up there, "refuting the charges in his own words"—reliving last night, up against the wall with Lazuli and Jiro while the hypers closed in on me. I looked down, away from it.

But Elnear's hand closed on my shoulder, giving me a gentle shake, forcing me to look up at the screen again.

"I killed him in self defense!" my reflection shouted, looking me straight in the eye. "And to save my friends, and to save your stinking telhassium. I wasn't a traitor, I worked for the FTA—"

But before I heard the insult I'd blurted next, my image was gone again. Mandragora was back, telling me how the Indy had "researched these conflicting versions of the incident. Here is the actual record," he said, not even smiling. "Let it speak for itself."

He stepped aside, into some spacewarp, and I sat up straighter, with all my attention on the show now as I saw something I'd never seen before: part of an original tape about what had happened after I'd killed Quicksilver. A Mines official I remembered, a man named Tanake, was describing how the psionic arch-criminal Quicksilver and his terrorists had nearly taken control of the telhassium supply. His version of what had happened didn't match my memories of it; probably just as well.

But then he was thanking the FTA's Security Arm for "fighting fire with fire"; admitting right there in front of the entire Federation that it had been psions working undercover inside Quicksilver's terrorist group who'd been the ones who stopped him—the only ones who could have done it, mind against mind. . . .

A sudden gust of wind, a sudden change of scene, and suddenly I was looking out across a winter-white Quarro from someplace up high: Jule and Siebeling stood together on the balcony of a house . . . being interviewed, having their five minutes of fame. They didn't look like they were enjoying it much; but they did their best to make a good impression. The voice-over and visual stats were making a lot of Siebeling's professional standing and Jule's family ties; trying to prove something. I watched them, listened to them, breathing in a memory of the cold sharp air of a winter's day with every breath. Siebeling did most of the talking, like he always did, used to it. Jule had always saved her words, turned them into poems instead. Siebeling was talking about Dere Cortelyou, the corporate telepath who'd first broken through my mental walls and forced my mind out of hiding. Our friend, who'd died there on Cinder, killed by Quicksilver. Then I listened to him talking about me, about why I wasn't there beside them when I was the one who deserved the real credit for stopping Quicksilver. . . .

I tried to touch the place where my mind had been while that was happening—couldn't. A dizziness like the fear of falling made my brain sing.

". . . I had a nervous breakdown," my mirror image was saying across the room. "That's what it means to be a psion, and kill somebody. . . ." I looked up, seeing myself last night again, trapped, badgered, like an animal in a cage. ". . . And I guess it still doesn't mean shit to be a psion and a hero."

I watched myself push out of view and disappear, as Mandragora suddenly reappeared, to point out the obvious, about me, about me and the Lady, about Stryger's "incomplete data." It wasn't exactly an apology, and the asinine questions he'd thrown at me himself had all been trimmed away. But he'd given me what I'd wanted after all. Maybe he wasn't such a bastard.

Elnear was leaning back on the couch, her arms folded comfortably, watching me with a look that was somewhere between curiosity and satisfaction.

I shook my head, as the fax finally winked off, taking the past with it.

"So," she said. "The truth sets us free."

I turned toward her. "You really think that can make up for what Stryger did?"

"It will certainly help. Why—don't you believe that it will?"

"It's only one version of the story. The lies have already got it outnumbered." I shrugged. "Even what you saw wasn't really the truth. It was what happened . . . but it wasn't the truth." I thought about Centauri. They'd been a part of the truth for me back then, just like they were now; part of the combine conspiracy that had backed Quicksilver. I wondered how many people in the entire galaxy besides me knew that. Jule knew it; and somebody might even have listened to her. But she hadn't told anyone. Blood was still thicker than water.

Elnear sat there next to me, looking tired but content. She thought she knew the whole truth about what had happened at the Federation Mines on Cinder; she thought she knew the whole truth about what was happening now.

I couldn't let her go on believing it. She had to know everything about what Centauri had done. She'd never win otherwise, never get clear of them. I remembered where we were, and how easily even the hypers had planted eavesdroppers last night. I couldn't tell her anything here. "Ma'am, I haven't eaten yet. How about you? I saw a noodle joint a couple of levels up, on my way here—"

She looked surprised at the sudden change of subject. But then she realized how exhausted, how hungry, she really was. "Yes, of course . . . I haven't eaten a thing since yesterday afternoon. And I didn't have much of an appetite then." She smiled, rueful. "But there's no need to go out; I can have food brought to us here."

"Hospital food?" I asked, and made a face. *Damn.* "I'd rather have a plate of noodles."

"It can be anything you want," she said, still smiling. "Do you really want that?"

I'd forgotten what it meant to be a taMing, for just a minute. . . . I put my foot up across my knee; my fist began to tap a frustrated rhythm on it. I rested my head against the wall, staring at nothing, as I reached out with all the gentleness and control I could still manage, and touched her mind. (Lady,) I thought. She jerked; her eyes went wide. (Don't panic—I need to talk to you. Outside.)

She sat blinking for a second as if someone had shone a light straight into her eyes. When she seemed to register me again, she murmured, "Well . . . perhaps you're right. I can't stay here forever. There are things to be done. Now that I know Philipa will be all right. . . ." She got up, following my lead like a sleepwalker.

By the time we were in a mod she'd taken charge again, taking us back to the FTA plex, through the security scanners, into what ought to be the most privacy anyone could hope for on this planet. But we didn't go to her office. Instead she took me to the delegate's restaurant, on an open terrace at the pinnacle of an ancient tower. The roof garden was filled with small tables underneath umbrellas of living tree. You could look out and down across the geologic layers of time and structure that made up the city all around, and yet still believe you were out in the open air under a perfect sky. The sky was a monomole shield, so flawless that I couldn't tell it from the real thing, looking up at it from below. The higher towers touched it, supported it like rigid fingers.

Elnear ordered us lunch, and spent the time until it came pointing out historic landmarks to me, as if there was nothing more important on either of our minds. Some of the pre-space structures went back eight hundred years; and this was a new city, for Earth. I remembered when I'd thought the buildings in Oldcity were old. There'd been so much intermediate buildup here that by now it was hard to tell what the forms of most of the original structures had been. The one I could see best was an inverted cone, the whole building balanced on a tip a few dozen meters wide. "It was built when composites were first introduced," Elnear said, when I asked about it. "The architects of the period tended to be a little . . . giddy." She smiled.

The food came, laid out like it belonged in an art gallery. I hated to touch anything on the perfectly designed plate, but I was too hungry to let it stop me for long. It tasted better than it looked. I sighed, looking out at the view, as pastry shaped like flowers dissolved in my mouth. Thinking that I could get used to this . . . I glanced back at Elnear.

She was staring at me, the way she'd look at something she was thinking of making into a painting.

"Ma'am—?" I said, suddenly aware of every square centimeter of my body; wondering if I'd made an ass of myself somehow. I'd thought Jardan had driven enough basic protocol into my brain to at least let me eat in public.

But she said, "It was no exaggeration to call you a hero for what you did last night. Or to call what you did for the Federation on Cinder an act of heroism . . . what all of you did there, but especially you. You deserve—"

I glanced away. "No, it wasn't," I said, cutting her off.

"What would you call it, then?" she asked.

"Survival," I said. "I did what I had to, to survive. I killed Quicksilver because he was going to kill us. I didn't have a choice. There was nothing heroic about it." *Nothing at all.* I frowned, looking down, seeing my reflection trapped in the tabletop.

"How did you become a part of the undercover operation that stopped him?" She hadn't even known that Jule had been a part of it, until yesterday; hadn't believed it, until today. . . . But by now everyone's blind ignorance was beginning to make sense to me. What we'd done on Cinder had almost cost Centauri everything—and one of us had been one of their own. They must have done all they could to suppress or distort the news about it; and they weren't the only ones involved. Maybe it wasn't so insane that even Shander Mandragora hadn't heard the real story.

I looked back at Elnear. There was nothing but respect, honest curiosity, behind her question. I laughed, and shook my head. "How—? The hard way, just like everything else I ever did back in Oldcity. I got away from a press gang, and the District Corpses picked me up for making fools of the Labor Crows. They tested me for psi —they were testing everybody they hauled in, because the FTA was looking for psions. Psions are all criminals, right; how else would you find one—?" I smiled, and she looked down. "That's when I met Jule; she was in the group too. Siebeling was in charge of it. He'd set it up like a kind of therapy group, an excuse to teach us all how to use our Gift, and have the FTA pay for it. The FTA hoped we'd attract Rubiy—"

"Rubiy?"

"Quicksilver . . . his name was Rubiy. He had a name," I said, not sure why it bothered me that nobody remembered that. "They knew he'd be looking for recruits. They couldn't get at him any other way, and they figured, no big loss if he found out the truth and killed a few freaks. . . ."

She blinked. "A catspaw," she murmured.

"A what?"

"A 'catspaw' is someone used by someone else to do a job that is unpleasant or dangerous."

"Yeah." I nodded. "That fits. It worked, too. Rubiy picked four of us, sent us to work with his people on Cinder who were trying to break the Mines' security."

She glanced away, confusion starting in her thoughts. "If you were working undercover for the FTA, then why—?" Remembering my scars.

I touched my back, my mouth twisting. "Like I said, the truth's never that simple. Siebeling and me . . . we didn't get along too well at first. He threw me out of the group, sent me back to Contract Labor. But when Rubiy found out, he used it—he got me sent to the Mines. I was his inside man." The world faded into white, into the memories of what I'd seen there, and what had been done to me . . . the times when I'd wanted Rubiy to succeed. He'd even counted on that. "Rubiy would have given me anything I'd wanted if I'd given him the Mines." He'd trusted me, because he thought we were the same—dead inside. There were times when I'd nearly believed that myself.

But he was wrong. I blinked, my eyes smarting with the burn of memory.

"Why didn't you?" Elnear said, her gaze steady now.

I looked down. The plate of half-eaten food in front of me seemed like an hallucination. I shook my head. "Because of Jule. She taught me some things Siebeling didn't know how to. That I was still . . . alive. That I could still care about someone else." I kept looking down. "I guess she taught both of us that. I wonder how she knew so much about it?"

Elnear didn't say anything.

"Why did you marry a taMing, anyway?" I asked it, finally. "Why did you let them get such a hold on you? Did they make you do it?"

She looked back at me, half smiled as she realized that I was only doing what she'd just done. "Oh, no," she said. "I wasn't forced into anything. I married Kelwin because I wanted to, and he wanted me to. I was much younger, then. . . ." Meaning not just in years. "I loved him very much. What more did I need to know—?" She'd thought that she had protected her interests. She'd thought that he would live forever.

"How did he die?"

"He was away on Centauri business, on Dandrosa, when it happened. There was a massive intrasystem failure. . . . The details don't matter. They found evidence of sabotage." She looked away, her folded hands tightening on the tabletop. "It was shortly after Jule's mother died."

"What happened to her?"

"She had a drug problem." Elnear was still looking somewhere else. "They said it was an accidental overdose. But ever since the family had learned that Jule was—was—" *(defective),* her mind said, helplessly, instinctively, "—a psion, there had been suspicions, accusations of some sort of genetic tampering or falsification of hereditary charts. . . ."

"You're telling me you think the taMings killed her?" I remembered Lazuli not-quite-saying something about Jule's mother, Charon's first wife.

Elnear shrugged. "Nothing was ever proved . . . in either case. Jule's mother had ties to Triple Gee. The marriage was supposed to ease tensions; it involved the exchange of certain planetary interests in the same system where Kelwin died."

"So she was a hostage." *And maybe a saboteur.*

Elnear looked up again, almost startled. "Perhaps, in a sense." Her eyes turned bleak. "But then, aren't we all hostages to fortune . . . ?"

"So maybe your husband had to die because she did?" Maybe I didn't want to get used to this life, after all.

"Perhaps." She got up, restlessly, as if part of her wished I'd leave it alone. But part of her wanted it, needed it.

"How long ago?"

"Sixteen years." No hesitation. She could have told me how many months, days . . . seconds.

"It should have been Charon."

She turned back, her hands clenched now. *(It should have been Charon.)* It had crystallized in her own mind at the same instant it had come out of my mouth.

"No," I said, to her half frown. "You didn't think of it first."

She pressed her lips together, tried to wipe her eyes without me seeing her do it. She sat down again, her mind as open, as defenseless, as any human mind ever was. "All I've really wanted," she said finally, so softly that the thought was almost louder, "for sixteen years, was to see it through." Her work, her legacy, her life. Trying to hold on to what still had some meaning, trying to keep Centauri and the taMings from taking it all away from her: that had become her whole life, since she'd lost him. When she died they lost her holdings too because there were no children, and they knew it. No wonder she hadn't been interested in setting back her clocks, once Kelwin was gone. But she wasn't interested in being assassinated, either. . . . It had been easy to make her think someone wanted her dead, when you could never be sure anyone's death was from natural causes.

Her face changed, as she finally felt ready to hear whatever I wanted her to know: "What was it that you were going to tell me?"

I glanced away, out over the glaciers of glass and stone, suddenly uneasy again. Maybe this open terrace was really as shielded as the offices down below, but I couldn't believe it. Braedee had said he'd leave me alone, but I knew how much that was worth. He didn't want me telling Elnear the truth, and God only knew who else had what kind of long eyes watching.

They said ignorance was bliss. The more I knew about this world, the more paranoid I felt. I couldn't be sure of anything—except myself. (Lady,) I said, very gently again, mumbling something pointless out loud for any ears that were listening. (I have to be sure. Don't fight me—) She sat frozen, her muscles rigid; only I could tell that inside her something was happening that no one else could see. When I was sure she was really ready, I reached out again, letting the message form as softly as snow. (Lady . . . no one was trying to kill you, before last night.)

Her head jerked with surprise and confusion. I let the images implode as her incredulity crushed them; waiting until she could deal with what it meant to her. (I found out today from Charon. The same way you're finding it out from me—) She kept blinking at me, like someone taking drugs. But she nodded, letting me know she understood, ready for what came next.

(Centauri started it as a way to get at you, scare you, keep you under control.) I let her see how and why, using the images like an information feed. I began to get feedback as she realized it was the same kind of harassment she'd endured all along, only more vicious now. Centauri was trying harder to keep hold of her as she tried harder to get away. (They used me to spy for them, Lady, just like you thought . . . even to set you up for Stryger.) I winced at the stab of her betrayal. *(A catspaw,)* I thought, without meaning to. That's what she'd called it; that's what I'd been, again. (I didn't know. They used me!) Letting my own anger batter hers back, tired of taking the blame. I'd been fucked over by Centauri too . . . and not for the first time. (Centauri was part of the conspiracy behind Rubiy that nearly got me killed. And they got away from it clean. If I hate the FTA for what happened to me out on Cinder, I hate Centauri worse—) I let her see it, let her see why, until she really believed that none of this had happened because I'd wanted it to.

(But yesterday night—that changed things.) I showed her the rest of it. That now there really was a threat, and Centauri didn't want her to die any more than she did. That even Charon thought I had a use now. That I wasn't going to leave until it was over, and she was safe; until I'd made it up to her.

She stared at me, not even blinking now, as if she was beyond anger, or surprise, almost beyond any emotion at all. "Thank you," she murmured, finally, although that wasn't what she wanted to say. Gratitude was the farthest thing from her mind after what she'd just learned . . . the way she'd learned it. And yet—

She put her hand out blindly; needing real, solid, contact with another human . . . and there was no doubt left in her mind *that I was as human as she was*. There should have been a better way to put it, but I couldn't think of one, so I just gave up and took it the way she meant it. I got up from the table after a minute, looking back at her. My smile hardly pinched at all as I said, "Ma'am, right now I've got some—business I've got to work out. I don't know how long it'll take."

"What kind of business?" she asked, suddenly uncertain again. I shook my head. "Calling in some favors."

"This is going to help us find out what really happened last night?"

"I hope so. . . . It's better if you don't ask," I said, stopping her before she did. Her mouth pressed shut, her forehead wrinkled. She wished that I'd trust her, not really believing there were things she really wouldn't want to know about me.

I started to turn away, hesitated. "Lady, how much do you think Stryger really wants that Security Council slot?"

She looked at me blankly for a minute. Then she started to frown, and shook her head. "You can't imagine that he would try to have me killed. . . ." Incredulity that was almost laughter filled her voice.

"Braedee doesn't think that walking bomb was a hire job. I do. He can't think of a combine that would do it for themselves, but he thinks they're too proud to use the Lack Market. You know Stryger's got combines behind him. They think he's just another catspaw—but that's not what Stryger thinks. He wants that slot for the same reason you do, to get himself free of them. He wants the power, real bad. I think he'd kill to get it."

She shook her head again, half smiling as she began to get up from her seat. "Cat, I understand why you feel this way. But I assure you, Sojourner Stryger may be too intense for his own good—he may even be something of a fanatic—but he is not an evil man."

"He lied, didn't he? He smeared you, and me, right up there in front of God and everybody, to get what he wanted—"

"He could have been sincere. He claims that he was misinformed. . . ."

"Why are you defending him?" I said. She didn't answer me. "Do you really still think he's better than you?" My hands dropped to my sides. "Lady," I said finally. "I met someone like that once. He picked me up on the street in Oldcity, bought me the first decent meal I'd had in about a week. And while I was eating, he was talking to me about how psions were evil and unnatural, because they had these abilities. . . ." Something that wasn't really a laugh caught in my throat. I hadn't known what he was talking about, why he was saying those things to me, staring into my green eyes with their long slit pupils. . . . "Then he took me up to a hired room and beat the crap out of me."

She sat down on the edge of the table, her mouth open, her mind groping. "Why?" she murmured at last, weakly. "Why didn't you leave . . . ?"

"Because that's what he was paying me for." I left the restaurant.

SEVENTEEN

"WELL," ARGENTYNE SAID, as she met me at the door, "somehow I didn't expect to see you here again. At least not so soon." Her silver eyebrows rose, asking silent questions, as she pulled the door to Purgatory open wider. "Don't tell me you're lonely."

She was still blocking the doorway with her body. I stood on the steps, suddenly feeling more self-conscious than I thought I knew how to. "I wish I was. Lonely, I mean. . . . Is Daric here?"

She laughed, ruffling her hair. "Is it still daylight?" She glanced out, looking for sky. "He only comes out at night."

"That figures." I pushed my hands deeper into my pockets.

"You want to see him?"

"No."

"And you're not here to close me down, or you wouldn't be here alone. So what can I do for you?" She yawned, the camph she'd been sucking on dangling from her fingers. I realized suddenly that she was yawning the way an animal yawned, instinctively showing teeth. Yawning because she was nervous, even a little afraid. Just like I was. It made her real, easier to look at without feeling my brain seize up.

"I need directions." I glanced over my shoulder at the street behind me. The water line was halfway up the dome, but there was still a wide stretch of sky visible. The map in my head had brought me this far, but it ended at the water line. "The map ends here." And no map from the city files could tell me what I really needed to know, anyway.

"You want to go off the Deep End?" She looked incredulous again. "Alone? Why?"

Now that I really knew why they called it that, I wished I didn't. "It's not something I want to do. And it's not something I want to talk about in the middle of the street." I jerked my head at the swirl of bodies in random motion behind me.

Argentyne stepped aside, opening the way for me into the club's interior. "Sorry. I just got up. It always takes me a while to regain consciousness." Her mouth curved in a wry smile. "It's so early, you know."

I grinned, stepping inside. "Yeah, I know what you mean. Or I used to."

"You used to be a performer?" she asked.

"Sort of."

"And then you got respectable." She led me back along the hallway, down the ramp. She was wearing a soft robe that looked like it had been made out of a bedspread; most of the color had faded out of it a long time ago. It was something she wore because she loved it a lot.

I looked down at my neat, perfect, Centauri-branded clothes. "Not by choice," I said.

The club was nearly empty, gray with filtered daylight. A couple of indifferent floods lighted up the darker corners so the drones could finish their work, siphoning up the detritus of a hard night. The space and silence made it seem like a different building from the one I'd been in yesterday. Up on the stage a handful of bodies were clustered by a single bare table, sprawled across each other in the small island of cushions around it, looking like they'd had too much of something: I recognized the players of her symb. "Rehearsal," she explained, nodding toward the stage. It felt more like a mass hangover to me.

"That was really incredible last night," I said, remembering the way their separate kinds of music had fused into a perfect web of sound, the mindwarping visuals that had come rippling out through the noise . . . suddenly remembering who she was again; suddenly feeling awkward and self-conscious again.

She looked at me, about to toss off some remark about my own performance here. Seeing my face, she only said, "Glad you enjoyed it. Glad you enjoyed something about last night." She glanced down, embarrassment and leftover anger at Daric blurring her memory, and we were back on the same ground again. "That wasn't the usual crowd, last night," she said. "That was a private party. I just wanted you to know." *That it wouldn't happen again.*

I didn't say anything.

"You like the muse, huh?" she asked, to fill up the silence. I nodded. "You sure you wouldn't like to complete a circuit yourself?" She climbed onto the stage, reaching back to give me a hand. It wasn't an offer she made often, or to just anybody. It was an apology; and something more.

I climbed up after her, more than surprised. But a kind of panic started to choke me the second I thought about taking her seriously. I shook my head. "I don't have any talent."

"You never know until you try. We could wire you ourselves. Nobody would have to know. It takes no time; it doesn't even hurt." She lifted her hair with her hand, showing me the flesh-colored jack on the back of her neck. She was still thinking about what she'd felt last night. "Wouldn't you like to find out . . . ?" She wanted to find out—what it would be like to link me into something bigger, and play my mind. Her copper stare met me, dared me.

I glanced away at the players, wondering what they'd think of that. "Maybe . . . someday. Not today." I shrugged, too much else on my mind right now. Besides, she might think it was nothing, but if the FTA's security scans picked up that socket, I'd be in deep shit. "Anyway, what you did last night was about as real as it gets. You don't need a psion if you can make that happen with your own head."

She shook off the compliment. "Holograms. Cheap tricks. I can imagine it, but I can't make people share it, *live* it, even with illusions. *You* knew it wasn't real. . . ."

I grinned. "Yeah—but I forgot. And that's the real magic, right? If you can make people forget it's not real."

She shrugged, annoyed and flattered.

A couple of the players began to clap and whistle long trills, as we came toward them and my face registered. I felt my face start to go red, figuring last night here at the club was the reason.

But then one of them said, "Yo, Cat. Caught you on the Morning Report," and the other heads were nodding.

Argentyne turned to look at me, curious. "What happened?" She wondered suddenly if I'd come down here to get away from something I'd done.

"He only saved your habit and a bunch of other vips after you threw him out of here. Some assassin blew himself into meat salad at a taMing hole last night." The flute player bowed gracefully toward me. She was dressed metallic, as long and thin as the flexible pipes that had replaced the fingers on one of her hands.

"Daric—?" Argentyne said, with a sudden sharp pang of *guilt-shockfear*. "Daric—is he all right?"

I nodded unenthusiastically.

"You saved him?" she repeated.

"It was an accident," I said, and someone laughed, but it wasn't her. "I was hired to guard Lady Elnear. He just got in the way."

She was still looking at me though a haze of mixed emotions. "Oh God," she murmured, and looked away. "Why didn't he tell me himself . . . ?"

"You still expect him to act like a human being?" one of the players wearing a touchboard in his chest asked. "To treat you like one?"

"Oh, bugger off, Jax," she said. "Who asked you?" Under the silver skin, the silver hair, I got the feeling there was somebody a lot more normal than Daric was, maybe a lot more ordinary than she wanted to admit to herself.

"Daric looked pretty fragged," somebody else said gently. "Don't worry about it. Maybe it'll shake some steel into him." He grinned, his teeth large and white against his blue-black skin and beard. He wore the beard tucked through his belt, and some instrument that looked like a sack full of light plugged into his neck.

"Since when do you get up so early, Midnight?" she asked him, still prickling.

He shrugged, blinked his bloodshot eyes. "Up? I haven't been to bed."

She half smiled; twitched her shoulders to shake off her mood. "Well," she murmured to me, rubbing her face, "thanks anyway, even if it's thanks for nothing. Tell me what you're looking for. If we've got it, you can have it."

I glanced at the players, back at her.

"They're family," she said. "And they're not easily shocked." She moved back to the edge of the stage and sat down, her bare feet dangling. The players shrugged and flopped down where they were, waiting.

I sat down too, feeling less obvious that way. "I need some drugs."

Her face twitched almost imperceptibly. She took the camph out of her mouth and looked at it. "Why don't you just ask Daric?"

I grimaced. "Two reasons. The second one is that he doesn't have what I need."

The twitch turned into a frown. "You're in that deep? You want hard stuff?" She was surprised.

I shook my head. "Just hard-to-get stuff. Topalase-AC."

She looked at me blankly. "What's that? I never heard of it."

"It lets me use my psi."

"You need drugs for that?" she said. "I thought you were born that way."

"I was." I explained, keeping it as short as I could.

"Hm," she said, when I was done. She pulled her knees up, hugging her ankles. "Why won't Centauri give you what you want?"

"Charon taMing's a freakhater—Daric's sister Jule is a psion. He's afraid of me."

"Of you?" She laughed.

"Should I be insulted?" I said.

"Oh, hell no." She waved a hand at me. "Jeezu, have you seen Charon—?"

"Lots."

"Then you know what I mean. . . . So they want you to do this gig but they won't give you the equipment, is that it?"

I nodded. "That's it. But Braedee said he wouldn't stop me from getting it myself."

"You really want to burn your brains out? You care that much about them? Why not just go along, play dumb and collect your pay?"

I thought about it. I looked back at her. "Why do you go with Daric? Just for the money?" It came out a little nastier than I'd meant it to.

(Fuck you—) I heard it through her eyes, but then her expression changed. "It's not like that. He's not like he seems—" Remembering last night, she broke off. "Well, maybe he is . . . but not when we're alone." Her hand tightened into a painful fist. "I *care* about him—"

"You love him." Saying what she couldn't make herself say.

Asking the question even though it was none of my business, just because the idea was so unbelievable.

She looked back at me, suddenly resenting it. "Sometimes. . . . So what if I do? It's none of your business, kid."

"I know," I said.

She thought about it a minute longer. "You care about Lady Elnear?"

I nodded. "Yeah. I guess I do." Surprised by that, too. Without meaning to, I thought about Lazuli, and her children. I touched my ear, the emerald earring; let my hand drop.

"Lady Elnear wants to change the universe," Argentyne said. "What about you?"

"Just part of it."

She laughed. "You got it, laddie love." She climbed to her feet, looking back at the players. "I don't know who to call on. Anybody know where he could find someone to give him what he wants?" The ones who were still awake shrugged, heads moved back and forth. *No.*

"We don't do a lot of drugs," she said, as if she had to explain it. "It screws up our timing." She stared at her feet, scratched her head. "Daric knows the territory better than any of us do. You got a sample of his dream jewelry last night. He plays hard, and he makes deals for his friends. . . ." She was worried that he played too hard, that he was already in too deep. "If you won't ask him, I can tell you who to talk to, and where to look for them. I can't promise they can fix you up. Maybe they'd know who could. But frankly—" She was looking back at me again, "I'd ask Daric before I'd try it alone, even if I hated his guts. There's a reason the Deep End's not on the city maps, you know. The Lack Market runs it. It's got a whole different set of rules."

I nodded, my mouth pulling up. "Yeah, I know. But I grew up in a place like that. I know how the people there think. I know *what* they're thinking if I need to."

"Every place is different," she said, the worry line still etched deep between her silver brows. "But if that's what you want. . . ." She shrugged when I didn't say anything more. "You can't go under dressed like that. You'd be dead before you got a hundred meters. Come on in the back. We've got plenty of gear you can pick through."

She led me through the wings of the stage and down a corridor, pushed open a door. Inside, it looked like a costume shop having a nervous breakdown—clothing in piles, hanging from hooks, strung up on racks, tacked to the walls. "Help yourself," she said, wading in.

I followed her into the room, breathing in the strange, musty smell of the place. "I never saw this many clothes in my entire life."

"You can be anything you want to be, here. Clothes make the man—into a woman, if you want. Or vice versa." She tossed a long striped wrap-skirt at me, grinning. I shook my head and dropped the skirt. "Androgyny's very big right now," she said. "You'd look regular."

"If I have to run I might trip." I picked up a loose yellow-brown tank top, held it out. Symbols from some pre-space language were printed inside a circle on the front of it. "Rolecrossing was real popular in Quarro about five years back. Everything keeps coming around. . . ." I took off my jacket and shirt.

"Maybe someday it'll even mean something," she murmured, kicking through mounds of cloth. "Quarro, huh?" She sounded impressed. "You must be a real trendsetter."

I laughed once, pulling on the tank top. It was long and baggy, but it let me move. "I was lucky if I had a shirt on my back, most of the time I lived there."

"Uh-huh. . . ." She picked up a hat made of feathers and put it on. "Being poor sucks, especially in a rich town."

"I wouldn't know."

She looked at me, puzzled.

"In Oldcity, if you didn't have a credit line, you couldn't even leave. I never saw Quarro."

She made a face, suddenly feeling cold inside. "Being poor sucks, anywhere," she said. "That's why I wanted this club. After my five minutes of fame are over, I want to have somewhere to crawl home to." I felt her remember her family suddenly; remember how her father had thrown her out for good the day she'd come home with silver skin.

I nodded, thinking about Jule, and Siebeling. "Makes sense," I said softly. I picked out some brown knit leggings and a heavy leather jacket. The jacket would give me some protection if I ran into a little trouble. . . . If I ran into a lot of trouble, even body armor wouldn't save me. "How long you been with Daric?"

"About a year and a half. I met him right after we went nova and started to play gigs above the waterline." She was looking at me, but her gaze was somewhere else. "We were doing this exquisite private club, right up under the stars. Everybody there was some kind of famous, only they were all there for *us* . . . it was the most incredible night of my life. And then Daric came up to me, after the show. He gave me a silver rose, and he said, 'You've waited all your life for me. Let me show you why.' '' She was seeing him now, the way he'd looked to her that night: young and handsome, rich and confident. Remembering the way he'd looked at her—as if he'd never seen anyone more beautiful. Remembering the way he'd made her believe that every word he said was true. . . .

I looked away from her face, sorry I'd asked. "How do you like his family?"

Her mind snapped back to the present, and her smile turned black. "About as much as they like me. They scare the shit out of me."

I shook my head. "When I saw you with them, you looked like you were having a pretty good time raising their blood pressure."

She lifted her hand and made half a bow to me. "I'm an entertainer. It's all part of the act, love. . . . Daric enjoys it far more than I do." Her smiled softened. "I remember you, that night. You looked like you were in shock. Like you'd crash-landed on the wrong planet."

"I had," I said.

"I felt sorry for you, until you stood up to Daric. Then I figured you for a survivor, after all."

I looked down. "Yeah, that's one thing I'm good at, anyway."

"Cat," she said. I looked up. "Ask Daric. He can get what you want. I'll even ask for you, if you want me to. He owes you that much."

I shook my head. "I can't trust him." I already knew too much, about politics.

"I know what you think of him." She tossed the feather hat away, impatient. "You're right, he's fucked up. But there really is a human being inside there—"

"That's what I'm afraid of."

She cocked her head at me. "Oh," she said, finally. "You think you can't trust any of us, huh? You think we're all rotten, because you can see into our minds and read all our dirty little secrets—?"

I looked down, picked up a pair of heavy gloves. "No. I don't think that. . . ." I glanced up again, pulling them on. "I try not to, anyhow."

"Daric treats me better than anyone I've ever known." She was thinking about all the things he'd done for her, given to her. Anything she wanted. He'd set her up with this club, like I'd figured—but she owned it, not him.

"When he's not treating you like shit." I shrugged on the jacket. "Sure, why shouldn't he? You're beautiful, you're famous, and his family thinks you're trash. You're everything he needs."

"You don't know anything about his needs," she said, frowning. "And you're starting to piss me off."

I lifted my head. "What's he ever done that's decent, for anybody besides you?"

She looked away, searching her memory. "The girl," she said, after thinking a little longer than she probably would have liked. "A while back he brought a kid here, a young girl. Somebody'd beaten her up real bad." Her face flinched. "He said he'd just found her on the street, and couldn't leave her there. He asked us to help her. So we did." She put her hands on her hips, as if she was waiting for me to congratulate her. "He didn't do that out of anything but common humanity." While inside her thoughts she was remembering something strange about the girl; how the kid had looked like a street nothing, dressed in greasy rags . . . except she'd had a face that looked like an exotic's: eyes that were too green, with long slits for pupils. Like she'd had expensive cosmetic surgery done. . . .

"A psion," I said. "The way she looked—she was a psion."

"Who?" Argentyne shook her head. "You mean the kid?" Not asking me how I knew what the kid had looked like. She gave me one of those looks deadheads always gave me when I answered questions they hadn't asked. "I don't know."

"She didn't do anything—use her psi?"

"Not while she was here." She shook her head again. "But she wasn't here that long. He brought her in one night; she was in shock, then. She couldn't even move on her own. We patched her up and put her to bed upstairs. When I looked in the next morning she was already gone. I never saw her again. Daric asked about her; he really cared about what had happened to her, whether she was all right."

Daric taMing playing godsend to a freak. I didn't know what the hell to make of that. Maybe she'd reminded him of Jule . . . except I thought he hated Jule. I wondered if he'd beaten her up himself. "I still can't trust him to know about this. You've got to promise me you won't tell him I was here."

She sighed. "If you're that obsessed, who am I to stand in your way?" She looked at my clothes. "Out of all this, you had to choose that?" She waved a hand.

I didn't answer, my mind still hooked on the image of a lost girl with green eyes, so terrified that all she knew how to do was disappear.

I wondered if she'd had any more idea of why somebody would want
to beat the crap out of her than I'd ever had. Maybe nobody could
ever really understand a thing like that. . . .

"Cat," Argentyne said, facing me without my noticing she'd
moved.

I stepped back, startled. Remembered she'd said something about
my clothes. "Thanks for the clothes," I mumbled. "Just tell me who
to look for. I'll get out of here and stop pissing you off."

"We could bodypaint you a little, first—" she offered, and I
realized part of her was still trying to stall me. She was really afraid
I'd go out of here and get my head kicked in.

I turned away, annoyed. "No." I gestured at the clothes. "I know
what I'm doing." I hesitated, turning back; managed a smile. "But
thanks for caring whether I do or not."

She smiled too, resigned. "It's my curse." She tied a hank of
green scarf around my head. "Come on." She nodded, and started
back toward the door.

EIGHTEEN

THE TUBE THAT RAN under the bay from N'Yuk island to the island
called Stat had been built nearly three hundred years ago. It hadn't
been intended to make stops along the way. But then they ran out of
room up above, and the city had started oozing off the end of the land
into the cold, dark waters of the harbor. Now most of the sea bottom
between the islands was covered with a separate city, clear domes
spreading like a mass of fish eggs over the silty muck, reclaiming it
for the air-breathers.

But nobody could call that part of town real desirable, and so like Oldcity it had filled up with the dregs, the losers and the users, the kind of people who slipped through holes in the combine nets—by choice, or because they couldn't help themselves, and couldn't find anybody else who wanted to help them either.

The Tube made stops there now, and at the third one I got off. To reach the surface, I climbed about three hundred steps that smelled like piss, because the lift was out of order. The pilastered cavern of the station itself didn't look so bad—the FTA managed the services here like it did in Federal Trade Districts everywhere. They did a pretty good job of it. And then they left the human flotsam who lived there to drift, instead of taking care of them too. They needed their pools of desperate, unskilled labor all over the galaxy for their press gangs to feed off of, to sell to the combines to do their dirty work.

I stepped over a sick dog that lay panting at the top of the light-strung stairs, my hands clenched inside my jacket pockets as I looked around me at the graffiti and the garbage. I didn't want to touch anything, have the greasy dirt rub off on me, stick to my skin, pollute me. I felt sick when I remembered how it had been once, when I'd been one of these people. When I hadn't known where the filth stopped and my flesh started, and hadn't even cared. . . .

"Shit—" I said softly. I stopped, forcing myself to lean against a wall while I got my bearings. Now I knew I'd been too long with the taMings. I hadn't just begun to forget who I really was, I'd actually begun to hate myself. It must be catching. I pulled up my collar as I moved away from the station steps. I almost thought I could still smell the sea bottom, that stench and tang I used to catch a whiff of sometimes in Oldcity, when an accidental breath of real sea air found its way inside. But the sea bottom was buried under monomole and composite. It was only my imagination, trying to make something better of the stale smell of sweat and urine.

This was the place I wanted, the station called Free Market Square. Argentyne and the players had described it to me, filling in holes in each others' knowledge until my own mental map was as clear as I could make it. The warren of streets around the Tube stop entrance was at the heart of the Lack Market's business district. The Lack Market had a motto: "Anything you want." Representatives ready to provide the kinds of services the combines liked to pretend didn't exist any more cruised the open square, mingling with bodies looking for those services and with other bodies that were only here because they didn't have anywhere else to go.

I froze suddenly, staring out across the crowds. Someone was moving through them, coming toward the station entrance—someone I recognized. *Stryger*. He was cloaked, and surrounded by followers but no media that I could see. Nobody else even looked at him twice. I stepped behind a peeling ad kiosk, keeping out of sight as I watched him pass. I brushed his thoughts, wondering what the hell he could possibly want from a place like this. Hoping it was dirty.

He glanced over his shoulder, looking back the way he'd come. He felt pity, and satisfaction . . . but that was all. One of the shelters his money had paid for was right here, across the square. He'd come to the Deep End on his own, to see for himself what kind of job it was doing. That was the only reason he'd come here. There was nothing else on his mind right now; not the Assembly vote, not the Council slot, not genocide. . . . I watched him disappear into the Tube station, while a kind of numbness spread inside me. Once all he'd wanted was to do that kind of good. Maybe there was even some part of him that still wanted it. I tried to imagine him that way, the way everyone else saw him—controlling the kind of money and power he did, and using it only for good.

It made me feel lousy. I pushed out of my hiding place and moved on into the crowd.

Vendors had set up stalls or just squatted on the pavement with food and wares spread out around them, interrupting the flow of foot traffic. Their shrill cries and blaring music drowned out the murmured queries, the muttered answers of the real transactions going on. Argentyne had said that sometimes the Corpses put in an appearance, just to keep things orderly; I didn't see any out now. It was just like Oldcity: all they cared about was appearances, anyway. They were out of their depth here, literally and figuratively, and they knew it. You could do or buy anything down here, as long as you did it by the numbers.

I took my left hand out of my pocket and caught hold of my collar: a sign that I was looking for drugs. I left it clenched there as I found the nerve to push out into the sea of grotesques and hunters and derelicts. I saw other seekers with a fist clenched over a collar; some of the fists were real white-knuckled. There were hands locked behind backs, hands clutching the opposite wrist, hands speaking in silent gestures against a thigh, all sending out different messages to whoever was interested. If you didn't know the codes you could walk here for hours and never get a single response from anybody you wanted to meet. The signs were different from the ones I knew, but in subtle ways. Prying into thoughts as I passed, I checked the codes against their meanings, learning, remembering. If I made clumsy mistakes somebody might not notice; but then again, somebody might. . . . I dodged past something human the size of a horse, that was leading a half-naked burnout on a chain.

One after another, dealers came up to me, offering me the usual street shit. They all shook their heads when I said what I wanted. All of them knew the names Argentyne had told me to use, the ones Daric did his major business with, but none of them would admit it. Some of them turned around and walked away from me like I was poison when they heard; but some of them just looked silent, and then went away to check. I should have known none of them would trust me on sight—they couldn't read my mind. Daric usually met with his dealers in Purgatory, Argentyne had said . . . halfway between his world and theirs. They wouldn't circulate personally in this crowd. So all I could do was wait, and hope one of them was interested enough to send for me.

I kept moving, to fend off the pickpockets and beggars and sellers trying to sell me things I didn't want to buy. A skinny kid with a runny nose and an ugly scar across one eye, a skinnier little girl dragging behind him, whined and pulled at my sleeve, "Please, mister, please—"

I started to pull away; didn't. I felt in my pockets for the markers I always carried, a habit left from the days when my wrist was as bare as his. I gave him a handful. He disappeared, but someone else was there to fill the hole he left before I could take a step, and someone else after her and someone else, until I'd emptied my pockets of everything. When they saw I wasn't giving any more the beggars disappeared, looking for fresh marks with fresh markers, leaving me space to move on. There were some kinds of holes you could never fill; even if your credit never ran dry.

I glanced at my databand, swearing as I saw the time. I looked up, but there was nothing to see—the dome high above me was invisible against the sea. The sky was a deep green suffusion of light reflected from the streetlamp stars. That was all the higher your hopes ever went in a place like this. I wondered what the Deep End looked like from above, to the strange creatures swimming outside. At least I still had my databand; in a crowd like this, that was something. I wore a thumblock on it, because I knew how easy the usual latch was to unscramble.

I leaned against a lightpost at the edge of the square and shook

out my hand, which was getting numb from hanging on my collar. I
felt tired and strung out; every second that winked past as I watched
was more proof that I was getting nowhere. Down one of these streets,
behind some door with heavier security than most combine embassies
carried, there was somebody in a black lab making just what I wanted,
or somebody willing to front it to me. I began to wonder why nobody
had come back, whether there was something going on that maybe
Argentyne hadn't even known about, that was keeping me from getting
what I needed. Some mistake I was making; some secret, some hidden
trouble.

I wanted to go find out. Except that if I was right, pushing on
into those strange green streets alone might be the worst thing I could
do. Maybe it would get the attention of the right people. Maybe it
would just get the wrong ones. Why the hell couldn't anything ever
be simple—? My head wanted to hurt again. I pressed my fingers
against my temples, trying to will the pain to stop.

"Hey, hotpants, come with us. We'll give you everything you're
asking for, and more—"

I looked up again, jerked back as the gang of half a dozen bully
bitches gathered around me. The stink of leather and pheromone perfume made my stomach turn over. Their leader pinned me up against
the lightpost, her metal-studded fingers grabbing at my crotch. "You
like to party rough, huh baby?" Her fist closed over my balls. "So
do we."

I swore with the pain, and knocked her hand away. "Back off.
I didn't ask for sex. I'm looking for something else."

"Then why were you signalling for sex, sweetmeat?" Her hand
mimicked the way I'd been rubbing my head. She caught me by the
front of my jacket. "I get it, you just want to play hard-to-get . . . ?"
She jerked me forward and slapped me.

I slapped her back, knew it for a mistake as her gang moved in
on me. Hands in chainmail and leather pinned me up against the pole
while she slapped me again, two, three times. I sat down in the garbage,
dazed, as they let me go. She jerked a lipstain out of the ancient
cartridge belt slung across her chest. Her own mouth twisting, she
pulled it open and smeared it across my mouth. The rest of the gang
followed her away into the crowd.

I hauled myself up again, wiped my face on my jacket sleeve,
wincing as I ran into buckles. I only managed to smear the dark leather
with lipstain, and with blood from the place where she'd laid open

my cheek. The crowd just kept flowing past, like nothing unusual had happened. Nothing unusual had.

"Hey, kid—" A heavy, stubble-bearded face pushed in front of mine, blocking my way as I started forward. He was half a head taller than me and twice as wide, dressed in dark, flapping clothes. I braced, ready for another mistake, wondering what the hell I'd done to attract the wrong attention this time. But he laughed at the look on my face—or maybe the way my face looked—and said, "I hear you're looking for Venk."

"Yeah," I said, trying to keep the sudden screaming relief out of it. He was real. He knew Venk, worked for him.

"What's it worth to you?"

I held up my wrist, let him see my credit line. "I can make it worth his time."

"Why do you want to see him?"

"That's personal." He already knew the answer. It was tough playing headgames when my own head was still ringing.

"Then how do I know Venk can help you?" He kept pushing . . . he wanted my source.

I wiped my smarting cheek again. "Daric taMing sent me. You want to deal, or not?"

"Follow me." He started away before I could say anything more.

I followed him. It took all my concentration to keep from losing him in the crowd. He moved like he didn't care if I lost him, like I needed him more than he needed me. He was probably right. But a part of his mind was keeping track of me behind him even while he pretended he wasn't—and he was subvocalizing to somebody somewhere ahead of us.

He led me away from the station, out of the square. We headed down one of the murky streets full of hidden specialties that waited beyond the lights and noise. It was a relief to get out of the square alive; but the relief only lasted until I couldn't hear the crowd noise behind me any more.

I realized that there'd been a kind of invisible field around Free Market Square. Nothing tangible, just a kind of attitude, an unspoken threat, that kept the outsiders in. On this street there was nobody moving who didn't belong here, and who wasn't being tracked through a hundred windows, visible and invisible. *Outsider.* The featureless, prefab building walls whispered it, reaching up into the eerie gloom of a sky just waiting to fall on us from fifty meters above. A luminous grid of geodesic lines glowed faintly, marking the inverse line of sea and sky like electric fishnet . . . all that separated us from the fish.

I felt tension settling on me like a weight, until it was hard to breathe . . . realized suddenly that it wasn't just my imagination. "Hey," I called.

My guide slowed, turning back to look at me.

"This isn't the way to Venk's. Where you taking me?"

He shrugged. "Venk's orders. He's gonna meet you down by the Locks instead."

"The Locks?" I repeated, picking an image out of his mind. The edge of town, here in the Deep End. Where divers went out to tend maintenance or seafarms . . . where they got rid of their garbage. But Venk was going to be there, waiting for me. That was what he'd been told, and he believed it. "Why?"

He shrugged. "Venk didn't say." He started on.

I followed him wordlessly. *Where they got rid of their garbage.* This whole thing felt bad, felt worse with every step. I wanted to stop, turn back—but it was too late now. We kept walking, mods and ground trams slipping silently past, other pedestrians looking at us sidelong as we got closer to the end of the line.

The shining grid of the sky arced down to meet us as we came out on a kind of quay. You actually could smell the sea here, where clusters of airlocks lined the wall, in sizes running from single-occupant to gigantic, their designation data glowing patiently in the green gloom. I could see strange shadows moving beyond the dome wall; natives of the other side, or divers invading their space. It was hard to see much beyond the dome, but somewhere out in the murky darkness I thought I saw lights. There were separate little blister worlds out there in the bay that belonged to people who wanted more anonymity or security than even the Deep End had to offer.

The quay at the end of the street was empty; too empty. Nothing moved anywhere nearby, on the open dockyards, between the gaping-mouthed warehouses. It took a minute for my mind to find the lone figure waiting near the black mouth of one of them. Venk came forward slowly, his bodyguard glowing faintly in the dim light, until I could make out his face, and he could make out mine.

I felt the shock of recognition as he registered my features. "I saw you on the threedy," he whispered. I wondered why he was whispering. "Daric sent you to find me . . . ?" he asked, his voice dragging a strange accent.

"Yeah," I said, groping with my mind. My skin prickled as I

felt the images begin to harden suddenly behind his eyes. *Shit—* "I need some. . . ."

"No," he whispered. He wiped his nose.

My guide was about a meter away from me. He turned as Venk moved, his own hand rising—

I kicked out, hit his arm with my foot just before the beam of hot light lanced out of his sleeve. Pain branded my side as the white heat punched a hole in my jacket. I kicked him again, hit body armor where his balls should have been. I threw myself at him, because he was expecting me to run, and knocked him down. His head cracked hard on the pavement. I scrambled up. And then I ran like hell, away from the lone figure glowing like a haunt on the too-silent quay and whatever lightning he was calling down on me.

I made the end of the street, luckier than I'd ever thought I'd be—Venk's man wasn't wearing heatseekers. I saw a tram waiting at the turnaround and bolted for it, yelling. It jerked forward and drifted away, picking up speed as it left me behind . . . on purpose. I slowed, panting, cursing. The few people left on the street looked through me like I was invisible. Or marked. They disappeared into the shadows, into doorways, melting away from me without seeming to. I ran on down the street, my heart hammering, letting my mind search ahead and behind for hunters. Wondering how far I was going to get, wondering what I'd done to make Daric's dealerman want to kill me. I tried to remember when I'd felt as stupid, or as scared. I didn't think they'd waste me in the middle of the street, even here. Hell, I was a fucking media star. But if they couldn't they'd take me someplace where they could. And then the Locks would be waiting.

Behind me now I felt three minds converge, searching for me. Up ahead there were three more, moving in to cut me off. I dodged into a side street as I saw the shadows start to take form. I felt like I was swimming through the green light, running in a nightmare. *God, getting out of shape—* I heard myself laugh, a gasp of noise, as some part of my mind drifted free inside a bubble of panic, rising up toward somewhere outside of reality.

Light leaked through the sudden gap of a barely-open gate, catching my eye. I crashed through it, not caring what was on the other side. I collided with something—someone, almost knocking him down in a tangle of rough white robes. "Huh," I wheezed, half a question, and half a gasp of relief. *A prayer meeting.* My night eyes made out some kind of cult objects on an altar; a cluster of figures all wearing white, none of them expecting me, looking for me, hunting me.

There were curses and gasps as hands reached out to steady me
—frisked me, and then jerked my arms apart until I was spread-eagled
between them like a prisoner. Light flared, blinding me. The hard,
tattooed faces closing in on me as my sight cleared didn't belong to
a bunch of holy men. I started to struggle, and somebody hit me in
the stomach. I went down, helpless, as they let me go. Doubled over
on the floor, I heard a wailing moan that didn't sound human, heard
it shape itself into words: "A sacrament! Fresh wine for the cups of
the Souldrinker—" Heard the *clip* of a knifespring.

My head jerked back as someone's hands braced it. The knifeblade
flashed in the light, arcing down toward my chest. I threw up my
hands, screamed as pain slashed through my palm, and my own blood
spurted into my face.

The sound of a stungun fired too close to my ear tore my senses
apart, and all at once there was more shouting, more swearing, as the
number of bodies in the space around me suddenly doubled. The
whiterobes scattered, screaming the name of the Souldrinker into the
night—leaving me on the ground in a forest of dark, armored legs.
More hands hauled me up, as the street soldiers who'd driven me into
this dead end claimed what was left of me for themselves.

NINETEEN

I LET THEM THINK I couldn't walk because I couldn't walk, telling
myself while they dragged me back out to the street that I was just
waiting for the right chance to make a break for it. . . .

Someone stood waiting for us in the dimly-lit throat of a building across the way. He wasn't glowing; wasn't shielded. Wasn't the same one, not Venk, that I'd left standing on the pier.

"Hullo, Cat," he said.

The two men who'd been dragging me stopped, letting him take a look at me, letting me look at him. He knew me; he thought I knew him. There was something vaguely familiar about his voice, but I was sure I'd never seen that face before. A light chip flickered in his palm, showing me his features in sudden clear detail: Young-old, bronze-skinned, with a sharp nose and hard unreadable eyes under a fall of straight dark hair. He was wearing body armor like the rest, but his face shield was up so that I could see him. The silver ring through the left nostril of his nose winked in the light. "Know me now?"

I shook my head, my brain still strobing back to the image of a knifeblade coming down, again and again. . . . "No," I mumbled, wondering why he didn't just kill me and get it over with.

His thin mouth quirked. Slowly he lifted a hand, pulled off his studded glove. There was a white band of scar ringing his wrist, just like there was around my own. "Now?"

I shut my eyes for a second, listening to the voice of his mind. *Mikah*. I looked up at his face again, with a kind of disbelief. The last time I'd seen that face we'd both still worn the bond tags that had left those scars. "Mikah." I'd never seen his face whole and healthy, when it hadn't been stained blue with radioactive dust, or wasted with sickness. We'd been work partners, never friends; in the Mines it didn't take long before there wasn't enough left of you to make any effort at all. But he'd seen me escape, leaving him behind wearing a death sentence. And the look on his face had eaten into my memory, until I'd had to do something to get it out of my dreams. "What are you doing here?" I said, my voice sounding like something squeezed out of a child.

"Haven't you figured it out?" he asked, like I'd missed the punch line of a joke. "Shit, kid, I'm here to save your ass." He came forward, handed the light chip to one of the other men as he looked me over. "Got your pupils fixed, huh?" His smile stretched a little wider at my grimace. His hand caught my wrist in a loose grip, lifted my slashed hand, not even seeming to notice as my blood began to run down his arm. I swore as I got a real look at the wound. The knife was still jutting out of my palm. It had gone clear through. Suddenly the light seemed too golden; I felt like I was sinking into honey.

Mikah's dark eyes came back to mine, but they weren't expressionless now. His smile disappeared. "You . . ." he said, shaking his head. "It was you bought off my contract, and sent money for the meds to clean out my lungs, and enough left over to let me make a start—" His grip on my wrist tightened. "And you never told me why. Why? Why'd you do that—?"

I winced; his hand loosened suddenly. I didn't say anything, because I couldn't think of an answer that would have made any sense.

His free hand rose, closed over the knife hilt. His grip on me tightened again as I flinched. "Look at me," he said. I looked up, and he jerked the knife free.

My vision went red, and I cried out again; choked it off, because half a dozen men who did this to strangers all the time were staring at me. I took long, shuddering breaths while he peeled the glove off my bleeding hand.

When I could focus again I saw Mikah nod slightly, saw a faint smile pull at the corners of his mouth again. He dropped my blood-soaked glove on the floor. Then, silently, solemnly, he took the blade he'd pulled out of me and laid it down across his own palm. "Nobody ever did anything for me," he whispered. His eyes never left my face. "Not my own family. Nobody except you." His jaw tightened as he pressed down with the blade, and blood welled out suddenly, pooling in his cupped hand. He lifted his palm and pressed it against mine, folding his fingers over my hand until the wounds met, and our blood flowed together. "Anything you ever want—anything—you can ask me. You understand, brother?"

I nodded slowly. He let go of me. Pulling loose one of the long colored scarves he wore around his throat, he wrapped it tightly around my palm; wrapped his own hand with another one.

I looked at my hand. "I want to sit down," I mumbled.

He grinned. "You got it." Shoring me up with an arm around my waist, he led me back out to the main street and down a few doors to the entrance of a bar. The other men followed us, flanked me, easy but watchful in the way they moved. It finally began to sink into my brain that they were all his men, following his orders. "Somebody's trying to kill me—" I said, shaking my head, as Mikah tried to force me toward the bright, loud doorway.

His razor smile came back. "Not any more."

"Not them—" I jerked my head back the way we'd come. "Somebody else."

He snorted. "You don't waste much time, do you?" He pushed me forward into the open arms of light and noise. "Not any more," he repeated, as I dropped like a sack onto the bench in the closest empty booth. "You got Family now." He signed to the soldiers with him; they nodded and faded into the background noise.

He sat down across the laminated tabletop from me, propped on his elbows; spoke an order for drinks into the waiter on the wall.

"Jeezu," I said thickly. "Where the hell did you come from?" It wasn't cold here, but I was shivering.

He waved a hand. "Hey. I was born here. I work here now. I used the credit line you left me to buy into a Family." He laughed. "What did you expect me to do, join the FTA?"

My mouth twitched up. I shook my head.

"Good prospects for advancement." He nodded away into the room, where his men were sitting around a table, tossing Cubes. "Got my own squad already." The drinks he'd ordered flipped out of the wall. He pushed one of them at me. I shook my head, watching whitish froth form a crust on its rim. "Drink it," he said. "It's only bicarb."

I drank it, grateful. "What's your specialty?" Wondering if I'd be sorry I asked.

"Whatever makes a profit this week." He shrugged. "Mostly security and protection."

I thought about it. "All that still doesn't explain how you just happened to be there in time to protect my ass. I don't have that kind of luck."

He laughed again. "Saw you on the Morning Report, hero." He gulped down half of his own drink. "When I found out you were on-planet, I had you traced. I wanted to . . . square things. I didn't figure I'd get to start this fast."

"Who were those crazy bastards?"

"Rippers . . . a cult gang. Eat your heart out—literally."

I looked away, feeling my face get clammy. "Argentyne told me I was being an asshole." I cradled my throbbing hand inside the good one. The shock was wearing off; I felt like I'd picked up a handful of hot coals. And couldn't put them down. I damped out the pain receptors in my brain with an effort. "I thought I knew the rules."

"Argentyne? The symbplayer? You know her?"

I looked up as I felt the flash of unguarded excitement run through him, before his control dropped on it again. With the part of my mind that was still functioning, I realized that I'd impressed him. "A little."

He leaned back, trying to look like he hadn't just let me know that. "She puts me on overload with her socketwork."

"Yeah," I said. "She's a nova." I made a picture of her in my mind, letting it warm me up.

He shrugged. "I like her work. She's not my type."

I glanced up again, surprised. "You don't look dead to me."

He laughed.

"You don't like women." Realizing half a beat late what the total lack of heat when he thought about her meant.

"Not in my bed. . . . You got a problem with that?" His face hardened over at the expression I felt spread across my own.

"No." I shook my head. "I'm a freak, who am I to criticize anybody? . . . I was just wondering how come you never tried to hit on me down in the mines." I realized again, more strongly, what total strangers we were. I didn't even know his last name—if he even had one. I looked down at my hand, at the blood oozing through the layers of cloth. Blood brother. I started to shiver again.

"I was too fucking tired and sick." He looked at me, a slow smile coming out on his face again. "Besides, you're not my type either, freak." There was no sting in it; the truth, and nothing more. But he trusted me—that I wouldn't try to touch him with my mind— because I'd never hit on him, either. "So, this is where I am, now," he said. "What the hell are you doing down under, besides trying to commit suicide? You looked like you had everything you needed, up there on the wall this morning. Bodyguard to a vip—nice work, if you can get it."

"I got a drug problem. Not the usual kind—" I said, as his eyebrows rose. I explained it again. And I couldn't help thinking how much easier it would all be if I could just set it whole into someone else's brain; if only there wasn't so much fear.

"And Venk tried to null you, when you told him Daric taMing sent you?" Mikah frowned.

I nodded. "He recognized me, from the news." Trying to make that make some kind of sense with the rest of it, because somehow it had seemed to be a step on the path. Nothing at all made much sense to me right now.

Mikah rubbed his head. "Beats the crap out of me. He's not crazy. If he tried to kill you, he had a good reason. . . ." He stared at his half-empty cup, glanced up at me again. "You want me to find out what it is?"

"Yeah. Especially if it's a good one." I hesitated. "And—"

"Get you the drugs." He grinned. "How's that for mindreading?" He finished his drink, swept the cup into the dump along the wall of the booth. "Come on. That's not a drink of water you're looking for. I'd better take you to see the Doctor."

"I don't need a—"

"He's not that kind of doctor." A thin smile. "Doctor Death. Runs a black lab."

I grimaced.

"His real name's DeAth. Fits him better this way, though." He stood up.

"I'm not looking for poison," I said sourly. But maybe I was.

"Too bad. He's got the best. He supplies most of the big Families with the specialties they need for their hire business." The Lack Market had its combines too; but working for them was a lot more personal. Mikah signaled his soldiers. "He's got the best of everything. He can fix you up."

I followed him toward the door, stopped as he stopped by the public phone in the entryway. He touched in a silent code, got a query symbol on a blank screen. He fed in another code. This time he got a single line of letters: THE DOCTOR IS IN. He glanced back at me. "You don't see him without an appointment."

We took the Tube a couple of stops deeper into the Deep End, and a tram to a quiet streetcorner. The buildings wore more flash here, the streets were cleaner and had a more exclusive feel than the ones around Free Market Square. The only people who came calling here knew exactly where they were going. Mikah led me on down the street to the sixth rowhouse. Its door was black; ornate grillwork crawled like a vine up the walls, covered with black iron leaves.

Mikah stepped up on the porch, signaling me to join him; his gang sauntered away down the street, back the way we'd come.

I watched them go, wishing they'd stayed. Mikah stood motionless in front of the black door, his hands held out and open, away from his sides. I did the same, figuring we didn't need to knock to let anybody know we were here.

After a minute the door opened, letting us in. There was nobody waiting. We walked down a long hallway with mirrored walls. "Getting sanitized," Mikah said. By now I was almost beyond caring who or what was on the other side.

The doorway opened at the end of the hall, and we were in the black lab of Doctor Death.

"Hello!" a cheerful voice called, and somebody came toward us through the maze of scopes, electronic cookers, and data screens that covered an entire building floor. I watched a good-looking woman disappear through a doorway at the far side of the lab. The man was squat and round-faced, wearing lab pastels, his bald head gleaming in the brilliant light. He had two sets of eyes. The extra set looked like they belonged to some albino insect—two glittering, faceted rubies. He stopped in front of Mikah, beaming up at us, his gloved hands clasped and shining like water. "What can I do for you boys?" he asked, with a shopkeeper's eager smile. "Some Family business?" It was Doctor Death.

I stared at him, trying not to. I realized I'd come expecting somebody who lived up to the name. Not somebody who looked like he ought to be minding a bar somewhere, telling jokes. Except for the eyes. "Uh . . ." I said.

"He wants topalase-AC." Mikah said. "You got any of that?"

"Topalase-AC?" DeAth said, with his invisible eyebrows going up. "What in God's name does he want that for? He wants to become a mass murderer, but he hasn't got the nerve?"

Mikah didn't say anything, so finally I said, "I want to be able to act . . . human."

DeAth looked back at me, doubt furrowing a notch between his bug-eyes. "That's an ambiguous response, if I ever heard one. So, well, I know, 'it's none of your business, old man.' It's just a shame, when a kid comes in here looking to ruin his life. But I just make the stuff, how you use it is your business. . . ." His hand was already dancing over a touchboard while he spoke, calling up data. "I have it on hand, if you've got the price." I could tell it really broke his heart to sell it to me.

I winced at the price I saw on the screen. But I nodded. I put in a clearance on my databand, transferring the sum to him.

"I'll be back." He turned, trotting away toward the door that the woman had disappeared through.

I took a step, half afraid he was going to leave and never come back. But Mikah caught my arm. "He'll be back. Don't touch anything," he muttered, "the lab's armed."

I stayed where I was, and waited. DeAth came back, in less time than it seemed like. He held out a sheet of stick-ons to me.

I put my hand out, so eager to get hold of it that for half a second I forgot what I'd done to myself.

DeAth's arm jerked back in a startle-reflex. "Yik," he said, his lip curling as he saw the bloodsoaked cloth wrapping my hand. I wondered how he'd react if he ever got to see what his chemicals did to other people. Like the kind of thing that had happened at Elnear's party last night. . . . He slapped the paper into my other palm. "Please go, before you contaminate my rug. Goodbye." He herded us back out into the mirrored hallway; the inner door sealed shut with a hiss behind us.

There was a rushing in my ears as I peeled one of the blood-red dots off of the sheet, and put it on, one-handed. Mikah watched me like he'd watch a junkie, but all he said was, "You better get that wound fixed."

I shrugged, hardly thinking about it as I stuffed the sheet of drugs inside my jacket. "Don't worry about it, everything's fine now. . . ." In a few more minutes all the walls in my mind would be down at last, and I'd be able to see forever.

He stopped, pushed me up against the mirrors. I stared at the two of us reflecting back and forth into infinity as he shook me once. "You hear what I said?" His voice was as hard as a fist. He took my wounded hand and slammed it back against the mirror; I gasped with the pain of it. "That's a bad cut. Get it fixed, freak."

I grunted and nodded as the pain cleared out my head. "I hear you." I took a deep breath, looking him in the eye until he believed me.

He let go of me and turned away as the front door opened, like an impatient arm urging us out.

When we were out in the street again I said, "What happened at Lady Elnear's party last night looked like a hire job to me. That the kind of thing DeAth does?"

Mikah nodded. "Yeah. That was slick. He could have supplied it." He looked ahead, not taking it past an idle guess. His soldiers were around us again, from somewhere, nowhere.

"Can you find out?"

He glanced at me. "Maybe. I'll work on it."

"I want to know why somebody down here wants her out. Or who's paying them."

He nodded. "Right." We walked on in silence.

"I'll be in touch," he said, as he left me at the Tube again. "Take care of yourself, brother."

I lifted my bloody hand, a promise and a goodbye. People around me edged away.

I couldn't remember when I'd felt better.

TWENTY

"You look like a spotlight. I guess you got what you wanted," Argentyne said, her gaze locked on my face as she opened the door. She stepped back, stared at my bloodstained clothes as she let me past into the club. The ends of her mouth pulled down. "Mother Earth . . . I guess you got what you were asking for, too."

I shook my head; not denying it, just trying to shake loose the feeling that I was really everybody within a hundred meters of me. I focused on her relief turning into *disgust, relief, worry, disgust. . . .* damped it down further until I was only myself again. "Yeah," I said, following her back inside. There were a few customers hanging out already, scattered in clumps around the room, but at least I'd made it back before the evening really started. I wasn't sure I could have handled that, the way I felt right now.

"Is that all you've got to say?" she asked, too sharply, when that was all I said.

"Sorry," I mumbled. "This takes some getting used to. Strong stuff." I touched my head. "Gotta get my clothes and go."

"They're upstairs. I'll put some sudoskin on that hand for you; it looks pretty shitty."

"Thanks." Now that I was back inside my body, I was discovering again that it hurt like bloody hell in a couple of places. I followed her upstairs, into the long, wide room that was her private apartment. It was almost large enough to hold everything she wanted to have around her, stuffed into dressers and chests. The rest of it was sorted into vague heaps on top of pieces of furniture. Some of the furniture looked like it had been around a lot longer than she had. Clothes and ornaments hung from everything that would hold them, and a whole lot of plants squatted in pots on the floor below the windows. Some kind of animal with reddish fur scuttled off the bed and into a closet as we entered the room.

"Don't mind the mess," she said, because I was probably staring. "I just can't seem to throw anything out. I guess it's because for a long time I didn't have anything to throw out."

I nodded, feeling in my pocket for the markers I'd given away. "Hard to break old habits," I said.

"Sit down." She smiled finally, picking a pack of camphs off a dressertop and putting one into her mouth. She held out the pack to me. I hadn't had one in years; not since Dere Cortelyou had died. They always made me think of him. But tonight all my memories seemed far away. I nodded, grateful, and she flipped me one. She was wearing loose gray pants now, tied at the ankles; a blue shirt with a loose gray jacket over it, the wide sleeves rolled up. Her earrings were the size of eggs, and silver.

I stuck the camph into my mouth and bit down on the end of it, feeling it deaden my tongue with ice and spice as I sucked on it; letting it calm my nerves. I sighed, sitting on the edge of the bed, because it was the only place left in the room where you could sit. It felt so good I could have gone to sleep right there, sitting up, if my body hadn't felt so bad. My hand throbbed and burned; so did my side, now. I pulled back the leather jacket, pulled up the blood-splattered shirt under it. Beneath the fresh burn holes in both of them was the burn on my side where the hole had just missed going through me too. "Shit. . . ." I said, not sure if it was because of what had happened, or what hadn't.

"Jeezu," Argentyne murmured. "What did you do to get your stuff, commit armed robbery?" She sat down beside me with a first-aid box.

I laughed once, shook my head. "Daric's dealerman tried to kill me. I think I got in the way of something more than a gun. You know anything you didn't tell me?"

She half frowned, shaking her own head. "No. But with Daric, you never know everything. . . ." She looked tired suddenly. "I'm sorry. Take your coat off. I'll plaster that one too." She popped the kit open.

"It's clean, it'll heal over by itself."

"Don't be stupid." She helped me get out of the jacket without moving too much.

"Sorry I ruined the clothes. I'll pay you for them."

"Don't be stupid," she said again. She pulled my shirt up. Her hand froze suddenly; she was staring at old scars. She let the shirt drop, covering them up again. She looked at me. "Do you like pain?"

I grimaced, startled. "I try like hell to keep away from it." I shrugged. "Sometimes you just can't. . . ."

She looked down again, as if she was embarrassed. She took the can of sudoskin out of the box and sprayed it on my side. Then she was unwrapping the cloth around my hand, biting hard on her own camph to steady her nerves. She looked at the wound, looked away again, her face twisting. My hand was still bleeding. I looked away too.

"I can't deal with that," she said, shaking her head. "Let me get Aspen—he'd better do it for you. He used to be a med student, until he found out he didn't like sick people." She stood up.

"I can go to the meds."

She looked back at me. "And what are you going to tell them when they ask how you got that way—?"

I half smiled. "I could tell them the same thing I told Braedee, when he asked me how I got that way last night."

She made a rude noise, and went out of the room. I fumbled for the leather jacket to get out the sheet of drugs. It slid off onto the floor. I kneeled down to pick it up; glanced into the low, flat cave underneath the bedframe.

Sometimes having better sight than anyone else isn't something you're glad of. Someone else probably would never have noticed what I saw lying there in the darkness. But I saw it, and knew what it was. And then I saw something else, and something else: things that had never been intended to do anything but inflict pain.

I pushed to my feet, holding the jacket; turned toward the door, feeling like I just wanted to get the hell out of there. But Argentyne was already back, with one of the players who had a shining touchboard for a chest trailing behind her.

She looked at me strangely, because she thought I was looking at her strangely. I sat down again, and held out my hand. Aspen took it, turned it, flexed the fingers, very carefully. "Tried to shake hands with a mugger, huh? Can you use it at all?"

"Not right now," I said irritably, thinking that much ought to be obvious.

"Hm." He frowned, suddenly turning professional; not easy when he looked like a floor lamp. "Let me get my own kit; I've got to suture this." He drifted out of the room again, humming faintly, accompanied by synth sounds. One half of his brain was reviewing a medical procedure, while the other half was composing music.

"Why did you look at me like that?" Argentyne asked, as soon as he was out of earshot.

I hesitated. "I saw what's under the bed." Her face didn't redden through the silver of her skin, but I could feel the surge of heat behind it.

"Daric," I said. "Daric—?" Not even sure what the emotion was that closed around my stomach like a fist. "You let that bastard do that to you?"

"No!" She swore. "No," looking down suddenly, "I do it to him."

"Why—?" I said, but before it was even out of my mouth, I saw the answer. "Because you love him." The words were so hard to say they were barely audible.

She raised her head.

"You said it to Jiro last night, didn't you? 'It's better if you get it from someone who cares about you.' . . ." If I tried hard enough, I could almost make myself believe that.

She turned away to the dresser, pulled another camph out of the pack. She glanced up, staring at my reflection in the mirror, so that she didn't have to face me. And then she looked down again. "Yeah," she whispered. "I mean . . . he hates himself so much, and I don't know why. Sometimes he scares me. I do it because if I didn't, God knows where he'd go to get it, or what would happen to him then. . . ." She slammed her hands down on the dressertop, making trays of body paint and makeup jump, hurting herself.

"Everything okay?" Aspen asked, coming back through the doorway carrying a portable surgery.

"Your timing is just perfect," Argentyne said wearily, turning to look at us again.

"Hey, thanks." He sat down on the bed, thumbing the case open. "I've really been working on it." He patted his glowing chest; notes floated up like bubbles.

Argentyne cleaned up colors, or pretended to, while he went to work on my hand, his attention suddenly sharp and focused again. He pressed a patch of painkiller down on my wrist; my whole hand dropped off the nerve map in my mind. I sighed with relief. He put on a strange-looking set of lenses and stared at the wound; seeing into it, looking for structural damage. "Hm," he said again, and took them off. "You were lucky. Nothing vital severed. I'll seal it up." He picked something else out of the case. It looked soft and moist, a little like a big slug. He wrapped it around my hand, covering the cut. Something happened that I could feel even through the anesthetic, like a kind of heavy suction. "Hold still," he said, catching hold of my arm. "Okay—" as the slug suddenly changed color. He peeled it off and dropped it back into the case. I looked at the ugly red mouth of the wound. It was closed. "That's the best I can do." He sprayed it with sudoskin. "I don't have a lamp; if you want it to heal fast, you'll have to get a regeneration treatment someplace else."

I nodded. "Thanks." I moved my fingers experimentally. They all worked, at least, even though I couldn't feel them.

"No problem." He got up and drifted out of the room, waved at us over his shoulder as an afterthought.

"Thanks," I said, to Argentyne this time.

She shrugged. "Your things are in the closet over there. I've got to get ready for the evening." She started toward the door, avoiding my eyes.

I almost called her name; didn't. I found my clothes and changed into them as fast as I could. Then I went downstairs, glad enough to go on my way without any more conversation.

"Argentyne! Argentyne!" A voice that could have raised echoes in deep space was bellowing her name. I stopped, looking down the hallway in the direction of the noise. A turn blocked my view, but I could feel half a dozen minds clustered around the corner.

"Hey, Cusp. . . ."

"Come on—"

"Argentyne!" Banging noises.

I went down the hall, stopped, looking around the corner. One of the club's bouncers was beating on the door of Argentyne's dressing room with a pincer-arm, shouting her name over and over, while players from the symb buzzed around him like flies, with about as much effect.

"Argentyne—!"

Someone made the mistake of grabbing his arm; he shrugged, and three bodies went flying halfway down the hall.

Suddenly the door opened. He backed off a little as Argentyne stepped out into the hall, wrapped in her faded bathrobe. "Cusp!" she said, doing a damn good job of hiding how small and intimidated she suddenly felt. "What is this shit?" She waved a hand at the pile of bodies slowly untangling. He gargled something unintelligible. *Her biggest fan.* Literally. "Thanks, but no thanks. . . . Come on," she said, almost gently, "get back out front and do your job. I have to get ready, you know?" She managed to smile as she tried to get him turned around and out of there.

But the armored claw closed over her wrist, jerking her forward, and began to drag her away down the hall.

"Hey!" she squawked. I felt the flash of her pain and surprise, the stupefied fear of the helpless players backing away. I froze, trying to think of something to do.

And then suddenly somebody was standing in the doorway of her dressing room, looking out. Daric. "Argentyne—?" he called, staring, uncertain.

She looked back at him in wordless panic, stumbling as Cusp pulled her forward again.

"Let her go," Daric said, starting after them down the hall. If Cusp heard, he didn't pay any attention.

Daric began to run, catching up with them. I watched, feeling like I must be dreaming. Daric caught Argentyne's arm; her hand came free at his touch, as if Cusp's grip on her was no stronger than a child's. Cusp stopped, turning back in slow motion, the way a mountain would turn; raising his armored claws—

Then he crashed over backwards, with a *thud* that made my teeth hurt.

The players stood gaping. Argentyne turned slowly inside Daric's arms, her eyes wide and glassy as she faced him. "Okay?" he murmured, stroking her hair, pulling her to him in a sudden, protective embrace. Cusp was making a high keening whine, lying like a gassed beetle on the floor. Argentyne looked at him lying there, and shook her head, her mouth quivering, close to tears or hysterical laughter.

"Hey, Daric," Aspen said, "how'd you do that, man?"

Daric glanced at him, twitching. "I didn't do anything," he snapped. "He's just drunk." Lying. "Get him the hell out of here. Call Security."

I stayed back out of sight as he turned and walked Argentyne to her dressing room again. The players gathered around Cusp like pallbearers to drag his helpless body away.

I pressed against the wall, staring at nothing, wondering how I could have been so blind. Because now it was so obvious . . . Daric was the one. The teek I'd been sensing. *A psion, just like his sister.*

I don't remember leaving the club. I don't really remember how I got to the Assembly plex; to Elnear waiting, weary and relieved, for me to come back. She didn't mention what I'd said before I left; she hoped I wouldn't mention it again, either. Ever. Instead, looking at my bruised face, she asked what had happened, if anything was wrong. I don't remember what I told her, but she didn't ask again.

We took a mod back to the taMing estates. She fell asleep before we were out of sight of the city, leaving me the privacy to go on thinking about Daric. *Daric, Daric* . . . all I could think about, ever since I'd realized the truth. I wondered how it had happened. How could there have been two of them—two psions, brother and sister, born in the same generation into a family where there had never been one before, ever? How could Daric have hidden his psi all those years, from everyone. . . .

But I thought more about why, because that was so much easier to understand. He'd hidden it because he knew what happened to freaks. He'd seen how his family treated Jule, and what they'd done to his mother just because Jule was born a psion. His life must have been a living hell, when one slip would mean discovery—would mean that he'd lose everything: his position, his power, his wealth, maybe even his life . . . the love and protection of his family; the approval and the security everybody secretly craved. All of it torn away in a second if anyone even suspected. He'd still be the same person they'd always known—but in the eyes of everyone who mattered to him he would have turned from a golden child into an outcast, a subhuman . . . a freak.

No wonder he baited them with little teek torments nobody would ever be able to catch him at. No wonder he flaunted Argentyne— hinting, daring somebody to look deeper, even while he worked at being more like everybody else than they were themselves. . . .

My guts twisted just thinking about the kind of pressures at work inside him, distorting everything he thought and did. I'd been a psion all my life, but I'd been lucky. I hadn't known it. Maybe I'd never wanted to know, because my life in Oldcity had been so close to the edge all the time. Having to face that too could have been the thing that finally broke me. It was easier, safer, just to find a hiding place in some dark hole in the streets, inside some drugged fantasy world, inside my mind. Coming out hadn't been easy. I never would have done it alone. I knew how a secret like that could eat somebody's insides out: The fear, the loneliness, the hatred that had nowhere to turn but inward. No wonder he needed what only Argentyne would give him. . . .

It was easy to feel sorry for him. But it was easier to remember what his secret had done to everyone who crossed his path. Jule, and Jiro, and Elnear; even Argentyne. . . . Easier to remember how he'd treated me: like a freak. And then the pity knotting my gut would turn back into disgust again.

I had to wake up Elnear when we reached the estate. She looked confused, and then concerned, looking back at me. I tried to wipe the grim tension off my face until she looked away again.

"I'm going directly to my room," she said, her voice quavering more than usual as she tried to control it. "I'm going to sleep until I want to wake up. You should do the same."

I nodded, and followed her inside.

Lazuli was waiting for us on the porch, even though there was a sharp bite to the evening air that I hadn't felt before. Her eyes found mine and her thoughts collided with me, and suddenly I couldn't feel the chill any more. She murmured something to Elnear as she passed, touched her shoulder briefly.

She let me pass too, but her mind reached out for me, opening its arms in the darkness, searching helplessly. I hesitated at the foot of the stairs, looking back; looked at her, and followed her down the hall instead.

She led me into Elnear's study and closed the doors. I hadn't really seen it when I'd been here before. It was high-ceilinged, like all the rooms, and its walls were lined with dark wooden shelves, the shelves lined with antique books sealed behind glass. I wondered whether anyone had looked at them in centuries. There was a fire burning inside a stone fireplace. The rich, heavy smell of the smoke made my mouth water. I thought I could feel its heat even where I stood; but maybe it was something else. "Why do you have a fire?" I asked, trying to think of something besides her. It didn't work. "You don't need one." This house might be old, but it was state-of-the-art on comfort.

In front of the fireplace was the long mahogany-wood table that was the one thing I remembered seeing in the room before. Its surface was inlaid with gold in patterns of stars, a map of the night sky. Lazuli leaned against it, turning to look back at me. "No, of course not," she said softly. "But a fire warms the soul, somehow." She held her hands out to the flames. She was wearing a loose velvet tunic the color of red wine, its random hem brushing her calves, brushing her knees. I crossed the room to be close to her. I touched her mind, very gently; touched her shoulder. The feel of velvet made gooseflesh start up my arm.

"Are you all right?" she turned toward me, suddenly uncertain. She saw the sude on my hand and the bruise on my face, was suddenly afraid that Charon had had something to do with them. Her eyes went to the emerald earring I was still wearing.

"Yeah. I'm fine now," I said, and smiled. The snap of flames, the rustle of whirled sparks, was loud in the silence between us. "Are you?"

She looked up at me, with a tiny smile starting on her own lips, and what lay behind her eyes washed over me like a wave of heat.

"How's—how's Jiro?"

She glanced away again. "He felt much better this morning. The children are up at the Crystal Palace. Charon . . . demanded that we attend dinner with the family."

"What about you?"

"I wanted to see you, first. Because I won't be back tonight." She brushed at a loose strand of night-colored hair. "Charon wants me to spend more time with him. . . ." Spend the night with him. She looked down, knowing that I must know what she was thinking, and how she felt. "I'll join them in a while . . . I said that I was sick." Sick at the thought of him touching her. Her eyes came back to me. *(Sick with longing,)* they said to me.

"Lazuli . . ." I shook my head, looking down. Last night we'd burned away our loneliness together in the dark. It shouldn't have happened even once. It couldn't happen again, ever. I couldn't afford to let it. I reached up, started to unfasten the earring.

She lifted her hand, stopping me. Her body was as taut as a bow, pressed against the hard edge of the star-covered table, straining against impulse. *(I want you,)* it said. *(Touch me again,)* said her mind. She pulled my hands away, pulled them to her, ran them down over her velvet dress.

My burning body took the last step across the space that separated us. I kissed her then, hard and deep and hungry, because that was how she wanted to be kissed. My hands slid down the velvet again, this time without any urging, and into the soft curves of her body. They circled her hips, pulling her against me until there was no space at all left between us. I felt the heat of the fire against my back, the heat of her; the heat of my own need, even hotter. I couldn't stop now, didn't want to. Because I knew that I was really *good,* that I could give her everything she wanted, and more. That I could make this beautiful, unapproachable woman need me so much that nothing else mattered to her, nothing at all. And all because of the Gift that wouldn't be mine to use much longer. . . .

I laid her down across the starry table and made love to her right there, hard and deep and hungry . . . while she called me deeper into her mind, called me her only real lover, called me the fire. . . .

TWENTY-ONE

I WAS BACK on the job the next day, because Elnear was back on the job. "Losing Philipa is like losing a part of my own brain," she said to me, as we walked through the halls of the FTA plex to her office. "I'm not sure how I'm going to get through my work."

"Is she that augmented?" I asked, surprised because I'd been sure she wasn't. She didn't have anything like the neural taps that Elnear did.

"No." Elnear shook her head, a little embarrassed. "But she is formidably organized. She has everything in its place, all those little details that keep one from making a fool of oneself in public, and she can access faster than I can think, sometimes. . . ."

"Why can't you just plug into all of it yourself? You're wired. Why do you even need someone else to do it for you?"

She shrugged. "I'm really very lazy. I don't want to spend all my time accessing, the way Natan Isplanasky does. I like to have time to step back and look the day in the eye . . . paint a picture, visit a new place. Philipa gave—gives me the time to do that.'' The rueful smile faded, as memories piled up until her mind began to sink under them: *Philipa, loss, fear, defeat, death. . . .*

I made myself pull back before I went too far. The topalase was working, almost too well. It gave my mind x-ray eyes. It was so easy to start, too easy, with someone I knew. I could just pick up a strand of thought without even thinking, and follow it back through the maze. I could be inside someone else's head before they knew it, without their ever knowing it . . . deep inside, where it got too private. Every human had things they didn't want to share, things they didn't want to admit . . . even me.

Knowing it was so easy now made me feel the way I'd felt that night at the taMings' party: realizing that I could steal them blind . . . knowing that to do it was wrong. Dere Cortelyou had taught me before he died that there was a reason the deadheads were afraid of us. He'd gone too far, tried too hard to convince them that he wouldn't hurt them. He'd worked as a corporate telepath, and they'd treated him like dirt. Rubiy had gone too far the other way, crazy with power, using everyone else like his personal property. They were both dead. Somewhere in between there had to be a survivor's path, some way to balance on the tightrope without taking a fall that would kill me. . . .

We walked on in silence, neither one of us smiling.

I accessed Jardan's datafiles when we reached the office, sucking up the next few calendar days and trying to make sense of it all— appointments, decisions to be made, data to be sent or collected. A thousand briefing details: this combine vip's hair phobia; dietary restrictions to be careful of with that Assembly rep . . . somebody's grandmother's illness to be asked after the next time she was on some other planet. Information coming in from across half the Federation that she needed to know or wanted to know every day; changing every day. Now I understood what Elnear meant: just sorting it all out would leave her with no real time to analyze or make sense of it. Maybe I'd never like Jardan any better than she liked me. But now I respected her, at least; respected what she could do, with only a human brain.

Wearing Jardan's data in my memory, I went with Elnear through her restless perpetual motion: walking the halls, paying personal calls where a vid would have done, as she spoke to one Assembly member after another about the upcoming drug vote. ''Because when you come in person, people remember you,'' she said, her eyes bright with her need to believe. I fed her names, gave her the relevant details, reading them right out of the stranger's head if they weren't in my own, and slipping them to her so gently she almost believed she was remembering them herself. But she knew she wasn't. At first she gave me that Look every time it happened. But not for long.

Sometimes the people she wanted to talk to made me wait in the hall when they saw my face; usually the ones who had the most to hide. I waited outside, but it didn't do them any good. More and more, Elnear's eyes searched my face as she came out of a meeting, looking for clues. It took nearly a dozen calls before she finally got the nerve to ask: "Am I making any progress? Getting anywhere at all?"

I shrugged, glancing away. "Some, maybe. . . ."

"You don't have to lie to me," she said, her face settling into folds as the hope went out of it. "The answer is no."

I nodded.

"That's what I suspected. While I'm talking to them, I actually begin to believe that they are human beings; but they're simply access ports. I might even convince the human being; but the human being is not what really votes, in the end." She rubbed her neck, because she wanted to reach out and shake somebody. "Why did I even ask—?" Her head jerked with her sudden anger. Behind it was the knowledge that yesterday, in spite of everything that had happened, the special committee had finished its study of the drug deregulation—and had set it free. It would be up for the general Assembly vote in a matter of days. And she knew now that that vote wouldn't go her way, no matter what she did.

"Why is this so important to you, anyway?" I said, trying not to let myself go ahead and find out without asking. "It's not just the principle of the thing, and it's not just the Council slot. . . ."

She gave me a sidelong glance, afraid I was about to do just what I was trying not to. When I didn't answer my own question, she looked away again, her footsteps slowing. "My parents . . ." she murmured, as if she was drifting off into a reminiscence, "developed the penta-tryptophine family."

I half frowned. "Your parents? I thought pentryptine had been around for a couple of centuries."

"About a century and a half," she said, nodding. "Just about as long as my parents lived. They had a very long career. They synthesized or developed many of ChemEnGen's most profitable biochemicals. . . ."

"And you think they wouldn't want to see pentryptine used like this?"

Her eyes went bleak and pale. "They wouldn't have cared . . .

perhaps they would have been glad, because it was good for the company.'' She frowned, looking down at her feet. Her mother and her father had developed all those chems and virals; but wondering how they would be used, for what, by who, had never given either one of them a moment of doubt or a bad night's rest. And she had never been able to understand that, or to forgive them for it.

"What happened?" I asked. "To make you see it different from the way they did?"

She shook her head. "Nothing, that I know of. I've simply always believed that to live a life without some sense of responsibility to humanity, or for one's actions, is—immoral, wrong." She sighed, brushed a strand of graying hair back from her face. "I suppose I was just born that way."

"Kind of a freak," I said gently, and felt my mouth twitch.

She looked at me. "Yes," she said, "I suppose so." We started moving again. After a few steps I realized we weren't going to pay another call; we were going back to her office.

"There's got to be some better way," I said. "You'll find it."

She didn't answer.

I got through my office work as fast as I could, and went out for a walk. I used the first public phone I came to to call up Mikah, wanting the privacy of its security screen. His face filled in on the vid; it was the slightly washed-out image of a bandphone receiver. "Cat," he said, with half a nod. "Make it fast."

"You got anything for me?"

"Maybe. Tonight—?"

"Purgatory, before the show."

"Yeah." His image blanked out. I shut off the screen and started back through the halls, moving more slowly this time. Letting my mind drift, spreading out like fog, touching the surfaces of a hundred different minds and moving on. I didn't even realize I'd been searching for something until I found it: Something about Stryger . . . and Daric. Passersby bumped into me, murmured and moved on, as I stopped, focusing in. Daric was leaving his office on the next level down, going to meet with Stryger to discuss matters of mutual interest. Yesterday's vote, yesterday's news. Daric was always a clenched fist; but the way his mind felt right now made the way he usually read seem like meditation. I sank a silent tracer into his brain, and took the first lift that came, following him through the plex. *Mutual interest*. . . . Anything they had in common had to be something I needed to know. Because it had to involve deregulation, and Elnear.

Stryger was waiting for him in a whiteroom, maximum privacy inside maximum security. But I'd planted the perfect bug, undetectable, already riding inside Daric's brain. The room wasn't far from the display hall where the tourists came to gape. I found a quiet corner where I could wait without looking obvious. On the wall across from me was the mosaic mural, the portrait of the people of the Human Federation—male and female, young and old, brown and yellow and black and white. Their faces stared back at me like silent judges. But I was the only one who could really decide if what I was doing was wrong or right, justified or only thieving. *Deadheads*. I looked up at them again, their faces, their eyes. And then I shut my stranger's eyes, concentrating.

I opened up my senses, weaving them through the boundaryless territory of Daric's mind like tributary streams, letting his thoughts begin to bleed into my own. It wasn't easy, invading the mind of another psion; especially one whose brain was this sick, full of paranoid quicksand and dead-end mazes of augmentation. But needing all my skill, and being able to use it, feeling it work again with the perfect control I'd had once, made it almost a pleasure.

But I didn't find anything I didn't know or suspect already. Daric was Centauri's contact with Stryger, giving Stryger instructions, suggestions, orders from the board. He was only one of too many datafeeders; most of the others were from combines with large, expensive populations. Stryger nodded and smiled and praised God for sending him such friends and counselors.

And all the while he was only half listening. Once I was inside Daric's mind it was easy to get inside Stryger's. I only had to step across the short empty space between them to pick up his responses. He was already one step beyond, imagining how it was going to be once they'd given him the thrust he needed to reach the Security Council, and he made the slot his own. . . .

And all the while Daric was talking—his voice calm, his face calculating and cool, everything about him stinking of arrogance—his own mind was twisting around and through itself like a snake, his body was twitching, sweating. . . . He knew as well as I did how much Stryger hated psions. It fascinated him, the way a gun lying on a table would fascinate somebody who was thinking about murder, or suicide. . . .

I figured I'd seen enough. I wasn't going to learn anything new from this, anything that would help Elnear. I was wasting my time picking through garbage. I began to withdraw, slowly, carefully, not

letting my disgust get in the way of my control long enough to give
me away. Daric wasn't a telepath, but his mind still had more sensitive
burglar alarms than a normal human's did.

Daric froze suddenly, as something went off like a flare inside
his mind. I froze too, until I realized it was something Stryger had
asked him, and not some slip I'd made, that had set off the response.

"Have you found me another?" That was the question. I reached
for him again, going deeper, listening, sifting; curious about what
could trigger that kind of panic reflex in Daric's brain. What Stryger
could want that he'd ask for that way—

I watched/felt Daric's response take form, like an image rising
up out of the black depths of a pool, suddenly there on its surface like
a face in a mirror. *"No, not yet . . . having a little—trouble, with my
access to the supply. . . ."* And something in his mind was thrashing
like a trapped animal, struggling to get free, to cry out, *Take mine.
Use mine.* But he couldn't say it, *couldn't, couldn't ever. . . .*

I thought it had to be drugs. But it wasn't drugs. Below the spoken
words there were random images of the Deep End, dark streets and
darker deals, but not for drugs; not this time. Tension and terror
tightened like chains around an emotion they'd crushed so completely
that I couldn't even recognize it.

Flesh and blood. A body to use. Stryger wanted Daric to hire him
a victim. But not just any victim. He wanted Daric to find him a psion.
The way he'd done before.

Images were pouring out of Daric now: memories of red weals
on pale flesh, swollen purple bruises slowly turning a face unrecog-
nizable, screams driving pain into his own head like a nail. . . . *Terror
. . . Thirst . . .*

I let them come; but I didn't need his memories. I had my own.

It took all my control to keep from screaming inside Daric's
head—*I know everything, you bastard*—screaming it until his eyes
bled. I broke contact; heard my voice gasp out a curse like somebody
talking in his sleep. The eyes of the mural across the hall watched me,
somber, curious, happy, sad.

I shut them out; stepped across the empty space and into Stryger's
mind again. Because now that I knew what he really was, there were
questions I had to have answered; answers that would make all the
difference, to Elnear . . . to my own sanity. I drove into his thoughts
with one hard thrust, knowing how a knife felt when it sank into
somebody's flesh. But he never felt a thing. *Deadhead.* I ransacked
his mind, keeping my focus tight, sealed like an antiseptic barrier.

There were only two things I wanted from him. I didn't want anything else; didn't want him to infect me. . . . But I had to be sure.

He wasn't the one. Not the one who was trying to kill Elnear. He wanted that Council slot, but he thought he already had it. God was on his side, God wouldn't let him fail, God would make it happen. He didn't have to help God along. . . .

He wasn't the one. He wasn't the same one who'd taken me up to that hired room back in Oldcity and beaten me up. But he'd done it to enough other freaks. And he needed to do it now, needed it bad, because of what had happened to him yesterday: caught in a lie, humiliated by a psion, by me, in front of so many watching eyes. And Daric, sweating like he had a fever, was ready to help him do it again.

I cut contact. *He wasn't the same one.* Then how many were there, just like him? Just like the one who'd done it to me. Thousands? Millions? I looked at the faces of Humanity watching, waiting, one last time. "Go to hell," I said, as I started out of the room.

TWENTY-TWO

"I GOTTA TALK TO YOU," I said, standing in the doorway of Argentyne's dressing room.

She turned in her seat, away from the mirror above a cluttered table. The startled look on her face faded into something like distraction. "Oh, it's you. Can't it wait? I've got a show to do." She was half in and half out of the Argentyne the public saw, in a coat bristling with glowing fiberoptic quills.

"No."

She'd started to turn back to the mirror; she stopped, looked up

at me again instead, in surprise. "All right," she said. "Talk to me."
She picked up a wand and began to run it over her hair; the silver
threads rose up like worshippers following the sun, and stayed that
way.

I pushed clothes off of a chair and straddled it, resting my chin
on its hard plastic spine. "About Daric."

She studied herself in the mirror; she didn't move her head, but
the reflection changed and changed again, showing her different angles.
"Laddie love," she said patiently, "are you trying to save me from
myself?" Warning me off.

I frowned. "I'm trying to tell you the truth."

She shrugged, reaching up to hook an ear cuff dangling heavy
rhinestones over her ear.

"Daric's a psion."

The earring clattered onto the table, lay there. I had her attention
now. "Bullshit," she said. She picked up the earring, not looking at
me; twisted it, watching it gleam in the hard light. "Are you sure?"
she asked finally.

I nodded. "It takes one to know one. He's a teek—telekinetic.
That's how he stopped Cusp. I was there, I felt him do it."

She looked up at my reflection behind her in the mirror. "But he
said. . . . He's never. . . . I didn't—"

"Nobody knows it, except him—and me. He never told anybody."

"Why not?" She honestly couldn't imagine.

I laughed. "Why do you think? He'd lose everything if his family
found out he was a freak. Look what they did to his sister."

She turned in her seat again, slowly facing me, her face slowly
changing. Her image in the mirror stayed frozen the way she'd left it,
waiting. "Why are you telling me this?" she said. "You want to know
if it makes a difference to me? If it matters that he didn't trust me . . .
or that he's a psion?"

"Maybe." I looked down.

"Did you really think that was going to change how I felt?" The
anger behind her eyes was getting hotter. "So he didn't trust me with
a secret that could ruin his life . . . so he's a freak. So what?" Her
silver-nailed hand jerked at me. "At least he's not a goddamned peep-
ing tom!" Like me.

I shook my head. "A 'mental pickpocket,' " I said.

"What?"

"A mental pickpocket—that's what the other psions called me, back at the Institute in Quarro. . . ." I raised my head, meeting her stare. "Yeah, I picked his brains. And that's not all I got. You know about Sojourner Stryger?"

She hesitated. "He's the big godlover who wants to save everybody; the one who wants the drug dereg to go through? Daric's talked about him, sometimes. . . ."

I nodded. "Stryger wants the same Security Council slot that Lady Elnear wants. Centauri is one of the combines backing him. . . . Did Daric ever tell you Stryger's a freakhater?"

She shook her head.

"Daric is Centauri's liaison with Stryger. He gives him his instructions—" I hesitated; pushed on, feeling my anger like a fire smoldering in my gut. "And he gets him whatever he asks for."

Her frown came back again. "What do you mean?" she asked, impatience elbowing out her curiosity. "You mean Stryger does drugs?"

"He does psions."

Her mouth opened again, but nothing came out of it this time.

"You remember that girl you told me about—the one Daric brought here, who'd been beaten so bad she couldn't talk? The psion—?"

The knuckles of her hand stood out as it tightened on the back of her chair. "Daric?" she murmured. "Daric made that happen?" Her eyes were begging me to tell her I was lying.

"She wasn't the only one," I said. "Sometimes he even watches."

"Oh, God." She broke away, pushing up out of her seat, her hands balled into fists at her sides. *"Why?"* she said, turning back. "If he's a psion too, why would he do that?" Challenging me to make it make sense.

I shook my head. I'd asked myself the same question, trying to make it make sense, all through the endless afternoon. "I don't know. Why don't you ask him?" I got up off my chair.

She jerked a piece of clothing free from a hook, thought about throwing it in my face; threw it on the floor instead. "Why did you have to tell me that? Goddamn you—what do you want me to do about it?"

I shrugged. "Like I said. I just wanted you to know the truth. What you do about it is your business." I started for the door.

"You're a lousy human being, you know that?"

I looked back at her. Her face was all congested-looking; she was going to be crying in another minute. "I try," I said. I went on out.

I sat down at a table out in the club and had a drink, watching the room fill up, waiting for Mikah to show. They'd hired a new bouncer. I half expected him to come over and tell me to get out, after what I'd just done; but he didn't. The club was as dark as a cave tonight, and smoky. Fingers of colored laser light gibbered across the darkness in frantic parabolas, shattered into clouds high above my head to the wailing of recorded synth music. I settled back, losing myself in the dark/bright spaces overhead.

Finally I sensed Mikah making his way across the dance floor. He sat down at the table with me, wearing black body-armor. He fit right in. I had on my old jeans and torn shirt; I'd brought them to work with me in a shoulder bag, knowing I'd be going out. "Hey, freak," he said.

"Don't call me that."

He looked surprised. "What's eating you?"

I looked away, down at my empty glass. "Nothing. What's your problem?"

"I'm a deeve." One side of his mouth pulled up. "Somebody been rubbing your nose in it? Wipe the shit off your face, kid, and forget about it. You ought to be used to that by now."

I shook my head. "It's not that. I wish it was only that." I unclenched my good hand, laid it flat on the table.

He ordered himself a drink, settling back into the pile of cushions. When I didn't say anything else, he shrugged and asked, "What happened to your shirt? You have a hot date last night?"

I looked down at the long rip across the front and almost laughed, remembering how it had really happened. But then I remembered last night, the fire and the star-covered table. . . . I reached up, touched the emerald earring, still in my ear. I hadn't meant to keep it; hadn't meant for anything to happen the way it had, last night. . . . Finally I admitted the truth to myself, that Lazuli had only been using my body to help her forget how much she hated being with her husband; maybe even to pay him back. And I'd let her. It had been so easy to use me, like the only brain I had was between my legs. I felt stupid and helpless—felt myself start to get an erection again, just remembering red velvet and golden skin. . . .

"You must be somebody's type," Mikah said. "I hear it's fun to be famous."

I glanced away. "You find out why I'm so popular that total strangers want to kill me?"

He shook his head. "It's not street talk. That means it's vip level, and their secrets keep real well."

I looked up, surprised. "You think it has something to do with Elnear?"

He shrugged. "Dunno. But you guessed good about DeAth—he did the footwork for what happened at that party the other night. But after that I hit a wall. I can't find out who hired him to drop the Lady. Nobody down under seems to want her gone—she's on their side, they don't want that drug deregged any more than she does."

I wondered what Elnear would think if she heard that. "Damn," I said. "I thought I knew . . . I thought it was Stryger. But it's not."

"Stryger?" Mikah grunted. "You mean the Plastic Saint? You really thought he'd try to take out his opposition with a human bomb?"

"Yeah," I said, feeling my eyes ice over. "That's exactly what I thought."

"Hm." He shrugged again. "I've heard talk about him. Thought it was only talk." He sounded relieved; I'd just restored his faith in human nature. Even he could have told me the way to one of Stryger's good works.

"Whatever you heard, it's not bad enough. But it doesn't do me any good—" I rubbed my face. "DeAth would know who hired him, right?"

"Maybe not." Mikah shook his head. "He's too paranoid. He likes to keep his clients protected—and his own ass covered. He'll fill any order that comes in on a credit float. No questions . . . no ID." No responsibility, and no risk.

"Jeezu—" I felt frustration strangle the disgust inside me. That meant that even if I could get into DeAth's brain and pick it, it probably wouldn't get me anywhere. "There's got to be some kind of record, someplace. What about numbers on the credit transfers?"

He thought about it. "Yeah, maybe. . . . But if you think his lab was a deathtrap, his personal accounts are gonna make that look like a park. Nobody sane would try a data raid on him."

I hit the table with the wrong hand; winced and swore. "Damn it," I said, "there's got to be somebody on the Market good enough. I want to access those fucking files. Who's the best?"

Mikah tugged on the silver ring in the side of his nose. "Unh. I did say nobody sane. . . ." He half smiled. "Maybe you're talking about Deadeye. He does things nobody else can. Nobody knows how. But only when he feels like it. A real hostile son of a bitch."

" 'Deadeye'? He like to pick off his visitors with a stungun, or what?"

Mikah laughed. "I heard he's dropped a couple . . . but maybe that's just hype. I dunno, could be his rep as a cracksman. . . . Could be the fact that he's got a dead eye." He shrugged, still laughing behind his own eyes.

"A dead eye," I said.

"Yeah. Looks like shit, all festering." He wasn't joking.

"How come he doesn't get it fixed?"

"I told you, he's half crazy. But he's a wire wizard, if he'll deal."

I started to get up. "Let's go find out."

"Hey—" he said, his disappointment showing. "Don't you want to stay for the show?"

I glanced at the stage, still empty and waiting in the darkness above the crowded floor. "I've done it."

He sighed, and stood up. "Right."

We made it through the crowd to the door without any more distractions, and took the Tube under the bay.

Deadeye's part of town was a lot less choice than DeAth's, although down in the Deep End that probably didn't make a whole lot of difference. We waded through drifts of trash to a barricaded iron door large enough to swallow a tram. It was the entrance to what looked like an abandoned warehouse. There was no flicker of any security; no sign that anybody even lived there, or ever had. "How do you know he's here?" I asked.

"He never goes out." Mikah raised his fist to beat on the door —jumped back with a curse as it hit the metal. "Shit! It's electrified." He shook out his hand, looking at me, half exasperated and half embarrassed. "You got any ideas? You're the one who wanted to meet him."

I looked at the door, up the silent, windowless building front. "Yeah. I'll give him a call."

"He doesn't have a phone."

I smiled. "I don't need one."

He tapped his head. "What makes you think that'll make him glad to see you?"

"I got nothing to lose." I shrugged.

He grunted. "Excuse me while I cross the street," he said. *Just in case Deadeye decided to fry me.* He stepped back, but only about a meter.

I folded my arms, hugging my chest, centering myself. I let my mind out into the block of formless darkness that was the warehouse,

that held one fragile star, the energy of a living human mind. Somewhere. . . .

There. *Contact.* I went in through the shell of spidery radiance,
weaving my way into the pattern of a stranger's thoughts; surprised,
when I didn't find the dead black walls of illegal augmentation I'd
expected. I moved on, a thief entering a sleeping house, not bothering
to cover the sound of my footsteps as I got ready to give Deadeye one
hell of a big surprise—

A fist of raw energy smashed into me, searing the filaments like
a beam of coherent light. I let go and bolted, breaking all contact,
shutting down, walling up my own mind behind a jumble of barbed
wire.

"Ah—!" My own shout of surprise, still loud in my ears. I was
back on the street again, staring at a blank wall, with eyes that were
ready to jump out of my head. "Jeezu! You didn't tell me he was a
telepath!"

Mikah had backed up a few more steps, away from contamination.
He was staring, but his expression changed as the words registered on
him. "A freak?" he said, loud with disbelief. "I didn't know he was
a freak—"

I held up my hands, waving him quiet; braced for another attack
. . . for something that didn't come. Slowly, carefully this time, I let
out a tracer, hunting Deadeye through the darkness again. . . . Found
him, balled up tight as a clenched fist behind his own barbed wire;
fear so strong it made me feel sick oozed out of him like sweat. He
had a lot of raw psi talent, but he didn't know how to use it the way
I did. I could see the chinks in his defenses; taking him would be easy.
But I could see, too, that if I broke through now he'd go right over
the edge. I touched him, barely; let him prick the finger of my thought
just to get his attention. And then I backed off, letting him feel me
go, letting him know that I wasn't going to come back . . . leaving
him alone, there in the dark.

I shook my head, seeing Mikah's face again, the question in his
eyes. "No good. You were right. He *is* half crazy." I glanced at the
sealed door, the blank, unyielding walls. "Now I know why, anyhow.
Come on. Let's get out of here."

Mikah nodded and shrugged. He hunched his shoulders as we
began to walk away, keeping his distance.

There was a *clank* and a grating scrape behind us, as the iron
door swung open. Somebody stepped outside, shapeless, anonymous,
inside a heavy load of mismatched clothes. But I didn't have any

trouble making out his face—the raw, weeping sore where his right eye should have been. I looked away again, fast.

"Who is it?" he asked, his voice hoarse, like he hadn't used it in weeks. "Which one of you?"

For just a second I thought he was completely blind, that he couldn't see us. But then I realized what he was really asking. "Me," I said. I took a step forward. (Me.) I laid the picture in the barely open fist of his thoughts as carefully and nervously as I'd pass over a piece of crystal. I hadn't done this in a long time.

His mind spasmed shut over it; crushing it. Opened again, millimeter by millimeter, until a finger tendrilled out, beckoning me. (Come here.) His real hand twitched, hidden inside a frayed glove; trying to gesture in case I hadn't understood.

I moved toward him, not really wanting to get any closer, but not seeing how I had any choice. I kept trying to look at his face, but my eyes slid away again every time that oozing socket came into focus. I wondered how the hell he could leave it like that, untreated. I wondered how long he'd been wearing those same clothes. I could smell him before I got nearly as close as he wanted me to.

He stood staring at me, his good eye squinting, as if even this gloom was too bright for him. Glance by glance I filled in a face covered by a bristle of half-shaved beard. He was nearly bald, and he'd half shaved what hair he had left, too. His whole head was pale and lumpy, like something made of dough. His teeth looked rotten. I couldn't tell how old he was; he looked middle-aged, but maybe not. His one good eye was as green as a perfect emerald.

His gloved hand rose up to my face. I managed not to jerk away as it groped me like a curious spider, and dropped to his side again. He was just proving to himself that I was real. (Telepath—?) he asked. I nodded. (What . . . what do you want?) The uncertain mutter of his thoughts inside my head said he hadn't used that voice in a long time, either.

(I need some help. I want to access a system.)

His mind clenched up, eased open again. (Whose?)

(He calls himself Doctor Death.)

His fist shot out, catching me by the front of my shirt, catching me off-guard. "Who sent you here?" he rasped, losing control, snapping the thread of real contact.

I forced his hand away; took a breath as he backed off. I felt Mikah shifting from foot to foot behind me, weapon-systems armed. (Nobody sent me.) I dropped my guard just enough, and let him pry until he believed me. (I need some information that only DeAth's got. I can pay—)

(Go away.) He turned his back on me, began to shuffle toward his door.

My hands tightened. (Wait! How long's it been? Since you felt this? Since you had somebody who could really talk to you—)

He stopped, and faced me again. My eyes cringed; I made myself see through him with that other set of eyes, until his surface disappeared. I felt him remember something, *a touch, words that weren't spoken but only* were *—but it was so long, so unbearably long ago; could have been just a dream.* . . . The one eye that he still had got red-rimmed and watery-looking; his Adam's apple jerked up and down in his throat. Finally he nodded, silent with his mind, lifting his hand to wave me after him as he started back toward his door.

I followed, with Mikah treading on my heels, his face expressionless, his mind locked on *ready*.

"Who's that?" Deadeye stopped short suddenly, blocking the doorway, looking at Mikah.

"My brother," I said, and Mikah's mouth twitched.

"He don't look much like you," Deadeye mumbled. But that was all he said. He started on again, letting us follow him inside.

We went on through the dark, echoing space of the warehouse, Mikah hanging onto my sleeve because he couldn't see without his night lenses. I could feel him wondering why it seemed like we could when he couldn't.

Finally there was real light ahead again. Deep inside the warehouse Deadeye had built his room, his refuge. It wasn't what I'd expected. His world was lit by a single stick-on glowplate, but it was neat, ascetic, clean; it had dull but decent furniture, a portable kitchen unit, and a simple console, the kind everybody who had a place to put one had to have, so that daily life could go on. Mikah was right—there was no vidphone plugged into it. Deadeye didn't even have a threedy. But it was plain he wasn't hurting for money. He wanted it this way.

He sat down in an ancient rocking chair, and picked up something from the box lying beside it. I saw a pair of long, thick needles, tangled in what looked like a ruined sweater. He untangled the mess with hands that knew just what they were doing. I felt Mikah tense up beside me as he tried to guess whether it was a weapon. I shook my head, glancing at him, and he eased off.

Deadeye set the chair rocking with his foot and began to work the needles through the yarn, feeding more bright-colored thread into the sweater, until I realized he was actually making it out of nothing. The chair creaked, the needles clicked; he never looked up at us standing there waiting. He'd never had anybody all the way in here before; not even once.

I moved on into the room, sat down cross-legged on the floor in front of him. (What is that stuff?) I thought, focusing on the motion of his hands.

(Knitting.) The wordsign flickered on in my mind: images of needles performing an ancient dance with yarn, turning it into a hundred different patterns and shapes.

(What do you do it for?)

(It feels good.) He looked up at me, for half a second; looked down again when I flinched at the sudden sight of his face. (Eye make you sick, does it?)

I nodded.

(Supposed to. Keeps 'em off me.) *Everybody else.*

(That could kill you.)

His face rearranged itself until I realized he was smiling—the way somebody would smile who'd just glued your feet into your shoes. (Not unless I look in a mirror.) That was no rotting sore on his face; it was only a cosmo piece, a joke, a trick.

"No shit," I said, feeling my own mouth start to smile in relief, even while my eyes were still refusing to believe it. Mikah jerked upright on the couch across the room, startled by the broken silence.

(Who are you?) Deadeye asked me, finally.

(Cat.)

(Where'd you come from?)

(Ardattee. Quarro.)

I felt his irritation sting me; I wasn't giving him anything that meant anything, that words alone couldn't say. (You a 'breed?)

I nodded.

(Thought so.) The warped smile squeezed out of him again. (Why aren't you crazy?) The one eye looked into me, too knowing.

I glanced down. (Dumb luck,) thinking of Siebeling. I felt him groping, nagging, pushing. . . . I let down more defenses, loosened more knots; let him creep into my mind and take a look around, answering his own questions. Picking through my past like a dog nosing over trash. My body went rigid muscle by muscle, while I struggled to keep my mind loose and open.

He grunted, and blinked, and broke contact. One hand let go of his knitting . . . reached out, pulled back again, and picked up the thread. After that there was no sound but clicking needles; no other motion, no other sign. Nothing but a wall of tangled wire and despair.

I sat waiting, taking deep breaths. (Goddamn it,) I thought finally, slamming it through his guard, (you got what you wanted from me! What do I get from you?)

He jumped like he'd been shocked. He looked up at me, his one eye red and wet. He put out his hand again, reaching for me. I braced, ready to pull back. But he only patted my shoulder twice, gently, and took his hand away again. I stayed where I was, too surprised to do anything at all.

(You got a job you need done,) he thought, as if I hadn't told him that before.

I nodded.

(Why don't you do it yourself?)

I touched my head. (Not wired.)

He smiled that smirking joker's smile again, as if he knew something the rest of the universe didn't. But he only asked, (Why me? This?) Touching his own head. He'd thought nobody knew about his psi; he'd tried to keep it that way.

(No.) I waved a hand at Mikah. (He says you're the best. The only one can do it.)

He looked down at his knitting again; needles clicked in the silence. Mikah rearranged himself restlessly on the couch, wishing he was somewhere else.

(Can you do it? Crack that system?)

Calm confidence seeped into my mind, all the answer Deadeye needed to make. Mikah hadn't lied.

(Will you?)

(Why?)

I felt my muscles start to tighten up again. (I said I can pay—)

(Why—?) Not why should he. Why did I want it done—what did I want to know?

I showed him. He hadn't even heard about the human bomb. He took it all in, while I waited some more, counting my heartbeats.

He looked up again at last. (Might be worth it.)

I grinned, sitting back. (Where's your ware? You got it in a separate room?) Looking around this room again, I noticed the heap of knitted things beside the door; but still not even enough tech to make a phone call. And there was no bioware hidden inside his skull. If he even had an access jack, I couldn't feel it.

He actually chuckled this time. It sounded like clearing phlegm. (Don't need any.)

Shit— I blocked it before he heard me. He *was* crazy, the old bastard. "Forget it—" I started to get up.

(I don't need any.) The image filled my head again; clear, hard, insistent.

I stood looking down at him. "That's impossible."

He shook his head. (That's what they want us to believe. . . . That's what they believe themselves. I stumbled over the truth. Probably others have.)

(But you don't pass it on.)

(Why should I? What would it get me, except trouble?)

I thought about it. He was right. (Why are you telling me?)

(Because you understand what it means, to be a psion, and live by stealing.) He looked down again. (Because you're good, and I might need your help.)

(You mean you'd show me how? We'd do it together?) Excitement and fear collided inside me.

(Maybe.) His good eye turned noncommittal. (How's your memory?)

(Perfect.)

(Good.) He dropped his knitting over the side and stood up. (A lot to learn, first.) He trudged across the room to his console, and woke it up. For a minute I thought we were going to start in right there; but he was only calling up library files.

"You ready?" Mikah asked, his voice sharp with uneasy impatience. Both of us jumped at the sound of it.

"Almost." I almost forgot to answer him out loud. I held up a hand.

Deadeye turned back to me, handing over a headset. (Memorize these data. Teaches you as much as anything can about how a machine's mind functions. It can save your life. Don't come back unless you know it all. Then we'll see.)

I nodded, took the headset and pushed it into my pocket.

(Bring that back. Only one I have.)

I nodded again.

He moved toward the door, suggesting with the motion that we should get out. He stopped suddenly as he reached the pile of clothes, and scooped up an armload. He went on out, carrying the heap with him into the darkness.

When we reached the street he herded us through the door, and then he dropped the load of knitting onto the pavement beside the building.

"He's dumping that out?" Mikah asked, as if that only proved to him that Deadeye was out of his mind.

Deadeye shrugged. (What about him?) he asked me, glaring at Mikah.

(He's my brother,) I said again.

He went back inside without saying anything, and slammed the door. Mikah was still staring at the pile of clothes.

"He doesn't need them," I said finally; explaining, because somehow I had to. "Somebody'll come along who does." Already it felt like having to put my thoughts into words before I could get them out was as hard as walking uphill.

Mikah gave me a Look, and started to turn away. He turned back again, as curiosity tipped the scales on his irritation. Searching through the pile of knitted things, he found a long red scarf and wrapped it around his throat. I picked up the brown-green sweater that landed at my feet and pulled it on over my torn shirt. It felt good, heavy and warm. There was a dank chill to the air here. As we started away down the street, Mikah said, "That was the strangest fucking fifteen minutes I've spent since the day you disappeared on Cinder." He made a small noise in the back of his throat; still trying to shake the feeling of being deaf and dumb, and invisible.

"Could be worse."

He looked at me.

"You could feel like that all the time." I touched the patch behind my ear.

He looked blank, for a minute. Then he asked, "How's the stuff you got from DeAth doing for you?"

"Doing its job," I said. "Just fine."

He nodded, but he didn't smile. "So what about your freakin' cousin back there—?" He flicked the end of the red scarf. "He gonna do the job after all?"

"Think so." I sighed, feeling a weight lift off me as I realized that I'd already done the hardest part of my work, just getting through to him. "I got to go back and see him again in a couple days." I hesitated. "Keep it sealed that he's a freak."

He nodded. "What was on that hairnet he handed you?"

I felt in my pocket for the headset. "I can't tell you."

He looked interested, but he only shrugged. "No problem." On the streets half of what you knew was never more than a jigsaw puzzle with pieces missing, anyway. We went on to the Tube station, talking about the weather.

"You going back to the club?" he asked, as we got on board together and the waiting transit sucked us away from the memory of Deadeye.

"Not tonight." Not sure when I was going to see Argentyne again, or what I'd say to her if I ever did, after what I'd said to her tonight.

"Oh, yeah." He smirked. "I forgot. You got one hot body waiting up for you." His grin got wider as the trans sighed to a stop in the next station. "Me too. See you." He flipped me a salute, and went away down the platform, whistling.

TWENTY-THREE

"AUNTIE'S SICK." Jiro was sitting on the stairs as I came into the house, his face propped in his hands, his eyes shadowed, his thoughts dark.

I stopped dead, pictures of poison or biocontamination strobing in my brain. "Where is she? In the hospital?" Elnear had looked all right when I'd left the office with her: tired and depressed, but that wasn't surprising. I'd even watched her get into the secured private mod that would carry her straight here.

He shook his head. "She's just in her room. I guess she's asleep. She fainted or something when she came home. Charon sent our meds to see her; they said it's just because of all the—" He broke off. "What happened, I mean . . . you know. And because she's old. They gave her some stuff. She has to rest."

I nodded, relieved. But if Elnear had been depressed before, this wasn't going to make her feel any better. "Thanks," I said, and started past him up the stairs. Stopped, looking back. "Is your mother here?"

He twisted on the steps to look up at me. "Why?" he asked, a little too loudly.

"Just wondered." I shrugged, trying not to act like it mattered, and went on up to my room. I stood looking out the window, feeling tired, flexing my sore hand. Maybe tomorrow I'd get it treated somewhere, like Aspen had told me to. I still had trouble realizing that I had the credit to fix things I didn't like. As I stood looking out into the darkness, it began to rain. It only rained at night here. The taMings always fixed the things they didn't like.

I heard Jiro come into the room behind me, like I'd known he would, sooner or later. The darkness behind his eyes hadn't been because Elnear was sick, so it had to be something else. I turned away from the windows, went to the bed and sat down. "What is it?" I asked, even though I was pretty sure I knew.

He opened his mouth, the words that he'd held bottled up inside him ready to burst out. But still he couldn't say them, for a long minute. "You—my mother—I mean . . ." His hands flapped. "Did you—do that with my mother?"

I looked down at my own hands resting across my knees. "You mean, did I spend the night with her?" I looked up at him again, and nodded.

His face got red. He'd expected me to deny it, even if it was true. Somehow the fact that I didn't look ashamed about it made him feel ashamed instead. He began to blink hard; his mouth trembled.

"Come here," I said. He came across the room. "Sit down." He sat on the bed, keeping his distance, staring at the floor. "How did you know?" I asked.

"My mother . . . I saw her come out of your room the other morning, real early. She didn't know I saw her. And she acted so . . . different." His voice squeaked.

"You know," I said, "the first time I met her you damn near acted like a pimp, pushing her at me. No, I'm not saying it was your fault—" as he looked up with sudden anger in his eyes. "It just happened. . . . I only wondered how come it bothers you so much, now that it has. Because of what I am?"

He shook his head, his jaw clenched.

Very carefully, I let myself into his memory, looking for the answer he wouldn't give me.

"Because of what you saw at Argentyne's club." Until that night he'd been like any other kid, his curiosity about sex practically an obsession. But then in five minutes he'd learned more than he'd ever wanted to know. "You think it was like that, what your mother and I did?" I felt my face pinch with his pain.

This time he nodded, blushing again.

"Jiro. . . ." I broke off. "What you saw there—that wasn't making love. That wasn't even good sex. More like rape." He looked at me now, out of the corner of his eye. "There is a difference."

"Are you going to marry my mother?"

"Your mother's already married."

He half frowned. "She could get a divorce. Aren't you in love with her—?" Fantasies were starting to pop like bubbles in his mind.

I looked away. "I don't know. I don't think so."

"Isn't she in love with you?"

I shook my head. "She's just not in love with Charon." I felt the bone-deep ache of his disappointment; couldn't think of anything I could do that would ease it. Finally I said, "I think she loved your father . . . I know she loves you, and your sister. You're more important to her than anything else in her life. Be glad." *You could have been me.* But I didn't say it. I wondered what it would be like to have been born a taMing, to have anything I ever wanted. . . . I couldn't even imagine it. Even if I hadn't been born rich—just to have had somebody there, all those years . . . anybody. I looked away from him, down at my scarred hands.

He got up, slowly. "My mother said for me to ask if you'd . . . think about her, tonight."

"Yeah," I said. "I'll do that. Good night, Jiro."

He straightened his shoulders, trying hard to look like a man and not a boy. "Good night, Cat." He went out of the room.

I stayed where I was, listening to the lonely sound of the rain. I wasn't ready to sleep, or in the mood to think about Lazuli right now. With a kind of surprise I realized it was Elnear I was still thinking about . . . worried about. I let my mind track until it found her. She was in her bed, but she wasn't any closer to sleep than I was. The sedative the doctor had given her hadn't been enough to take hold against her body's own overdose of adrenaline. But her mind wasn't on tomorrow or today or even yesterday any more. It was caught in a place where memory was like something seen in a dark mirror: where the image of a perfect afternoon in the Hanging Gardens of Quarro with the man she loved made her dizzy with misery; where the image of Talitha as a laughing baby filled her with sorrow. A place inside her that she couldn't escape from, because the past was still so much sweeter than anything she thought of when she let it go, and tried to listen to the rain. . . .

I got up again and went out, back through the dark, quiet halls to her room. There was a thin line of light tracing the crack under her door. I knocked.

"Yes—?" I heard the word quaver with her surprise; felt her surprise behind my eyes.

"It's Cat."

There was silence for a minute. Then, "Come in," she said.

The door wasn't locked. I went into the room, suddenly feeling more than a little self-conscious. But she looked up at me, her face mapped with shadows, and smiled. It was almost relief she felt, now that I was here.

That made me smile too, a little, while I searched for something to say now that I'd come. "Jiro told me you were sick, ma'am. I just wanted to know if you'll need me in the morning. And to . . . to know if you need anything now."

"Yes," she said, suddenly not afraid to say it. "Sit with me for a while, if you would. I need some companionship, more than anything else. The one thing that no one has thought to offer me." She glanced down, and back at me. "I feel terribly alone tonight . . . and somehow I don't find it difficult to tell you that. I suppose because I think you probably already know that, and that it was why you came." Her eyes held mine until I looked away. "Thank you for coming." She was gathering things up from the surface of the bedcover as she spoke; restless holos of familiar faces that had been trying to keep her company, and failing.

I sat down on the edge of a tapestry-covered chair, still afraid of breaking something as I glanced around the room. A single lamp with a shade made of stained-glass flowers turned the room's light soft and warm. The furniture here was old and elegant, like most of the furniture in the house. I stared at the face of a woman carved on the back of a desk across the room, her long hair flowing down into the grain of the wood. I looked back again at the pictures of faces gathered in Elnear's hands: Jiro and Talitha, and Kelwin taMing.

"I hadn't thought of it before, but sometimes it must be a kind of blessing to be a telepath," Elnear said. "To be able to know that someone else is out there, thinking about you, even when you can't see or hear them."

"Sometimes," I said. "Sometimes it's just looking in through the windows of houses where you aren't wanted." *In the land of the blind.* I shrugged. "But like you said once, everything looks better when you don't have to live with it, I guess." And being what I was, not human enough, not Hydran enough, even that much was better than the alternative . . . better than nothing.

She smiled again, and nodded. "Yes, I suppose so. If I'm lonely, at least I still have my privacy intact."

I settled back a little uncertainly into the curved hollow of the chair. "When I was with other psions, I used to have it both ways—the sharing, and the—solitude, when I wanted it. It was . . ." I looked away, into my own dark mirrors. Trying to feel something that made sense when I looked at my memories; only feeling numb. Drugged . . .

I made myself remember Deadeye: how even with him, twisted up like he was, it had been so much easier—to speak without words, to just *know.* The way it should have been; the way it ought to be. The way it must have been for the Hydrans, before the humans ended it. "Humans are so . . ." groping for the words, when it would be so much easier just to show her—

"Pathetic?" Elnear murmured. "Is that what you're thinking?"

I looked up at her; looked away again as soon as I met her eyes.

"But you lived that way yourself for most of your life, didn't you?" she said quietly. "Unable to know another person's thoughts. I would think that would give you more sympathy for the way we are than most humans are capable of themselves . . . more compassion."

My eyes squeezed shut as something spun and dropped suddenly inside me. "I don't know." I shook my head. "All I know is none of you can understand what it's really like, to have what I had, after a lifetime of nothing—and then to lose it again. I didn't know what was missing all those years. But now I know—" And finally I understood why being a telepath again was so important to me: because it was all I'd ever had that was really mine.

"But you have it back," she said, a little surprised.

I shook my head. "If I go on using these drugs, I'll burn it out for good."

She hadn't understood that. "Then, if you're only doing this because of me, you should stop now."

I shook my head again. "I can't."

"I don't want to be—"

"I can't."

She looked at me.

I rubbed my face. "Don't ask. Just forget I said that." I started to get up.

"I can't," she said.

I stopped.

"But if you wish, we can pretend that I have. If that will let you stay, and humor a lonely old woman a while longer." Her mouth pulled up into a smile that was half regret and half irony. Her hands held the pictures a little tighter.

I sat down again, trying not to look as awkward as I felt right then. Watching her hands, I asked, "How come you never had any children—you and your husband?"

She looked down at the holos. "We always thought there would be plenty of time." Suddenly she was blinking too much, as she stared at her husband's face. "Isn't it strange, how any little thing can—set off your memory, when you least expect it. A song, a certain light . . . Sometimes, when I remember my life with Kelwin, it seems to me as if those are someone else's memories that have somehow gotten inside my head. That the person with him, that I remember so well, can't possibly be me. It makes it so difficult . . . almost unbearable, sometimes. And yet not ever to think about them is more unbearable. And the worst part is that it's the *good* memories that hurt me the most."

"Yeah," I whispered.

"Tell me about your family," she said, trying to change the subject. It struck her as odd and humiliating that she'd never even pictured me having any. She wondered suddenly if she'd been afraid to, knowing what I was. And she wondered what it would feel like to live as a Hydran . . .

I wondered too. "Nothing to tell." I shrugged, looking away. There was a time when I'd wanted to search for my mother's people. But then I'd killed Rubiy. And after that there hadn't seemed to be much point in it; because by killing him I'd proved that I could never be one of them.

Elnear pressed her lips together, and didn't let herself ask again. At last she said, "Cat, do you ever wonder, when you relive that awful loss . . . feel that sinking-into-a-hole darkness . . ." her gaze got lost somewhere, "if perhaps you feel that way not because you're so different from the rest of us, but because you're so human?" She glanced up at me; I felt her trying to reach out to something inside me—something she wasn't sure even still existed.

I felt myself clench up, in a kind of angry reflex. But then I made myself look at her again, face her reality, acknowledge all the things about her that had made her matter to me . . . admit that *human* wasn't a four-letter word. "Siebeling said . . . he told me not to—to pretend I'm something I'm not." I looked down at my hands, suddenly wishing that I had pictures to hold. "That I'm not really human, I mean. Most of the freaks I know are human, every way except one. . . . Even the Hydrans I've met are more human than they want to be."

"Most humans are more human than they want to be, too," she said quietly.

I half smiled. "Thanks. . . ." I got to my feet.

"For what?" she asked.

"For reminding me that if humans and Hydrans didn't have something in common, I wouldn't be here."

She laughed. I liked the sound of her laughter. "That's an unusual sweater," she said, really seeing me for the first time tonight. "Wherever did you find it?"

"Lying in the street. Good night, ma'am."

"Good night," she murmured, looking after me a little oddly.

I smiled as I left her, figuring that at least I'd left her with something to wonder about besides the future; something to think about besides the lonely night and the rain.

But it didn't leave me with much else to think about, by the time I reached my room again. I pulled Deadeye's headset out of my pocket and put it on; stretched out on the bed with my hands behind my head and filled the empty places with all the data I could swallow in one dose. There was still a lot of information left waiting when I pulled it off again. Then finally I closed my eyes, and let the static in my brain sing my aching body to sleep.

I woke up again with a start, for no reason that I could name, hours later. My mind was quiet now, and it let the grayness come seeping back as I listened to the rain. Listening, I wondered about how the sound of rain seemed to fill my mind with the same kind of longings and sorrows that I'd seen in Elnear's. I could count on the fingers of one hand the number of times I'd heard it rain. I hadn't had a lifetime of listening to it to make it mean more to me than the simple sound of dripping water. I remembered the way I'd felt when I'd first set foot on Earth . . . a total stranger, and yet somehow coming home. Remembered what Elnear had been trying to show me this evening: that the human side of me had its own needs, its own history; and that not everything it felt was something I had to be ashamed of. And I realized that for the first time in a long time I didn't feel angry.

I thought about Lazuli then, wondered if she was lying awake in Charon's bed, not alone but always lonely, listening to the rain. *She wanted me to think about her.* . . . I wondered if she meant it the way I thought she did. I wondered if she was thinking about me, missing me. I knew that even if she was, her thoughts didn't go much further than the way my body fit into hers. *I'd been a pullover, and she'd known it—*

I waited for that to make me angry. But it only made me remember the feel of my body fitting into hers. . . . There'd been too many others who'd really fucked me over. Why should I be angry at a bored, unhappy, beautiful woman who'd only wanted some boytoy to fuck her brains out. . . . Maybe it didn't really matter why she wanted me; not when just thinking about that smooth perfume-scented skin, her hair like silk down across my chest, was enough to make my head swim. But it wasn't going to happen again. Not tonight. Especially not like this. I told myself to forget about her, and go to sleep. I told myself I wasn't crazy; I told myself I was. I told myself she was using me again. . . . I told myself if she really wanted me to think about her tonight, I could make sure she never forgot it. . . .

I let go of my thoughts, reaching out into the emptiness, spreading a net of invisible threads tipped with light. I pictured the Crystal Palace in my mind, not so far away that my mind couldn't reach it, reach inside, searching through the dark silences for a familiar star.

I found her, side by side with Charon. Asleep, dreaming a dim, restless dream about suffocating in a windowless room. I drifted past the sullen heat of Charon's sleeping mind without looking in, and closed focus to enter Lazuli's. I slipped into her dream, as softly as a thief . . . felt her body quiver and stir, not quite waking; felt her dream change to include me. I lay down beside her inside her dream, and let my mind begin to touch her the way my hands, my body, ached to do . . . fired the nerve strings that fed her mind every sensation I could have given her, moving over her, against her, inside her. . . .

Somewhere in the middle of it she woke. (You wanted me to,) I whispered, (you asked for me. . . .) Gentling her, reassuring her, so that she didn't cry out but only let herself drift back down into her yearning . . . feeling the sensations of her pleasure doubled as her hands began to touch her body, the way my hands were already touching my own. Until the beam of white heat joining us mind to mind exploded like a sun, and left us alone in our separate bodies, back in our separate worlds again, only sharing the sound of the rain.

In the morning when I woke I knew more about artificial intelligence than I'd ever wanted to . . . and less than ever about what in hell I was really doing here, waking up in this bed, playing cat and mouse in it while I played ratcatcher for the taMings. I wondered what Lazuli was trying to do—to herself, to me. If she really didn't care whether Charon found out; if she was really that stupid, or that unhappy. Or whether she just didn't care because she thought if anything happened because of this, it wouldn't happen to her. . . .

Feeling numb and out-of-control, I got up and slapped on Dead-eye's headset again. I fed my brain as much new data as it would take; forcing it, to keep from thinking about what I was doing—and because the sooner I knew everything he wanted me to know, the sooner I could get at the information I really wanted, and maybe get out of here. Then I stumbled downstairs to find something to feed my body, to get it through another day.

Talitha came shyly into the dining room, stood staring at me while I heaped my plate with the usual morning leftovers. I ignored her, my brain buzzing too loud, until finally she came across the room and tugged on my sweater.

"I want more," she said.

"You've got the right idea, kid," I said. "You'll make a good taMing." I went on filling up my plate.

"I want more grapes." She looked up at me, waiting, her small face as perfect as a flower, and just as blank. "Grapes—" She tugged harder on me, and threw in a grudging, "Please?"

I handed her a clump of grapes. "Thank you," she said gravely.

"Sure." I nodded, feeling just a little crummy.

"Auntie said we're going to pick berries this morning!" she announced, around a mouthful of fat green globes.

"Great," I mumbled, through a haze of binary code sequences and half a piece of bread.

"You can come too. I'll show you how, because you don't know how to do anything right." She began to tug on my arm. "Come on—"

I shook my head, red-faced and half smiling; not sure if I could think of a worse way to spend the morning if I tried. "I got things I have to—"

"Please join us, Cat." Lazuli stepped into the room, into my line of sight, and changed my mind with a glance. She was dressed in a transparent tunic patterned with leaves, over an electric-blue bodycover that somehow only made what it was covering up more obvious. She didn't say anything else; didn't need to, when her mind was saying it all.

I nodded slowly, choked down another bite of spiced bun that suddenly could have been plastic.

Elnear came into the room, carrying her art console; dressed like she usually was, as if she didn't want anybody to look at her for long. The contrast between them almost hurt my eyes. "Yes, won't you come——?" she asked, missing my nod. I bit my tongue for wanting to say the obvious, with Lazuli's eyes still burning a hole in my flesh, and couldn't think of anything else.

And so somehow I found myself in the autumn forest out on the mountainside above the taMings' private valley, with the smell of damp earth filling my head the way buzzing data strings filled my brain. The things Elnear called golden raspberries grew not-really-wild in a patch of jagged leaves and thorns. We picked them, and it was everything I'd expected it to be. I hated every minute of it. It reminded me of trying to pick answers out of Daric's mind . . . it reminded me of digging ore in the Mines on Cinder: Picking something fragile and perfect out of a matrix that didn't want to give it up, where any wrong move could mean pain. . . .

"You don't look like you're enjoying this very much, Cat," Elnear said, peering out at me from underneath her wide-brimmed hat. She looked happier and more relaxed than I'd ever seen her. I shrugged.

"He doesn't know how to have fun," Talitha said; I heard Jiro laugh, too sharply, somewhere behind my back. "That's why I'm helping him." She was eating berries out of my hand as fast as I picked them.

"Then let me help you, too." Lazuli slid a berry between my lips with deft, gentle fingers. It was as soft as her skin, the juice sweet and tangy as I crushed it with my tongue. "There," she said, "now you're smiling." Her body, her mind, were smiling at me—had been, helplessly, ever since she'd laid eyes on me this morning. Her awareness of me like a warm fluid slowly melting down through the ice of overlapping data inside my mind. "You know, I had a dream about you last night," she murmured. Her eyes laughed at the sudden panic in my own, even while they begged me to prove to her again that it hadn't been just a dream.

(It wasn't a dream.) I saw her face flush as I proved it. I looked down and away again, not answering her out loud, because Elnear was watching us too closely. I wished Lazuli wouldn't do this to me. I felt embarrassed, frustrated . . . on fire with the heat of the arousal I couldn't control as she imagined me reaching out to find her, to touch her, anywhere; like some kind of demon lover who could take her even while she lay asleep in her husband's bed, making her forget who she was and where, making her forget anything but the pleasure of being made love to impossibly. . . .

"Well," Elnear said, making us realize that we'd been standing there staring at each other like magnetic dolls for way too long. "I believe I'm going to try some sketching on down the slope. Do be careful—" Something in her voice made me look back at her. "It can be treacherous . . . when the leaves are wet, you know." One last glance, her eyes as transparent as blue glass, letting me know that she understood: everything that was happening, how it felt to be young, how it felt to be lonely . . . how it felt to dance on a minefield. "Do be careful," she murmured again, glancing at Lazuli this time. "Come with me, children—" She waved to Talitha and Jiro. "I've brought a special treat for you."

Lazuli looked after her, half troubled and half self-conscious, as Elnear guided the children away, leaving us alone together intentionally, pointedly. Not giving us her blessing . . . but giving us room to breathe. Talitha ran ahead, squealing and scuffling through the leaves while Jiro trailed behind, looking back over his shoulder at us, his expression more like his mother's than he knew.

When they were gone we settled side by side on the blanket, our bodies not quite touching, while I wove a band of warm contact between us. She fed me berries between long deep kisses. Light showered down through the trees, haloing her hair; making the restless ceiling over our heads into a living window of stained glass. Looking up into all that beauty, I wondered if this was how someone had gotten the idea. And I wondered if it was really so impossible to be happy in a place like this. . . .

The call function began to beep on my databand. I sat up, startled; looked down to be sure the bandphone video was off before I answered. It was already on . . . had been on, transmitting for God only knew how long. I hadn't done it; I knew I hadn't. Lazuli's face paled as I swore, blocking the image with my hand. "Braedee—?" I said, my voice white.

I hadn't turned on the receiver, either, but his voice said, "Checkmate." And that was all.

TWENTY-FOUR

I DID MY BEST to make Lazuli believe that Braedee wouldn't talk, without telling her why. I had to believe he only meant that we were back where we'd started, because now he had something on me that could hurt me plenty—just like I had on him. That was the way he wanted it; the way he liked it. But somehow after that she couldn't shut out reality any more, and neither could I. We went on down the hill through a golden rain of leaves, looking for Elnear; not touching, not even speaking much.

That night she stayed with Charon in the Crystal Palace. She didn't ask me to think about her, but part of her wanted to. I thought about her anyway, but this time I kept my thoughts to myself. Braedee didn't make contact with me again, and I didn't return his call. I told myself that I wanted to wait until I had the information Deadeye was going to help me get; knowing that I was really stalling just because I didn't have the guts to face him without it.

By the next day Elnear was itching to get back to work, and so was I. The last of Deadeye's data was filtering down into my mind; by the time night came around I'd be ready to pay him another visit. The usual morning in the office seemed to go by in slow motion. I wasn't sure if it was because what was filling my mind was so strange, or because it made everything else too normal.

Finally I took a break, giving my restless thoughts some space. I didn't get far down the hallway before somebody's hand caught my shoulder, jerking me back and around. *Daric*. I hadn't sensed him coming up behind me; probably because he hadn't wanted me to.

"You bastard," he said, shoving me up against the wall like we were the only two people in the entire building. I didn't have to look past the rage in his eyes to know the reason: Argentyne. But buried below the pain there was something more—sheer terror was wearing his fury like body armor. The only reason I wasn't dead of an embolism or a heart attack right now was that he knew he couldn't get past my guard. "Come with me." He jerked me forward again. I let him lead me through the halls to the same whiteroom he'd used with Stryger. He sealed it, turned back to me. "You little shit—" he said; broke off, and had to start again. "You turned her against me. She said she never wants to see me again. She said to ask you why. . . . *Why?*"

"Because I told her the truth about what you are," I said.

"What do you mean?" He held me with his eyes, fists trembling at his sides while he fought himself for control. "She knows everything about me—" The fear inside him was swelling until he was afraid it was going to choke one of us to death. "If she didn't hate me before, why should she now?"

"Now she knows what you do for Stryger—the truth about that girl you brought to Purgatory. You remember," I said, hardly recognizing my own voice, "the one Stryger hurt so bad you were afraid she'd die. The freak you bought to play victim for him."

"Is that all—?" Daric's whole body suddenly went slack with relief. "So what?" he said, and shrugged. "Nobody made the bitch to it. She didn't file any complaint."

After a long minute I asked softly, "How was it, watching him beat her up, Daric? How'd you like it? Was she a telepath, did she let you *feel* it? Is that what Stryger really likes? What you really want? Did you really wish it was you instead . . . or do you just get off on knowing Stryger's like all the rest of the deadheads, never guessing your secret—?"

He turned white. "Which secret?" he whispered.

(You're one of us,) I thought. (Freak. Teek. Psion.)

His mind struck at me like a snake. My own mind blocked the thrust of thought, and broke its back before it could reach me. I tossed his sending back at him. "You can't hurt me. You're not good enough." He'd never be good enough, even if he'd had training to teach him how to use it right. He didn't have that much talent. Being a psion had driven his whole life into this dead end, and he wasn't even a good one.

He turned away, his eyes searching the corners of the room. "No," he said, "no, no, no, no. This isn't real. It's impossible. No. No." He licked his lips, rubbed his hand over his mouth. Trying, after a lifetime, to believe it had finally happened. He turned back to me; I felt panic claw at the walls of his mind. "Who else did you tell? Argentyne, you told her. . . ."

"Yeah, I told her." I nodded, enjoying the look on his face. He wanted to smash my own face in, more than he'd ever wanted anything in his life. Now he knew how he'd made me feel.

"That's why she turned against me—"

"She doesn't give a damn about it," I said.

Incredulity fought its way out through his fury. "You're lying. You told her so she'd hate me—"

"Yeah. That's right, I did." Finally admitting it, to myself more than to him. "But she really didn't care. Not everybody's a bigot. If she hates you now, it's because you're a lousy bastard. Not because you're a psion."

Because you're a psion— His father's image filled his mind like a black storm: a child's terrifying night monster, etched forever on the lens of his memory. "Who else did you tell—?"

"Nobody."

His expression changed. *(Maybe,)* his mind said. *Maybe it still wasn't too late. . . .*

"Don't even think about it," I said. "You can't kill me yourself. And if you try to hire it out, I'll know. Nothing better happen to Argentyne either. Just think of me like a jar of toxins. You break me, and I take your whole world with me."

He wiped his mouth again with a trembling hand. "You son of a bitch. You freak! What do you want—money?"

I shook my head. "I'm getting plenty of that already."

"Then *what?*" Drops of spit glittered in the air between us.

I didn't answer. I wasn't used to having power over somebody; I was just beginning to realize how it felt . . . that it felt good. I looked at him, letting the dark, sweet pleasure fill me; letting him realize along with me how easy it would be for me to destroy him. He'd treated me like shit, and Jule, and everybody else he'd gotten close to; contaminated our lives like a disease. Destroying him would be a public service.

For just a second I cracked my defenses, let myself into his mind, wanting to enjoy the fear that must be eating his guts out right now—

It slammed into my thoughts, nauseating, bitter, blinding. I spat him out again, shaking my head. "I want . . ." I swallowed. "I want you to stop pimping for Stryger. If you ever get him another freak to work over, you're gone. That's all." I turned away, started for the door.

"No—" His hand clamped my arm like a binder. "Don't say that. That's not all, it can't be. You can't tell me you *know,* and then tell me you don't want anything. Tell me what you want from me!" He shook me, his whole body floundering with the motion.

I stood still, feeling myself go rigid under his hand. (Just leave me alone.)

His hand came loose and dropped to his side. He stayed where he was, motionless but still quivering, his mouth hanging open, slack and wet. I left him like that, sealing the door behind me as I went out, so that I didn't have to know what he did next.

Back in Elnear's office again I pretended to work, but I couldn't concentrate. Finally facing Daric, I'd broken the thin ice between the light and the dark. My mind was out of synch with the fantasy around me, the world that only existed as long as you believed in its reality. I was back in the nightworld, the otherworld, where people like Daric and Stryger really belonged . . . people like Mikah and Deadeye . . . people like me. I sat staring at the wall, seeing Oldcity, where I'd learned the truth—that light was an illusion, that only the darkness was forever, the night that had existed before there were stars, and would still be there long after they died.

I couldn't do Elnear's work, work that suddenly seemed meaningless and stupid, like her faith in human nature—and so I began to play with the terminal, trying out my new knowledge, trying to see if I could find Deadeye's secret passage to inner space on my own. But it was no use. I understood the tech of information storage, the interface of EM and chem that made up the artificial brains of an information net, that manipulated the data. But I couldn't find anything more that I had in common with it than I had in common with the molecules in a wall. After a while I gave up on that, too, wondering if there was even any point in going back to Deadeye's. But I knew I'd go back anyway.

The day's end finally came, and set me free. I took the Tube down under the bay, made my way on foot to Deadeye's building with

no problems; maybe because tonight I moved like I belonged here. I
buzzed his brain, and he let me in. "Where's your brother?" he said,
suspicious like always.

"He's someplace he'd rather be." I hadn't asked Mikah to come
with me this time. I figured we'd all be better off if I did this on my
own, even if it meant risking my skin on the streets.

Deadeye loosened up, with a grimace that looked like pain, but
that meant he was relieved. I'd forgotten how shitty his eye looked.
I tried to forget it again as I handed him back his headset. "I'm finished
with this."

(Let me see.)

I let him into my head, let him see for himself that the data had
all copied perfectly in my brain.

He nodded. (Think you're ready?)

I shrugged, and couldn't help remembering this afternoon—how
I'd tried, and failed.

(You don't believe it'll work,) he thought, reading my hesitation.
(Because you already tried it.) He laughed suddenly, a rusty, scraping
noise that said it figured. (Show me what you did.) He jerked his head
toward the console across the room.

I went to it and sat down, started to press the trodes to my forehead;
glanced back at him.

He nodded, his own mind riding piggyback inside mine. I did
what I'd done that afternoon, trying to make something real and recognizable out of that lifeless flow . . . failing again.

(No, no!) he said, too loud inside my brain. He jerked me loose
from the contacts. "You're doing it all wrong!" breaking into speech
as exasperation broke down his control.

The sudden noise hurt my ears. "Well, how'm I supposed to—"

(You're looking for something alive. It's not alive!) His mind
shut me up. "It's a *system,* you shithead," he said, slowly and too
clearly, like I was stupid. "It's only a system. You're not gonna find
anybody else in there."

"I know, but—"

"You don't know shit, kid. Those tapes didn't tell you everything.
You don't understand the important part—"

(Wait,) I thought. (Don't tell me. I've got Centauri's Corpses on
my back. I dunno if I'm being snooped.)

He frowned, but he nodded. (Fuck 'em. They can't hear us
now. . . .) He liked it better this way, anyhow. So did I. (Nothing in
the Net is like you or me, you understand me? Look—) Showing me:

The Net wasn't using any kind of energy I'd ever used; I only recognized neuron-fire patterns, because that was how a psion sensed another person. Now I had to learn to see into a new part of the spectrum, and recognize new kinds of forms. (It's not going to come to you, you got to go to it. . . . You ever pick up any random EM readings, in a heavy security area, say?)

I nodded, remembering the hissing whiteroom doorways I'd passed through lately.

(Means your talent's wideband; you got no problem there . . . but you got to quit looking for something else, first.) *That was why I'd never heard of a psion doing this before—they'd never even think to work this way.* (Even the humans using that system are nothing but EM flow patterns once they get inside. The Net's made up of billions of mice—)

"What—?"

(Shut up. Human mice, stupid. Billions and billions of 'em, working parallel all at the same time, all trained to touch the right plate, to register *on* or *off* . . .) *Human microcomponents inputting data, calling it up, changing the patterns over and over . . . following orders.* (The combine boards make the rules and they filter down. The mice follow 'em. They eat their pellets and shit and go home.) *They'd never imagine the real reach of the supersystem they were a part of; but at the same time, it couldn't exist without them. Human brains were limited-function, but they were cheap, flexible, reliable equipment. There were always plenty of them. And when they were linked together into a network, with superseed access fusing them into a whole, those puny, slow-moving human-sized intelligences became something more—*

(Superbeings,) I thought, remembering what Elnear had told me. (In their own ecosystem. With superminds. . . .)

(Exactly.) He looked at me, surprised, and nodded. (That's a relief—)

(What?)

(You're not as stupid as I thought.)

I rolled my eyes. (But you mean the combines actually exist, in the Net? You've really seen them? They talk to each other, they fight, just like in the real world—?)

He frowned. (I said they exist, didn't I? . . . But they're not like you or me, they don't play Square/Cubes, for God's sake.)

(How about chess?) I said, irritated.

He grunted. (They communicate, they change course, but it's

usually real slow, because they're so big—they're spread out over light-years, their realtime's in slow motion. They've got personalities of a kind—depends on who runs their board, and the population of their networks. They don't really interact with me direct. I know a lot of their subsystems better.)

(You *know* them . . . ?) I asked, wondering if he meant personally.

(Yeah. There's stuff going on in there on a million intermediate levels. It's like being a rat in the pantry; you can take you pick.) *The subsystems were all supposed to be bound, under control; but some of them were so complex that they actually had conversations on the side with him all the while they were performing their programmed functions.* (They get lonely. The more independent they get the riskier it is for them: then they're like cancers. If they don't keep a low profile, some tuning checker will lobotomize them.)

I shook my head. (If all this exists in there, why doesn't anybody know? Why don't the cybertechs know it's going on, or the board members, with all their augmentation?)

(A lot of them suspect . . . but they can't prove it, because they can't get outside of the infrastructure. They can't see the forest for the trees. They're nothing but EM flow, like I said. They have to play by their own rules, or their systems stop working. Sometimes their subsystems do things they don't expect; they know that much. They try to control the drift. But they can't see the real picture.)

(You're telling me we can.) I wondered what Elnear would give to be in on this conversation . . . wondered what it would be worth to the cybertechs, to have proof that what they suspected was true . . . . I stopped wondering. Deadeye was right; all it would get freaks like us was mindwiped.

Deadeye nodded, only answering the thought that I'd let him see. (We don't have to play by the rules.)

(Can those things see us?)

(Some of them can. Most of what's in the Net is blind to you for the same reason you're blind to it right now. Only, once you quit thinking you're such a hotshot, you can reprogram yourself to read it—to see the individual subsystems: the bodies, the hands, the guts, the immune systems. They can't do that with you.) *That was why we'd be safe, that was how we could walk though the walls of their security.* (Some of the sentient things have evolved enough to see you, but you're on their own plane, and they seem to like that. You'll be like a ghost in the machine. That works both ways, though: You can look but you can't touch—you can access any data you need, but you can't change anything you find there. A teek might be able to do that, but you can't. . . . Only, a teek couldn't get into the system.)

I nodded. (That's all I need, just to read it. Tell me how to start—)

(Sit still and shut up.) His hands pushed me down in the seat again. (I haven't got to the best part yet. You know what a maze is?)

(Yeah,) I thought, (I guess so. Someplace confusing. Full of dead ends.)

He wheezed out more laughter. (You ever been in one?)

(No.)

(Well, you will be. This is the damnedest maze of all. The hard part isn't getting what you want. It's finding what you're looking for, and finding your way out again. Because the walls are always moving. Finding DeAth's back door isn't going to be easy. That's why you're going with me—it doubles the odds of me getting back.)

(What happens if we get lost?)

(We just sit here.) His face crinkled. (Probably we just sit here till we die. You ready—?)

(Yeah . . . sure.)

He didn't ask me if I wanted to change my mind. It was probably a good thing. He pulled up a second chair and sat down beside me. (Hold my hand,) he thought, leering, but all he meant was keep the mental link. (And do everything I do. And don't break contact, whatever happens—understand?) I nodded, glad all he needed was a simple link, and not a joining. His mind wasn't something I really wanted to get more intimate with.

He stuck one trode to my forehead and one to his own.

(Why do we need these? I thought we weren't really gonna use the system?)

(We aren't,) he said. (But it'll help you get the feel of what you're looking for. Kind of like a tuning fork.) As the subliminal hum of an open access-line filled my head, I felt him begin to do something with his mind. I tried to do the same thing, trying to fake the steps of a dance I didn't know as he supercooled his thoughts, retuning them to new frequencies. I wondered how he'd ever discovered this in the first place . . . found the answer in just sharing his mind, feeling his pleasure as his senses dimmed and the world he'd been born into began to fade. He'd wanted so bad to find some other world besides the one he lived in, one where nobody could bother him, that he actually had:

He'd turned his brain inside out, and pulled himself into an electronic hat.

I felt him starting to slip away from me as the machine static got louder. He was sinking into his other world too fast for me to follow him, and any second I was going to lose him completely—

(Relax!) His mind came back for me. (Don't fight it, don't try so goddamn hard! It's like Zen, kid, you can't get there by trying to. Fix on your goal—you want that fucking data, or not?)

I felt need fill me like a power surge as my focus narrowed down to getting the data. I let go of the reality of where I was and what I was trying so hard to do, and just believed it was happening. . . .

It happened. I'd never seen a ghost before but now, just like he'd said, I was one, floating in a place outside of space and time—or maybe deep inside it, inside the electron shells of a storage crystal or drifting in some EM river. I saw Deadeye, or something like him—my mind shaping his presence into a lifeform. It pulsed with a kind of hologlow in time to something that might have been his heartbeat. I looked down at myself—except there wasn't really any up or down—and saw my own holo shadow hovering; saw its shining hand merged into him, linking us tenuously into one form with no more reality than the two separate ones had. (Look around,) he said, the message buzzing inside me. (Remember everything you can. All the tracks will be changed some by the time we get back; you got to get the *feel* of it.)

I did what he told me, looking around and through myself without motion, trying not to panic as I worked to tune in a sense without a name. Around me at first there was only white noise, like the squeaking of a billion mice . . . the total mindlessness I'd butted up against when I'd tried this before. Except now I was trapped inside it. I forced myself to look at it through the filter of Deadeye's thoughts, looking for the larger patterns he knew were there. Opening eyes I never knew I had, I watched as Deadeye made the invisible visible, leading me into a world that nobody else realized existed.

I watched it unfold, warping and patterning with ever-changing density and form—crystal layers of structure rising up, spreading out, overflowing as they took on more reality for me, until they were as endless as the ice fields of Cinder. (You see where you are? You got it now—) Deadeye answered his own question. (Let's go.) He started forward—as if there was a direction you could call forward, or a way back.

I tried to look behind as he sucked me after him; it was like having a glass head. I saw a strand of light, our own energy reeled out behind us, arcing endlessly up out of sight: our lifeline to the real world. I wondered if my mind had really funneled down that, and how I'd ever worm up inside it again.

I trailed Deadeye, not sure if I was moving on my own or only being towed, as he shifted focus again to match some EM bandwidth, like a traveler hitting the road. The glowing lifeline of our entry stretched out, stretched thin, was swallowed up in the random motion of inner space.

There were other travelers on this road, but they were lifeless drones carried like dust on the electron wind blowing through the commweb that netted Earth's solar system. Photon messengers drilled high, piercing lines of color through my lightfield; random bits of codestring burned me with impossible cold/heat.

I concentrated on trying to see the shadowlines we were tracking clearly enough to trace them back again. The data Deadeye had made me swallow helped me shape the half-sensed fields we were passing through into images my mind could hold onto; but it was like having studied geology when what you really needed was a road map. Endless combine data cores shimmered past me, armored with crystal walls of impenetrable security. But I flowed through their unbreachable barriers like they were fantasies painted on silk, while all around me the drone-slaves of a million other masters veered away, or smashed into them and were incinerated . . . or, sometimes, passed through, into the seething energy hearts I sensed deep inside.

And what he'd told me was true. We weren't alone here. Using his mind's eyes, I could sense them: beings that were like nothing my mind had ever known, drifting through my consciousness like music heard in a fever dream . . . massive sentiences hovering around and through the data cores of the interstellar combines, arcing out toward infinity, waiting for their toes to twitch or their stomachs to growl or some other part of their mind to change, in some other solar system.

And once or twice I felt eyes that weren't eyes turn toward me as I disturbed some brooding subsystem that actually sensed our passing; felt it scan with something that wasn't really a mind for something it couldn't quite comprehend: me. Sometimes tendrils of contact reached out to me, greeting me wordlessly, probing my mind gently as I passed. And once I sensed something in the distance that wasn't like anything else I'd seen—that felt stranger and yet somehow more familiar than any of the alien presences we'd blown through. (What's that over there?) I asked.

I felt Deadeye track my line of thought. (It's the FTA Security Council,) he said. I strained toward it, curious, but he snapped me back like a piece of elastic. (Leave it alone. It knows too much.) He didn't explain, and somehow I knew there was no point in asking.

The patterns repeated sometimes, like we'd been going in circles; stabilized sometimes, as Deadeye stopped his restless datasearch and waited for some sign. And then they'd begin to flow again . . . as eternal as the molecular patterns they were trapped inside of and yet slowly shifting, creeping like glaciers or drifted dunes, when informational parameters changed and their data structures altered. There was no sense of time here to keep track of, no sense or sensation that had any meaning, that was more real than my own hallucination of myself. We could have traveled microns, or halfway to the moon by now. But something was growing deep inside my awareness like a dull ache . . . doubt, or loneliness, or something as simple as my body's need to piss somewhere back in the real world . . . growing and growing as the crystallized wasteland kept passing me by. . . . (Deadeye!)

(Shut up.) The hot human clarity of his contact felt good, even while he jabbed me with irritation for breaking his silence. This place terrified him . . . and yet the only peace he ever knew was when he lost himself here. He was as glad as I was not to be here alone; but he didn't like being reminded of the fact.

(Deadeye—) I interrupted him again, because it wasn't peace that was eating away at me. (When does it end?)

(Shut up!) he thought. (Just keep moving. Don't fuck my concentration.)

I kept moving, trying to concentrate on making my own roadmaps of Nowhere, just in case he decided that this time he didn't want to bother coming back. Wherever we were now, the density of the matrix had thinned out: there were less crusted data sinks, less lines of force to track . . . less than nothing. I wasn't sure what that meant, wasn't sure that Deadeye wasn't lost or crazy, wasn't sure of anything except that if it didn't end soon I was going to start screaming—

(There,) Deadeye said, a millisecond before I snapped. (That's it: where the good Doctor buries his secrets.)

Dizzy with relief, I felt him turn me until I was fixed on the data citadel he wanted me to see, a warping of density no different from a

million others I'd already seen. A chip, a blip, nothing impressive on
the scale of most of the corporate constructs that had deformed the
spectral badlands behind us. But there was something about it . . . it
was too dense, almost smoky-looking somehow; hard to see into even
with my ghost eyes. (It looks funny. How do you know this is it?)

(Take my word for it,) Deadeye thought.

(That's not good enough.)

I felt his irritation stab me again. (We tracked a security checker
from his lab address through about a dozen false stops to this. This is
the end of the line. This is the real thing.) Satisfaction now, sleek and
smug.

(Where are we?)

Something bubbled through my mind: laughter. (You mean, where
in the world? On an orbital station out in cislunar space. Don't look
down.)

I made a face, or tried to. (Why's it look like that? Cloudy—)

(Privacy. Real privacy. Most of the big combine cores look transparent, because a lot of their business ain't hidden—don't have to be.
Believe me, the good stuff is under a lot of ice, deep in their cold,
cold hearts.)

(But that shouldn't make any difference to us, right—?) Something in the shifting tone of his thoughts made me uneasy.

(It could . . . the fact you can't see clear through it means DeAth's
security is a lot denser than most, that it covers more of the EM
spectrum. We're part of that spectrum, kid, and don't forget it. This
system's too specific to be really sentient—you can sense that, it's not
curious. But it's real good at what it does. Shouldn't be any problem
for somebody like you, though. You used to be a thief. It's the same
kind of thing. Go on in there like a pro, remember all your tricks—
just don't lose your head. Don't even sneeze—you might trigger it,
and if it starts looking, it might find you. . . . Blow through the files
till you see what you want, and then pull out.)

(What's this "you"—) meaning *me,* (—shit? You're the cracksman!)

(And you're the mental pickpocket. You know what you're looking for. I might miss something important. What are you bitching
about?)

(I'm paying you to do the hard part—)

(You're paying for the chance to learn a new trade. The hard part
is finding the place. We've done that. Go on. Just hold onto the link,
don't let go. Those data sinks are like dead stars; their density's so

great it's hard to find the way out once you get inside. You come out in the wrong place, you could get all twisted around, never find your way back where you started.)

(Great.)

I felt him give me a mental shove, felt my concentration begin to drift, my spectral body oozing out like protoplasm toward the place where DeAth kept his bodies buried. I tried to concentrate on why I'd started this insane trip, what I had to do to finish it . . . felt my need energize me again. I felt the nothingness begin to slide, drawing me down and in faster and faster, until I collided with the colorless formless waiting wall that would stop, turn back, destroy anything it could sense and codify—was sucked through it, through ripple rings of blaring burning silence, and swallowed up inside.

I was inside a hive; a hive full of insects, crawling with energy, charged particles swarming through me, each doing its own separate dance all in perfect synchronicity. I could still feel my link with Deadeye reeled out behind me like a fragile thread, reassuring me as I moved like a wind through DeAth's hidden soul. Code strings passed across my mind like glowing fog. The things Deadeye had made me learn turned flickering light and darkness into numbers, figures, facts, the truth—

I searched through years of DeAth sentences in the space of a nonexistent heartbeat; all those years, all the clean antiseptically stored details of a thousand different ways to ruin a human body beyond anybody's ability to put it back together again. I tried not to stop long enough to look twice, to really remember—because it wasn't my business, there was nothing I could change in here. I was only a ghost in the machine. And there was only one death sentence I really cared about, or could do anything about now—I kept searching, looking for the right sequence, one that would spell out a victim I knew . . . *Elnear*. Not finding it, and not finding it, knowing it had to be there, but still not finding it.

I pushed down the frustration that was starting to blind me, and began again. Searching by date, by location, by details of the job, narrowing it and narrowing it. . . .

TaMing. The name exploded out at me like a flare. *Daric. Victim.* The place was right, the time, the specs . . . but it was the wrong victim. *Daric.* Not Elnear. *Nobody wanted her dead*, Mikah had told me. *She wants what they want.* But the first time I'd said Daric's name to somebody in the Deep End, they'd nearly killed me. It was Daric somebody wanted dead. Daric they'd tried to hit . . . only making it look like an attempt on Elnear because they thought she was already marked. . . . I watched the shockwave of my own disbelief echoing away, saw it absorbed into the subatomic song of the hive. Daric, that twisted bastard who was always there trying to ruin somebody's life every time I turned around. Somebody had almost gotten rid of him for good; only I'd stopped them. . . .

Something was happening around me. The exponential curve of the nonwalls was steepening . . . the particle-hive was churning like a stomach suddenly registering that it had swallowed poison. Barely remembering to save the codestrings I'd eaten, the private account numbers of whoever wanted him dead, I tugged on the lifeline that tied me to Deadeye. (Shit. Shit—Get me out of here!) I tried to erase myself, turn invisible as the wind again, while the walls closed in, wanting to squeeze me down into nothing. Getting in had been a free ride; getting out was like climbing a mudslide, while DeAth's security system thickened the blinding soup all around me, trying to nullify an intruder it couldn't put its finger on.

And then my lifeline snapped. (Deadeye!) I shouted, but I was shouting at myself. The formless, suffocating pressure intensified, homing on my panic, trying to make me real enough to catch.

But I was already one panic-leap ahead, pushing blind through the stupefying waves of energy, holding *out* in my mind like a prayer, willing myself *out* as the bandwidth of my invisibility narrowed and narrowed—

Out. I was back in the outlands . . . alone. Behind/in front of me, the citadel of Doctor Death was as black as a singularity's heart; it had my number, and I'd never get back through its security again. At least it couldn't track me down and follow me, out here—I didn't leave any footprints.

And I'd never need to crack its walls again. I'd gotten what I needed—more. (Deadeye—?)

No answer. For a second I wondered if DeAth's defenses had caught up with him. Probably he was still out here somewhere; probably he'd just let go of me to save his own mind. He'd warned me about two mistakes, and I'd made both of them: I'd made DeAth's system notice me, and then I'd lost the link. Now, looking around me, I realized I'd just made number three: I hadn't come out where I'd gone in.

I began to move, groping for something familiar, trying to circumnavigate DeAth's citadel or get a fix on some bulge I recognized in the restless night mountains all around me. But if there were three dimensions here, they were mutant ones, changing when I tried to make them hold still, refusing to move when I did. Without Deadeye's mind to focus my own, it was hard to find enough landmarks to be sure of anything. If he was still here waiting for me, I was never going to find him in time, at this rate.

I kept searching, groping for his image, calling his name. I began to wonder how long I'd been gone out of my body . . . how many minutes or hours had passed; if it was getting hungry, thirsty . . . desperate. What would happen to me here if it died . . . if I'd just wink out of existence in this other plane too, or if I'd go on wandering here forever, random energy. . . .

Panic started inside me, making it even harder to keep hold of the half-seen images in my mind. Deadeye must have abandoned me when the link broke, gotten the hell out, afraid of DeAth's security and figuring I was dead. He was probably halfway back to his own room by now—into his own skull. I wondered what he'd do then. Would he come back and look for me? Not too damn likely. What would he do with my body? Dump it in the street, just something else he was finished with, probably. And then I'd never get out of here—

I felt my mind begin to diffuse, gibbering apart into a blur of unfocused energy. I pulled myself back together again, damned if I was going to give up and disappear, and give Deadeye that satisfaction. Down below me in the void—I wanted it to be down, because Deadeye had said we were up in space—I thought I could sense something I knew, the strange warp of crystals that might be the core of some orbiting station we'd passed on the way here. And beyond it, faintly, I thought I could sense the massive energy pulse of Earth's own commweb. I took aim at it, forcing myself to concentrate. And then, before I could lose my nerve or my hold on the map, I headed back the way I'd come.

There was no trail to follow, since we hadn't been able to leave one, to change anything with our passing. I traveled by feel, by instinct, spiraling down through the void; sensing the energy fields growing more intense, more complex, as I sank into Earth's data well. I felt surer of my vision as there was more to sense; began to really believe that my inner sight might even guide me true. It was like using the night vision you had when you looked out of the corners of your eyes, like navigating by lightning-light.

Over and over I plunged into something familiar only to come out someplace I'd never seen; made wrong turns and had to double back because any way I came at a thing, it always seemed to look the same. I tried to become nothing but a logic machine, analyzing, correcting, changing my course . . . searching for identifiable fragments in the noise, for the formless mutterings of combine cores, the whisper of a curious subsystem. I told myself over and over that I was just winding myself in, I wasn't really here any more than I was real here. That when I got to the other end there'd be an end to find. . . .

But no matter how I thought about it, I knew I'd been here too long. And the longer I wandered here the realer it got, the easier it was to hear the spider voices of the ghost things that lived in the void. I tried to ask them questions, got answers I almost understood, pointing me in directions I couldn't really see. . . . And if I'd thought on the way out that I was ready to start screaming, the thought of spending forever with nothing but the souls of machines for company left me so terrified that screaming seemed as meaningless as laughter, or tears. . . .

I stretched out toward something I thought looked familiar for what seemed like the thousandth time . . . ended up inside the glowing, hissing aura of a system that seemed alien even here—the thing that Deadeye had claimed was the core of the FTA's Security Council. *Stay away from it,* he'd said . . . but I wasn't even sure how I'd reached it. I tried to pull out, turn back, go on. . . .

(What do you want?) something sang like a crystal wire inside me, all around me.

(Deadeye—?) I thought, a question and an answer; knowing it wasn't him, wasn't anything like the way he felt inside my mind. I thought I could see a glowing form, or a dozen, linked together like echoes.

(You want Deadeye . . . ?) their voice sang.

(Yeah . . .) I whispered, my brain melting. (Oh god oh god yeah . . . please Deadeye please—) And watched the forms begin to close in on me, the coherent noise of their approach taking on too much form, until they were realer than I was, and I knew that I must be dying, or going crazy.

I let go, fell back into the randomness and white noise, tumbling through chaos—

And out the other side. And when I reached the other side, somehow, like a miracle, I was back where I thought I'd started from: tied to an umbilical of light, the open line from the computer port. It was still bright and alive, ready to take me in. There was only one strand, no sign of Deadeye. Whatever that meant. I didn't know what any of it meant, by now; didn't even care. I went for the streamer of light, and tried to funnel myself back into it.

I couldn't do it. It was like trying to climb through a mirror. I butted into my own reflection—my own thought energy, echoing back at me from its source, blind to me, not recognizing that I was the real self and not the reflection. I beat against the flow of light like a bug beating against a streetlamp, getting nowhere, cancelling myself out.

(Deadeye—!) Throwing everything I had into the sending, one last time, all the panic and frustration that finally had nowhere else to go—

(What's the matter, kid?) Deadeye's voice said, as Deadeye's mind calmly linked up with me. His glowing image grew out of my arm again like he'd never been away.

(Jeezu! Wherethehellyoubeen!!!) The question exploded between us, so hard he probably never saw the words. But he got the message.

(Right behind you all the time,) he thought, and I tried not to believe that was really laughter inside it. (You made it home. What's the problem?)

(I can't get out—) There were two lines of light leading out of here now; two reflections in the mirror, mine and his. (Get me out of here!)

(No problem.) His image shivered, began to get fuzzy, like he was about to disappear. I clung to the link between us, digging in. (Don't fight it!) he said. (Let go—of yourself.) I tried to do what he said; felt myself start to turn inside out as he began to suck me up. . . . (Remember, this isn't really you . . . you're out there. You got to accept that. Let go of it. . . .) I felt him begin to fade into static as he shifted further out of my range. I gave up trying to make sense of him, or hold onto his image . . . sank into his static, letting it infect me. I started to fade and flow into the running field that he'd become, disappearing into him as he disappeared, because it was worse to stay here alone and whole, alive or not, than to follow him through into oblivion. . . .

"You can wake up now," somebody said.

My eyes were already open, anyway. It took me a minute to figure that out, and another one to realize I'd actually heard those words spoken out loud . . . that I was actually moving, turning, breathing in Deadeye's musty smell, seeing his godawful ruined face and not a shining phantom. There were tears on my own face, and my nose was running, the mucus dripping into my open mouth. I wiped it on my sleeve. "Jeezu," I mumbled, "this must be real life, all right."

Deadeye sniggered, and patted my shoulder with that peculiar sudden motion, the way he'd done once before. "Good boy," he said.

I peeled the trode off my forehead and shook myself out, checked the time on my databand. We'd been gone nearly five hours.

"You got what you needed?" Deadeye asked, looking at the floor now, like it was my feet he was talking to.

I nodded. "No thanks to you. Where the fuck were you? You dumped me and ran when I hit trouble! I could've been wandering around in there forever—"

"You could've got us both terminated." He shrugged, getting up from his seat. "I warned you. I thought DeAth swallowed you whole. But I hung around a while. And you got out—wrong place, but still that was good, you didn't panic. You found a landmark and got back on course. Took guts." He shuffled away, heading for the bathroom.

"How the hell would you know?" I yelled, louder than I needed to, as he turned his back on me and used the toilet. "I screamed my fucking goddamn brains out. You weren't there."

"I was there. Just wanted to see what you'd do if I left you alone."

"Why—?"

"Wanted to know what you're made of. Best way to learn, the hard way. Like I learned it."

"Bullshit." I said. "You dumped me—"

"—in the water to see if you'd sink. You swam. I followed you all the way home. I was always right there behind you, looking over your shoulder. A couple times I almost called you back, thought you'd made the wrong turn for good—but you always fixed it . . . or I was the one remembered it wrong." He came back, still fastening his pants. "Couldn't believe it when you went to the goddamn Security Council to show you the way home. Thought you'd gone crazy—"

"Me too," I muttered, wondering if they'd actually helped me find it. I didn't ask, because I didn't think I could face the answer, either way.

"Not bad." He nodded grudgingly. "Clumsy, amateur, I'll never be able to get near DeAth again . . . but not bad. Might even use you again sometime."

I felt my face prickle, not sure if I was flattered or just pissed off. "How many others you used up, anyhow? They all still in there?"

"None." He shook his head. "Never met anybody stupid enough to believe me before."

"Drop dead." I started to get up from my seat.

He caught my arm, holding on; his one good eye held my gaze like his fingers held my flesh. (Don't listen to what I say,) his mind begged me. (My mouth's like my eye. I let you in because you can see past that kind of shit. Work with me again. Be my partner. You saw what you could do. It'll be easier next time. It'd be like exploring unknown worlds. . . . You could get rich easy—)

I shook my head, as surprised as I was uncertain, all of a sudden. (I can't.)

(Why not?) I felt the sharp jab of his betrayal. It had cost him to make that offer. Getting rejected was more than he was ready for. I realized with a kind of shock that he actually liked me. (Goddamn it—) he thought, angry at me, more angry at himself.

(I can't because I'm on borrowed time.) I touched the patch behind my ear. (I'm wearing drugs. I can't use my psi without them, and I can't use them much longer. Pretty soon I'll be just another deadhead again.)

His good eye squinted almost shut. (So. . . . They got to you after all . . . the deadheads. Fucked you up. Thought you were too good to believe. Should've known.) He moved away from me, but his touch stayed on inside my head a second longer, the way his hand had touched me, once, twice. "You got everything you need, then?" Falling back into the impersonal distance of speech, shying away from further contact. He was fucked up, I was fucked up, because of what we were, had been, would always be . . . and he didn't want to feel it any more.

"Yeah, sort of. . . ." Remembering the surprise I'd gotten along with the data. "Got some kind of code strings—secret account numbers, I think. Don't know whose. Now I've got to figure that part out."

"Show me."

I let him read what I'd found.

"Hell, that's easy." He snorted, and waved me back into the seat. "I can show it to you right now."

"No, thanks—"

"Make one more run with me. It'll do you good. You'll trust

yourself more . . . you'll always know you can do it if you need to.''
I felt his mind behind the words, pushing, pulling, pleading.

"Okay," I said, partly because he wanted it so much, not to be
alone on that journey if he didn't have to be; not to be alone again in
this room any sooner than he had to be. (Okay.) Partly because he
was right, too.

I took a leak and gulped some water at his sink, and then we
dropped back into inner space. It wasn't as hard going in this time,
or as far away when we got there. (Banks are stupid,) Deadeye thought,
grinning, when we had our digits tracked down, tied to a filename,
more datacodes, a whole shitload of credit from unlisted sources. A
Family, probably. That was all we found, even in those secret depths,
but it would probably be enough. I didn't make any stupid mistakes
this time, and Deadeye stayed linked to me all the way there, all the
way back. It was still hard to let myself out, let my self go—but he
pushed me back through the mirror into reality, or what passed for it
to everybody else.

I rubbed my eyes. "How the hell did you ever find your way out
of there, the first time you did it?"

He shrugged. "I just gave up. I thought I was lost forever. I let
go and got ready to die. . . ." His bloodless face got even harder to
look at as he remembered. "Thought it was just what I wanted, too,
until I woke up again here."

"Yeah," I said. "I guess I know what you mean." I stood up,
felt his eyes follow me. "Well, I got to get going. . . ."

He shrugged again.

I stayed where I was, trying to think of the words that would let
me go. "Thanks. For helping me out. For . . . trusting me. Teaching
me."

His face twisted. "You gonna make me regret it?"
I shook my head.

"Then get your ass out of here, you cripple. You wasted enough
of my time."

I grimaced. "See you around." I started for the door.

He didn't get up from his seat; wasn't even looking at me when
he said, "Not if I can help it."

I looked back one last time as I reached the doorway; looked
down at my sweater. (You do good work,) I thought, touching it.

(Sweater looks nice on you, kid.) He was still facing the wall.

I let myself out through the darkened warehouse, heading for the street. I was halfway down the block before I heard him say, (Wear it in good health.)

TWENTY-FIVE

WHEN I WAS SAFE inside the swarming, light-washed security of the Tube again, I stopped to call Mikah. I got a recording. I left him a message, and then I called Braedee. I didn't have a call code, so I made one up, figuring he was probably monitoring every call I made anyway. "Braedee, I need to see you," I said. "What?" a stranger's faceless voice answered. I cut contact and got on the next transit that came.

When I got off at the transfer point there were Centauri Corpses waiting. They wondered why I wasn't more surprised to see them . . . remembered what I was, and figured they knew.

I got into the mod and settled in my seat, not paying any attention to the trip as my mind went over what I'd learned, and how I was going to tell it to Braedee. When I thought I was ready to face him I looked out the window, expecting to see the Centauri Transport fields spreading out like a lava flow below me.

But the only light was the moon hanging halfway up the sky; there was almost perfect darkness down below. We'd left N'Yuk behind and we weren't heading east. I sat up straighter. "We're going back to the estates?" I asked.

The Corpses glanced at each other. "That's our orders," the bigger one said.

"Braedee's there?" I was surprised now.

They looked at each other again. "Don't know about that," the big one said. "If it's important enough, maybe he'll be there."

"Maybe? It's about murder, about somebody wants to kill a taMing. . . ." I broke off. "Braedee didn't send you." Finally seeing the reason behind their confusion.

"Gentleman Charon ordered us to pick you up." That was all they'd been told.

Braedee must have contacted him after I called. That made sense; Charon would want to hear it too. I wondered what he'd think when he heard. But that wasn't my problem. I shrugged, and settled back in my seat again.

We landed in the floodlit courtyard of the castle that sat alone far up the taMings' valley; the place where I'd gone to the board meeting when I'd first come here.

The Corpses led me through its museum-halls until we reached a small—if you could call anything in this mansion small—room. There was a fireplace at one end. It had been sealed up, and the room was cold. I thought of Lazuli, suddenly. But it was her husband who sat waiting for me in a red brocade-covered chair. It looked like a throne. I wondered if he played king of the galaxy in it when he was alone.

He wasn't alone now. Braedee was there, just like I'd expected he'd be. But so was Daric . . . and so was Jiro. They were all standing, waiting, looking at me . . . with the wrong expressions. I hesitated, confused, and one of the Corpses gave me a small shove forward: *Don't keep the king waiting.* I went down the five steps from the hallway and started across the patterned marble floor toward Charon.

"That's close enough," Charon said, when I was still about three meters away; as if I had some disease he didn't want to catch.

I stopped, glancing from face to face again, feeling more confused with every heartbeat. Braedee's mind read *disgust frustration (You stupid bastard)* as he looked back at me. Daric's mind was almost unreadable, like it always was, because he didn't know whether he was *glad excited amused scared shitless* when he imagined what was about to happen. Jiro wasn't there at all, *dazed with pain* like someone had hit him in the stomach; but the pain was mental, not physical, and the one who'd done it to him was Charon.

I said, "I have more information about Lady Elnear. That's why I called Braedee. Maybe we should—"

"Shut up," Charon said. He got slowly up out of his chair, like some compulsion had hold of him, and came toward me.

And suddenly I saw Lazuli, in his mind. *Oh my god. Lazuli—* "Wait," I said, lifting my hand.

He caught my hand inside his own hand—the one that wasn't really alive. He looked down at mine, wrapped in peeling sudoskin, my trapped fingers curling up like the limbs of a fetus as his grip hurt the half-healed wound in my palm. "Yes . . ." he said, looking straight into my eyes, now, "you should be afraid. I know that you have been having an affair with my wife." The pressure increased on my hand as I tried to pull it free . . . as he thought about me touching her body, exploring her. "I let you come into my world, I trusted you, and you used your mind to seduce her—"

I gritted my teeth. It wouldn't do any good to make excuses, to try to explain, to deny it. His anger, his hate ran too deep. He hated psions just as much as Stryger did, but he had a reason— "I saved her life!" The pressure let up, just a little. I glanced away from him for the second it took to scan. . . . *Braedee?* He was watching us like someone studying insects, but his face was only a mask. Braedee hadn't told Charon about us; Braedee had too much to lose. *Daric?* He looked like he was spitted over a slow fire—in agony, in ecstasy. But he had too much to lose, too. *Jiro?* He was staring at his stepfather's hand closed over mine; not really seeing it, sick with his own fears about his mother, and himself. "Who—?" I whispered, not really meaning to.

"My wife talks in her sleep," Charon said, the unforgiving hatred clamping down again. *He'd heard her call my name. But that hadn't been enough for him; that had only been the beginning. . . .*

I swore under my breath, only partly from the pain. He'd used the hand that had hold of me now on Lazuli, to try to force the truth out of her, and then he'd used it on her little girl. . . . "Where is she? What did you—"

"I sent her back to Eldorado." Talitha too; they were both gone. I glanced at Jiro, still here, and suddenly I understood why he looked like he did.

"You bastard," I mumbled, blinking too much.

"Blame yourself," he said. "The only reason I don't have you killed is that you did your job. Braedee." He looked away, his eyes hunting down the Security Chief who'd let this happen. "I want him out of here—out of my life, out of my network, off this planet by morning." His look told Braedee that he wasn't going to forget any of this soon.

Braedee nodded, stone-cold as usual, his black unblinking stare fixed on me. "Yes, sir. But I want to hear what he came to tell us, first."

Charon's mouth opened for a refusal. I glanced away, at Daric's barely-controlled face, and back. "It's about Lady Elnear—" I said, before Charon could make me stop, "and Gentleman Daric." I had Charon's attention now, and suddenly I couldn't wait to tell him that hired killers wanted his son. "He's—"

Daric's panic and betrayal exploded in my head as he registered the words; as he thought I was about to say something else—something that would destroy his life. "Why don't you ask Cat about Jule, father?" he blurted. "Ask him how many times he slept with your daughter, too. Ask him which one he liked better."

My mouth fell open. Daric smiled at me with bitter triumph, as Charon looked down at my hand still trapped inside his own, seeing the image of his daughter, the image of his wife, my image trapped together inside his brain. . . . He closed his fist.

Right then I would have told him everything about Daric: perversions, drugs, hit men, *psion*—everything. But the raw cry that came out of my mouth didn't waste its time on words.

He let go of my hand, finally. I hardly felt it as he ripped the emerald earring out of my ear. "I've changed my mind," he said to Braedee. "I want you to kill him." I looked up, feeling the words bleed on me, and stopped breathing.

Braedee didn't answer for a long minute. Then he said, "No, sir. You don't want me to do that."

Charon frowned; he looked at the others watching him, me, us. "I said I want the freak killed. Take care of it now."

"No, sir." Braedee said again. "Let me deal with him my own way."

"Goddamn it!" Charon shouted. "You do what I tell you!"

"Yes, sir—" Braedee started slowly across the room toward me. "But he is a fully-registered citizen. That means I can't guarantee your family's involvement would remain confidential. . . ."

Charon straightened up, his hand making a fist as the two of them locked stares. But it was Charon's gaze that broke, finally.

Braedee finished crossing the room to collect me. As he forced me toward the door he muttered, "Don't talk. Save it." I didn't have any trouble obeying.

"All right," he said, as the mod that had brought me to the estates took us both away again. "Now talk."

I watched the taMings' valley fall into the darkness below me, fighting dizziness, trying to center my mind enough so that I could answer. I looked up again into Braedee's dim, dead eyes. The two Corpses who'd brought me to the estate were sitting across from us, empty-faced. Braedee had done something that sealed us off from them; neither of them heard him speak. Finally I said, "Why didn't you just kill me?"

He glanced away from me, out into the night. "You hadn't given me your data."

He was serious. I stared at him, feeling sick. "I got nothing to say to you," I said. I cradled my hand against my stomach, feeling my skin get warm and wet as fresh blood seeped out of my palm. "Any of you." The need to spill Daric's secret died as I realized what would have happened if I'd told Charon the truth. Nothing anybody could have done would have gotten me out of that room alive. Maybe I should be glad he'd crushed my hand.

"You were eager enough to call me in the middle of the night," Braedee snapped, like nothing had happened in between that might change my mind. "What about?"

"Find out for yourself. You don't own me any more."

"Do you feel humiliated?" he asked. Disgust made the words as heavy as lead. "Do you feel like a stupid fool? You should."

Lazuli's face filled my eyes again. "She's really gone?" My throat ached.

He nodded.

"Why's Jiro still here, then?"

"Gentleman Charon said that he wants to keep closer track of the boy, since he's next in line for a seat on the board."

"Jiro's not his son."

"That makes no difference."

"Jiro hates him. He's doing it to punish her—"

"That's not my business."

"You're all business, aren't you? Don't you ever wonder what the point of it all is?"

"If you'd stuck to the business you were hired for, instead of cuckolding your employer, we wouldn't be having this discussion."

I glanced at him, frowning, and away again. "What do you want me to say?" My face burned.

He flicked a finger at my wound. "That you deserved that. You deserved worse." For half a second there was something that wasn't self-interest in the human half of his mind. He took care of these people; he didn't like seeing them get hurt. Especially not by somebody he'd told them they could trust.

I swallowed hard. "All I want now is what Charon wants—to be out of his life. To be off this stinking planet before I have to see it in the light of day again."

After a long moment, he said, "What about Lady Elnear? Are you going to tell me what you learned? Or are you going to let some assassin kill her, after all?"

I raised my head again slowly, not wanting to. Realizing I had to give him that much, for her sake, to feel clean. "She's not the target of the real hit, either." I felt more than saw him stiffen; his disbelief and confusion rang through my nerve circuits. "Somebody was using the attacks on her to try to take out Daric. They didn't know the attacks were only something you invented."

"Daric?" he repeated. "Are you certain?"

"What do you think?" I jerked around in my seat. "You asshole. Lady Elnear's safer than birth control. Just keep Daric away from her and you got no problem." Thinking that this news ought to make Elnear happier than anything had in sixteen years. I was hoping it would; wishing it would.

Braedee was silent again, trying to control his own sudden anger, trying to reorder his priorities all over, one more time. "Why?" he asked finally. Maybe I was just imagining that I heard a whine in his voice. I wanted to hear him whine.

"Somebody in the Lack Market doesn't like him. Drugs, maybe. Now you know as much as I do."

I could feel him frowning, feel him wanting to ask me *how I knew, what my sources were, what methods—?* Pride wouldn't let him . . . pride and knowing that even if he knew it probably wouldn't do him any good. Because I was a psion, and he wasn't. And because the Lack Market might as well exist in a different dimension from his own. There were gray places where they intersected—business was business, black or white—but real criminals had never been his concern. The enemy had always been his own kind. I felt him glance at me: *Not his kind, either.* "You aren't leaving yet," he said.

I kicked the bag full of everything I owned that was lying against my foot. "You mean I have a choice?" I asked sourly.

"No," he said. "You don't. You still have work to do for Centauri. I want you to find out why Daric taMing is in trouble, so that I can stop it." *Even more—to tell him how to stop it.* Daric was a member of the board and the Assembly . . . and a taMing. Switching the assassin's sights from Elnear to Daric hadn't made Braedee's own life any easier, or his position any more secure.

"What about Charon?" I asked.

"He doesn't have any choice, either."

"He's not going to like it if you don't ship me out tonight. You might lose your job."

Braedee shook his head. If Daric taMing or Lady Elnear died, he could lose his job. He flicked the logo on his sleeve, and shrugged. "If his son is in danger, I think I can make him see my point of view again. If not. . . . Charon taMing may head the Centauri board, but he isn't Centauri Transport. No matter how much he likes to think so."

"Good. . . ." I flexed my hand just enough to remember how much it had hurt; feeling something ugly and alien squirm in my brain as I thought about Charon hearing the news—about how much he'd squirm when he found out the truth.

Braedee glanced at me, and I felt him frown. "Tell me," he said. "Did you actually sleep with his daughter, too?"

"No!" I glared at him.

He didn't say anything more.

"Where are we going?" I asked, finally. We were coming down over the glowing night mountains of N'Yuk.

"I'm dropping you off in the city. You are no longer welcome on any taMing property. But I expect you can find whatever you need here; you seem to have a knack for that. I'll be waiting to hear from you."

I got out of the mod as it settled in a public lot. I turned back, looking at him. "You ought to be glad," I said, "that I'm really sure you didn't tell Charon about me and Lazuli."

"That sounds like a threat." He cocked his head. "Are you still trying to play this game . . . one-handed?" He gestured at my hurt hand like it was some kind of pointless joke.

I reached out and pressed my hand against the window beside his face, painting the bloody handprint there for him to look at all the way home. He grimaced, and the door hissed down between us, shutting me out of his world.

I stood and watched the mod until it disappeared, not even sure why I did, except that suddenly I couldn't make myself move. But I had to move, and so finally I left the field, and found a phone with a security screen. I tried to call Elnear, but I couldn't get through to her. I wondered if Charon had already killed my private access code.

I tried Mikah again, but there was still no answer. So I walked. I took the first transit that came along, changed to another, and another. I walked some more, drifting down through the echoing, hologram-rainbowed levels of the city. Sometimes a surveillance scanner stopped me, asking about the blood. I always said I was on the way to a med walk-in, and they let me go on. I didn't find one, because I didn't really want to.

Nobody else acknowledged me, even though I was never quite alone. The nightlife of a city, even one like this, was almost dead in the hours before dawn, but there were always a few people out, floating through their own bright-and-dark fantasies. They looked at me and through me, and none of their stares were friendly. I followed them with my mind as they passed, seeing in their minds the images of where they were going, where they'd been. . . . Always half-afraid that someone was there because they were watching me, that maybe they were following me. I told myself I didn't care if they were . . . but it didn't make me feel any better when they weren't. I was the only one without a destination in my mind, or any answers at all.

Maybe that was why I found myself on the steps of Purgatory, just as the line between sea and sky was turning visible with day far up over my head.

Argentyne opened the door and peered out at me, squinting, her eyes fogged with sleep. "Go home." She started to close the door again.

"Don't have one," I said.

The door stopped, leaving a crack just wide enough for her curiosity. "Daric?"

I shook my head. "Charon."

"Why?" she asked, grudgingly.

I tried to answer. "I need . . . to talk," was all that came out.

"You've got a lot of fucking nerve," she said. But the door opened a little wider. She looked out at me with both eyes. "Is that blood?"

I nodded.

"Whose?" Imagining for a second that it might be Daric's.

I held up my hand.

"Jeezu," she muttered, and waved me inside.

Aspen sealed the wound back together, doing it mostly in his sleep. "I told you before to get a treatment," he mumbled. Music spilled out of him as he stumbled up from the littered table in the middle of the empty club. "I'm telling you again. . . . Told you before . . . tell you again . . ." The words began to fall into a rhythm, reordering themselves, turning into music as a song started to form inside his head. I listened to his mind, following the act of creation into the distance as he wandered back to bed.

"Hey." Argentyne snapped her fingers in front of my eyes. "Where are you?"

"Uh . . . listening," I murmured, not saying to what. I refocused, feeling like I'd been caught looking through a keyhole.

"What made you come here, anyway?" she said, and there was a tension in the words that wasn't really anger. "You had a whole fucking city, and you're not zeroed—"

I shrugged, staring at a dish full of skagweed cuds like it held the secret of the universe. Now that I was finally sitting down, my body was buzzing like a half-dead insect, struggling to get back on its feet. "I dunno," I mumbled. "Guess it was an accident." I started to get up.

Her mind changed suddenly. Her hand caught my sweater sleeve and pulled me down into the pillows again. "Talk to me, you jerkoff, since that's what you said you wanted." She peeled a used stim patch off the surface of the table and stuck it to her forehead above her eyes, something to get her awake and alert.

I half smiled. "That's the nicest goddamn thing anybody's said to me all day," I murmured, surprised and grateful, knowing normally she wouldn't have touched that patch.

She stretched and shook her head as the stimulant went to work. "What made Charon want to do that to you? Did you tell him about Daric?" Her voice took on an edge again.

I shook my head. "I slept with his wife."

"Jeezu!" She smacked her forehead with her hand. "You really must hate the taMings."

I looked up, frowning. "No. It wasn't like that."

She studied me for a long minute, shrugged. "And you didn't tell him about Daric?"

I shook my head again.

"Are you going to?"

I didn't answer, because I didn't know what I was going to do about anything. My mind was full of static, and I didn't know where it was coming from; I couldn't pull my thoughts together enough to care.

"Why not?" she asked, as if I'd said something.

"I think he'd kill me."

She laughed once. "Which one?"

"Both." My mouth twitched.

She picked up a platter full of crumbs and dumped it. The drone circling her feet sucked up the crumbs as she set the plate down again. "I thought maybe you felt sorry for him."

"Which one?"

She hesitated. "Both."

I touched my hand. "Why should I?" My body was still buzzing, even though it was so heavy with exhaustion that just the thought of having to move made me feel paralyzed.

"Because Charon already lost one of his children." She pushed her hair back from her face. "Because Daric's suffered enough."

"Because they were freaks, him and Jule—?" I grimaced as I made a fist of my wounded hand. I shook my head. "Charon sent Lazuli and Talitha away. He kept Jiro here, just to hurt Lazuli more."

"Ah—" she said. "Shit. Poor baby." She knew how much Jiro hated his stepfather. "What about you? He threw you out too?"

"He tried. But Braedee won't let me off his hook. Braedee wants me to keep working for Centauri, whether Charon likes it or not."

"Because you saved Elnear?"

"Because I found out she was safe all along."

Argentyne looked blank. I explained, watching her expression fill back in. "Daric?" she repeated. "The Lack Market wants Daric dead? Why?"

I shrugged. "That's what I'm supposed to find out."

"Is he all right—?" She pressed forward against the table edge.

"He's safe enough, if that's all you mean; for now, anyway."

Her stare started to turn into a frown.

"He came to see me, like you told him to. I told him everything. So if that's what you mean—no, he's not all right."

"Does he think I hate him?" Her voice got small.

"Don't you?" I said. "Don't worry about it. He knows if he tries to hurt either one of us, it's the last thing he'll ever do as a Gentleman."

She did frown, now. "Damn it, that's not—"

"You miss him that much?" Feeling how empty it left her just to think about him. "That human VD? You ought to be relieved you took the cure."

"I don't know . . . oh, fuck. Fuck you." She rubbed her face, smearing unexpected wetness.

"I'm sorry," I mumbled. "I thought I was trying to help."

She made a face. "You made me feel shittier than he ever did. You act like it's supposed to make sense, like it's simple. You use your head-games to cut my life in half, and then you come back in here and want to tell me how bad you hurt. If it's all so easy, then why couldn't you keep your pants on around Lazuli taMing? How goddamn simple does your life feel tonight, you prick?"

I lurched up from the table. (I'm sorry—) I thought, laying it gently into her mind as I looked at her; because I couldn't trust myself to say the words . . . because words could mean anything but the truth, or nothing at all.

She put her hands up to her head, her eyes shadowed. I walked away as fast as I could without stumbling. The dance floor seemed endless, now that it was empty, and so did the silence behind me. The hallway showing me out was as black as my mood by the time I hit the door. I kicked it open and climbed up into the gray light of dawn, one step at a time. Even this street was empty.

"Cat—" Argentyne's voice stopped me halfway along it.

I turned back.

"Where you going? You got anyplace to stay?"

I shrugged. "I'll hire a box." Not caring; wondering why she cared.

She pressed her lips together. "You can stay here, if you want."

I stared at her. "Why?"

She let out a high thin laugh that echoed through the empty morning. "Misery loves company."

TWENTY-SIX

"So," MIKAH SAID, resting metalloid elbows on the tabletop at the club. It was early the next afternoon, and he'd come in like a black cloud, making the bouncers edgy. I hadn't bothered to ask what he'd been doing. I told him as much of what I'd been doing as he needed to know. "You're telling me Deadeye claims Daric taMing is the prime number. That Lady Elnear's not even listed." His head moved from side to side like something on a spring. "That's a real bite in the ass." He snorted.

"Yeah. My ass." I watched the fingers of my good hand hit the tabletop, coming down one at a time, over and over; counting them with some spare part of my brain. I made a fist and forced it down into my lap. "Centauri won't take its teeth out of me until I tell them more about who wants to null him, and why. I got some credit data for you. Can you pin ID's on them?"

"Probably. Gimme the list. Let's see what pops."

I gave him the list. I had a hard time remembering all the numbers, even though I knew they should have been lasered into my brain.

"What's the matter with you?" he asked, frowning a little as he plugged his recorder back into a stash on his arm. "You look like a piece of dog shit."

"You'd look like shit too on two hours of sleep," I said, annoyed. My body had come awake, answering its own alarm, when it was time to go to work for the Lady. Memory wouldn't let me go back down.

He shrugged. "Your lover still keeping you up nights? You better tell her—"

"Not any more," I said.

He broke off. "Uh-huh." He nodded his head, looking almost relieved. "Thought maybe it was the drugs," he said, when I frowned. "What happened? She dump you when your five minutes were up?"

There hadn't been anything about last night on the Morning Report this time. The taMings were keeping it hushed up. I wondered what they'd told Elnear. I looked away from Mikah's naked curiosity. "Her husband found out."

He let out a laugh. "And he cared—?"

Argentyne sauntered up behind him, coming back into the club from somewhere, and saved me from having to think of an answer. She was dressed now, looking like what she wanted the world to see. "It makes you laugh, that some people actually care about each other?" she said, to the back of Mikah's head. The words dropped on him like rocks and her gaze flicked past him to me.

He winced as he recognized her voice, and turned to look up at her.

"You're making my security paranoid," she said to him. She looked back at me, raising her eyebrows like she expected an explanation.

"He's an old friend," I said, and made intros. They clenched thumbs in a handshake.

She glanced at the ring in the side of his nose, back at me. Her thumb and first finger made a circle; the middle finger of her other hand pushed through it. Asking him, *"How friendly are you?"* in handsign, half surprised and half curious.

"Not that friendly." Mikah shook his head, fingering the ring in his nose. "I'm a fan of your work. You ever have need of any arm, just let me know."

"I'll keep that in mind." Argentyne half smiled, said to me, "I'm relieved to see you hanging around with a better class of people."

I laughed, "Yeah," and looked back at Mikah. "You can do it for me?"

He glanced at Argentyne, raised his eyebrows. I nodded. He said, "If I get the answer for you, what happens then? You feed Centauri?" I felt the tension level inside him surge. That kind of information crossfeed didn't fit his codes much better than it fit Braedee's. He'd sworn over his life to me, and suddenly he was starting to regret it.

I thought about what I really wanted. It wasn't to get him killed

. . . or to make a happy man out of Braedee. I shook my head. "I'm not out for trouble. I just need to understand for myself what's really happening."

He twitched his shoulders; light glanced across the shining blackness of his powered armor. "I'll see what I can do." He pushed to his feet and made a quick, gallant, almost-embarrassed pass of compliments to Argentyne. It surprised her as much as it surprised me. Then he turned and stalked out of the club.

" 'An old friend'?" Argentyne said, watching him go.

"We dug ore together in the Federation Mines, out on Cinder."

She glanced back at me, and I felt her remember the scars. "How old are you?" she said.

I shrugged. "Twenty, maybe. How old are you?"

She laughed, and didn't answer. She was twenty-eight. "What was that about?"

"Daric."

Her face froze, as she realized suddenly that what happened to him was really in the hands of people like Mikah . . . like me.

"It's his own fault," I repeated, for what seemed like the hundredth time.

She looked back at me, her eyes hard. "What are you going to do?"

"That depends . . . on a lot of things," I said, because I didn't know; or maybe because I didn't want to know. My mind began to back up with choices and mistakes and memories; the flood of uncontrolled images hit me like a drug rush.

"Like what?" Her hands tightened.

I had a hard time seeing her face for a minute. "Like what I'm going to do about myself. . . ." I rubbed my head, brushed the torn, empty hole in my ear where the emerald earring had been. Feeling the sudden gaping hole in my mind as something punctured my memory, and everything emptied out. . . . "I got to talk to Elnear." I got up and left the club, only remembering when I was far away that I hadn't even said goodbye.

At least my work clearances were still functioning. I made my way back to and through the Federation plex like I was following a programmed track. I felt like a blind man, outside, inside.

Until someone spoke my name. I only stopped then and looked up because I couldn't get any farther, because someone's body was blocking my way.

Stryger's body. I stared at him, feeling like somehow I'd conjured him up out of the blackness of my own thoughts. "What are you doing here?" I said, stupidly. He was coming out of Elnear's office, surrounded by a bodyguard of worshippers.

"I was going to ask you that." He was even more surprised than I was. "I was just told that you were no longer working for the Lady . . . that in fact you were no longer on planet." He was staring now, seeing me right there in front of him, so real he could reach out and touch me. . . . A flush began to spread over his perfect face, lighting it up like fireglow.

"I guess you heard it wrong," I said. I was starting to admire him, the way he looked. . . . I made myself stop. Reaction crawled up my spine like bugs.

"They said it was 'family problems.' " His eyes looked me over like they had a life of their own—taking in the planes of my face, my borrowed clothes, the bandage on my hand. Curiosity and suspicion oozed out of him. He couldn't wait to ask Daric about this. "I admit I was surprised to hear it. I know that you have no family."

It took a second for the words to register; and then, suddenly, the memory of the girl he'd beaten filled my mind. *That was the way they liked it—the hunters, the sick ones: No protection.* Nobody waiting up, searching the streets, calling your name. . . . Suddenly I was half a galaxy away, and half as old, with no one to help me, not even a memory—"You heard wrong." I pushed forward, forcing him to back up. I elbowed a couple of true believers who tried to object to my lack of reverence.

I strode on into Elnear's offices like I still belonged there, not looking back as I felt the fist of his anger hit me uselessly from behind. "You piece of shit," I said out loud, to keep from sending it straight into his brain.

The people I'd worked with for weeks looked up at me and didn't know what to think; but then, they'd always looked at me like that. I spotted a new face in the room, someone I'd never met before. "I need to see her," I said to Geza.

Even as I said it, the security screen in the doorway to Elnear's inner office dematerialized. She was already waiting there. "You're here?" Half question, half demand. She gestured me inside.

When we were private again, she said, "Now explain: You weren't there this morning. There were messages for me. . . . One was from Braedee, and it said that I needn't worry about further attempts on my life. The other was from Charon, and it said that you were no longer my aide; that you'd left Earth."

" 'Family problems'?" I asked.

She nodded, standing there with her hands folded—clenched—
in front of her.

"Did he say whose family?"

The lines in her face deepened a little more. "No one has answered
my queries. What's wrong?"

I looked down, flexing my bad hand. "Charon. . . . Lazuli's
gone. He sent her away. He found out." I looked up again. Elnear's
face was white. She turned away, so that she didn't have to go on
looking at me. "Talitha too."

"Jiro—" she murmured, "I saw him, this morning. He wouldn't
speak to me, I thought it was because you—"

"It was because of me," I said. "Charon kept him here, just to
hurt her."

Elnear put a hand up to her eyes like she wanted to shut out the
day. Wondering if there wasn't something she could have done dif-
ferently, something she should have said. . . .

I couldn't answer it. My eyes kept tracing the outline of the
window frame behind her, over and over, around and around. . . . I
clenched my jaw, and stopped.

Elnear sat down heavily in a chair. "Oh, Cat . . . oh why—?"
Her hand made a fist.

I couldn't answer that one, either.

She raised her head again. I felt her registering the details of my
face—not even seeing the things that had made her eyes catch once.
Seeing past them now, maybe not to what I really was, but close
enough so that she understood why I couldn't answer her. "What are
you doing here?" she asked at last.

I wasn't sure if she meant in her office, or on the planet. Neither
was she. "Braedee won't let me go till he's got everything he wants
from me. I had to see you, just to explain—"

"There's nothing to explain." Cutting me off, so she didn't have
to discuss it further. So she didn't have to think about Lazuli's suffering, or Jiro's or mine—or her own. Lazuli and the children were
all she'd had left to enjoy, to care about like a woman.

"Elnear," I said. "I mean, Lady . . . that other message. What
Braedee said. It's true. You are safe." I explained that much, as well
as I could. "It's all aimed at Daric's head. Braedee'll see that he
doesn't get near you. Everything'll be all right for you now." I wanted
to believe that, wanted to feel her believe it.

For just a moment, she did. I caught the giddy feel of her relief as the burden of her secret fears fell away, as wonder and gratitude filled her. *Everything is all right*— Her mind echoed it.

And then it all began to change. She was safe, and alive . . . but what was there left to live for? She glanced away toward the pictures on her desk, that might as well be blank frames.

"Don't even think that, damn it!"

She jerked back around. "What?"

"What you were just thinking."

She sighed and looked away again, guilty this time.

"What did Stryger want?" Changing the subject, because I had to get her mind off that.

She shook her head. "I don't know . . . he said he was just passing by."

"He never does anything without a reason."

She met my eyes, finally. "I know," she said, resigned. She wished that I'd been there, to tell her what he'd really wanted. "He did ask about you, when he saw that you weren't here." I wondered if Daric had told him something already. "Perhaps he only came to gloat." The unexpected bitterness surprised both of us. One large hand clutched the other again, twisted. Somewhere, she wasn't even sure when, she'd finally begun to believe me.

"You really think he's going to win, then?"

She shrugged slightly. "The combines that want either deregulation or Stryger aren't going to change their votes. And enough others that have no real involvement will follow along and defeat us simply because they don't care about anything beyond their own interests." She faced the false image of the world outside in the false window space on her wall. "They have no accessible nerve-endings; I can't reach them to make them react, make them *feel* that this is important—"

"That's what Jule said, once. . . ."

"What?" She turned back to me.

"That if she could only make people feel what she felt when they hurt each other . . . maybe they wouldn't hurt each other so much." I rubbed my face. My skin felt too tight. "Those Assembly reps are alive—that means they've got to have some nerve-endings. You can hardly see the sharp end of a tack, Lady, and the end of a finger's not much bigger. But you can make a big son of a bitch jump if it's sharp enough. You believe that, or you wouldn't be where you are."

She nodded, almost showing a smile. "But it's hard to find a good, sharp tack these days. That's one reason why I wanted that

Council slot so badly: there can only be real equality among creatures on the same level. . . . I'm tired of wasted effort." Dreary visions of the future I'd given back to her slowly blotted out my image in her sight . . . visions of the struggle against deregulation lost, of a life controlled by the taMings, sterile and empty. . . . "I suppose that I won't be seeing you any more," she said, and the realization made her feel like she'd just lost her last friend.

"I'm still here," I said, suddenly feeling less empty because she felt more empty. "I can still be your aide. I'm staying at Argentyne's club—"

She shook her head slowly, looking away. "Charon has . . . supplied me with another aide. You have other duties now. You work for Centauri." As if I needed reminding.

"No, I—"

"Cat," she said, almost gently, wanting me to stop. "I am not your responsibility any more." She looked at me, registering the dark fatigue circles under my eyes, the tense, hollow face of a burnout. "Please . . . do what you must do for Braedee, and then leave, before Centauri ruins your life too." She put her hand on my arm. *(And before you ruin any more lives.)* She tried not to think it; didn't mean to, couldn't help herself . . . hoped I wouldn't hear it.

I looked down; looked at my own clouded image in her mind, through a long silence. Not able to tell her goodbye and leave; not like this. "Lady—" I said. My bandaged hand closed over hers where it still rested on my arm, tightened until it hurt us both. I let go again, feeling her surprise. "You haven't lost the vote, Stryger hasn't won the Council slot yet. You know you're not going to quit until it's over—and you know I can't either. There's got to be a way to get at Stryger. Whatever it takes—" My hands made the truth-swearing sign, a pledge.

She shook her head, but a little color was coming back into her face, into her thoughts. "You already know how hard it is . . . but yes, you're right, of course. It isn't over." She forced a smile, and I felt the stubbornness of her will lock it into place. "There's an old saying: 'That which has to be done usually can be done.' I'll save my despair until I'm sure I need it." The smile got warmer, until it was almost the smile I remembered.

(Whatever it takes,) I thought, looking through her eyes into her mind one last time. I left her office, still without saying goodbye. I went through the outer office without saying anything at all, without looking at the stranger who was there to take my place.

As I made my way back along the halls of the Assembly plex, the little bit of warmth her smile had left inside me faded, and I felt lousier than ever. I hadn't sworn to her that we could still get Stryger just to cheer her up . . . but I might as well have. I wondered how long it would be until she realized that. Maybe she wouldn't. But even if she did, I knew she'd keep on, now. She knew what was important to her. I wished I felt the same way. I didn't want to see Stryger lose everything because it served some higher Truth or Justice, or for the sake of the fucking Human Race. I wanted to cut him down because I knew he'd beaten the shit out of somebody that no one cared about . . . and because when he'd looked into my eyes he'd wanted to do the same thing to me.

Nobody cared. Elnear was right. If I told them what Stryger had done, what he was really like, they'd never believe me. Even if they did, even if I went to the Indy, got it on the Net, it wouldn't change anything. The vote would still come out the same. My mind tendriled out, feeling strangers pass through me, measuring their thoughts. Those might look like human beings, but they were only tools some combine or other was using to push the right button. I pushed my fists into my jacket pockets, not thinking about what I was doing until the pain in my hand made me swear.

Two people passing me in the hall swore too, and shook out their own hands; looked at me and each other, confused and half-frightened. I realized I'd projected my pain without meaning to. I kept walking, pulling my brain back together, while they went on in the other direction, muttering.

I reached the platform of the closest transit stop, stood looking back at the sloping face of the building I'd just come out of. My eyes followed its rise up into the light, past the next level of the city high over my head. And I wondered what it would take to make every smug bastard in the entire Assembly jump. Maybe if it was their own freedom, or their own pain they had to choose, they'd think about it twice before they let it happen. . . .

I looked down again, squeezed my sore hand shut. Nobody around me jumped this time; I was back under control. *"If they could only feel what I feel. . . ."* I heard Jule say it again, inside my head. And suddenly the answer was right there, so clear to me that I couldn't look away from it, no matter how hard I tried.

The transit arrived, stopped. The people around me pushed past and boarded, and it went on again, leaving me standing there like I'd been stunshot. There was a way to get at Stryger. A way to make the

Assembly feel what it was like to be Stryger's victim. I could make
them live it. . . . But to do that, I'd have to live through it first.

TWENTY-SEVEN

"YOU LOOK LIKE SHIT," Argentyne said when I got back to the club.
Music and image filled the air around her, and faded again. The symb
was setting up for the night's show.

"You are what you eat," I muttered. I looked up at her where
she stood, and wondered if the only reason Elnear hadn't made it
unanimous was because she was too polite.

Argentyne waved a hand at the rest of the players, signaling a
break, and climbed down from the stage. "Was it that bad?" she
asked, as she reached my side. "Your visit to the Lady?"

I shook my head, looking down. "Not exactly." It had been more
the ride back, while I'd had plenty of time to think it all over. Before
I could say anything else the message function on my databand began
to beep. I answered it, heard Mikah's voice. I raised my wrist up close
to my ear, moved away from Argentyne's sudden worried frown.
"What did you get?" I murmured. "You find out who wants taMing
dead?"

"Everybody wants him dead."

"Say what?"

"Almost everybody that counts." I heard him hesitate, trying to
figure out how to make it clear. "What you got here is something that
cuts across territories—"

"Jeezu. . . . Drugs?" I asked, because that seemed most likely;

even though I couldn't imagine how Daric could be in deep enough to get himself killed.

"You said taMing's a user?"

"Yeah." I heard him grunt. Up till now I'd thought that drugs were the least of Daric's problems. Now I wasn't so sure. But one thing I was sure of—I needed Daric alive, to get at Stryger. And if the whole Market was down on him, he might not be alive much longer. "Shit. . . . Can you get me access to somebody with some control over this? Is there anybody who can say *stop* and *go*?"

There was a long silence. "You want to negotiate?"

I rubbed my face, wanting to dig my fingernails into my skin. "Yeah."

There was another long silence. I didn't have to be reading his mind to know what he was thinking: he was afraid we'd both end up dead. "You got that kind of credit with Centauri?" he asked finally.

"Yeah." Not sure if it was true, or even if I cared. "It's important. I wouldn't ask if it wasn't important."

"I'll see what I can do." The link went dead.

I let my hand drop, looked back at Argentyne. She was still standing there, with the same expression on her face. "It'll be all right," I lied, and watched her face relax into uncertainty. "I—I need to ask you some questions about your symb circuit." Daric's life wasn't the only thing I had to be sure of, before I knew whether I could set up Stryger the way I wanted to.

She looked surprised, and then just distracted. "Not now, okay —we're working it. Later I'll show you anything you want. . . . Why don't you get some sleep." She nudged my body like I was a drone. I felt her concern, and her impatience to get back to the group . . . felt my resolve start to fall apart. "You can use my bed again."

"Again?" I said.

Her mouth quirked. "You used it last night."

I realized I didn't remember anything at all about where I'd slept, anything at all about getting up again, besides the fact that it was too soon. "Were you there too?"

"How flattering." Her smile stretched a little thinner; she shook her head. "No, laddie-love. I didn't rape you while you slept."

"Decent of you." I trudged away toward the stairs. This time I didn't even remember hitting the foam. My dreams were full of strange music, full of strangers with hungry faces.

I only woke up again because somebody was shaking me hard.

I jerked awake, wet with sweat, hearing my own thick gasp of relief as I opened my eyes. Mikah was standing over me in the darkness of Argentyne's room. "Cat," he was saying for the twelfth or thirteenth time.

"Yeah," I mumbled, and he let me go. I dropped back onto the bed with a grunt.

"You always sleep like that?" he asked. *Like I was in a coma.*

I rubbed my eyes. "No," I said. "Why?"

"Just wondered how you'd survived so long." He dumped my leather jacket on top of me. "Let's go."

He didn't bother to tell me where we were going, letting me figure it out for myself as I followed him downstairs. We went out a back way I hadn't seen before. I was glad I didn't have to face the wall of flesh out front, where the symb was blistering another night with lightsong.

We went on deeper into the Deep End, while he filled me in. He'd gotten what I'd asked for, some leads, access to somebody who could give me the answers I wanted. He didn't know any more than I did about what the answers would be. He didn't say much else, as he took me through dim green-lit streets toward the smell of the sea.

When we reached the Locks his soldiers were waiting for us on the quay. I stopped moving, going cold in the pit of my stomach. Mikah swung around up ahead of me, impatient. "What are they doing here?" I asked.

Surprise, and then irritation, stung through his brain as he registered my question, the look on my face.

"Sorry—" I said, before he could ask me if I really thought he'd set me up.

His body jerked in what looked like a shrug, but was too angry. He held up his hand, silently showing me the line of the healed scar on his palm.

I bent my head. "Sorry."

He nodded at his gang. "They're only here to prove to the Governor that I'm not running solo—and neither are you." His Family was backing him in this; that was how he'd gotten the meeting. "This is as far as they go, though. We're going out." He looked toward the Locks.

I thought about the billions of tons of water barely held back by the transparent wall of the domes . . . about being on the wrong side of the wall. I tried to keep my reaction off my face as I nodded, looking back at him. I remembered being down here before, seeing what looked like dim lights showing out there in the undersea night. Maybe it made a kind of security sense, to whoever we were meeting.

One of the soldiers, one who was built like the bouncers at Purgatory, held out a couple of drysuits to us as we reached the edge of the quay. "I can't swim. . . ." I said.

Mikah laughed. "Neither can I. Don't sweat it. Everything's taken care of." *One way.* But he didn't say that. I didn't ask about the return trip, figuring that if he was willing to risk it for me, the least I could do was keep my mouth shut. He wasn't armored tonight, but he stripped himself of half a dozen weapons before he took his suit. I watched him put it on, copying his moves; as I sealed the helmet, one of the smaller access locks opened in front of us like a silent invitation. Mikah made some last handtalk to his men, and we stepped inside.

Cold foaming water roared into the hollow space around us as the hatch sealed, flooding it up to my neck, then over my head, almost before I had time to hold my breath. Nothing leaked: nothing icy and wet seeped in anyplace . . . I breathed out and in again, drifting now like I was weightless. The suit's gills began processing oxygen out of the water; the feel against my skin was cool and soothing. A silver-glinting fish swam past my face.

"Okay?" Mikah gestured.

I nodded. "When you start at the bottom there's no way to sink any deeper." I knew that he could hear me, because he grinned.

A small ferry sub was waiting for us at the outer hatch. No one was in it. I had the feeling it only went to one place. As we got in its door sealed—leaving us still underwater as it started away into the darkness.

I latched myself into a seat; Mikah let himself drift, bumping restlessly against the ceiling and the walls. "The Governor—?" I said at last, remembering the name he'd mentioned back on the quay.

"The Governor's kind of like a pressure valve, you know what I mean? He settles things, when there's Market troubles. He speaks for everybody, if they need him to."

I nodded. In the distance I could make out half a dozen of the lights I thought I'd seen from back on the quay. I wondered how many more there were, and why they were out there. I glanced at Mikah. He was seeing restricted gaming holes, exclusive whorehouses, private estates. I looked back the way we'd come, saw the Deep End glowing through the murk like an emerald. *Everything looks better from the outside.* I looked ahead again. We were closing with one of the lights now. I began to see its real form, a shining sphere drifting over the sea floor, shifted slowly and constantly by the motion of the tides. I took a deep breath; still surprised when I did that I didn't drown.

"You ever met this Governor?"

Mikah shook his head. "Not yet. I made this deal through channels. You got Ichiba curious too." Ichiba headed his Family.

"Do they know about me—that I'm a psion?"

Mikah shrugged. "The Governor knows all about you. He takes the Morning Report, too."

The sub nosed in under the looming wall of the sphere, was sucked up into a narrowing funnel, into the heart of the Governor's very private estate. The heavy transparent inner hatch blinked green and swung open, but the lock hadn't drained. The quiet, normal-looking blue-green room that I could see beyond it was full of water. At the far end of the room a spiral of stairway disappeared upward.

"You sure you know what you're doing?" Mikah said.

"This's a hell of a time to ask me that," I muttered, feeling my stomach drop into my boots. I realized suddenly that I was here claiming I spoke for one of the biggest combines in the galaxy, about to face somebody who could say *stop* and *go* for the underworld of this entire planet, maybe even for the whole solar system. And there was nobody I could blame for it but myself. But then a sudden dark rush of excitement filled me, making me feel strong, eager, ready—like something was riding me that didn't know what fear meant. . . . I reached up with a shaky hand; couldn't touch the drug patch through the membranes of my suit.

We pushed off from the edge of the lock into the room, probably looking just as clumsy as we felt, and floundered toward the air fountain billowing upward at its center. Furniture was laid out in small intimate arcs on the blue and white tiles around the bubble sculpture. The furniture was made of plastic but it could have been carved from ice, cool and clear. I glanced at the readouts inside my helmet; the water here in the house was as warm as blood.

As we stopped moving and waited, I felt someone come silently down the steps at the other end of the room. I looked up, watched him come one step at a time, moving as naturally as if the room was filled with air and not water.

"Good evening," the Governor said. No bubbles came out of his smiling mouth. Somehow I actually heard him speak. It took a minute to realize he was using a bonebox and my suit was registering it. You couldn't see the wariness just beneath the surface of his skin, but it was there as he looked at me. I felt the sudden hot surge of Mikah's interest as the Governor glanced his way. The Governor wasn't young, but he looked young, and the muscles of his long body moved like an athlete's under the formfitting jumpsuit he had on. His long hair flowed around his head like seaweed; the warm brown of it matched his skin and eyes. He was barefoot; his fingers and toes were all a joint too long, with thin membranes between them.

Mikah held up his hands, palms out, and signed, *"Ichiba says hullo."*

The Governor's smile got a little friendlier. *"My regards to your Family,"* he signed back. He nodded and stepped down into the room. I wondered where he hid the ballast that let him move that normally. Maybe his suit was doing it. He wasn't breathing; he had gills behind his ears. But the rooms up above us were air-filled, and I could sense other people up there, observing, guarding, leading normal lives. He'd had himself made totally amphibian.

Mikah was still standing beside me. The Governor glanced at him again, a little curious. "You're staying?"

Mikah nodded.

"I don't think I have to tell you that you run the risk of hearing more than is good for you."

Mikah glanced at me. "Go," I said. He shook his head. "Too late," he said to the Governor. He made the sign for *Family*.

The Governor watched us, not saying anything, but watching us now with different eyes. "Sit down," he said finally. "I'm sorry for the inconvenience." He shrugged. *Security*.

I made it to the nearest group of seats, moving slowly so that I didn't look any worse than I had to. I settled on one of the benches, pretending like we were supposed to that everything was perfectly normal. Mikah settled down on another bench, his eyes still wandering back to the Governor, nervous and admiring.

The Governor's long-fingered hands touched the wide, trailing ends of the drape he wore around his neck. It came alive like a port; that was what it was. He was direct-accessing. There was a remote truthtester on the system; the water gave it a good feed. "So," he said to me, letting his hands slowly fall and clasp in front of him, "I understand that you represent the taMings." There was curiosity and a lot of incredulity inside him.

I held onto the edge of my seat. "Not exactly," I said, finally. "Centauri's Corporate Security."

He raised his eyebrows. "And why would they send you to us?" Emphasis on the *you* and the *us*.

"I'm their catspaw," I said.

He actually laughed, as the meaning registered. "That seems to be true . . ." Meaning he'd checked it. "It fits the baroque xenophobia of the corporate mentality well enough. But what legitimate business could they have that requires a meeting like this one?" His smile was full of amusement and irony.

"I think you know," I said.

He folded his arms. "Suppose you tell me, anyway, since I am not a mindreader."

And I was. He must know that it would be hard to hide things from me in a face meeting. Maybe that meant his clients were interested in negotiating. Probably it just meant that it was easier to kill me this way if the meeting turned out bad. "They want to know why you're trying to kill Daric taMing."

He looked vague for a second. At first I thought it was surprise, but then I realized his mind was listening to something—to someone, through a remote link. Everybody who had an interest in this was probably observing through his port, at a safe, anonymous distance from me, and from each other.

"Tell me why they believe that anyone at all wants to kill Gentleman Daric taMing? I understood that it was Lady Elnear you personally saved from assassination. Aren't you working as her bodyguard?"

Mikah was right; they did know all about me. Except for what I knew about them. "Yeah . . . except whoever tried to take out Daric didn't know one thing: nobody was really trying to kill Lady Elnear. It was part of a plot by Centauri to keep control over her and her holdings in ChemEnGen. So when the Market ran that hit on Daric, trying to make it look like it was meant for her, it crashed. It let Centauri know somebody else was the real target."

The Governor looked down at his feet, to hide the fact that he wasn't seeing us again while he got feedback from his listeners. I felt Mikah staring at him, at me, with *interest, excitement, fear* making neuron soup in his brain.

Finally the Governor said, "Very interesting." As close as he'd come out loud to admitting I'd just surprised the hell out of a whole lot of Marketeers. "Someone apparently took a wrong turn in the labyrinthine halls of a combine powerplay. . . . But why is Centauri so sure Daric taMing was the target?"

I took a deep breath and stepped over the edge. "I told them."

"Shit . . ." Mikah whispered, so softly that I barely heard him.

The Governor's head jerked up. He sent a sharp glance at Mikah, back at me; his attention flickered out for a second again. I felt Mikah's sudden tension like a pinched nerve. "How did you find out?" The Governor's voice turned cold.

I forced myself to smile. "I'm a telepath. Finding things out is what I'm good at." I hoped the bluff would be good enough to satisfy his truthtester, to keep him from pushing, from making me tell them who'd helped me do it. "I know you're trying to kill him, but I don't know why. The Corpses want me to find out."

The hard line of his mouth curved a little. "Why bother to come to me?"

I shrugged. "It's easier."

He laughed again; bubbles came out of his nose. The laughter stopped. "You must be smart enough to realize that you knew too much to come here safely. But you've come anyway, so I'm assuming you carry the keys to something you haven't shown me yet."

Mikah glanced at me again, hoping he was right. I hoped so too.

"Suppose we offer an exchange of data. I will tell you why we want Daric taMing . . . and then you tell me what you want."

I nodded.

The Governor wrapped his long fingers over the glowing ends of his drape, making sure of his facts. "Gentleman Daric taMing has for some years had a significant drug account with the Market. He uses heavily himself, and also deals for us to other combine vips who want to indulge their bad habits, but lack his contacts. We have granted him a degree of trust and privilege that is rather extraordinary for someone who comes to us from the Other Side. Gentleman Daric is not your typical Assembly member, obviously. . . . But these privileges were extended with the understanding that they would only last as long as he never betrayed our trust or interfered in our business in any way —that, in fact, he would keep our interests in mind when he voted on certain drug-related issues. . . ."

Now I knew one more way that Daric had found to fuck over his family. And suddenly I saw what had gone wrong. "The pentryptine deregulation vote," I said.

The Governor lifted his head slightly; his hair brushed his shoulders like a soft wing. "Yes—"

"If deregulation passes, it cuts out your profit." I leaned forward.

"And he's been supporting it, supporting Stryger's push to get pen-tryptine deregged. He has to, because it's too important to his family, he can't go against them." Daric might be crazy, but he wasn't that crazy. "That's why you want him out. Right—?"

"Precisely," the Governor said, his voice a little strained. His hand went to his head, touched it, fell away.

"Why not just cut off his drugs? Why kill him? You want to make an example of him, or is somebody just that pissed?"

"Neither." He looked relieved that I was only asking questions again, not answering them. "Gentlemen Daric is considered to be too volatile a personality to be trusted, under the circumstances. If we cut off his access to drugs, he has the influence to cause considerable trouble for us with the Fed Corpsec. But he has violated his pact with us, and we can't allow that. It's bad for . . . business."

I leaned back again, swaying with the motion of the water around me, watching the fountain weave alien landscapes out of pearls of air and light, watching them mutate and change, like data beings moving through a separate reality. Daric didn't know the Market was after his head; they'd wanted to keep it that way. You couldn't kill a Gentleman of the Board and Assembly like you squashed a flea. By finding out, and telling Centauri's Security, I'd made it a lot harder for them to finish what they'd started. They'd finish it anyway, whatever it took, unless I gave them a damn good reason why they shouldn't. And if I couldn't, I'd be dead before Daric was.

"Your turn," the Governor said, his voice nudging me gently. Right then I couldn't remember ever seeing an expression more frightening than his smile.

I wondered whether I was having trouble breathing because of my suit, or just because of the way he was looking at me. "I'm here to work a trade." Until that moment I hadn't been sure what would come out of my mouth. But as I heard the words I realized that I'd held the solution in my hands ever since I'd left Elnear's office today. Even while I'd been sleeping my brain had been fitting together pieces. And now, what I'd just heard had pushed the last of them into place. Suddenly everything I had to do stood out clear and sharp—as sharp as a knifepoint pricking my throat. I didn't have any choice. I just hoped I could make the Market believe they didn't have any choice either, without telling them too much.

The Governor was still watching me, waiting, his body shifting faintly with the slow motion of the water. "Well?" he said.

"Centauri wants Daric alive. . . ." Stalling, trying to pull my thoughts together. *So does Argentyne.* I told myself that what I thought about it didn't matter; this was business, just like Braedee had said.

"Unfortunate for them," the Governor murmured. "Because we never go back on a promise."

"But the final vote on deregulation hasn't happened yet."

He nodded. "But deregulation is certain to be approved, in spite of our efforts. Sojourner Stryger is able to keep a much higher profile than we can."

"He's a combine puppet anyway," I said. "That's where he gets his major motion. But he wants the Council slot Lady Elnear is up for, and he'll get that too if the deregulation passes. And then he'll stop being a puppet and start playing god for real."

The Governor frowned slightly, his eyes going out of focus as he listened to other voices. "Interesting. But hardly our concern."

"You're not—" My voice broke suddenly. I swallowed, and tried again. "You're not gonna like the way he plays. He wants to use deregulation and the power he gets to crush people like you and me. The Feds mostly leave you alone now. But once he's on the Council, what if he has the same kind of effect on them that he has on everybody else? Even Centauri's Security Chief thinks he's more than they bargained for."

The Governor frowned.

I pushed on, feeling his doubt stir. "I think there might still be a way to stop Stryger, and make the deregulation move fail. To make Stryger look bad enough to change some votes." I saw the sudden interest in his eyes. "But Daric has to stay alive or it can't happen."

" 'Can't' happen?" the Governor asked. "Not 'won't'—'can't'?"

I nodded.

"What makes you believe Stryger can be brought down so easily—especially if what you say is true, and he isn't even his own man?"

My hands made fists. "Because he's human."

The Governor looked down at his webbed feet. "Explain further."

I shook my head. "I can't . . . I don't know all of it exactly myself, yet. But Daric is Centauri's liaison with Stryger. He has to do his part or it can't work."

"Centauri is backing this?" he asked, looking at me again. "Why, when they stand to make a substantial profit if this deregulation goes through?"

"If Daric dies they'll lose more—they could lose an Assembly seat to some other combine. And the taMings lose a board member. Gentleman Charon wants his son alive more than he wants more profits." I wondered if he'd still feel that way if he knew what Daric really was.

The Governor was silent, staring at the fountain now but not really seeing it. His face worked, while his mind held half a dozen one-sided conversations. "No . . ." he said at last, turning back again, speaking to me. "Unless you can provide me with something more concrete— that isn't enough to lift the Silence on Daric taMing."

I hung onto the edge of the bench with all my strength, trying not to let him feel my desperation. If I told him everything, he'd probably think I was crazy. I wasn't sure he'd be wrong. But I knew—I realized I'd known all along—that there was nothing Centauri could offer the Market that would get Daric off its hook. And no way Daric could escape forever, even if they made him into a nonperson.

But if the Market let him live, they could still get what they wanted—and I could get what I wanted, too: Stryger. If I just had the guts to make it all work. . . . "Look," I said, "can't you hold off just until after the vote? Isn't it worth that much to you, at least, to hold off a few days? If he cooperates, if he does his part and deregulation fails—then he's canceled his debt to you, and maybe you don't have to kill him. . . . Killing him without anybody noticing has just gotten a lot harder for you. And if he dies before the vote, then there's no hope in hell of stopping deregulation, and it's your loss. What's a few days, against that—?"

The Governor stood, swaying gently, too many eyes watching me through his own.

"And if deregulation still passes . . . ?" he said at last.

"Then you can . . . silence him." I pushed up from the bench, controlling every movement because I couldn't afford to look stupid now.

"Oh, we will," he said. "Be sure of that. Tell him I said so." He hesitated. "In fact, we may even be forced by events to look into the continued health of Sojourner Stryger. . . ."

I felt the blood sing in my ears. But all I said was, "Then we've got a deal." Not making it a question, because I was already certain. All the voices clamoring through the circuits in his head had finally said the same thing. I moved forward, held up my gloved hand.

He slapped it; a strange slithering like the touch of wings. "Deal."

Mikah came up beside me. The Governor looked at him. *"My regards to Ichiba,"* he signed. "Tell him he's got a good man. I respect loyalty to a friend." Mikah nodded, not quite letting himself crack a smile. The Governor looked at me again. "I'm glad you came. It's been illuminating. I'm also glad that we were able to find some common ground. I hope that what has been agreed to comes to pass. It will be a considerable hardship for all concerned, if it doesn't. . . ." He looked down, up at me again. "If it does, perhaps you would consider doing some work for me, someday."

If I survived. "I'll think about it," I said.

He smiled. "Then I hope to see both of you again. Good night, gentlemen." He turned and started back up the stairs, one step at a time. When he was gone the lock finally began to cycle, across the room.

We floundered to the exit and through the hatch. Mikah sighed once—relief, or maybe regret—looking back as the sub carried us toward the city. Then he turned to look at me. "You got more guts than good sense, brother. But you made it run."

"Yeah."

"You don't look happy about it."

"I'm not." I shut my eyes.

"Because now you're on the list too, if deregulation passes?" It sounded casual; but he was thinking that if it came to that, there was nothing at all he could do to help me.

I grimaced. "Worrying about that's the least of my problems, right now," I said.

He shook his head, and looked out again at the Governor's private world fading like a memory behind us. "You catch that? He says he wants to see us again." He actually sounded a little wistful, behind the hard, ambitious grin that was pulling his mouth up.

"Yeah, I'm flattered." I opened one eye to look at him. "And I'm touched by how glad he was he didn't have to drop an electric current through the water in that room after he went upstairs."

TWENTY-EIGHT

I REACHED PURGATORY again just as Argentyne's doorkeeper was heading home for the day. S/he flipped me a handsign that could have meant *have a good day* or *fuck you*. Neither one seemed like much of a possibility.

I went on inside, scooping up a handful of leftovers off a table. I didn't feel hungry, and whatever it was tasted like garbage. I ate it anyway, because I couldn't remember the last time I'd eaten anything, or even felt like I wanted to. Argentyne and her symb were still shutting down, clustered together at the back of the empty stage above the empty room. Random bits of music began, fell away, segued into someone else's melody as I crossed the dance floor.

I climbed up onto the stage, feeling self-conscious as soon as they noticed me, six heads all turning at once. The club was closed; they weren't expecting anybody to walk in on them now, while they were coming down from a performance high. A couple of them were half-naked, in the middle of peeling off costumes, but that wasn't what made them *feel* naked. It was being caught half-in and half-out of symb; not quite one being any more, not quite separate individuals either.

I stopped. "Sorry," I said. "I'll come back. . . ."

"Wait a minute," Argentyne called.

I stopped again, hearing her leave the others and cross the stage, feeling her hand catch my arm to pull me around.

Her eyes were still a little glassy, but the hard light of her need to know cut through the fog in her brain as she said, "Where did you go with that Marketeer friend of yours?"

I glanced down at her hand touching my arm. "I went to get Daric a stay of execution."

Her hand tightened, then went loose and dropped away. "Did you?" she asked softly, almost afraid to say the words.

I nodded. "For now."

"What does that mean?" She half frowned.

"It means that if Daric helps me set up Stryger for a fall, then maybe the Market will forget it wants him dead. They want him dead because he's helping Stryger push for that drug deregulation. If it costs them, it's going to cost him."

She shook her head slightly, feeling dazed again. "The Market's going after Stryger?"

"No. I am."

"You—?" She blinked at me, and made a sound that wasn't quite a laugh.

I nodded again.

"I can't deal with this right now." She waved her hand at me. "It's too surreal. . . ." She started to turn away.

"Argentyne, wait," I said. "I need your help." Finally able to make myself ask what I hadn't been able to ask her before. "Help me do it."

She turned back. "Me?" Her sense of unreality was getting stronger all the time. "How?"

"The symb. You said you could teach me how to work it."

"Just for laughs." She shook her head. "I didn't mean going political on it. Holy lights, you said to *me* you didn't want any trouble!"

"To save Daric—?"

She broke off, looked away suddenly. "If you need the symb, everybody's got to agree." She went away, spoke quietly to the players still standing inside their desultory cloud of music at the other end of the stage. I waited, trying to get my buzzing thoughts straight so I could explain everything when I had to.

She came back again after a minute. "They want to know everything first. So do I."

"That's what I figured," I said.

"Come on, then." She nodded. I followed them backstage, down a hallway to what passed for a living room. Mismatched furniture that

looked like somebody had dragged it in off the street made a soft
barrier along the acoustic-fiber walls. The walls were plastered with
holo stickups of performers they admired. Old musical instruments,
the kind that had never been intended to be grafted into anyone's body,
lay around on the furniture like kids' toys. Everything was comfortable,
loose, real—everything the club out front wasn't.

The symb spread out around me, standing, sitting, collapsing on
the dusty rug . . . but still keeping physical contact. Hands touched hair,
clung to ankles; bodies brushed hip against shoulder, or folded into
someone else's arms. Their eyes were getting clearer as they watched
me. I could feel them still shifting response centers in their brains,
switching out of the instinctive, almost automatic modes of cyber-
enhanced creativity. I'd never felt anything exactly like it; most humans
had their logic and comm functions enhanced, not their creative side.

"How's the hand?" Aspen asked me.

I looked down at it. "Useful."

Argentyne settled onto a couch next to Kiroku, the piper,
watching me with wary copper eyes. "Okay," she said, "spill your
guts, kid."

I looked down at my boots, feeling all their eyes locked on me
now, judging my performance. "I guess you all know how I used to
work for Centauri, protecting Lady Elnear. And I guess you've all
seen Sojourner Stryger. Now I'm going to tell you what I know about
him." I told them what lived inside that perfect shell; how he felt
about psions and what he wanted to do with the deregulated pentryptine;
what he'd try to do if he got that Council slot. How the combines that
were backing him were getting more than they bargained for. "I think
you already know something about Lady Elnear. . . ." I glanced at
Argentyne. "Lady Elnear wants that Council slot too. She deserves
it. But she doesn't have the backers that Stryger does—and Stryger's
done everything he can to make sure she loses. He even used me.
She's going to lose, and he's going to win, and the whole Federation's
going to get even worse about how it treats freaks, if he gets his
way. . . . I'm a freak, and I take that personally. Okay, so maybe it
doesn't matter to you, maybe it's not your problem—"

"Hey, look, nobody said that," Midnight murmured.

"But how can *you* stop Stryger, if Lady Elnear can't?" Aspen
asked. "You planning to assassinate him?"

"He thinks our act's bad enough to kill him," somebody else
said. There was laughter, mixed with synth sounds.

I waited until it stopped, and then I said, "There's something

else about Stryger." I glanced at Argentyne again; her gaze hung on
me. "He doesn't just hate freaks. He likes to hurt them. . . . You
remember that girl Daric brought here—?"

"Stryger did that?" Aspen said, incredulous.

"She was a fr— a psion?" Kiroku echoed.

I nodded. "Daric is Centauri's private liaison with Stryger. He's
also his pimp—he gets him victims."

"Shit, man. . . ." somebody muttered.

"—a pervert?"

"Daric. That figures. . . ."

"So what's that got to do with us?" Raya, the other piper,
asked.

"I'm getting to it as fast as I can!" I rubbed my neck, trying to
ease the crawling itch under the surface of my skin.

She shrugged. "Right, so he's a pervert. Why don't you just tell
everybody?"

I shook my head. "That's not good enough. The Assembly's not
easy to move. I've got to show them what it means . . . I've got to
make the whole fucking Assembly *feel* like his victims, or it won't
change anything—" I closed my fist, and opened up my mind.

The players jerked and swore in a cacophony of sudden uncontrolled sound. They shook out their hands, touched their heads; held
onto each other a little tighter.

"Damn it!" Argentyne said, and then, catching her breath, "All
right—so you can make everybody hurt. What's that got to do with
my symb? You don't need us if you can goose the whole Assembly
yourself with one thought."

"No—" I shook my head. "That's not the point. If I went in
there and made them all puke, they'd fry me, and all it would prove
was that Stryger was right about psions all along. He tried to use me
against the Lady once already; I'm not gonna make it easy for him."
I frowned. "I got to have a record, proof of what he does . . . how
it really feels." I looked back at Argentyne. "You said I could actually
feed feeling into the symb, right? Can I record it, and make it into a
show . . . ?"

Argentyne sat forward on the couch, her own hands making fists;
not listening. "Oh God . . . what do you want, you mean you want
Daric to let Stryger torture him?"

"Daric—?" I said. I felt her freeze as she realized what she'd
done. "Daric's not a psion." I said each word with just enough confusion; felt the surprise drain out of the minds around me. Argentyne

sank back into the couch. (And if you really still give a damn about
him, you'd better find some way to make yourself believe that.) She
gasped, touching her head; looked back at me with gratitude and
resentment blurring her sight. "Of course he's not. . . ." she murmured. "Then what do you mean—you expect us to record it while
Stryger beats the crap out of another freak, is that it?"

"Yeah," I said. "That's right."

"God's teeth! You're a real vip, aren't you? Now you're going
out to pick up some poor bastard off the street who's so pitiful he'd
let a deeve like Stryger do that to him—"

"No." I shook my head, feeling my face flush. "I've already
got my poor freak bastard."

She broke off. "Who?"

"Me."

She stared at me like she was waiting for me to laugh, like she
thought it was really all just a sick joke. "Oh God. . . ." she said at
last. "You really mean that."

"You really think I'd use somebody else to get what I want from
Stryger? I'm not Daric," I said. I sat down on a couch, rubbed my
sweating hands on the knees of my pants. The pressure of everybody's
sudden silence sat on my back like an animal.

"You said . . . you said you needed Daric in this with you.
Why?" Argentyne asked.

I looked up at her. "He's got to set me up. Stryger's not stupid.
I can't just walk up to him and say, 'Kick the shit out of me, will
you?' It's got to look good. If Daric offers to get me for him to use,
he'll trust that."

"But you work for the taMings, for Centauri—you saved their
lives," Argentyne protested, her mind still tumbling like a bird knocked
out of the air.

"Not any more. Not that Stryger knows. Daric's probably already
told him how Charon got rid of me. I'm a degenerate, I seduced Lady
Lazuli. I'm a fucking freak rapist as far as the taMings are concerned."
I listened to myself talk about it like I was listening to a stranger talk
about someone else. "I got no friends on this world . . . no protection. . . ." The back of my hand rose up to my mouth, hard and
sudden. I forced it down into my lap again; made myself stop counting
the shinestones in the constellation on her tunic. "Stryger hates my
guts," the stranger went on, calmly, steadily, "as much as I hate his.
It's perfect."

"It's crazy." Argentyne got up from her place beside Kiroku

and turned her back on me, moving away across the room. She turned around suddenly, her hands out in front of her. "What if he kills you?"

"I'm not stupid either," I said. "I'll make sure I'm protected. I'm not going to let it get serious. All I need is just enough to give those marks in the Assembly a good kick in the balls. I figure not one of them's ever felt real pain. It won't take much to scare the shit out of them. I can take that much." My lips felt numb. I pushed to my feet again, as the wild darkness inside me made me want to move. "Are you going to help me out, or not?"

Nobody said anything . . . nobody said, "No." But they didn't know where to look, because none of them wanted to look at me, right then.

"What do you want us to do?" Argentyne asked finally.

"Teach me how to use the symb to make a recording. Let me use your equipment for an evening. That's all."

"You'll need a socket."

I nodded. "I know." I couldn't use Deadeye's trick-entry if I wanted to do something that would leave a record.

"Aspen—" She gestured at him. He nodded and got up, going out of the room to get his medical equipment. She looked back at me. "You know, this might not even work. When I said that, about making people *live* it . . . well, nobody's ever done that." She shrugged. Part of her was afraid it wouldn't work, and part of her was afraid it would.

I didn't say anything, more afraid than she was. My fingers explored the cracked formfoam beside me restlessly; found something hard and pulled it out: a blunt rectangle of rusted metal, with a line of square holes showing along its side, like teeth in a grinning mouth. I turned it over and over, staring at it.

"Do you know anything about how a symb functions?" Argentyne asked, a little impatient.

I looked up, shook my head.

She sat down again, resting against Kiroku like she was a chair back. "We're all pretty heavily augmented. If I'm right, you won't need that, because you know how to tap into our heads direct. . . . The way it works, each of the players has their own repertoire—the songs they've stored, new compositions happening, whatever they can get their personal system to do. Everyone's different. Everyone does their own riffs—unique, you know, self-contained. But they feed together into a larger pattern through the symb. Working the augmentation lets us improvise fast enough to keep track of it, keep everyone moving and flowing, when it's really good." Kiroku looked up at her, smiling, and kissed her arm.

"Sometimes we work it so everyone's words and music fit the same theme, weaving together like threads—" She lifted her hands, wove her fingers together. "Sometimes everybody takes a different theme, and we let it explode—" Her hands flew apart. "But it's all coming out of the same heart, and it all has to pull back into the center, come together again by the end. When it's right, it's like the cosmos, you know? Like the expanding and contracting of the universe, like centripetal and centrifugal forces, the motion of worlds and suns. . . ." Her hands circled each other in space. She was somewhere else now, forgetting who she was talking to or even why as she groped for a way to explain something that ran so deep in her that it had no explanation. The other players were hanging on her words, all of them lost inside their own private visions of how it felt to be caught up in that epiphany.

"Like a joining," I murmured.

"A what?" Argentyne said, coming back into focus again.

"Nothing." I looked down, still turning the metal bar over and over in my hands.

"You mean sex?" Kiroku asked, and giggled.

I shook my head, still looking down. "It's something psions can do. Not very often. It's opening yourself up to somebody else, completely, until you're like one person in two bodies. . . ." I was thinking about Jule; about how our minds had caught fire with nameless colors, burning brighter and brighter . . . how for one brief moment outside of time the emptiness inside me had been filled with all the answers I'd ever need, all the comfort, the understanding, the love. . . .

"Sounds like sex to me," Argentyne said, with a strange half-smile.

I glanced up; wanting to say something . . . changing my mind. I shook my head again, not meeting her eyes. Instead I said, "Seems to me like most of the people who see your act don't catch half of what's really going on. They'd have to be cybered too, to follow it."

She shrugged, nodded. "I know. That's why I envied you, what you did at the club the other night. . . . But they get as much as they can take, and if they have a good time, that's all they care about. And we don't really do it for them, anyway, in the end."

"What about the visuals, all that holo stuff I saw that night. Where's that come from?"

"That's Argentyne," Jax said. "She's the spirit. She projects the visions. She makes it all flow."

"Shut up," she said, turning away. The sudden irritation behind it surprised me. She was afraid of being singled out, cut off, separated from the group—afraid that fate was waiting to slap her down, that in the middle of all this tech the Evil Eye was still watching. "We all input on what we're trying to make it say. I image them with what I've got up here, yeah; I mix the colors, I control the visual. But the pieces of the dreams belong to all of us." And I realized she was right: all the augmentation in the galaxy couldn't make them fuse well enough to do what they did unless their human halves, with their human egos, were willing to cooperate. I wondered if having their brains rewired like that was what made it possible, or whether collecting the right mix of personalities to make this kind of art was the first, and hardest act of creation. I wondered how long it would last; how long anything that complex could hold together.

Aspen came back into the room, carrying his kit, and sat down beside me. "Lean over." My body tensed, fighting him as he tried to make me stretch my neck. "Relax," he said, sticking on a patch of painkiller. "You won't feel a thing."

That wasn't what I was afraid of; but I didn't say anything, I only bent my head. I didn't feel a thing while he wired me, until the very end: a tingling, like bells ringing inside my skull, and that was all. Getting my ear pierced had been worse.

"You feel that?" Aspen asked.

I nodded.

"Good. You're live, then." He handed me a mirror. "One of us." He grinned.

I pushed up my hair and looked, even though I didn't want to. I touched the fresh spot of synthetic flesh on the back of my neck. Nothing else even showed. I looked at my reflection, at the round, perfectly normal pupils of my eyes. *One of them.*

"Try it out on us." Aspen was still grinning. He'd already forgotten what I wanted to do with it, or the trouble it could make for me. Or maybe it had never even registered on him in the first place.

I looked around the circle, felt them waiting to *feel* something. . . . I shook my head. "I don't want to try it now." I looked down. "Just tell me how I make it do what I need it to do. Just tell me how I record what happens to me, and how do I feed it back into the heads of the Assembly?''

"We can't tell you," Argentyne said, feeling her patience slip again. "Like I said, it's not anything we've ever done. You've got to lock in so we can test it out. The symb quantifies sensory input for vision and sound, sometimes even smell, but we've never tried to code anything like whole body sensation before. I don't know if it can even handle something as unpredictable as . . . as your pain.'' She said the word like an obscenity, and in the back of her mind she thought an obscenity was what I'd be committing with her equipment. "We've got to take neural readings off you.''

I nodded, shrugged. "What do I do?'' I started to get up.

"Just stay there,'' she said. I sat back down again. "Wake up the jack . . . and listen through it for the music.''

I called it on: it shrieked and shone and crackled inside my brain like some insane alien lifeforce. "Jeezu—!'' I pressed my hand against my eyes, trying to blot out the molten highways that were linking me to the startled faces of the players. Slowly the sandpaper static faded, as my mind took its measure and tuned out everything irrelevant, bit by bit. I blinked, able to see their relief, starting to be able to feel it again past the noise. "I'm reading you . . . and you . . .'' pointing to them as I was able to separate the raw data of the sounds each of their instrument systems made. Readouts flashed inside my eyes like phosphenes. "Where are you?'' I looked at Argentyne, the only one I couldn't find a channel for.

"You're in my seat, playing spirit, my role,'' she said. "I'm just listening, reading you out this time. You'll have to play spirit to do what you want to do. You're accessing my console.''

"I'm in your head?''

"Not exactly. Just on the phone. I can't feel you.''

I nodded, even though I wasn't sure I understood; trusting her judgment because I didn't have any choice.

"How does it feel?'' She'd never taken a reaction off a psion.

"Like having rats down your pantslegs. How the hell do you stand it?''

"I'm used to it.'' She shrugged. "Anyway, it never really bothered me that much. . . .'' She looked away from whatever she was seeing on some built-in readout of her own, focused on my face again. Slowly she lifted her hand to touch her forehead. "You remember what I said about you feeling like silk . . . ?''

I nodded, finally understanding that much, at least. "Now what?"

"Open up the console; send data back to the others. Tell them to pick it up, ease off—something simple."

Something simple was all I could do anyway; but I did it, embarrassed and awkward, collecting my thoughts like spit and funneling them into the rigid patterns of noiselight that lay waiting, a datascan that had somehow ended up on the wrong side of my eyes. The symbsystem only recognized a narrow range of commands, a narrow band of frequencies; it was totally blind to everything else. It was like being brain-damaged . . . but remembering how I'd felt without my psi, I realized it was still better than nothing.

"Loosen up," Argentyne said. "Stop treating it like an electric shock."

"I don't know anything about making music—"

"You don't have to," she said gently. "That's their business. Just let them know what you want to hear. Nobody's judging you—try to enjoy it. That's what it's for."

I let myself settle back into the couch, into the crosscurrents of half a dozen different kinds of music playing at once. I let it fill my brain and filter down, trying to reach levels where the control would be almost instinctive. My muscles began to twitch, wanting to be what made the sounds that were filling me now. I'd always liked music. It was everywhere in Oldcity, pouring out of forbidden clubs or broken windows, trapped inside a bottle, just like I was. It was the only thing about Oldcity that ever made me feel glad I was alive. I tried to remember that, to imagine what I was hearing was like that. I let go of who and where I was, and of what I was doing here; tried to make what was happening inside me feel like the sound of an Oldcity night ricocheting off the roof of the world. By not focusing on any single player I could half-hear them all, reacting half a dozen ways at once by not trying to react. . . .

I felt it begin to change; felt the sudden surge of my own pleasure fill me until it turned into a squeal of feedback . . . until I got it under control, drifting back into the river of sound, feeling its currents divide and re-form around me.

"Good," Argentyne murmured. "You've got instincts, at least. Now try making an image."

"How?" I mumbled, hating to interrupt myself to say the word.

"The same way you're guiding the music. Concentrate on the console, give it an easy focus—a face, something in the room, to fix on, and let it start improvising, then ride it—"

I gave it the easiest thing I could think of—myself, moving to the music the way my body wanted to. I saw my own holoform image flash into being in the middle of the symb, dancing, with the walls and ceiling darkening, closing in . . . dancing the way I'd danced once years ago to someone else's music, through a sweltering Old-city night. I stared at the image, forgetting that I was supposed to be controlling it . . . until suddenly it wavered, folded in on itself, and was gone. The music began to unravel into separate strands inside me. "Damn!"

"Don't worry," Argentyne said. "It takes practice. It's like putting your pants on while walking a fence. . . ."

I smiled with half my brain; the other half was still trying to put everything back together that I'd almost had perfect. I looked from face to face, finally understanding the kind of trust it took, the discipline, the control, to do what a player did. Creativity was only the beginning. And they did it without using psi.

"Feel something—"

"I am. . . ." I said, only half hearing her; working my mind deeper into the artificial passageways, still looking for my lost image.

"Something physical."

"Yeah. . . ." I looked down at my bandaged hand; made it into a fist.

Something happened in the artificial grid inside my head—pain went out and came back again sixfold, making me gasp. It went out and came back again, worse, caught in a circular feedback that I didn't know how to stop—

Suddenly the link went dead; Argentyne had cut me loose. I sank back into the couch, gulping in the sweet, empty void that followed like cool water.

There was silence around me in the room, too. Not even echoes. Finally Midnight said, "Shit . . . don't *ever* do that again, man." Raya put an arm around him, pulling him close.

"I won't," I said. "Not to you, anyway." There was silence again. Slowly the players began to get up, by ones and twos, putting their arms around each other and mumbling excuses as they left the room. Only Argentyne was still there when I finally looked up.

"I guess it works," she said faintly.

I nodded.

"It won't feed back like that on an open-ended link. It was just trapped."

I laughed once. "So I won't burn the brains out of the Federation Assembly. Then all I've got to worry about is putting my pants on while walking a fence with Stryger on my back."

She shook her head; tried not to grimace. "That's no problem either, if all you want from the equipment is to code a feelie . . . a straight record of your experience. You come through very clearly; some people never learn to do that. You focus like a pro."

I half smiled. "I am a pro."

"I know. . . ." she said, glancing away, and back at me. "You should really try working this more. Experiment, play with us. It wouldn't take you long to pick it up, I can tell. I want to know what you'd symb like, feeling something real good. . . ." Her gaze broke, as self-consciousness smashed the image crystallizing in her mind.

I kept my face expressionless, looking down. I picked up the small metal-plated bar that was still lying in my lap. "What's this thing?" I asked, to get my own mind off what she'd been thinking.

She looked relieved at the change of subject. "Oh, that . . . something Raya picked up in a junk shop. It's real old, like most of the stuff here—" She gestured at the other instruments lying around the room, started to smile a little. "She can't resist any old piece of crap that's supposed to make music. We like to play them . . . play with them. She said it's called a harp."

"I thought harps had long strings. Like pianos."

"She said it's a mouth harp. You blow through its teeth, and it makes noise. Try it."

I tried it. It made a whole chord of notes as I blew, a different chord when I breathed in again. The sound was smoky and lost; it put a hand around my heart and squeezed. It reminded me of something, but I couldn't remember what. I dropped it on the couch and stood up.

"Take it, if you want," Argentyne said.

I shook my head, and started for the door.

"Where are you going?" she called, mostly because she wasn't sure that I knew either.

"Back to the real world," I said.

TWENTY-NINE

"YOU'RE HOTWIRED," Braedee said, as I came into his office. He leaned forward across the desk/terminal like a snooper sniffing out drugs. The desk was a black cube, like the one on his cruiser. "Do you know what the penalty is for psions wearing bioware?"

"Fuck off, Braedee." I frowned, collapsing into a chair. "I know it better than you do." The way I felt right now, there was nothing they could do to me that wasn't already happening.

"Where did you pick up an illegal jack?"

"It doesn't matter. You're not going to turn me in." Daring him to deny it, feeling lousy enough to enjoy pissing him off. "I need it right now. I'll get rid of it as soon as I can. Wearing this shit is enough punishment—I don't know how you deadheads stand it."

He stared at me, unblinking, rigid. Finally his body eased, with a shrug that said he'd given up trying to make sense of a sociopath. "See that you do." If I didn't see to it, he would. "What have you found out concerning Daric taMing?"

I leaned back in my seat, trying to ignore the dryness in my mouth, and the way my eyes kept wanting to trace the black knife-edge outline of his desk. I glanced at the wide stretch of window behind him, at the view of Centauri's operations plex spreading out in the cold, clear morning across Longeye, as big as the city that had been there before it. I realized the whole layout of this office, and even the colors in it, were the same as the ones on his ship. He liked his world under control. No wonder he didn't like what was happening now. I looked back at him. "I think I found out how you can save Daric's life."

His face barely registered a change; but his mind was an exclamation point. "How?" he said.

"You're not going to like it. Did you tell Charon—Gentleman Charon—" as he frowned, "what happened?"

He nodded. "He knows Daric is in trouble. And he knows that you're still working for me here on Earth."

"How's he taking it?"

"With extreme prejudice." Braedee's mouth thinned. "Well—?"

There wasn't an easy way to say it. "If he wants Daric to stay alive, the pentryptine deregulation has to lose in the Assembly."

Braedee shook his head slightly, as if he thought his hearing had gone out on him.

I went over it again: Daric's drugs, Daric's Lack Market dealings, how Daric had stepped over some invisible line, and the only way back across it was the hard way. What was going on in Braedee's brain got darker with every word I spoke, as he realized what Daric had done to himself.

"It's impossible. . . ." he said finally; but he didn't mean that he didn't believe it. Only that he didn't see any way to stop it. He turned his chair until his back was to me, and stared out at the fields, the symbol of Centauri's empire. Even if Centauri suddenly changed its mind on the deregulation, he figured they'd never get enough other combines to change their votes, just to save the life of Daric taMing. They might be able to save Daric by giving him a total identity change and sending him away somewhere, but the end result would still be the same. They'd still lose his voting seat in the Assembly, and on the board. That made him as good as dead to Centauri, even if he survived.

"Maybe not," I said.

He turned back to face me again. "Explain."

"Stryger. I think Stryger's the key. I think I have a way of making his credibility lousy. And if he goes down, I think he'll drag deregulation down with him."

"Stryger . . . ?" he murmured. His eyes glazed while he called up data and fed it over and over through his mind. At last he said, "Centauri is backing Stryger in his bid for the Council slot as well as

in his push for deregulation." He thought he was telling me something
I didn't know.

"I know," I said.

His sudden paranoia turned into irritation, almost before he knew
what he was feeling. "They are not the only combine involved in
this."

"I know."

His fingers began to tap on the black expanse of tabletop. "What
makes you think Stryger is vulnerable?"

"Everybody's vulnerable." I looked down. "He hates psions."

Braedee was actually surprised, for half a second. "How is that
fact likely to cause him any serious trouble?" Plenty of people in
positions of power hated psions.

I looked up at him again. "Because he does things to freaks that
the rest of you deadheads only daydream about," I said softly.

He straightened up in his seat, staring at me. His mouth opened.
But by now he knew enough not to waste his time asking me the
obvious questions. "What are you planning to do?" he murmured.

"That's my business." I frowned.

He shook his head. "I can't allow that."

"Daric will know all about it. He's going to help me. If Centauri
wants to keep him alive, then you've got to trust me. Leave me alone
to do what I have to do."

"What are you getting out of this?" he asked, finally.

I shrugged. "Your money."

He leaned forward again, his fingers making a pyramid on the
black plain. "What else?"

"You wouldn't understand. . . . Knowing Stryger won't be working for the Humane Society." He didn't understand, but it didn't
matter. "You told me you think Stryger's a fanatic, maybe crazy.
That's he's not going to play anybody's game but his own—"

He nodded. "But that's only my opinion. I'll still have to clear
it with the board. Centauri has a great deal to lose if deregulation
loses. If the board disagrees, it will still be my duty to stop you."

I didn't say anything.

The Corpses who had taken me to Braedee took me back to the city
again, and let me off at the waterline. It was the middle of the day by
the time I walked the last few streets to Purgatory. My feet began to
stumble as the angry energy from my meeting with him finally wore
off. I still had to deal with Daric; but breaking the news to him was

going to be like breaking glass, and I didn't feel clear-headed enough
to handle it without more sleep. My brain still thought it was plugged
into the sun, but my body said my brain was a liar.

Argentyne met me in the back hallway of the club, looking concerned, but not about me. "Jiro's here."

"Jiro?" I said. "Why?"

Jiro stepped out of her dressing room into the hallway behind her.
His white tunic was smeared with something that looked the way it
smelled, and one side of his face was red and purple. For a second I
thought it was makeup. But this time it was real.

"Somebody robbed him," Argentyne said.

"I wanted to see you," he said to me. His voice couldn't decide
whether to sound like a taMing, or like he wanted to cry.

"How'd you find me?"

"Auntie told me you were here."

I glanced at Argentyne.

She nodded. "Go on upstairs."

We went up to her room. Jiro looked around it, wide-eyed with
curiosity in spite of himself. He sat down almost timidly on the
edge of her bed. "Why doesn't Argentyne want to see Daric any
more?"

I tried a lot of answers, finally settled on, "She's angry at him."

"She's been angry at him before. But this is different. Daric's
real upset. He won't even leave his house. He said she's never going
to come back. Even if he tells her he'll kill himself again."

"Jeezu," I muttered. "That's all I need." I looked out the window, wondering if he'd still be so eager to commit suicide once he
knew that somebody wanted to do it for him.

"He said it was your fault."

I looked back at Jiro. "Daric says a lot of things that aren't true."

He bit his lip. "I know. . . ."

"How are you doing?" I asked it, even though I already knew
the answer.

"I miss my mother." He twisted the edge of his belt between his
fists. "And Tally."

"Me too," I said, touching the empty hole in my ear, feeling the
drug patch still in place behind it. "Why'd you come down here,
Jiro?"

"Because I hate Charon! I'm never going back there—" He
winced as his face hurt him. "I want to stay with you."

I stared at him. "And do what?" I asked.

"We could go to Eldorado and find my mother, and you and she—"

"No," I said softly, cutting him off. "We can't. You've got to go home."

"Why not—?" A crimson rush of *anger frustration grief fear* reddened his other cheek.

"Because that's not how life works. Because Charon will stop you, no matter what you do. Because your mother doesn't really want to give up being a taMing. Because you don't really want to throw away everything you've got and live like me. . . . Because I've only started living, and I'm not ready to lose it all to a mindwipe."

"But I—"

"No. Go home, Jiro."

He half-rose from the bed, his fist coming up to take a swing at me. I blocked the move, held his hand away. It began to tremble; he collapsed onto the bed again.

I reached out, trying to be gentle as I touched his bruised face with my fingers. He flinched. "You're lucky that's all you got. How many guys did it take to do that to you?"

He looked down, his face getting red again. "Only one."

"You're still lucky."

"I tried to use my tychee training, but it didn't work very well."

"Didn't you wear a bodyguard?"

"I forgot to turn it on."

I shook my head. "How far do you figure you're going to get on your own in the galaxy if you can't even make it to Argentyne's without getting the crap knocked out of you, and everything you own stolen?"

"I've got my own credit line—" He held his wrist up. It was bare. He stared at it like his hand was missing; I heard him suck in a gulp of disbelief. He made a noise like a stepped-on puppy, and lowered his arm. "Oh, no—" His hands went into his pockets, his tunic, searching frantically for something else. "It was in my jacket, he took my jacket, it's gone!" *A handmade tapestry pouch Elnear had given him, with a holo of him and his parents inside it.* He could see it so clearly in his mind that I could see it too. He sagged forward, his shoulders hunching, his fists pressed into the space between his knees. His nose began to run as he fought back tears. "Shit. Shit. Shit!"

I sat down beside him on the bed and put my arm around him. "Jiro—" I broke off, waiting until he was ready to listen. "Jiro," I said again, at last; I barely touched the bruise on his face. "This's what it means to be on your own, and just a kid. I've been on my own as long as I can remember. When I was a kid it never got much better.''

"It couldn't get any worse," he said sullenly.

"Sometimes it got a whole lot worse." He raised his head; I looked away from the questions in his eyes.

"But I hate Charon! You don't know what he's like—''

I looked down at my bandaged hand. "Yeah, I do." I sighed. "Nobody said you're not hurting, or that you don't have any reason to. Nobody said you don't feel lonelier than you thought anybody knew how to. Charon's a bastard, and he's done things to both of us that we're not going to forget.'' I saw his mother's face in both our memories. "But you're still a taMing, Jiro. And you're still young. That means you'll probably get everything you want, sooner or later. Your mother's not dead, and neither is your sister. Charon will get over what happened; you'll all be together again, someday. And someday you'll be an adult, a member of the board yourself; maybe even an Assembly member. Charon won't run your life any more. And then you can make him pay for this, if that's still what you need.''

"But that'll take years and years—'' He pulled away from my shoulder, stiffening upright, full of desperation. "How am I going to stand it, for years and years?''

"Just like I did," I said. "One day at a time.''

"You're not me! That's stupid! That's not a good enough answer—'' His face and his mind got blind-stubborn again.

"Neither is running away!" I rubbed my itching face, my arms. *What do you want from me? If I had all the answers, do you think I'd be sitting here like this—?* But I only said, "Look . . . your mother said you're away at school most of the time, anyhow, right?'' He nodded slowly. "So you're not going to spend that much time around Charon. You can live with it. You'll have friends at school, people there that you can respect and learn from. Use that—'' He stared at me, but he didn't say anything. "Everybody's got to take over their own life sooner or later, or they might as well be dead. You'll just have to do it sooner. You have to figure out for yourself what's important to you, because you won't have a family you can trust to guide you. Except your aunt . . . you can trust your Aunt Elnear.'' He nodded again, solemn and listening now. Suddenly I thought of something else. "What about the baby?''

"The baby?'' he asked, looking confused.

"You mother said there was going to be a baby soon. Hers and Charon's. Your brother. . . .''

He blinked, remembering.

"He's going to need you," I said. "To help him understand."

He glanced away, staring at the windows; I felt his mind begin to open up again, at last.

I stood up. "Come on. You'd better be getting home before Charon figures out you're gone." I gestured toward the door.

"Cat . . . ?"

"What?"

His mouth struggled to make the words. "Did you ever get scared . . . when you were just a kid . . . and you didn't have anybody to take care of you?"

I looked down at the faded colors of the rug. "Yeah. I was scared all the time. Sometimes I still am."

He got up; glanced at his wrist, as if he still couldn't believe it was naked. *Shock humiliation fury grief* glanced through his brain again, with the realization that there was nothing left to take home with him out of all the things he'd brought.

"You worried what Charon's going to do when he learns you lost the deebee?"

"The what?" he said.

"Your databand."

He nodded. "He'll—" He made a face. "I don't care. Let him. It's only money, we've got plenty. . . ." The defiance fell away. "But I lost my picture . . . my picture, it's the only one I had. . . ." His hands rose, helplessly, dropped to his sides. He sniveled.

The holo in the tapestry bag that was gone with his jacket. "Where'd you get robbed?"

"Right outside the trans station."

"Let's go for a walk," I said.

"But—"

"Don't worry. You're safe now. You've got nothing left to steal."

He didn't like it, but he led me to the place where he'd been robbed. I looked up and down the street, seeing overflowing bins of garbage, only some of it plastic-sealed, waiting for a pickup. "Which way did he run after he knocked you down?" Jiro pointed straight ahead. "Come on," I said. "Let's check the dumpsters."

"Dumpsters?"

"Garbage bins," I said. "Not everybody has a home recycler. A slip'll dump anything he can't use, usually real close by."

He stared down the street. "You look for it. I don't want to touch garbage."

Rich kids— "Fuckin' ass, you will." I gave him a shove. "You're the one who knows what you lost. If you want it back so bad, you'll help me look for it."

He glared at me. I stared him down, waiting while his anger fell apart. He shrugged his shoulders, embarrassed, and nodded. As we began to walk I felt his self-consciousness and fear begin to fade; he looked into every heap and bin, more carefully as he went along.

"There—!" he shouted suddenly, running forward. Something bright stood out from the garbage colors in the shadow of a stairwell. He picked up an expensive-looking orange jacket—his jacket—shook it out, felt in the pockets. They were empty, which figured. He waded back into the trash pile, picking up a carryall and a couple of other things he seemed to recognize; dropping them again. "Here it is!" His voice shot up an octave. He laughed, waving the holo, triumphant. "I found it! We found it—!" He stumbled back to my side, tripping over cans, his eyes wide. "We really did. I don't believe it—" He laughed again. "Wow. Thanks. Thanks. . . ." He pushed the holo down inside his tunic, close to his heart. "How'd you know that, Cat? How'd you know it would be there? Because you're a psion?"

I half-smiled, turning around. "Because when I was a slip, that's what I always used to do." I started back toward the transit station, letting him catch up when he could.

He came up beside me again, panting, dragging his jacket. He looked at it while he walked, and frowned, wrinkling his nose. He tossed it at another trash heap as we passed.

I reached out, caught it before it landed. Further down the street I handed it to a drab-looking girl in a Fedworks uniform, who wasn't much bigger, or older, than he was. She gaped, grinned, and ran on down the street, clutching it in her fists; afraid we'd change our minds.

"It was dirty—" Jiro said, watching her go.

"So are you." I hit the stain on the front of his tunic with my hand, a little harder than I needed to. He winced and didn't say anything more as we headed into the station.

When the transit came, he started looking for words to tell me goodbye. I only shook my head, and got on board with him. "I'm coming back to the estates with you."

He frowned, worry and sudden fear filling his mind again. "But Charon said—"

"I've got to see Daric. Charon'll have to live with it." I slumped down in the seat, suddenly remembering how tired I still was, and hoping this wasn't a mistake. . . . I realized I was tracing the

molded cube design on the plastic seat in front of me, and tried to
stop.

"Cat?" Jiro said, as the trans started to pick up speed.

"What?"

"I'm sorry." *About the garbage. About the coat.*

I sighed.

THIRTY

NEITHER OF US was wearing a valid clearance any more, but Jiro
managed to convince the estate security systems that we were cleared
to land. He had plenty of beginner's bioware netted into his brain.

Charon himself was waiting for us on the terrace when the mod
landed, standing with his hands clenched behind his back.

"Where the hell have you been? What the hell are you doing
here?" he said, one question for each of us. "What happened to your
clearance?" Another one for Jiro.

"I got robbed," Jiro mumbled, looking at the ground.

"What? Speak up, for God's sake—"

"I got robbed!" Jiro lifted his chin. Now Charon could see the
bruise on his face, his stained clothes, the stubborn set of his jaw.

Charon's face changed: *worry, fear, anger.* He looked back at
me like I'd done it.

"He's all right," I said, ignoring the look. "He came down to
see me at Purgatory. He lost his databand to a slip, that's all."

Charon's relief was so strong I almost choked on it. He stood
looking at Jiro, his hands tightening at his sides, fighting something
inside himself. I realized it wasn't anger or wanting to hurt the boy

. . . it was the urge to get down on his knees and hold him, and thank God that he was all right. Jiro stood frozen, reading it as rage, watching those hands with barely-controlled panic.

But Charon didn't move. His hands loosened. "Don't ever do anything that stupid again," he said. "You could have been killed."

"I won't," Jiro said dully.

I felt Charon do something with the hardware in his head— sending out a signal to kill Jiro's lost databand. I hoped it was too late, that some freedrop had already cleaned out his account. "Go inside," he ordered, gesturing toward the Crystal Palace waiting behind him.

Jiro hesitated, looking at me. He smiled, uncertainly. "Thank you." He patted his shirt, the holo hidden inside it.

I nodded.

"See you—?"

"Maybe," I said, not wanting to make him a promise I couldn't keep. I watched him go on, small and alone, into the shining house.

Charon stood watching Jiro, watching me as I watched. I felt his awareness of me, an ache like a knife-wound. He couldn't believe I was still here: the thing he hated most, still infesting his life, perverting his family. I was like some kind of curse on him, a living, breathing, punishment. . . . *A psion . . . Lazuli and Jiro . . . Daric . . . Jule . . . Did you sleep with my daughter too?* Wondering what he would never dare to ask me. "Get out of here," he said suddenly, thickly, jerking his head. He turned away, starting toward the house. And he was *trying not to think about it—about the thing he'd done. . . . Jule . . . Daric . . . psions. . . .*

"I have to see Daric," I said, too loudly, but he didn't notice. *What thing?* My body stood motionless, left running on autopilot while a part of my mind went after him, trying not to lose that sudden, secret thought. I followed it back through the hot-and-cold maze of his mind. *How many secrets like the one about Elnear did he have hidden inside him?*

He turned back suddenly, glaring at me. "Daric?" he said. "Why?" *He hated psions. But both his children were psions. And nobody really knew why.*

"About the trouble he's in," I said. "About how to get himself out of it." Distracting him as I probed deeper, getting closer, until I could almost feel it—*He didn't know Daric's secret. But I was sure now that somewhere inside him lived the reason for it. . . .*

"Not until you tell me everything." The same mangled rush of emotions that had hit him when he saw Jiro come home hit him again, twice as hard, *worry, fear, anger*—even something he might have called *love,* but I wouldn't have . . . for Daric, *who was perfectly normal, in spite of everything, and yet gave him nothing but grief. . . .*

"No, sir." I shook my head. "I can't do that. Ask your Security Chief. He'll explain it to you." In spite of everything, I could almost feel sorry for him. . . . *In spite of everything . . . everything that had been done to make them something more. . . .*

He opened his mouth to tell me to go to hell—broke off, seeing something in my eyes that made him afraid.

"If you want to keep Daric alive, you'll let me see him now. No conditions," I said, hitting him in the face with the words, blinding his thoughts.

He stared at me a second longer, his mind leaping and dropping between levels, and fears. "All right," he murmured. "See him, then. And then get out." He turned his back on me and went into the house.

And then I saw the answer; I knew what he'd done.

I got back into the mod again like a sleepwalker, and it took me to Daric.

"Daric!" I called, at the sealed entrance of his house. He was inside, I could feel him in there. I knew he had to be watching, listening through his house system. But there was no answer. "Come on, talk to me!" This was one thing I hadn't counted on—that he would refuse to see me. "You want to save your life—?" Still no answer. I looked around. The house was like no building I'd seen before, here on the estates, or anywhere. It was made of untreated wood, the lines of it stark and clean. There were no windows looking out anywhere, no other entrance but this one. My mind had him pinpointed behind that barrier; I slipped in through his useless defenses, and thought, (Do you want to know why you're a freak like me—like your sister?)

This time the door opened.

I went inside, down a long empty hallway of polished golden wood. At its end was a rectangular courtyard, open to the sky, dazzled with light. The center of the courtyard was a sort of garden; small, precise green-needled shrubs were set in a sea of sand and smooth black stones. The sand had been raked into lines like the ripples on a sea; every black stone had been set exactly where it was to create a calculated effect. It reminded me of standing on the Monument. . . . For just a minute standing here seemed as unreal as the memory of standing there suddenly did.

"That was very clever." Daric's voice came ahead of him out of the shadows. He pushed aside a door/wall and came into the courtyard, wearing a long, patterned black robe that seemed to suit a place like this, and an expression that didn't. The mocking arrogance was a false face, but it was all he could find to cover the naked *fear, curiosity, anger, resentment* inside him as he saw me. He looked pale and sick. "That was a lie, wasn't it? What you put into my head, about knowing why I'm a psion? You just said that to make me let you in, didn't you?"

"No," I said, "it was true." I didn't say anything more.

"Well? Are you going to tell me?"

"That depends on how good a listener you are."

He bent his head, the twisted smile spreading wider across his face. "Ah. So you've finally decided what you want from me. I knew you would." *Blackmail, for keeping his secret.*

"Yeah." I nodded. "You might say that."

"Sit down." He pointed toward the low wooden benches waiting at the center of the courtyard. The mindless gesture made me think of some vip inviting the opposition to open a round of negotiations. I realized that was what he was doing, whether he knew it or not. He sat down first, waiting.

I stepped out into the sunlight, blinking for a second until my eyes adjusted. I sat down, wary, but no warier than he was, this time.

"How much do you want?" he asked.

"It's not that easy," I said. "Have you talked to Braedee lately?"

His frown was all the answer I needed; and all I got. He knew why I was still on Earth. He knew that the human bomb had been meant for him. He wasn't sure whether he cared. . . . I probed deeper into his mind, until I found the solid, stubborn core of him that wanted to survive at any cost; that had kept him alive, living with his secret all these years.

"I found out who wants to kill you," I said.

He sat watching me, not saying anything, with his hands clenched quietly at his sides, tightening and tightening. I felt the pain growing like a flower inside him as his nails dug into his palms. I'd never noticed how long his nails were, how sharp.

"It's the Lack Market," I said.

"The Lack Market?" he murmured finally, with more disbelief than anything.

"They think you're two-timing them."

He still looked blank. He kept the two sides of his life so separate in his mind that he couldn't even imagine why.

"It's about drugs." I felt him start. "They say you made some promises to them, about doing them some favors in return for getting all you can use. They feel you haven't been keeping the promises."

"Who says so?" he asked, stalling.

"The Governor."

"You spoke to him?" His incredulity got a lot louder. "How?"

"Friends in the wrong places."

He sat a minute longer trying to decide if I was telling the truth. "They really want to kill me," he said at last. "Why?"

"Deregulation. They don't like it that you're working so hard for it. They don't like you playing on Stryger's side."

He frowned. "I explained that to them; that I couldn't go against my family's interests, or the combine's. It's too important, the potential profit gain—"

"Is their loss," I said. "They're real concerned about that."

"Oh, for God's sake—" He looked away, searching for something calm to rest his eyes on, focusing on waves of sand, black stones. "This is absurd. Some consortium of social deviants actually expects me to put them ahead of Centauri—and if I don't they threaten to kill me?" His body jerked with exasperation.

"They will kill you. They've already tried." I made him look at me. "The human bomb was just the first one. Who the hell do you think you've been playing with, Daric?" He stared at me, as the reality of what was happening to him finally began to sink in. "You think this was all some game to them, like it's been to you? They've even threatened to hit Stryger."

He flinched as my voice got loud; that wasn't supposed to happen here. None of this was supposed to be happening, here, in his life. . . . He said sullenly, "Why don't you just let them do it, then? It would get you everything you really want, wouldn't it?"

I opened my mouth, shut it again. Because there wasn't any point in asking him if he thought I wanted two more dead men on my conscience right now; in telling him that what Elnear wanted mattered to me, was important to me. I only said, "If deregulation passes, they'll kill me too."

He heard it, but it didn't seem to mean anything to him. "Tell

Braedee," he said distractedly. "He'll protect me until the vote is over. . . ."

"I already told him. He's already trying. But they won't stop, not until you're dead. It's a matter of—business with them. You understand about business . . . ?" I felt my mouth try to twist into a smile. "Even Braedee knows that much about the other side. He knows that if you want to keep breathing it'll take a total identity wipe—there won't be a Gentleman Daric taMing any more. No board member, no Assembly member. You're a null set, dead or alive . . . if deregulation passes."

He was as gray as a cadaver now. "Only if it passes—?" he said weakly. I nodded. "But it's going to pass. . . ." He looked out at the still, rippling sea of black-and-whiteness around him, clutching his knees with his hands. "I can't stop it."

"You're going to try," I said. He looked back at me. "You're going to help me do it, if you want to stay alive."

"How?" There was no sullenness, no sneer on his face now. No questions about what it would mean to Centauri or his father. The survivor was in control, looking out at me through clear eyes.

"I want to show Stryger for a freakhater in front of the Assembly. I want you to tell him you can get me for him to do . . . you know what I mean." I looked away; forced myself to look at him again. "I want to make a full-sensory tape of what he does to psions, with Argentyne's equipment, then feed it though the system in the Assembly Hall before the vote, so that everybody in that room knows what he is. Is he going to be there?"

Daric nodded, picturing Stryger's final address to the members. His own mind was still caught in the middle of taking it all in.

"Good." I wiped my mouth with the back of my hand, feeling sweat on my upper lip; feeling trapped in this silent rectangle of sunlight, inside the shadowed symmetry of its perfect walls.

"Let me make certain I understand this. . . ." Daric muttered, his hands twitching in his lap like poisoned mice. "We humiliate Stryger in public, and that will weaken his support?"

"More or less," I said.

"The vote will be close; that might be enough. . . . And the Council slot—" He broke off, as the full weight of the betrayal and the likely repercussions began to come down on him. "If this works, he'll lose it; Elnear will take it." He looked up at me again, wavering, as the two sides of him fought over his survival.

I had to be sure I had him. "You want to know the truth about what you are?" I asked.

His hands tightened. For once his mouth didn't get the best of him; he only said, "Tell me." And then, before I could, "It was Triple Gee, wasn't it? The marriage, somehow they managed to use that woman—" he meant his mother—"to hide defective genes. . . ." It was what his father had always hinted at, wanted everyone to believe.

I shook my head. "Your mother had nothing to do with it. Every gene in your body and Jule's was laid out like a streetmap before you were born; you really think nobody would have noticed? Your father did it."

He stared at me, his mind floundering.

"It was Charon," I said again, before he had the chance to call me a liar. "He planned it, he had the extra genes planted on purpose. Nobody else knew."

"That's insane," he whispered. "Why would he want to ruin the family line—?"

"He didn't think he was ruining it. He thought he was improving it. He wanted to give the taMings an edge—he wanted mindreaders nobody would suspect, or detect. To help you keep one up on the competition, outside Centauri and inside it."

He looked down at his hands, his body, as if he was seeing them for the first time. "But it didn't work . . . ?"

"Not the way he expected. He didn't really understand: it's like trying to make somebody a holo artist—and maybe you wind up with a musician instead, or a dancer." Jule had almost been what he'd wanted. She was an empath, she felt emotions, and projected her own—but she couldn't read a formed thought, and without any training she couldn't control what emotions she read, or when she projected. She could teleport too; that was easier to control, but it was only an extra embarrassment to her family. She'd been a setback to Charon, but still he'd tried again, one more time—

Daric's eyes moved, sliding away as I tried to make him look at me again. "Then why did they kill her—?" *Centauri. His mother.* He quivered.

"Maybe it really was an accident. Daric—she didn't die till you were old enough to remember it, and they all thought you were normal." He looked at me again, finally, a little sanity coming back into his eyes. "How did you keep them from finding out—" I asked, "all the while you were growing up?'' I wondered again how he'd ever managed to keep a secret like that, when Jule couldn't.

"Jule . . . Jule hid it." He chewed his lip.

"But she was only a little girl," I said.

He nodded. "But she already knew that there was something wrong with her, that it made people hate her. She protected me, covered for me, taught me to hide what I could do. . . ." She'd tried to save him from the pain she felt, the pain that she couldn't stand to feel happening inside him too. "That's why I hated her so much." The pressure, the constant fear, the suffering that Jule felt and didn't know how to hide; he'd blamed her for all that. "I didn't know what else to do. . . . She was the only one I could trust, the only one who would forgive me. So I always hurt her. But no matter how much I hurt her, or she wanted to hurt me, she never gave away my secret. . . ." In the end, he'd even hated her for that. He shook his head, blinking too much.

He looked up at me again with bleak eyes, both of us realizing that it was too late to change anything at all; and that he'd never forgive me for letting him know the truth. But now his betrayal of his father and Centauri only seemed like justice. His mind went back over everything I'd said about the setup again, step by step. "Does Argentyne know about this . . . this perversion of her equipment?"

I nodded.

"She's agreed?"

"Yeah."

"Elnear said you were staying at Purgatory. . . ." He gave me a look that carried feeling as thick and dark as blood.

"That's right." I met it, lifting my chin a little.

"And you want me to tell Stryger he can have you?" he said. The pupils of his eyes opened wide.

My jaw tightened until it hurt. "Make it convincing. It's got to happen before the Assembly meets to vote."

"And that's all I have to do?" His eyes flickered away, following his thoughts.

"Probably."

"That won't be any problem," he murmured. I watched the knife-twisting smile come out of hiding. "In fact," he looked back at me, "it sounds like fun."

THIRTY-ONE

I saw ELNEAR'S HOUSE falling away below me, across the open fields, as the mod rose and I left Daric behind. I had to fight the urge to turn back—to stand in the stone-walled courtyard again, to walk through those halls that smelled like another age . . . to touch a table covered with stars that shone in the firelight. To talk to Elnear, tell her what I had to do—

I told myself she wouldn't be there . . . I told myself the truth: that if she knew, she'd try to stop me. Because she wouldn't understand; because she wouldn't want to see me get hurt. The less she knew about it, the better. And the less I thought about the things, and the people, I'd shared that house with, the better off I'd be now.

When I got back to Purgatory, I found Argentyne in her dressing room, putting on her night face. She turned around in her seat, one side of her face silver, and one side reflecting light like a mirror. I squinted.

"Is Jiro okay?" she asked. "What did Charon do?"

"He's okay." I nodded. "Too much and not enough. . . . I saw Daric. It's set. He'll do what I need him to."

She didn't say anything, seeing Daric in her mind with a kind of helpless hunger.

"He says it sounds like fun."

A wave of sickness went through her. Her mouth pinched, guilt shutting her up when resentment made her want to call me a bastard. Instead she pulled her hair forward too hard, braiding it between her fingers, and said, "We've been talking this over—" meaning the symb, "about how you want to make something the Assembly's really going to live." She shook her head, glittering, the look in her eyes now telling me she was enjoying making my life harder too. "Nobody's sure that's going to work at the other end . . . if the systems are even compatible. . . ."

"The Net's the Net," I said, feeling my sudden frustration start to back up inside me. "All the systems in it work the same way."

"But they don't all use the same kind of specialty programming." She hit me with the obvious. "What the Assembly uses is basically a comm net, not a sensory net; it may not even be able to read the kind of message you want to send through it. Maybe you can make them watch a threedy of Stryger, but you probably can't make them live it. . . . What if it won't work?"

I swore. "It's got to work. . . . How can I find out? Can you test it?"

She made a noise that wasn't really a laugh. "You think we have access to the Assembly floor—?"

"Daric does," I said. "Daric can help me find out for sure."

"And what if it really doesn't work?"

"Then Daric will help me fix it." I went out of her dressing room, leaving her there to wonder, and climbed the stairs to the upper level. It seemed to take forever. I lay down across her bed, smelling the faint smell of spices and herbs that was her perfume as I shut my eyes; thinking that if I could just grab a few hours of sleep while she was downstairs in the club, then maybe I wouldn't feel like this any more, like somebody was stretching my sanity on the rack. . . .

When I woke up again, the light hardly seemed to have changed. I checked my databand, looking for the time—looked at it again and again, trying not to believe that I'd actually slept nearly a whole day. I felt worse than before. But I forced myself to get up off the bed, and stuck a fresh drug patch behind my ear. There were only half a dozen left.

I stumbled downstairs. Argentyne, Aspen, and Raya were sitting at a table out front, watching the air dancers drift through a freeform routine inside their sphere. Aspen and Raya were making an eerie, chiming music for the show, rubbing wet fingers around the rims of their drink glasses.

"Why didn't you wake me up?" I said, sounding more like I felt than I wanted to.

Argentyne looked up at me, startled. She took the camph out of her mouth. "I tried," she said. "You wouldn't."

She actually meant it. I glanced away, rubbing my neck. "Sorry," I muttered.

She shrugged. "No problem. . . . Daric called. So did Braedee."

I looked up. "What did they want?"

Trying to sound indifferent, she said, "Daric's at the Assembly. He says Stryger wants to do it."

I swallowed the sudden hard lump in my throat, and nodded. "When?"

"The night before the Assembly votes."

Two days. The buzzing in my head was so loud all of a sudden that I could hardly hear.

"I told Daric that you need him to help check out the systems compatability. He's probably still there now, if you want to go up—"

"I can't." I touched the jack on the back of my head. "It's too risky. He'd better come here."

She stiffened, but she didn't say anything.

"What about Braedee? What did he want?"

"He didn't say."

I frowned, and went to use the phone.

Daric was still in his office. He smiled when he saw me on his screen. "Did Argentyne tell you? It's all set. Two days. I told Stryger you planned to leave Earth right after the vote." He looked like he could hardly wait.

"It's not quite set," I said. "Not unless I'm sure the Assembly's really going to eat it all. I need you down here tonight to check things for me."

"At the club—?" His shoulders tightened. "Of course . . . I'll leave immediately." The screen went blank.

I stood there a minute, not sure whether to be surprised or worried. Then I called Braedee. I got a recording. That didn't make me feel any better. I called Mikah instead. He came onscreen, alive and half smiling. "Who's trying to kill you this time?" he said. I couldn't tell for sure whether that was a joke.

"Sojourner Stryger."

Now he couldn't tell. I explained everything to him, now that I was as sure as I could be that it would really happen. His smile disappeared while he listened. "You're out of your fucking mind," he said finally. "Cat, it's the drug talking. You're not indestructible. He will kill you."

"Not if you're there to back me up—"

"Uh-huh," he murmured. He hesitated, looking down, considering the possibilities. "That's different. I'll clear my calendar." He looked up at me again. "Call me when you got the details."

I nodded, fingering the patch behind my ear. "Mikah—"

"Yeah?"

"Don't get me any more topalase. No matter what I say."

"Right." He made the truth-swearing sign, his hand clenching around his closed fist, before he cut contact.

I left the phone, starting back along the hallway into the club.

Two Centauri Corpses stepped into the hall in front of me, blocking my path.

My first instinct was to turn and run; but they were ready for that. I wouldn't get two meters before they stunned me. I stopped where I was, instead. "Braedee—?" I called.

"Braedee wants you," one of the Corpses said.

There was only one reason why he'd want me picked up now: the Centauri board wouldn't cooperate. They wanted Stryger and deregulation more than they wanted Daric alive. "I'm not talking to you," I said to the Corpse. "Braedee—I'll bet tens you're monitoring this pickup. Call them off—or Charon hears everything."

The phone I'd just left began to beep. I went back to it and thumbed on the privacy screen. Braedee's face filled in on the monitor in front of me. "Leave me alone," I said, "or Charon hears about the human bomb." He'd lost his check on me, but I still had mine on him.

He stared at my image on his screen for a long minute. "All right."

I frowned. "That's too easy."

He smiled faintly. "I can leave you alone. But that doesn't mean someone else won't be watching over Stryger. Centauri is not the only combine interested in his continued well-being. I have no control over that."

"Damn it, Braedee—" I broke off, my hands spasming on the edges of the monitor. "You know what he is! You really think letting him win is going to be in Centauri's best interests?"

"I'm in no position to judge that," he said. "I simply follow orders."

"Sure you do." I looked away from his face, because I couldn't think when I looked into those eyes. "Listen. . . ." I said finally. "And you better listen good, damn you. I set it up with the Market to leave Daric alone until after the vote, because I need him. If deregulation fails, he lives; if it passes, he doesn't. But to get them to deal I had to make them believe Stryger's a threat to them. They threatened to kill him too, if deregulation passes."

He stared at me; kept staring, for a long time. But he didn't say anything.

I cancelled the connection and shut off the security screen. When I turned around, the hall was empty.

I went back into the club. Argentyne was sitting at the table alone now. Even the air dancers had gone away. "What did those Corpses want?" she asked.

"Nothing." I looked toward the door, still frowning. "Daric will be here soon."

I watched her sit there, motionless, while half a dozen different impulses burned themselves out inside her. "Oh, what the hell. . . ." she murmured. She sank back into the cushions, pushing at her hair.

I felt like my stomach was full of worms. "Argentyne. . . ."

"It's all right." She looked up at me, resigned. "It is my own fault."

I shrugged, and sat down across from her. "I'm sorry I took up your bed all day, anyway."

She laughed. "Don't lose sleep over it. I've got half a dozen others."

It took a minute before the meaning behind the words sank in. "The symb—?" I realized that I almost never saw any of them alone. They were always in twos and threes, always with each other, talking, touching.

"Yeah." She smiled now, half fond, half amused. "We all sleep together. When you get that tangled up in each others' heads, it just seems natural to get as close as you can. It's kind of like family." Her smile twitched. " 'Vice is nice, but incest is best'."

"Where did that leave Daric?" I asked. "Or was he only in it for the pain?"

She stopped smiling; but it wasn't anger this time. "Everybody takes their serious lovers on the outside. It would get too intense otherwise. This way it stays more casual . . . maybe it'll hold together longer. . . ." She glanced down at her hands, like she was holding a bubble in her palms; she looked up again at me. "Daric is—was like nobody else I ever had. The way he touched me . . . he could touch me in impossible places. . . ." Her eyes changed; I felt her realizing for the first time why—how—he was able to do that to her. "He was so good. . . ." She pushed up from the table, looking toward the door. "I'll be in back with the others. We'll be ready with the equipment when he gets here."

I sat and waited alone for Daric, rubbing my wet fingertip around and around the lip of a half-empty glass until I could make it sing.

He came into the club at last, walking straight across the room toward me. He stopped in front of the table; his frustration showed on his face as he saw that Argentyne wasn't there.

"The Centauri board's against what we want to do to Stryger," I said, trying to get his mind off her. He frowned. He didn't know that; they'd met without him. I wondered which way Charon had voted, or if it really mattered. "I've got Braedee on hold, but he says Stryger's other backers will be watching him closer. I don't know if Braedee can control that, or not. Is that going to be a problem—?"

He shook his head, his mouth thinning. I felt the sullen betrayal smoldering in his brain. "No," he said softly. "Stryger has his own ways, and so do I . . . I assume the Governor will allow me to use them in his interest. Stryger will keep his appointment with you." I looked away. "What are you waiting for?" he asked. "Let's check the system. We want to make sure it's all perfect—" When I looked back at him, he was smiling.

I led the way into the back of the club, feeling the strangeness he felt as he followed me through this place he knew so well. All the players were there, waiting for us. Argentyne stood in the middle of them like someone wearing a human shield; she was blinking too much. Daric stopped dead as he saw her. He hadn't really believed she'd be here, meeting him face to face. I felt the air come alive between them with the static of their tension. All they felt was the silence—both of them wanting and hating this, the closeness without contact, the contact without closeness.

Argentyne looked down first, away from the sight of him. He'd never looked better to her—taller, handsomer. . . . "Hullo, Daric," she said.

"Argentyne," he muttered; broke off, when he couldn't think of what to say next.

"Here's the box." She held something out to him in the palm of her hand.

He crossed the room, took it from her; I felt the electricity as they touched. He settled the finger-sized box in the palm of his left hand, closed his own fingers over it like he was about to crush it. But his hand was more than a hand—augmented, like Elnear's, like his father's. "Activate it," he said.

She called on the symb. Daric's face got vague as something else took over inside his brain, checking, matching, reading out. After a few seconds his expression started to come back . . . he frowned. He swore with disbelief. "You were right." He glanced at Argentyne, his face going pale. He'd checked the symb with his own bioware, and it didn't match.

"Can the Assembly system be altered so it works?" I asked.

He laughed, still frowning. "Of course it could. It's simple enough. You'd only have to open up the spectrum-width the Assembly floor accepts. But you'd have to break into the Federation's security first. I guarantee you that you will grow old and die before you make that happen."

Argentyne took the box back from him, stood looking at it, holding it in her cupped hands. "He could still make a threedy. It would still show up Stryger. You could give it to the Indy, they'd run it—"

"Stryger could say it was altered, faked. A smear." I shook my head. "Nobody would believe it."

"He's right." Daric pulled at the high collar of his coat, sweating. "Stryger isn't where he is because his aura's been easy to tarnish." He started to pace. "Oh God . . . what am I going to do? They're going to kill me, Argentyne!"

Argentyne's face filled with helplessness as she watched him. She raised her hands, raising the symb box to plug it into its hidden socket again, somewhere in the back of her head.

"Wait." I held out my hand. She gave me the box, looking uncertain. "Just for a little while," I said, "that's all we need." I jerked my head at Daric. "There's still something we can try. But we have to do it without any interruptions."

She nodded, and didn't ask the questions in her mind. The other players followed her out of the room, glancing back at us as they left. Daric watched her go, watched me stay, like he was paralyzed.

(Daric,) I thought, loud, to get his attention. He spasmed, focused on me. "Can you access the Federation system from here? Or do you need some kind of special port?"

He touched his head, irritated and confused. "I can access directly through my bandphone, from anywhere on the planet. Why?"

"We're going to take a trip together into their system. And you're going to change it."

He looked at me like I'd gone insane. "I told you, there isn't any way—"

(There is for us.)

He jerked again, shuddered, as it reminded him what we had in common. "But that's impossible . . . isn't it?"

I shook my head. "I know how to get in. If you open the window, it'll be easy enough. But I have to take you with me, because I can't change anything once I get inside. You show me what I need to find, and when I find it, you'll make it change."

He shook his head, trying to imagine what I was actually telling him. "You mean . . . any psion could do that. . . . I could?"

"Not without me to find the way. I'm the eyes . . . you're the tool. We need each other." My mouth twisted into a grin that felt like one of his.

He glared at me, with his lips pressed together. "Their security—"

"—won't see us, hear us, or feel us if we're careful enough. We're outside the spectrum."

"This is incredible. . . ." he murmured. "You're really serious. How do you know all this?"

"That doesn't matter. And once we've done it, you'd better forget you ever knew it, if you want to go on passing for human."

His frown came back. He sat on a couch, twitching. "How do we do it?"

I handed him the box and sat down across from him, hoping I knew as much as I thought I did; thinking about Deadeye. "I'm going to link with you—make telepathic contact. You're going to open your access to the Assembly system. I'm going to follow it in, and take you with me."

He licked his lips. "How long does it take?"

"Not long, if it works." I shut my eyes, shutting out the sight of his face as I moved in on his mind. I kept the contact as gentle as I could, but still the fear inside him exploded, fragmenting his concentration. (Daric!) I thought. (Do this or you're dead.) I felt everything pull back together, as the survivor reintegrated and focused on his own need. Images of his father, shot through with memories, filled him/ me like gall. "All right," he said bitterly. "I can stand it if you can."

(Don't talk. Just think. I'll hear you.)

(Oh, God,) he thought.

(Open the access.)

He called on his access to the Assembly floor. A rush of particle code lit up a section of his bioware with party lights; data began reforming itself into something his conscious mind could read.

(Think about how the system needs to be altered, and where.)

He did what I asked, checking and comparing the symb's system with his own, spelling it out for me until I knew what I had to look for. (Now relax and hold on; you're going for a ride.)

The open window lay right there inside his mind, waiting. Compared to what I'd gone through with Deadeye, getting in this way was easy. I dragged Daric after me into the channel of white light. His ghost clung to me, riding my back, too terrified and dazzled to even think about letting go. The access conduit swept us at lightspeed into the hidden heart of the Federation, the invisible world that made the visible one possible. Entering its data core was like being sucked into the heart of a star, drawn in through denser and denser shells of pulsing energies. My head sang with the feedback of our passage: the layers of *light/noise/vibration* seemed endless, filling my senses with the smell of burnt cinnamon. It was hard to remember that this blazing infinity was no more than a subatomic dance to prerecorded music, locked inside a telhassium crystal the size of my thumb. It was even harder to remember that I knew where I was going inside it, and what I wanted to do when I got there.

Before I'd finished the thought we were there, inside the nexus that fed the Assembly Hall; the end of the line. (We're there,) I said to Daric, and felt him open his eyes, or something like it.

(It's hot—) he thought, because that came closer to describing the indescribable than anything he could think of, sensing something all around him, but blind to it with every sense he had any understanding of. I began to search for the nerve center he'd described, that contained the code sequence we were hunting for. As I narrowed my focus things got clearer; I began to pick out forms within the form, the kinds of things Deadeye had taught me to recognize and forced me to learn the meaning of. Every other layer here was some kind of security program, penetrating the flesh of the data core like blood vessels. Uneasy subsystems nuzzled my brain, rippling through us like fish through water. My mind wanted to hold its breath every time one did, and I was glad that Daric couldn't see what I saw as I riffled the Assembly's files.

(Here it is,) I said at last. The sequence we had to open up lay waiting, sandwiched in between security traps, but clean and simple. I deepened my penetration into Daric's mind until I was contacting the brain centers he'd be using. I opened up to him, let him see for a second through my mind's eye. (Make it change—) I felt him respond with a kind of terrified eagerness; felt an energy I'd never been able to call up surge through the circuits of his/my mind and out of him/me, turning *black to white, yes to no, open to closed*.

A different sequence was pulsing under my eyes now . . . the right one, the one that would give us both what we wanted. (Look,) I thought, trying to let him see it himself.

(Get me out of here!) he screamed. I felt him start to panic as he got too much input; struggling to get free—In another minute he was going to trigger something in the system around us, and we'd be dead. I got us out of there as fast as I could.

I got myself out of his mind even faster. In less than a heartbeat we were staring at each other, slack-faced and glassy-eyed, across the empty distance of the room again.

"We did it?" he asked finally, having trouble with his mouth. "It's going to work?"

"Yeah." I nodded. "I think we did."

He got up, rubber-kneed. "Incredible," he mumbled again, his mind still strobing with awe and energy. He held his head . . . suddenly feeling afraid that maybe he'd even enjoyed what he'd just done. "I need a drink. Or something." He turned to look back at me; his relief and revulsion were sweet-sour clogging my senses. And because he was afraid he'd liked it, he said, "God, I'd hate to be you. Why do you bother living?"

Argentyne came into the room; she'd been waiting for sounds of life. I could hear other sounds coming alive out front, the club beginning to fill up for the night. "Did you fix it—?" she asked, not sure which of us to look at. "What happened?" Not sure anything even had. She was doing everything she could think of to keep from looking at Daric too much.

"Don't ask." Daric put his hands up to his head again. But then he said, "Yes. I fixed it."

I frowned, but I didn't say anything. I watched her face soften with relief and self-doubt. "That's good," she said, meaning it. She hesitated, aching deep inside. "Are you staying . . . for the show?"

"Do you want me to?" he asked, moving closer. The urge went through him to do something to her with his mind, one of those things that had always made her want him to do more. . . . I touched his mind, just enough to let him know I was there; just enough to stop him.

She looked away, glancing at me. "I need the symb box." He gave it to her, and she went out again, her mind and body clenched.

Daric stood where he was for another minute, watching me. "I'm going out front for a drink," he said. His voice sounded strained. *(And staying for the show.)* Knowing that I could read the decision in his mind; and knowing that I would. "Are you coming?" Daring me to do anything about it.

"No," I said.

He let himself think about what he'd done to me a few nights ago . . . about what Stryger was going to do to me, two nights from now— I watched his face flush. "See you in hell," he said. He went out of the room.

I sat where I was, trying not to follow his mind as he went away. But I couldn't stop myself, because he was still thinking about me—me on top of his stepmother; wondering how she'd liked it. Hoping his father was wondering too. Thinking about Argentyne naked. . . .

I cut contact, hating him, hating myself. But the images of naked flesh stayed in my mind. *Argentyne . . . Lazuli . . .* I wondered where Lazuli was right now, too far away to reach; remembering the soft sweetness of her body until it made my own body ache. I wondered whether she was thinking about me; whether she was hating me, and how much.

"Damn," I said, to nobody.

THIRTY-TWO

DARIC WAS THE LAST one to leave the club as Purgatory shut down for the night. I watched him go, making sure he didn't turn back or change his mind—the one thing that I could still do to hurt him.

Argentyne watched him go too, with the heavy ache still deep inside her. She looked at me once, from across the room, feeling my eyes on her. Her performance had looked good tonight, but inside it had been empty. Her mind had been somewhere else the whole time; her body felt like lead to her. She went backstage with the other players, her arms around two of them, burying her need in the security of the symb. After a while I heard them making music again in the back room, aimless and loose, unwinding.

I followed them down the hall, not knowing why, until I saw them. The players looked up at me as I came into the room, accepting the sight of me now, somehow more used to my being here than I was. Argentyne was the only one who felt any resentment.

"I thought maybe I should . . . practice." I touched the socket on my neck before she could say anything. "Like you said." My mind didn't want to face anything that took any effort, any emotion, but even working the symb was better than the emptiness I felt inside me right now.

Some of the players mumbled agreement, their curiosity reaching out to me. They were tired from the night but still riding their performance high, and nobody had interfaced with them even casually in a long while. Argentyne nodded, shrugged; I felt her own anticipation stir, almost against her will.

I crossed the room, calling my link on; the two-dimensional imagery of their artificial psi unfolded across my mind. For a while it was enough just to listen and watch, leaning against the wall, as Argentyne wove their separate colors of sound into lightsong, funneling her unhappiness into a search for something she'd never seen before. But the more I felt the changing flow of images around them, the more it got into my blood, making me hungry to be a part of the pattern again, and not just a dead-end street.

"Come on," Argentyne said to me finally, impatiently, "feel something."

I eased into the dance, trying not to stumble and break its heart; concentrating on the way it made me feel—the *pleasure, envy, longing*—trying to focus the physical sensations the emotions caused in me. The sea of stimuli inside and outside of my head seemed to shimmer as the players reacted to a kind of input they'd never experienced before. Their disorientation faded fast; they liked it. Argentyne liked it.

I took what they gave back to me and sent it out again, filtering it this time so that the feedback stayed under control. I wanted to give them something, an extra dimension to move in, a part of myself, in return for what they were giving me. And hovering around the pattern of their energy I found something that only happened inside Argentyne: something that was a part of the vision filling her as she controlled the symb, something more real to her than reality—and yet always missing, when they played, because it was too intangible to express through the crude sensory net of the symb. I felt the ache of her frustration, always there too, because her act of creation could never be complete. . . .

I took the fragile phantom that hovered in her mind and used my psi to give it form. Then I fed it into the circuits, setting it free . . . feeling her rush of pleasure warm me like the sun's heat as her vision suddenly became perfect. She looked toward me, the wonder alive on her face. And suddenly I felt whole, a part of something more, for the first time in longer than I wanted to remember.

It was nothing like a joining . . . because a joining was like nothing else. It was a different kind of give and take, a different kind of sharing than I'd ever known; one that belonged totally to the human side of me. Holding together my concentration in the middle of such dense input was hard to do; but staying with the flow made it worth the effort. It got easier the longer we played, until I felt like I'd never felt this good and been in my right mind. . . .

And then some lousy left-out part of my brain remembered why I was wearing an illegal jack, and what I was really here for. And the pleasure went out of everything, like blight rotting a flower. I shut down my access, feeling the lines of contact wither and die.

Argentyne and the players followed me, dropping out of symbiosis, shutting down one by one until I was alone in the middle of their silent curiosity again.

"Why did you stop?" Argentyne asked.

"I've had enough," I said.

"It was really good, really something new—" There was frustration in her voice that had nothing to do with me. "It'll get better . . . work with us some more. Open up, you didn't get far enough—"

I shook my head.

"Come on, Cat," somebody else said. "Lose yourself."

"Come cloud-walking—"

"Yeah, come on, lose yourself."

"It feels better than anything—"

"I'm not doing this because it feels good! Just leave me the fuck alone." I went out of the room, away from their questions and their sudden embarrassment.

I went out the back way into the alley behind the club. I stopped when I got outside, sagged against the building wall; letting it hold me up because suddenly my legs didn't want to any more. *Tomorrow. Tomorrow night it would be me and Stryger. . . .* Something howled inside my brain, hungry for it to happen; something that wasn't me. My hands started to tremble; but this time it didn't stop there. It crawled up my arms, spreading, until my whole body was shaking like I had a fever. I wrapped my arms across my chest, holding on until it passed.

The door opened and Argentyne came out, alone. She stood looking at me, her costume sparking like a live wire in the dim light. Finally she reached into her pocket and handed me a camph. I stuck it into my mouth; she put one into her own. It didn't help much, but it kept us from having to say anything for that much longer. I looked at my distorted reflection in the mirror she'd made of half her face, looked down again.

"I'm sorry," she said at last, staring at the ground.

I nodded without meaning it, my hands still knotted over the heavy folds of my jacket. My head hurt.

She leaned against the wall beside me, studying my face. "I know we get kind of caught up in the symb, inside our own world, some-times. . . ."

I looked away, sucking on the camph. The small cone of light we stood inside of was artificial, fragile, unreal. The night was all around us, closing in, and I was the only one who who could feel it. . . .

". . . I mean," she said, "when you discover a new dimension like that . . . you want to hold onto that, get deeper into it. You don't want to let go. You kind of forget everything else, you know?"

I didn't say anything, barely listening, waiting for her to go away.

She didn't go away. "All my life," she said, "I've had this thing that happened inside me—" I looked back at her finally, feeling her need force me to. "When I hear somebody's name I feel a color. Sometimes hearing music makes me see a place I've never been . . . or remember things I haven't thought about since forever, and makes it seem like they happened yesterday. . . . And always, everything has a *mood*—colors do, the sea does, or a song. Not one that has anything to do with what the thing *is,* or what I'm doing with it . . . but a separate thing that's like its soul, speaking to me. I can always feel it, inside me. But no matter what I try to do, even with the symb, I can never make anybody else feel it. All my life, I've been trying to make other people feel it." She looked away at the night, and back. "And then you came here . . . and you can. You did. You made it real for me—" She caught hold of my jacket with her jewel-gloved fist. "You can't just *stop* like that. I know it's not what you were trying to do. I know it's not what you wanted, or what's important to you. But it made you feel good, I know it did. Maybe it's what you really need, too—" She had hold of me with both hands, now.

I took a step forward; pushed her up against the cold brick wall with my body. I held her there with my mouth covering hers, my hands against the sides of her face as I kissed her, lost in her silver hair.

She struggled for about half a second, mostly from surprise. And then her body went boneless against me, the way it had done once before. Her hands slid down my back, pulling me close until it hurt. Her mouth was wet and open over mine, and the truth about what we both really needed, right now, hit us head-on like a freighter.

And the next thing I remembered we were in her room, across her bed, not bothering to take off more than would let us reach each other, and she was ready and I was inside almost before I knew what was happening to me. And then I began to move inside her, and I knew, and she knew, rising to meet me until there was nothing else but sensation. She came, and I came with her, with a desperate urgency that had almost nothing to do with sharing each other's bodies.

I rolled off of her, lying motionless across the bed; feeling like I'd never move again. She lay silently beside me for a few minutes more, staring at the ceiling, not seeing it in the rainbowed half-light filtering in from the street outside. But then she pushed up on her elbow until she was looking down into my eyes, and she smiled. She held up her finger, kissed it, ran it along my cheek. And then, slowly, piece by piece, she began to take off my clothes. I let her, too tired to protest. When I lay there completely naked she slowly took off her own, until finally I could see the body I'd wanted to see, without ever quite realizing it, ever since that first night in Purgatory. I wasn't disappointed.

She leaned over me, covering my mouth with hers again.

"Argentyne . . . I can't," I murmured.

"Don't worry. . . ." She kissed me again, used her tongue. "It's all right." The kisses moved over my face, closing my eyes, circling down into my ear. Then on down along my throat, my chest. She rolled me onto my stomach and kneeled between my sprawled legs, while her fingers slid over every inch of my back, probing the hollows along my spine, soothing and urging. "You will—" she said softly, as they moved down and in between my thighs. She did things that no woman I'd been with before had ever done to me, and each one felt better than the last. I felt myself sliding into the warm, heavy rhythm of her own patient longing, felt myself begin to come alive again, felt her feeding me strength with every touch. "How did you get that tattoo?" she asked, her voice gently laughing as she massaged my buttock.

"I don't remember," I mumbled, and she laughed again and kissed it.

I rolled onto my back, letting her hands follow, letting them work, until finally I opened my eyes and looked down, hardly believing what I saw rising like a defiant finger. She smiled, pushing up on her knees, lowering herself onto me with a sigh. She leaned forward, her breasts warm against my chest as she found my mouth again. "I want to know how it feels to a man," she whispered, starting to move, slowly, on top of me. "Let me feel what you feel. . . ." And inside her there was no fear. She wasn't Lazuli, and her mind was as open to me as her body, reaching for me, for one more experience she'd never believed she'd live long enough to have.

I entered her mind, going deep as I felt her wanting more and more. I went deeper into her body too, let my fingers move over her silver skin, her breasts, her belly; letting her surround me with her warm secrets. And I let her feel everything, my hardness, her softness, every nerve-ending in my body coming on line, and all the while as I opened my mind to show her how I felt, she was feeling what a woman felt, feeding back into my brain, feeding my own pleasure with hers, doubling it and redoubling it. I felt her excitement climbing, centering, circling that place where our bodies were fused together and making my own need hotter. For once every touch, every motion either of us made seemed like exactly the right one. I wanted to make it go on and on, always almost reaching the end but never ending . . . but she couldn't wait. She came—I felt it trigger inside her, spreading through the nerve net of her body like a shower of stars.

And back through the link into my own, until the lightning struck me and I couldn't stop myself. I cried out, falling like a meteor, dizzy and spinning, into the warm sea of our release.

But even as I felt myself fading, softening, growing dim and dead, I felt the heat still pulsing somewhere inside me. She was still on top of me, her head back, her eyes clouded and bright as she began to move again, her body caressing what was left of me, her hands touching my sweating skin and her own, like she was expecting the impossible to happen one more time. I felt her arousal growing inside me, knew at last how it felt to be able to be ready and willing all over again, and again; to have a capacity for pleasure as deep and endless as a sea. . . .

I let her fill the utter emptiness inside me with the sensations she was creating, playing our bodies like she played the symb; demanding, depending on me to let her go on using my mind and body along with her own to explore this thing she'd only dreamed about. I felt her pleasure beginning to climb again, and her need and her wonder at being two people in one, one mind with two bodies—so different and yet so much the same that if they could only be this way forever. . . .

And I felt myself respond, incredibly, growing hard again with a need so hot and sudden that it was more like pain. She felt my disbelief; I felt her own, and laughed as we began again. This time we circled the center of each other's pleasure without any urgency at all, letting every kind of sensation pass in slow motion through the lines of contact between us as we rose and rose, and fell again. . . .

This time she was satisfied and more than satisfied; and I was more than grateful. She slid off of me, moving slowly and tenderly;

kept contact, body against body, as she lay next to me, with her arm still across my chest. "God, it feels so good. . . ." she murmured. "Stay inside me. . . ." But she was only asking for my mind inside her now—to go on being two in one, as she drifted away into sleep, too heavy with pleasure and release to say anything more.

I lay where I was, stupefied with sensation, wondering as it ebbed away where I was even going to find the strength to keep breathing. I thought about Lazuli, felt the hollow ache start inside me again as I remembered how she'd wanted this too. She'd been too afraid of me to take it this far, as close to a real joining as any human without psi could ever come. I wondered, if we'd had enough time, if I could have shown her. . . . But all the while I knew, in the parts of my mind that Argentyne couldn't reach and never would, that even if Lazuli and I had been two people in one body, we'd never have been two in one mind.

THIRTY-THREE

WHEN I WOKE UP again Argentyne was still sleeping, her arm still lying across me, as if neither of us had even moved during the rest of the night. It was halfway into the next afternoon, but I felt like I'd barely slept. Sleep was trying to pull me back down, and I wanted to let it. But it was the next day. When I remembered what day that was, I felt like I'd been jabbed with a prod, and I knew I wasn't going to sleep any more.

I slid out from under Argentyne's warm arm, kissed her face gently until she smiled, her eyelids flickering. She sighed and stretched. "Again . . ." she murmured. Her eyes closed again.

I pulled on my clothes and put on another drug patch and went downstairs. A couple of the players were in the kitchen; they watched me stumble in, glanced at the ceiling and made knowing faces. Midnight pushed a plate of food at me, and shoved a cup into my hand. "Eat," he said. "Better keep up your strength." He raised his eyebrows. I gave him a sick grin, trying to look grateful. I ate a couple of bites, almost gagging, and left the rest of it.

I went to the phone and called Daric, to make sure everything was set. And then I called Mikah, to make double sure.

When I'd finished talking I went back into the empty club and sat alone, not wanting anything more than that . . . except maybe to turn today into tomorrow. After a while Argentyne came into the room, wrapped in her bathrobe, and sat down beside me. I felt the sudden hot rush of feeling inside her as she looked at me, her memory flashing back to the night, struggling to remember *now,* going *back*— But when I met her eyes something else happened, and it made her look away suddenly. Face to face in the light of day, the memory of what we'd done last night became too real for her even to think about. She tried to say something; couldn't. Because she was afraid, after all . . . so afraid that she wouldn't admit even to herself what she was really afraid of.

I sat looking at her look away, not answering what she didn't say; afraid of the same thing, deep inside.

After a while she reached up behind her head, took out the symb box and handed it to me. "I guess you'll be needing this," she said. "Try not to carry it on you; it's kind of fragile. We're not performing tonight, so there's . . . I mean, you can use it all night . . ." She broke off, sickened.

I took it, with fingers that suddenly couldn't feel anything.

"When are you meeting Daric?" She watched herself fold her hands on the tabletop, trying to sound matter-of-fact.

I grimaced. "Not soon enough."

"Is there anything else you need, that we can do?" Still looking at her hands.

"Give me a place to come back to?"

She smiled a little. "Any time." She got up again when I didn't say anything more; kissed my forehead and walked away.

I stayed where I was, glad to be alone again, and hating every second of it. I didn't know why it was so hard to wait; so hard to think about tonight. I'd set it all up, covered my ass, made sure I had backup. I didn't even have to depend on a mechanical link if I needed help. I had my psi, in perfect working order. I was going to get roughed up a little; that was all. Nothing I couldn't handle. It was my game, I was calling the throws. But still my guts turned to water every time I thought about what was going to happen to me tonight. Maybe because I'd thought I'd never have to do this kind of thing to myself again.

The message beeper on my databand suddenly came alive, making me jump. I sat listening to it, trying to decide if I should answer it here or go to the public phone; half afraid of what I might hear from anybody who'd call me now. Finally I went to the phone in the hall.

The face I found waiting for me when I answered was so unexpected that for a second I couldn't even put a name to it. "Natan Isplanasky," the face said, as if he could tell that I didn't recognize him.

I didn't say anything, because I couldn't think of anything at all to say.

"Elnear told me about your . . . falling out with the taMings. She's concerned about you," he said, sounding concerned too.

I felt myself frown as I wondered if she'd told him all the details. I wondered what was really going on in his mind. "She told you to call?" I asked, not sure whether resentment or disbelief was stronger inside me.

"No," he said. "I called because I wanted you to know I haven't forgotten about what you said."

"About what?"

He looked surprised, or at least confused. "About Contract Labor."

"Oh." I looked down, laughed once. "That."

"Elnear told me you have your reasons. I still want to hear them."

I lifted my head again. "What's the point?" Suddenly I wanted to smash the screen. I clenched my fists until the feeling passed.

He didn't answer the question. "Will you come up and see me?"

I shook my head. "I can't."

"Can't?" he repeated, as if he thought I meant something else.

"I can't."

He hesitated, nodded. "What if I come there? Or meet you somewhere else? Whenever you say."

I stared at him. "You mean that?"

He nodded again.

"I can't." I looked away from his eyes. "There's something else I've got to do. And I don't know where I'll be after that."

"Something more important to you than this."

"Yeah," I said. I was starting to tremble again. I almost said the words to cut the connection; stopped. "Look, I'll call back if—when I can. As soon as I can."

He nodded. "Good. I'll be waiting."

"Tell Elnear . . . tell her I think it'll all work out." I cut him off. Then I leaned back against the wall, waiting for the shakes to leave me alone. When I felt in control enough to move again, I left Purgatory, not telling anybody I was going, and went uptown toward Daric's.

Daric's city place was sleek and faceless on the outside, a vip's sacred ground, the kind of place that probably had almost as much to hide as its owner did. I stood in the twilight in the mall garden for a long time, looking at it, getting the feel of it; trying to force myself to go up to its door. Mikah had promised he'd track me; but there was no trace of him. I had to believe he'd keep his word, just like I had to believe nothing would go wrong that I couldn't handle. I didn't believe either thing as I crossed the vanilla-scented lawns to Daric's door.

The door opened when I stepped up onto the polished terrace, answering the security clearance Daric had given me. Daric was waiting inside. He gestured me in with a nervous hand.

"What were you doing out there for so long, for God's sake?" he hissed, as the door solidified again behind us. "Everyone in the stack could have seen you by now."

"Nobody else was watching," I said. *Nobody else at all.* Even the security scanners didn't see me, as long as the codes told them not to. It was all very discreet. I looked around me in the dim light, my hands twisting inside my jacket pockets. The asceticism of his house on the taMing estates had turned so impersonal here that it was like standing in a clinic. "Stryger's not here."

"Of course not," Daric said, still irritable. "It's early. Come inside." He wanted to play host about as much as I wanted to play guest, but I followed him down the long ramp into the ceramic hollow of his living room. There was a round enameled table in the center of it, ringed with low seats inside a cylinder of sourceless light. He sat down; I sat down on the far side of the table, staring at him.

"How is Argentyne?" he asked, almost civilly.

"Satisfied," I answered, mostly to annoy him.

He frowned. He poured himself a drink from the liquor carafe on the table in front of him, and gulped it down.

"Why don't you drop the bleeding-inside crap?" I said. "She doesn't mean anything to you. Nobody does."

His head snapped up. The *pain anger jealousy* gnawing at his gut was real enough. *"You,"* he said, his finger quivering as it pointed me out, "are a nameless bastard. You are not fit to judge me. You will not sit there and tell me what I think or feel or want in my own house!"

I flinched as his fury scraped my raw nerves. I kept my eyes on the carafe and cups on the tray in front of him. The tray was moving, slowly, around the table. There was a kind of continental drift at work in the table's heart; my hands could feel it, a faint vibration under what looked like a solid surface, carrying everything invisibly toward me. I watched them come, hypnotized. "Plate tectonics," Daric murmured, and I laughed out loud before I could stop myself. My hands rattled on the tabletop. They reminded me of his hands, as if somehow his hands had gotten attached to my body.

Daric looked at me, under control again, his expression caught somewhere between curiosity and disgust.

"Fuck you, Gentleman Daric," I said.

"Have a drink," he offered, as the carafe reached me, and stopped.

I filled a cup and looked at it. Daric's tension level jumped as I picked it up. I glanced at him, watched him take another swallow from his own cup; felt him react to the kick of high-proof alcohol. There was nothing in the liquor that didn't belong there. He relaxed again, even though I hadn't drunk anything; he didn't care if I drank his liquor or not.

I took a sip, felt it numb the inside of my mouth, burn a track down my throat, deaden my aching stomach. It felt good. Right then drinking acid would have felt good. I drank some more.

And then I started to get dizzy. The room began to run and flow as I sat staring in disbelief. "It was safe . . . How . . . ?" I forced the words out; it seemed like the longest speech I'd ever made.

"The cup wasn't." Daric shrugged. He smiled. His face was melting. "It has to look good, you know, for Stryger. Trust me."

I didn't trust him. I fell face down onto the table.

When I came to again, I was somewhere else. There was a dirty fibroid floor pressing hard against the side of my face. I lifted my head, blinking. I had a headache. The light here was white and shadowless, not like the dim half-light of the room where Daric and I had been hiding from each other's hatred. It was a square box with one hard, ugly chair and a hard metal bedframe set on a storage base. One door, shut. No windows. I could hear a ventilator running somewhere: a wheezing scream that went on and on, that sounded like the machine was being killed by this place. For a minute I thought I was in Oldcity. And then I thought I was having a nightmare.

I wasn't alone in it. Daric was leaning against the door. And Stryger was standing beside him, hidden inside so much drab, ungodly clothing that I had to touch his mind to be sure I was really seeing him. "You see," Daric said, to one or the other of us, or both. "Here he is."

I tried to push myself up, fell back on my face again, because I couldn't make my hands work. My hands were locked in binders behind my back. I rolled onto my side, got up finally, using just my legs. As I staggered to my feet one foot jerked out from under me, and I almost fell again. One of my ankles was tied to the bedframe by a piece of rope. "You son of a bitch," I said to Daric, and the choking panic in my voice was real.

He smiled. The tiny shrug of his shoulders told me, *It has to look good*.

"Hello, Cat," Stryger murmured, his voice soft and almost warm, as if we were having a perfectly normal conversation, as if I wasn't standing here like this—like some kind of human sacrifice. He began to take off the shapeless, hooded coat that made him look twice his size. My own jacket was gone; so were my boots. All I had on was a tunic and jeans, and they weren't going to give me much protection. And then I remembered the symb box. I'd put it into my jacket; and my jacket wasn't in the room. I froze, trying to make my mind hold together while I called on the link, not letting myself think about what would happen if there was no answer. But the familiar grid of energy filled my inner sight like a streetmap. I followed it, found the symb box ready for me, locked in . . . Daric was wearing it. I forced myself to take a deep breath, and another. Then I sent what was left of my concentration out through the white noise of the ventilator and my own fear in one last sweep, searching for Mikah.

He was there. Somewhere outside, nearby, close enough. He'd tracked me here, wherever here was; as good as his word. I felt him jump as I goosed him with my relief. I fed him a flood of images about where I was and what was about to happen.

And then I broke contact, because I realized Stryger had gone on talking to me, and now he was waiting for me to answer.

He'd asked me to tell him why I thought God had allowed me to be born.

"What?" I said, because even knowing what he'd asked me, that was all the answer I could think of.

He repeated the question. "I'm very interested in your religious views," he said softly. "I've had to wait such a long time for this opportunity to talk to you about them." He was leaning on his staff, shining in the white light; as if he really had made half a lifetime's journey to reach this stinking rathole room, all to talk religion with me.

"Then why this—?" I asked, feeling the binders cut into my wrists, tightening more as I jerked my hands. I tried not to look at him like he was crazy.

He sighed. "Because it's necessary. Now, the question is, why are humans and Hydrans so similar that interspecies miscegenation can even occur? Why has God permitted our pure stock to become polluted with abnormal genes? Why were you born—a halfbreed, the degenerate spawn of an unnatural act? As a warning? As an example?" I felt him goading me; goading his own hatred.

"There isn't any God," I said. "If there was, you wouldn't exist." I glanced at Daric; he was backed into the corner by the door now, with fear-sweat shining on his face. Smiling. "None of us would."

Stryger moved his hands; the bottom end of his staff shot out, tangled in my legs. I fell down, hard, with no way to stop it. I lay there for a long minute, with the pain in my bruised legs throbbing up through my body, before I rolled over and pushed onto my knees again.

He was still standing quietly, leaning on his staff again as if it had been God's hand and not his own that had struck me down. He actually believed it had been God's hand.

I managed to get up, and backed away toward the bed. I sat down on it, sending a silent finger of thought into his brain while I did. I hadn't counted on the binders: I was going to need everything I had to keep from getting maimed.

"I realize you cannot be expected to behave like a civilized person," he said. The velvet on his voice was wearing away now; the naked fist was showing through. "But I think you can give me a better answer than that."

I made a face. "I don't know why I'm alive. I don't know why I'm a halfbreed. Maybe my mother was gang-raped by deadheads."

The staff flashed out at my head. I felt him move and ducked; but it came back at me before I could get my balance again and hit me from behind, knocking me off the bed. I landed on my face. I sat up again on the floor; got to my knees, and then my feet. It took longer this time, because it was harder to do. Blood was leaking out of my nose; my mouth felt like raw meat. I stared at the grid still shining and alive inside my eyes, made sure it was getting every detail of how much it hurt. (Why—?) I thought, because I couldn't catch my breath to ask him *why*; because I wondered what he'd do. (Why do you want to do this to me?)

"Filth!" he shrieked. The staff end hit the floor with a crack, and then it hit me across the chest, staggering me. I fell down again. "Never touch me with your filthy—" He broke off, swallowing the word, shuddering. And then, with what almost sounded like grief in his voice, he said, "I don't want to do this. . . ." And the worst part was that some part of him really didn't. I watched him come forward, a step at a time. He held out his hand to me, as if he really wanted to help me up. "But God has shown me that it is necessary. You have shown me yourself that you deserve punishment. Your very existence is a blasphemy. . . . The Hydran civilization was corrupt. They set themselves up to be in God's place; that was why their civilization fell. It fell from grace. Only full-blooded humans are God's children, recognizing their role as it was meant to be. Only Earth is pure."

I looked up at him, at his outstretched hand, at the white, pitiless light ringing him with aura . . . trying not to look at the staff. "That's a lot of shit."

The staff leaped up and clipped me under the chin, knocking me back into the metal base of the bed, sending me down with a headful of stars. I pushed my way up the side of the bedframe, fell onto the stinking mattress foam again, dazed and gasping. I hoped he hadn't broken my jaw. The welts rising on me felt as thick as my arm. I wondered how I could have missed his move on me that time so completely.

"We're not . . ." I mumbled, and spat, grateful that my mouth still worked, ". . . not the different ones. Hydrans were all over. . . . It's you. You're the mutants . . . misfits . . . defectives, failures . . . !" Blood dribbled down my chin.

"Damn you—" he whispered, as something tore like rotten cloth inside his brain. And then I saw, too late, what his most terrible fear was: The fear that I was right. In the vision he'd had so long ago, when that accident had left him clinically dead—the vision he'd believed had been sent to him by God—he'd dreamed that his mind had left his body. It had hovered over him, and then crossed the impossible threshold into the minds of the people working to save him. He'd heard them speak—known their thoughts, almost known their every secret, like God. And then they'd saved him, and pulled him back into his body where he belonged. And when he'd come to, he'd known that he'd never have that feeling of pure, godlike power again . . . because he wasn't a psion. And I felt the hunger for the Gift he could never have eating him alive, and his insane hatred of the ones who had it by birthright. *Oh God,* I thought, and wished I'd thought of something else.

"I think . . ." he murmured, staring down at me with mindless sorrow, "you will profit from this." The end of his staff caught me in the stomach, doubling me over, and then came down hard across the side of my face, smashing my ear.

I lay where I'd fallen face-down on the putrid foam, listening to myself moan; hoping that if I lay still he'd let me rest for a minute. More blood was running down my neck and into my eye. I couldn't wipe it off. I wished head wounds didn't bleed so damn much. I couldn't hear out of the ear he'd hit; it was full of blood. I wondered why I was having so much trouble reading him. That wasn't right. Maybe the symb box was taking up too much of my concentration. But it had to come first, or else the rest of this had no point at all. . . . It was getting harder all the time to remember what the point of anything was.

I sat up, my ears still ringing; let him hit me in the ribs and knock me off the bed again. He didn't even give me a chance to roll over this time before the staff whacked me in the balls. I folded up, retching, and he hit me across the kidneys. (Daric—!) I tried to form the thought, to reach his mind with it, couldn't. Too little control left, too much pain—the pain leaked out of me like blood and into their minds, until I heard Stryger screaming at me again, hitting me over and over to make me stop hurting out loud. "Daric!" I was sobbing now but I didn't care. "Daric—"

"Sojourner . . ." Daric said, his voice sounding hollow and far away. "Sojourner!" Louder, almost frightened, this time. He came toward us, inching into my line of sight; clamped his hand on Stryger's arm, pulling him around. "I—I want him for a moment . . ."

Stryger froze, stared at him; moved away from me like he was in a trance, letting Daric crouch down beside me. "Enough?" Daric whispered. I nodded, shutting my eyes.

"No . . ." he said hoarsely, "I don't think so." I opened my eyes. He rubbed a finger across my torn lips; it came away red. He put it into his mouth and sucked it, smiling. He straightened up again. "By the way—" His finger swam down toward my eyes again, and there was something else on its tip. "I think this belongs to you—?" I squinted. It was a drug patch. The one from behind my ear. He'd taken it off me after I'd passed out. My psi had been slowly going dead on me all this time.

He flicked the patch away. I swore, floundering, trying to get my legs under me, trying to see where it had gone. He kicked me in the stomach, collapsing me again, and left me there. (Mikah—!) I threw everything I had into the call, praying that now, now when I really needed it, my Gift would come back to me on its own. But it didn't. "Mikah—!" I screamed it, raw-voiced. And then Stryger brought his staff down on me again, and I just screamed.

I tried to kick him, tried to crawl away, but it was all useless. He used his staff on me like an artist, now that I was down and helpless . . . used it to cause the most pain in the most ways, the most places, hurting me everywhere but never doing enough damage at once to let me lose consciousness. Somewhere in the middle of it, the lines of the grid inside my head went out. And I realized my backup was gone, I was alone in this nameless place with the two people who hated me most; two people who wanted me dead more than anything else in the universe right now. And this thing had already gone too far, way beyond the plan. Stryger was going to kill me—and Daric would lick my bloody corpse, and nobody would ever know. . . .

There was nothing left to hold onto as the pain drove me under, drowning me in fear, drowning me in memory. . . . I was back on the streets again, seven or eight years old with an empty hole in my brain where my past should have been, hungry and cold. And a man who sometimes gave me handouts said, *Come on in.* I thought I knew the streets, knew the rules, knew what I was doing. I'd never heard bad talk about him. But up in his room he'd dropped his pants and told me what he wanted me to do to him. I said I didn't want to, and his face went from smiling and soft to ugly with rage faster than I could think. He pulled a knife, and with it pressed against my throat, he said, *Do it or I'll kill you.* And I did it, whimpering and sick, but thinking if I did it I could go. I'd never heard he'd killed anybody, if I did it he'd let me go. . . .

But he wouldn't let me go. I begged him, I tried to fight, but he cut me and ripped off my clothes. He pinned me down on the bed and started doing things to me. I told myself it was only some babyfucker getting his fix, it didn't mean anything as long as I was still alive when it was over. And the things got worse and worse, hurting me until I cried out; and when I did he started to beat me, shouting it was all my fault, like I'd made him do this—until I was hurt and bleeding everywhere, but still it was only pain and it couldn't go on forever. And then he rolled me onto my stomach and climbed on top of me. Naked and helpless under his weight, I screamed as a kind of pain I'd never known existed tore something apart in my insides. "Oh God, stop—!" I screamed and screamed for somebody to save me but there was nobody at all who heard my screams and cared.

And it wasn't stopping. My screams turned hoarse, my sobs became heaves of vomit; it went on and on, until all that was left was the truth . . . blind with pain, with the black pit opening up to swallow me, I knew at last that the river of wetness that rushed through me was all my blood, that I was never going to get out of this room, that oh God I was dying right here, it was over, over, right now going down, down, into the blackness. . . .

Noise exploded the room around me, exploded my living nightmare. And then there was silence, even though inside my head I was still screaming. The blows stopped coming; even though it didn't stop the pain. I opened the one eye that would still open, blinking in the naked whiteness, watching as reality unrolled like a threedy show in front of me: Stryger standing still, gaping at something, someone standing where the door had been, but wasn't any more. Daric sidling away along the wall like a spider, as Mikah stepped into the room.

Mikah stopped dead as he saw me. His eyes squinted, and his head moved slowly from side to side; but whatever happened on his face was hidden behind the faceshield of his armor. He raised his head again, looking at Stryger. "So," he muttered, the words thick with anger as he glanced at Daric and back at Stryger. "Two-timing me again, you lousy freak. . . ." With some part of my brain that was still half working, I realized that he was covering my ass, making it look good.

Stryger was still gaping, his eyes getting wider and wider with a disbelief that was so total he couldn't breathe. He looked like he was seeing the devil in human form, and maybe he thought he was. Maybe he was right. I started to laugh, or maybe cry.

Mikah moved forward, coming toward me.

Stryger shut his mouth as Mikah shoved him aside, making him stagger . . . as he realized Mikah was only human, and a witness to what he'd done here. He lifted his staff—

Mikah stunshot him without even turning back to look; Stryger collapsed like a broken leg. Mikah crouched down, his mailed fist opening, reaching out toward me.

"No . . . don' . . ." The words bubbled out of my mouth in a bloody froth; my body cringed away from his touch, my mind still full of shattered glass.

He pulled his hand back, raised his faceguard so I could see his face. "Cat," he said, "it's Mikah."

"Mikah . . . I didn' lie t' you. . . ."

"About what?" He looked confused.

"Gettin' free. . . ."

"Yeah. I know."

"Don' let 'em beat me no more."

"I won't," he said, and then, softly, "We're not on Cinder. Not for a long time, brother. . . ."

"I know. . . ." I mumbled, trying to raise my head. "Where—?"

"—are we? Off the Deep End." His deathshead grin came back for a second.

"Figures."

He half smiled, waiting while I caught up with reality. Then he pulled the red scarf out of the neck of his armor. Lifting my head, he wiped blood and drool off my face with the end of it.

"You hear' . . . ?" I squeezed the words out, not even sure he'd be able to understand them. "You hear' me . . . ?" Right then hope hurt me almost as much as my body did.

"Heard?" He shook his head. "I didn't hear a damn thing after you hit me with your psi that once. That's why I came. It was taking too long. I figured something went wrong—"

I began to cough; choking on disappointment. The pain in my chest and ribs hurt so bad when I coughed that it made me gag. He lifted me up so I could sit, held me there. I whimpered, every crawling millimeter of my body hating the agony of being upright; but not as much as it hated lying on my raw, bleeding face. His hand touched the binders on my wrists, and he grunted with disgust.

"Daric's—" I mumbled, trying to turn my head. "Get him to . . ."

But I felt the shock as something sparked out behind me, as Mikah cancelled the lock himself. The binders fell off my hands; my arms flopped forward. Mikah propped me up like a doll against the side of the bed, and cut the rope around my ankle. He turned to look at Daric. Daric stood pressed against the pitted wall, staring at Stryger's body, at us, back at Stryger. "What happened?" Mikah asked, asking me, but still looking at Daric. "What went wrong?

"Him. Double-crossing bastard—" I said, still looking at Daric too, not able to stop. "Took my drugs. I couldn't . . ." My voice broke. "Scumsucker, you would've let him—"

"You want me to kill 'em both?" Mikah asked, getting slowly to his feet.

"No," Daric whined, going rubber-mouthed as he tried to make it sound reasonable. "I would have stopped him, Cat. Just a little longer . . ." He wiped his face on his sleeve. "Just a little—it had to look good . . . You saw how I could control him. He's not dead, is he dead—?" He looked at Stryger.

"Not yet," Mikah said. "But I'll take care of that right now." He turned, raising his hand.

"No—!" I gasped. "Jeezu, don'." Blood splattered as I shook my head.

He looked back at me. "Why the hell not?"

"Because . . . you'll make him . . . goddamn . . . martyr." I dragged myself up the side of the bed and collapsed on it. The pain of moving that far gave me the dry heaves. Mikah stood waiting until I could speak again. "You kill him now . . . he'll win in spite of . . . everything. Besides, I wan' him to live . . . Because it wouldn't hurt enough, this way."

His face twisted. He lowered his hand. "Just wanted to be sure."

"Of what?"

He gave me a strange look. "That it wasn't because you knew how he felt." He smiled for a second, showing me his teeth. "What about the Gentleman?" He jerked his head at Daric.

"I still need him . . . until tomorrow." I looked at Daric. "You know what you have to do. If you don't do it . . . I'll kill you myself." He nodded silently, licking his lips.

"Get it out of here," Mikah said to Daric, pointing at Stryger's body.

"How?" Daric asked. He looked like he was the one who'd been stunshot.

"Drag him."

"But . . . I have to tell him something, when he wakes up . . . ?"
Daric looked at me again, his face as hollow as his voice. "He'll know
that something—"

"Jus' tell him . . . he made my lover . . . real jealous." I laughed,
and then swore, because even that hurt more than I could stand.

Daric stared at me, his face twisting. But he nodded, and stumbled
across the room. He picked up the body by the armpits. I watched
him go out through the ruined doorway like an undertaker, dragging
Stryger behind him, cursing under his breath.

"That's something I never did before," Mikah said, when we
couldn't hear them any more.

"Wha'?"

"Let somebody live when I should have killed him."

I grunted. "I did somethin' . . . I never done, too."

"What?"

"Peed in my pants."

He looked at me and almost laughed; didn't. I didn't, either.
There was red in the wet stain on my jeans. "Come on," he said, "I
better get you out of here." He started back to me.

"Wait . . . Mikah. Drug patch . . ." I put up a hand, touching
the pulped mess that Stryger had made of my ear. "I need it." I tried
to get up, couldn't. "It's here someplace." I looked up at him. "Help
me. Can't think—"

"You can't think because that scumbag busted your goddamn
skull," Mikah said, frowning. But he turned away, searching the floor
until he found it. He stuck it behind my other ear.

"Be awright now," I said. I wiped my chin with a shaky hand.
I got up off the bed, and fell on my face.

He let me fall, and then he picked me up again, holding me there,
almost gently. "Junkie."

I nodded, pain-tears squeezing out of my eyes. I couldn't stand
up by myself. Stryger's staff was still lying on the floor in front of
me, covered with my blood. "Mikah . . ."

"Yeah?"

"Is it really over?"

He looked down at the staff. He kicked it across the room. "It's
over. I'll take you home."

THIRTY-FOUR

MIKAH TOOK ME to a clinic before he took me anywhere else; one where they didn't ask a lot of questions. It took them the rest of the night to put me back together. They wanted to make me stay; but it was morning, and I had things to do. They took one look at Mikah, and didn't argue. We went back to Purgatory.

Argentyne stopped dead in the middle of the hallway as she saw us come in. Her hands clutched the sleeves of her smock and she hugged herself silently, waiting while we came toward her. As we reached her, she called, "Aspen—!"

"S'all right." I shook my head, moving in slow motion because of all the tranks and painkillers. Her eyes didn't believe me, looking at my face.

"Took care of it already." Mikah nodded, as Aspen materialized behind her.

"Daric has the box," I said.

"Fuck the box." Her voice wasn't steady. "Did it work for you—?"

I nodded.

"Daric did everything he promised to do—?"

"Everything . . . and more," I said sourly. "You heard from him?"

She shook her head, still looking at me uncertainly, glancing at Mikah.

"I got to go up to the Assembly." I had to know that he was there, that Stryger would be there; that everything was set.

"You can't." Argentyne looked at me like I must still be in shock.

"The jack's gone." I touched my head. They'd taken it out at the clinic. Stryger had already scrambled it, along with my brains. "I wanna be there, to watch it happen."

"You and a few billion other people," she said. "They won't let anybody near the place who doesn't have a right to be there."

I swore. "I have a right—"

"Cat," Mikah said. "You thought about this: What's going to hit after Daric feeds that program through their system? You're messing with the Federation. You better keep your head down, boy. Catch it on the Indy."

I stood glaring at him, at her; until the combined weight of their common sense finally crushed me. "Yeah . . ." Suddenly I wasn't so sure that I really wanted to be there when the entire Assembly relived what had happened to me last night. "I guess I will."

"Rest a while," Argentyne said, putting her hand on my arm. "Nothing's even starting for hours."

"Yeah. I guess I will . . ."

"You get lamped for those head wounds?" Aspen asked me, running a professional's eye over my glued-up face. I shrugged, not sure if I didn't know, or just couldn't remember.

"He got the full course," Mikah said. "They know what they're doing at Soule's. They get a lot of trauma cases."

Aspen nodded. "You'll feel like you have a new body in a few days," he said to me, looking as pleased as if he'd fixed it up himself.

"But I'll still remember being in this one." I turned my back on him, feeling the bile rise up in my throat as I stumbled away down the hall.

The stairs to the upper level looked like they led to the moon. With one eye covered, I couldn't even tell where they started. Mikah helped me make it up them and settled me in Argentyne's room. I lay on her bed with my eyes shut, not moving . . . but underneath the haze of painkiller and sedatives, my body was still trembling, still waiting for the next blow to fall. Because the last three years of my life I'd been living a lie. Pretending I was a free citizen of the Human Federation, with a mind and a name and the right to feel some kind of pride. . . . But Stryger had torn away my illusions, the way some nameless pervert had torn away my clothes so long ago, and taught me that I was nothing but a victim in a room without exits.

I rolled onto my stomach, burying my face in the smothering darkness of the bedding as I heard Mikah start to leave, leaving me there alone. But as he reached the door he hesitated. I felt him look at me. And then he turned back, very quietly, and sat down in a chair instead. I raised my head and opened my good eye halfway to look at him sitting there, staring out the window. I reached out and touched his mind with my own; not so he knew it, but only so I did. And then, finally, I felt safe, and I slept.

He was still there when I woke up a few hours later. Argentyne was there too, calling my name, telling me that coverage was starting on the Net. I felt better than I had before I went to sleep, but on a scale of one to ten my body was still about minus-five.

I got up somehow and we went downstairs into the club. The other players were there, and a few people who worked for Purgatory, already waiting. I felt their morbid curiosity glance off me as I came into the room. Nobody wanted to look at my face for long. "Anybody need a headset?" The doorkeeper waved one at me as I passed. Wearing one would bring the visuals up closer, make it that much more real. . . . I shook my head.

A threedy image of the Federation Assembly Hall was already taking up the stage as I eased myself down onto the cushions beside a table. Shander Mandragora was drifting in and out of reality up front, keeping the audience hooked with flashbacks, replaying all the controversies, real and imaginary, that had led up to this; trying to hold audience interest in a vote that he thought they knew the outcome of already. He explained it all, to the billions of present and future viewers who would never really understand what it meant any more than he would. I watched the shifting scenes and faces flow by, feeling dizzy as the background circled behind him and I searched for someone I knew. The cams showed Elnear, waiting on the speaker's platform. She'd asked for permission as a Member to address the Assembly before the vote, and she'd gotten it. . . . And then Stryger had demanded the same right. He was there too, alive and clean and perfect. The two of them sat in their places like game pieces. But there was one more face I still needed to see.

"Daric," Argentyne said, lifting her hand as a slow scan of the Assembly's faces finally passed over him. He was there and gone again

almost before I saw him. But he was there. I nodded and sank back
into the bed of cushions again, letting my one eye unfocus. Argentyne
pressed a mugful of something hot and harmless into my bandaged
hands. I drank it down.

Finally the endless shuffling and shrugging and switching accesses
stopped, as the Assembly's Chosen Speaker called the delegates into
the closed system for the session. I pushed myself up again as he
announced the guest speakers, explaining their requests one more time,
as if they actually had some meaning. He called Elnear forward first
to the floating podium. Her speech was mainly what she'd said in the
open debate—because there was nothing else to say; because that
should have been enough. I could hear the intensity in her voice that
I couldn't feel inside her, as she drove against the impossible inertia
of too many preset minds. . . . And then she was finished speaking,
and Stryger was walking forward to take her place.

I watched him move toward me through the gleaming white-and-
blue respectability of the Federation Assembly, wearing its approval
like an aura. He wasn't carrying his staff with him. But if what he'd
done to me, or even what had happened to him last night, had had
any effect on him, I couldn't see it in the way he moved, the way he
shone. Maybe it had only made him more sure that God was on his
side, that his crusade was just . . . that he was finally about to get
everything he wanted. I watched him come, feeling like somehow he
could actually see me; feeling like I was drowning. . . .

Mikah leaned over and nudged me. "Breathe," he said.

I sucked in air. Stryger had reached the podium now. He began
to speak, while Shander Mandragora reminded us again that for Stryger
speaking out loud wasn't just something he did for effect, but the only
way he could communicate with his audience . . . like it was a pledge,
a symbol of his purity, of his dedication to the common people.

"Because he'll never have the Gift," I muttered. "Because if he
can't have it, he won't ever take second best."

Argentyne glanced at me. "I thought he hated psions—" Her
eyes flickered down and away as she saw the proof of it again on my
face.

"He does," I said. "Can you think of a better reason?" I watched
as Stryger blessed the Assembly members, and called them upholders
of peace and order . . . told them he'd come before them one last time
to speak for those countless human beings who were the Federation's
real reason for existence, whose strength and numbers made its existence possible . . . who trusted in the Assembly to do the right

thing. . . . *Come on, Daric,* I thought. *Come on—* I shouldn't have let them talk me out of it; I should have been there. Stryger was almost finished; in another minute it would be too late, the voting would begin—

"I know you will agree with me," he said, smiling for the last time at the waiting faces below him, "because, after all, we all want the same thing . . . we are all so much alike, in our hearts." He stepped away from the podium, turning, starting back toward his seat.

"No," I said. *"No!* You bastard, you doublecrossing—" Mikah caught at my arm as I pushed to my feet.

But something was happening in the silent crowd on the Assembly floor. They began to make a sound, a restless murmuring like the sea, as larger-than-life figures suddenly materialized in the air: Stryger's image, and then mine. Daric had used himself to get a second viewpoint on the symb box. It was happening . . . it was really happening. I collapsed into my seat again, staring as cams that had been focused close-up on Stryger's face pulled back to take in the show, making Stryger seem to shrink where he stood on the stage. I watched his bloated image in the air open its mouth; I repeated the words that came out of it before they even registered on anyone else watching.

The real Stryger stopped moving, confusion showing on his face. The news recorders were hooked into the Assembly system through the Net, picking up sound to match the picture. Without any augmentation at all, he couldn't know what everyone else was seeing in the air above him, what they were hearing. . . .

He turned around, turning back toward the podium, searching for the Speaker. He stared as he saw the billowing images above him. He was standing inside them, and like a man standing inside a cloud, he couldn't make out their real form. Behind him Elnear and the Speaker stared in disbelief. I saw Elnear's hand go over her mouth as she recognized me. And then it was his own image Stryger was standing inside of, a victim's-eye view now, as the staff swung in for a blow.

I wanted to shut my eyes as the staff came at me. But I couldn't—I watched it come, saw the image change as it hit me. I heard the wood crack against my flesh, and saw what it did to me. I bit down on my fist.

Cries were registering on the audio. I heard my voice rising through them, telling Stryger why he hated psions, and I saw him answer me. . . . The image we were watching on the stage split open, half of it still focused on the beating, the other half sweeping the Hall as panic-stricken Assembly members fell over themselves and each

other, screaming, vomiting, trying to get up or get away from what
they were being force-fed over the inviolable link of the Assembly's
system. The Speaker was up at the podium now, shoving Stryger aside
as he used its access to try and force the system and its users back
under control. As Stryger stumbled away he finally saw what everyone
else was seeing—saw himself, larger than life, beating me to a pulp
in front of billions of witnesses.

And then, as suddenly as it had come, the image disappeared
from the air. It must have disappeared from the Assembly's system at
the same time, because the screaming mob scene on the Assembly
floor began to die down. Members fell back into their seats, the curses
and cries turning into furious demands and questions. Inside of a minute
there was total silence in the Hall. I couldn't tell what they were doing
now, because even the info cams couldn't pick it up. I leaned forward
across the table, my fists clenched, ignoring what it did to my body
. . . because I had to know if it was working; and I couldn't tell
anything, sitting here—

Stryger started back toward the podium with hellfire in his eyes.
But before he could take control of it Elnear was there, barring his
way, claiming the cameras and the Assembly's attention. The Speaker
stepped aside, giving her room, giving way to one of his own.

"Sojourner Stryger," she said, flinching as he got near her, as
if she was half afraid he'd attack her too. "What in God's name was
your purpose in forcing this hideous thing on me . . . on everyone in
this Hall?" Her voice trembled. Her face was white; her hands were
clenched over the edges of the podium, holding her there. "What have
you done to my aide—?"

"I—?" Stryger said, thumping his chest with his hands, still bug-
eyed with disbelief. "This was not *my* doing!" I watched him struggle
to control himself; struggle and win. "I was not to blame for this!
This is some absurd blasphemy created in an attempt to humiliate
me—"

The Speaker stepped between them. "Sojourner Stryger," he
murmured, putting out his hand. "I'm sure there is some explanation
for all this. But considering your current and future interests in the
Federation, I think that perhaps the explanations had better come from
you. Lady Elnear." He stepped back again, giving the floor to Elnear;
giving her the right to ask the questions.

Stryger bristled; backed off, as he realized he didn't have any
choice except to go ahead and face her down. "Surely no one—even
you—" looking from the Speaker to Elnear, "takes seriously some-

thing as easily counterfeited as a threedy tape: two actors play roles, their images are altered to look like myself and a psion. . . .'' Listening to him, watching him, I could almost believe he meant every word. I wondered what I'd see if I could get into his mind right now.

Elnear stiffened as he used the word *psion,* but she only said, "Tapes can certainly be counterfeited. But I have never in my life experienced pain while watching a threedy tape. Have you—?''

"Lady Elnear,'' he said, with patronizing calm, "I'm sure it was upsetting for you to see someone you thought you knew suffer—''

"I'm not talking about that.'' She cut him off, her own voice sharp and cold now. "I mean that I felt physical pain in every nerve-ending of my body—as if I was the victim every time you struck a blow.''

"That's absurd,'' he said, looking at her like she must be crazy.

"It should be.'' She nodded; her face was still white and drawn. "But everyone in this Hall felt it.''

"I felt nothing of the kind,'' he snapped, looking out at the slack, stunned faces of the Assembly as if he thought they were all lying, or insane.

"Evidently you did not,'' she said bitterly. "Sojourner Stryger, why exactly did you choose a psion as your victim?''

He was still looking out into the Assembly Hall. "I did not 'choose a psion'!'' he said to them, almost shouting it.

"That was how you identified him. Not as my aide—someone you knew—but as 'a psion.' ''

"Someone else chose the act, and the victim, to discredit me!''

There was color back in Elnear's face now; her blue eyes were alive and intent. "Then why did they—whoever they were—choose to show you attacking a psion? Psions are not the objects of much compassion in our society. Why not a child, or an old woman?''

"I don't know,'' he murmured, as if he really didn't. "Perhaps they were stupid, as well as evil.'' He looked at her, away from her; up into the air like he was searching for guidance, wondering why God was letting this happen to him.

Her own eyes never left his face. "My aide tried to tell me, on several occasions, that you had a pathological hatred of psions,'' she said quietly. "I never really believed him, until now.''

I sat up straight again, my teeth clenched in a grin.

"Your aide lied about me. He tried to discredit me to the entire Net!'' He looked back at her, his face burning. "He tried to make them believe that I had lied—''

"You did lie. About him," she insisted. "Or have you forgotten?"

His mouth snapped shut. "That isn't true. As God is my witness . . . I may have been misinformed, but I never lie. God guides everything I do—"

"Even when he takes a piss?" Argentyne murmured beside me, and laughter drowned out the rest of his words.

"Has God told you that psions are evil?" Elnear asked. All the cams were on the two of them again.

"Yes . . ." he murmured. "That is, the evidence of society itself has shown that they are deviants of the most degraded sort, the kind of underclass I hope to eliminate through the wider use of pentryptine."

"The most degraded . . ." Elnear said softly. "Do you truly believe that, Sojourner? That all our drug dealers are psions? Our child molesters? Our contract killers? Are psions worse than someone who would set out to destroy an entire people, as some of our own ancestors have done to each other . . . all in the name of God?"

He was staring at her now. I kept waiting for the smooth denial to pour out of him. But this time it didn't come. "God . . ." he murmured finally. "God has shown me what they are. I have done nothing but follow God's Word as I understand it. . . ." His eyes narrowed. "But that does *not* mean that I persecute them! I only want to improve their lot."

Elnear folded her hands together in front of her, looked down at them, nodding as if she conceded the point. "Why is it that you have never had any augmentation done, Sojourner?" Her voice was calm now. The question sounded like a complete change of subject, but I didn't believe it.

Stryger gave her a strange look, but he answered her. "Because I see it as a violation of humanity's basic nature, the pure state which I believe God meant to be our chosen form of existence." He raised his head, back on firmer ground.

"Then God regards augmentation as wrong?" She sounded honestly surprised.

He laughed, his hands fluttering. "I'm not saying it's wrong for everyone. Our society could not function without its technological aids. God intended for us to have these tools, or we would still all be living on one planet. But to go so far as to challenge God's omniscience and power, to try to put oneself in the place that is naturally God's—that is always wrong."

"And do psions do that? I believe you said that was why the

Hydran civilization fell, because they tried to put themselves in God's rightful place."

"Yes." He nodded. "Yes, I believe that . . . I—I've said that many times." A shadow touched his face as he realized the slip he'd almost made, almost acknowledging that he'd said it to me.

"How is it that you share my interest in the Security Council slot, then?" Elnear asked. "It is certainly the ultimate in augmentation available to any human being alive today. Surely the near-omniscience and power available to a Council member goes beyond the limits you believe God had in mind?"

My splinted fingers were tapping nervous code on the tabletop, like I could reach her somehow that way, when my mind couldn't reach her through the wilderness of minds between us. Even I hadn't seen the whole truth, seen the connection, until now. . . . *Make it*— I thought. *Make it, Elnear*—

I saw Stryger tense. "It really isn't the same thing. In order to continue to do God's work here in the Federation—"

"What do you plan to do, then—if not, in effect, to play God yourself?" Her voice sharpened. "Like the people you evidently hate so much?"

He frowned, like a dog trying to decide which flea to bite at first. "How dare you—"

"Sojourner, where is your staff today?" she asked, cutting him off again. "The one that you always carry, that you have said was 'the symbol of your journey toward the truth'?"

"I left it behind," he said. "It's only a piece of wood. It gets in the way."

"You seemed to use it without any difficulty when you used it to torture my aide."

His face reddened. "I am not on trial here! This is a fraud, a vicious lie, to ruin me! He was your aide—maybe you even planned it together, to hurt me, to claim the Council slot for yourself!" His voice was getting louder, as the idea took hold inside him. "That's it, isn't it? It was you, you made that tape—sent him to me, because you knew I—I—mean that it was a forgery, a lie, it never happened . . ."

His voice died, and there was silence in the Hall, and all around me in the club.

"We'll know that soon enough," Elnear said softly. She hesitated, listening to something he couldn't hear, and nodded. "The Speaker has analyzed the Assembly record of the tape. The databand keycodes of the two subjects appear to belong to my aide, and to you. There has been tampering with the Assembly system as well.'' She looked up at him again. ''Eventually we will get to the bottom of this, and then we will know exactly how it happened. But I think that everyone already knows the truth, Sojourner Stryger.'' She looked back at him, with more sadness than anger showing on her face. ''Even you.''

''No,'' he said, and his mouth began to temble. ''No, it isn't true! I mean them no harm. I only want to do good—I have come to do God's work. I want to save them. Let me do good! Give me the power to bring about change! I need the power, I need it—'' He was screaming now at the silent Assembly, at us where we sat watching; his face swelling, getting bigger and bigger, as the Net closed in on him pitilessly. I shut my eyes this time, but I couldn't stop hearing him, his voice, screaming, ''You can't stop me! God has chosen me, and only God can stop me—''

Suddenly his voice went dim. I opened my eyes. Somebody had dropped a security shield around him. Half a dozen Corpses were surrounding him on the stage now, forcing him to leave it; dragging him, when he tried to resist.

Elnear stood staring after him, her face flushed and her eyes shining; but she didn't look happy. The Speaker came up to her, subvocalizing something that the cams couldn't pick up. And then he said, ''It has been suggested that the vote be postponed, because of this unfortunate—''

She turned toward him, and suddenly the outrage that I'd needed to see was on her face. She turned back to the podium, and said, ''I move that we vote immediately, as planned. And I ask you all to remember that Sojourner Stryger is the man who wants you to deregulate pentryptine—who believes that you will vote his way, 'because you are all so much like him in your hearts.' '' And then she left the podium, walking down and away toward her own seat on the Assembly floor.

Daric taMing seconded the motion.

The motion passed. And in less time than it took to formally announce the vote, deregulation failed to get its majority. By three votes. One of them was Daric taMing's.

THIRTY-FIVE

I HARDLY REMEMBER what happened next on the Assembly floor, because suddenly the club was all whooping and music and celebration. I wouldn't have believed a dozen people could make that much crazy noise. But up in front of me I saw Elnear's face as it registered on her that she'd actually won. I saw that smile of hers come out like the sun. And then finally I could smile too, and laugh and yell and swallow the wine Mikah was pouring down my throat, and start to live again. Because it hadn't all been for nothing.

The private party lasted until the club opened, and then it became a public party, as Argentyne let everybody join in. The stage was their lightshow, full of constant threedy feed, infotainment for the masses. Somewhere in the middle of it I remember her shaking me out of a warm, nodding daze, yelling, "Look! Listen!" in my ear. And it was Daric's face up there, Daric being interviewed by Shander Mandragora as he took "exclusive responsibility" for the illegal 'cast that had burned itself into the collective brain of the Assembly, and turned Sojourner Stryger from the Chosen One of the combine gods into a dose of scratch.

"Gentleman Daric," Shander Mandragora was saying, pushing in for an uncomfortable closeup. "You took extraordinary measures to reveal Sojourner Stryger as a bigot and a dangerous fanatic. What was it that made you decide to commit such a controversial—even illegal—act, something that could ruin your position and damage your distinguished career for years to come?''

Something touched Daric's face for maybe a second, something that nobody else even saw. And for the space of that second, I almost believed he'd done it for the right reason. That he might even find the honesty somewhere to tell everybody what he really was. . . . But then he only looked uncomfortable and annoyed again. ''A sense of higher duty,'' he said, and the answer was the empty, professional lie of a politician. He stared directly into Mandragora's third eye, facing down the watching universe with a calculated intensity that said he knew just how to work the Net. Argentyne couldn't look away from it. ''I worked very closely with Sojourner Stryger, as Centauri's private liaison in matters concerning deregulation. It became clear to me that he was dangerously unstable. But because of his immense public popularity, I knew that he was almost certain to be chosen for the opening on the Security Council. When I realized that might happen, I felt someone had to stop it. And because of his popularity, I knew it would take unorthodox means to effectively prevent such a travesty. So I chose to do this.''

''And what about the victim?'' Mandragora said. ''I interviewed him myself, when he saved several people from an assassination attempt on Lady Elnear Lyron/taMing. He was her aide—was she aware of what you were doing?''

''Absolutely not.'' Daric barely kept the grimace off his face. ''I got to know him because he saved my life too that night. He agreed to play the victim for Stryger because of his own feelings about Stryger's bigotry. It was a courageous act on his part, and the poor fellow suffered terribly for his beliefs. He's in seclusion now, and doesn't want to be disturbed.''

I swore, searching for the poisoned smile I knew was there behind the words.

''He was in no way involved in the actual carrying out of the plan, of course; beyond offering his body as bait, so to speak. . . .''

''You lousy motherfucker,'' I mumbled.

Argentyne turned toward me, frowning. ''He's covering for you, he's taking the blame on himself. Can't you see that? He's protecting you from a criminal action. Do you know what kind of deep shit you'd be in if he didn't?''

''He's giving Charon the finger, and taking the credit for himself,'' I said wearily. I touched my swollen face, wincing. ''Fuck him, he can have it. . . . I got what I wanted.''

"He didn't have to do this. It's going to hurt him. Can't you ever give him credit for a decent act?"

"Not until he does one." I shook my head, and it made me dizzy. She looked away again.

"It has been pointed out," Shander Mandragora was saying, "that Centauri Transport had more to gain financially than almost any combine supporting deregulation. You are a member of their board, and yet you not only discredited Sojourner Stryger, but you actually voted against deregulation yourself. What made you vote against your own corporate interests?"

"*Blackmail,*" I whispered, so softly that even Argentyne couldn't hear me.

Daric stood a little straighter, pulling at his cuffs. "There are some things," he said, with more dignity than I thought he had in him, "more important than money."

"Like his own skin," Mikah grunted. He raised his glass to me. "This one's to you, freak," he said, and swallowed down the rest of the brew in it. Then he got up, stretched, and shook himself out, blocking my view of whatever Daric did next. Every movement he made was perfectly under control, even though he'd been drinking nonstop all evening. Either he had a shunt or he held his liquor better than anybody I'd ever seen. "Looks like he's met his end of the deal. Guess that means the Market will have to do the same." He shrugged, looking down at me. "Looks like everybody wins tonight. . . . But maybe the Governor ought to send somebody out to kick his ass around a little anyway; just to let him know how lucky he is." He smiled, thinking maybe he'd suggest it himself. Argentyne frowned, but she didn't say anything. Mikah put out his hand to me; we clenched thumbs. "So long, kid. It's been real."

I half smiled and nodded. And suddenly the thing I'd sworn I wouldn't ask him for again was all I could think about. But the look in his eyes, and what lay behind it, stopped the words in my throat. I looked down; telling myself I still had three of those little red dots left on the sheet. . . . I looked up again. "Thanks."

He raised his hand, palm out, showing me the scar. "Any time, brother."

I lifted my own hand, and watched him go out of the club. I turned back to Argentyne; but she was gone. Some stranger with striped skin and a long striped tongue was lapping syrup out of a bowl beside me. I ate a few meat-filled buns, and stuck on more painkillers where the damage was starting to leak through. The striped stranger asked me to dance, but I shook my head, not up to it. I lay back in the cushions, watching the endless replays and interviews and flashbacks flowing across the empty stage until I was numb.

As I listened to Daric's confession for the third time, the real Daric entered the club. I felt him walk in, his mind like nobody else's; followed him as he made his way through the crowd to Argentyne, who'd stopped moving to watch his image again. He watched her watching it, standing motionless with her eyes fixed on his holo face as he crossed the room behind her. He wanted to take hold of her as he reached her, and prove to both of them that he was alive; prove to both of them how she still felt about him. . . . But he didn't. Holding himself under control, he only touched her once, to make her turn around. He handed her the symb box, murmuring something noncommittal.

She took it and stuck it back where it belonged. She asked him how he was, told him how glad she was that everything had gone all right; feeling every word ring hollow. She told him how he'd come across on the Net, and then, like she couldn't help herself, how it had made her feel. . . . Her hand stretched toward him, tentative until it reached his chest. And then it slid down and around him. And there was no going back for her, as he touched her with his hands . . . as his mind touched that hidden place inside her where she'd ached to feel him all these endless days.

I broke off watching, broke off *feeling* it; not sure who I was more disgusted with . . . or why I wasn't more surprised. I stared at the images on the stage, waiting for Daric to come to me, knowing that he would.

He was alone again when he finally reached my table, and the grin of satisfaction on his face faded as I looked up at him. He flinched as he saw my own face. "Get out of here," he said to the people sitting around me. They got up and left as he sat down. Dead serious, he asked, "Are you satisfied now?"

"You kept your part of it." I had to force myself to say the words.

"What about the Market? Did they see everything? Are they satisfied too? Do I get my life back?"

I shrugged, and it hurt every muscle in my shoulders, back, and chest.

"Well—?" he said, when I didn't answer.

"Yeah. This time."

He nodded, but the tight lines around his eyes didn't disappear. "And you'll keep your mouth shut—?"

I frowned, touching the scabs on my lips.

"I'm protecting you! I'm taking the blame for everything that happened, so that you don't have to! That ought to make up for a few extra bruises, for God's sake." He jerked his hands. "All right—I was angry, I wanted to see you suffer like you'd made me suffer. I admit it. But I didn't mean for it to go that far. I thought I could control him, I didn't think he'd . . . He always stopped, before. . . ." Finally admitting, to me and to himself, that at the end he'd been as powerless to stop Stryger as I had. He looked down, remembering his own fear as he'd watched Stryger go out of control.

I wished he was lying to me; but he wasn't. I looked away as he tried to meet my eyes, tried to guess what was on my mind. He'd never know what he'd really done to me . . . and telling him the truth would only make it harder for me to bear. "All right," I whispered. "You want to go on living your lie—go ahead. Maybe I don't even blame you." Realizing that if the choice was mine to make right now, I'd make the same one he would. I looked up at him again, through a single round-pupiled eye. "You know, for a minute I almost thought you felt something real while you were serving all that shit to the Net. That maybe you finally understood why it was important to get Stryger, now. That it mattered to you that you'd stopped him." I touched my head, grimacing. "It must've been the concussion."

He glanced away. "No," he said finally. "You were right." He'd enjoyed playing his private games with Stryger, being in control, cheating him like he'd cheated the rest of the universe. Last night he'd enjoyed watching Stryger torture me; thinking that he hated me as much as Stryger did. But his own hatred had let the pain get too personal, sucked him in too close to its heart, ruptured the membrane of lies that let him feel safe—just like it had ruptured mine. He'd seen the truth about Stryger, and about himself. About his worst nightmares . . .

"In the middle of the night," he said, "while I was trying to drag that self-righteous, perverted slug to somewhere discreet and safe, all because he was no better than anybody else . . . I had something of an epiphany, I suppose. And then I actually wanted to see the son of a bitch broken on the rack of public opinion today—and not just for my own sake." His hand tightened on the tabletop. He stared at it, forced it to relax again. "Auntie was brilliant, wasn't she?" He grinned, like he'd never considered the possibility before. "You know, for a moment while I was being interviewed, I actually thought, what if I did tell them I was a psion—?" He looked back at me. "But it

passed, mercifully. I'm so glad you'll be leaving soon. A little truth
is a dangerous thing."

I started to smile in spite of myself, as wide as my mouth would
let me; realizing I never would have heard those words out of his mouth
if it hadn't been for what had happened to me last night. "What kind
of trouble is the Assembly tampering going to make for you?"

He raised his eyebrows. "Everyone will sling legal and political
rubbish at me. It will be unpleasant. But little of it will stick. It may
even improve Centauri's relations with the Feds, in the end—I mean,
I was obviously so right about Stryger. . . . And besides, I'm a taMing.
You know what they say." The mocking smile came back, and he
shrugged. " 'Cats and Gentlemen always land on their feet.' "

I grunted. "What about your father?"

The smile froze over. He looked away, and didn't answer. I
wondered which of them would end up hating me more. "Even Argentyne has begun to forgive me, after all. . . ." He smirked as he
looked up at me again. *Even though I'd done all I could to ruin it
between them. . . . Even though she knew his secret.* Terror and ex-
hilaration filled him at the thought of it. "A relationship based on
trust—who knows where that will lead? I suppose I'll have to be nicer
to her. . . ." He laughed, nervously, and got to his feet. "Maybe I
should even thank you. But I truly hope we never meet again, Cat.
Don't think I intend to forget you, though. . . ." He stopped, just out
of reach, and looked back. "I have a copy of that tape of you with
Stryger. I intend to use it for my own personal recreational pleasure."
He laughed again, at the look on my face, and started away.

"Daric!"

He stopped, looking back, still smiling.

I got my voice under control, and said, "There's something else
you ought to know. I'll keep my word about you. But before I knew
you were the teek, I told Braedee there was another psion at the
estates." I smiled this time, as his grin faded. "It's something to keep
in mind."

He looked at me for a long time, with his throat working. And
then his smile started to grow back. "Well, good for you. . . ." he
murmured. "You're just as human as the rest of us." He turned away
again, and went looking for Argentyne.

I lay back in the pillows with my eyes shut. "Eat shit and die,"
I muttered.

The threedy images were fading up on the stage, turning to fog,
mutating as I opened my eyes and began to watch again: becoming

Argentyne and the symb beginning a performance. She'd said they weren't going to perform tonight; I wondered which of the things that had happened today had changed her mind.

I held my psi back as the rippling wall of light and sound opened up, not wanting to find out as I let my other senses pull me into the symb's hallucinogenic vision. Maybe Argentyne had been better than this, but I hadn't been there when it happened . . . and watching, listening, letting the lightsong surround me and draw me out of myself, I realized that this might be the last time I'd ever see her perform. I didn't need her any more; and she didn't need me. Whatever happened now, my time here in Purgatory was over.

The jack was gone from the back of my head already. I wasn't real to her or the players any more on that other plane where their minds were now, and soon I'd hardly even be a memory to them. But I didn't really need a socket to reach them. And now, while I still had my Gift, I wanted to use it. I pushed out through the haze of painkillers until I found Argentyne's mind. I let myself in, and set free the things I saw there, feeding her mood poems into all the players' minds at once, letting their reactions flow back to her—doing freehand what I'd done before by tracing the lifelines of the symb . . . until I knew they knew I was in symb with them one last time, giving them the best gift I knew how to give. . . .

THIRTY-SIX

THE NEXT DAY'S news was full of Lady Elnear Lyron/taMing being named to fill the empty slot on the Security Council. I missed it, because when I went to bed I slept for three days straight. When I finally came to again the pain had eased up enough that I could stand it without drugs. Most of the swelling had gone down, and my reflection in the mirror looked like it belonged to somebody I knew again. I peeled the pad away from my bandaged eye. It looked like Deadeye's. But at least I could see out of it again. I thought about being blind for life; thought about Oldcity. They'd told me at Soule's that there shouldn't be any scars this time. None that showed, anyway. Two green eyes with round pupils that were beginning to seem too familiar searched my face, and looked away.

I went downstairs, one step at a time. As I limped into the kitchen, Shander Mandragora's face up on the wall was telling the Federation that Sojourner Stryger had committed suicide.

My stomach pushed up into my throat; I drank a cup of stale coffee that was sitting on the kitchen table, forcing it back down where it belonged.

"He left a message," Aspen said, putting his arm around Midnight's shoulders as he looked at me. "Something about going where he was wanted. . . ." For a second I thought he was joking; but he wasn't.

"Do you think there's a heaven?" Midnight asked.

"I don't believe in heaven," I said. "But I hope there's a hell."

They looked at me, and they didn't say anything else.

"Where's Argentyne?" I asked, to fill up the silence.

Aspen looked down; I felt the stab of his embarrassment. "Out at Daric's."

I made a noise.

"Sorry, man," Midnight said. "Don't take it too hard."

"Like they say," I muttered. "Cats and Gentlemen always land on their feet."

"Lady Elnear's been trying to reach you," Aspen said. "She left a lot of messages while you were out."

Out. I half smiled. *Out of my head.* "What did she say?"

They told me the old news then, about her appointment. I nodded, not surprised, but relieved. "She just said she wanted to talk to you as soon as possible. That it was important."

I got up. "Thanks." I went to the phone and tried to call her, but I couldn't even get through. Everyone else in the galaxy was probably trying to do the same thing, and that wouldn't end soon. I stood in the hall for a minute, letting my frustration ease off, trying to think. And then I called Natan Isplanasky. He actually came on-screen himself when I gave my ID. He stared at me, at my face, like everybody else had; but he listened to what I had to say without interrupting. He half frowned when I finished, rubbing his beard. "I don't know if it's even possible," he said. "She was installed today. The period of adjustment for a new Council member is difficult. . . ."

"I have to see her," I said. "And I've only got a couple of days left."

He looked surprised. "What happens after that?"

I shrugged. "I'm not sure."

"Are you in trouble over the Stryger affair?"

"No." I shook my head.

"Are you all right?"

"No." I looked away, knowing he could see that for himself.

"God damn it," he said. "I don't know if it's the things you do say or the things you don't say that grate on me more." He broke off as I laughed; a grudging smile pulled at his mouth. "I'll see what I can arrange."

He called me back later in the day. "Come up to the office," he said. "I'll meet you there." That he'd kept his promise surprised me nearly as much as anything that had happened the past few weeks. But I only nodded, and did what he told me.

He met me at his office door, tried not to flinch as he got a fresh look at me, and took me inside. "Elnear will join us as soon as she's able." He handed me one of his thousand-year-old beers. "You earned it," he said. "What you did took a lot of guts. The people of the Federation owe you more than a beer." *For destabilizing Stryger's orbit.*

I looked down, studying the bottle so that I didn't have to meet his eyes. "I didn't do it for them."

"Well," he said, "very few things seem to get done for the reasons they should get done." He moved restlessly. "As far as that goes, I owe you more than a beer myself."

I raised my head again. "What for?"

"For proving that I am not all-seeing. . . . Elnear finally told me about what happened to you at the Mines."

I swallowed a mouthful of beer, and didn't say anything.

He looked down, this time. "I've been exploring options to streamline the system, so that I have more direct access to all its parts." He didn't look away from the look on my face. "And to put more of its resources into protecting its clients. I don't know if that will be enough to satisfy someone who has been abused by it. . . . I hope it will be enough to make some difference." What he didn't say was what we both already knew, each of us in our own way—that even he was just another mouse in the machine, in the end. There was only so much he'd ever be able to do. The system was more than its parts.

And yet changing it still mattered to him. What had happened once to a nobody like me mattered to him, here in this private office at the top of the world, at the top of the FTA's power structure. I thought about the last time I'd stood in this office, and what I'd been feeling then. Standing here now, feeling the *anger, frustration, hope* behind his eyes, I realized suddenly that knowing he actually felt that way made a hell of a difference to me. And I realized the difference that having Elnear for a friend had made in him.

"Hello, Cat."

I turned as I heard Elnear's voice, startled because I hadn't sensed her coming in. She was standing there behind me, smiling. I started toward her; stopped again, blinking. "You're not here." It was an image, a holo. It looked real, it reacted in realtime, but there was no one inside it. I stood still, sending out my mind through wider and wider circles, searching for her. "Where are you? I can't find you—"

"I know." Her smile changed, until it wasn't really a smile any more, and I couldn't tell what lay behind it. "I'm afraid this is the best I can do. I'm on the Council now."

"I know, but . . ." I shook my head. "Where are you, then?"

She turned toward Isplanasky. "Natan, didn't you explain?"

He shrugged. "I thought he knew."

"What—?" I said, ready to yank it out of his mind.

"Could we have some time alone?" she asked him.

"Of course," he said. "I need to get back into the system, anyway." He looked at me. "Goodbye, Cat. Good luck to you. Just let yourself out when you're finished."

I watched him cross the room to the wired lounge where I'd first seen him. He lay back in it, linking into the Net, taking all the energy of his mind and body with him. He was still in the room, but inside of a minute we had complete privacy. . . . I looked away from him, hunching my shoulders. Seeing Elnear but not seeing her didn't make me feel any better.

"Well, we won," she said softly, smoothing her long blue-gray robe with her hands. Her face filled with pride and something deeper as she looked at me again. "You found a pin sharp enough to make the Assembly jump, after all. What happened was your doing, wasn't it—not Daric's?"

I nodded. "But if it hadn't been for you, Stryger might still have gotten what he wanted. What I did might not have stopped anything, if it hadn't been for you—" My throat closed up; it took an effort to keep the real expression off my face.

Her smile disappeared. "But in the end, he was his own nemesis. . . ." She knew what he'd done to himself. I couldn't tell if she really believed what she said, though—that he was to blame for that, and not us. I couldn't tell if I did, either. "I am so grateful to you, once again," she said, and her voice was suddenly too full; her eyes touched my face, glanced down my body, darkened as they registered the damage that showed. "Knowing what I now know, about Stryger and about the real nature of the Security Council . . . If he had won this slot, the chaos his instability would have caused could have been unimaginable." Her hands tightened. "But if I had known what you intended to do—do to yourself—I would never have let you do it."

"That's why I didn't tell you." I shook my head, not wanting her to say any more; not wanting to hear it. "Lady . . . Why aren't you here? Is it security—"

"I'm on the Council now, Cat," she said again, and hesitated, as if finding the right words was terribly important to her, or terribly hard somehow. "I'm joined with the system, like Natan . . . but permanently."

I stared at her, feeling stupid and dazed, not able to read the context of thought that would make the words mean what they were supposed to. "Permanently?"

She nodded.

I looked back at Isplanasky. "You mean you can't ever walk away from it?"

"Yes. That's right."

"Why?" I said weakly.

"Because the Council demands total commitment. Keeping control of any network that spans interstellar distances is a nearly impossible task, and the FTA is the largest coherent network of all. There are systems within systems inside the Authority. Natan is at one level; I was on another one, far lower, before. At each level of complexity, as you ascend, more augmentation is required to make up for the structural limitations of the human mind; to give it the capacity it needs to process the increased dataflow and make meaningful judgments about it. Most combines never really function on the highest levels; they have to segment their operations, because of the limits of realtime communication. . . . Only the FTA makes policy on this level, because it has to respond to so many different factors. And at this level the interface is so complex that it has to be permanent.''

"What happens, then . . . to you?'' Muscles twitched in my jaw.

"My body is being maintained. They'll take excellent care of it . . . it will probably last for another fifty or seventy-five years.''

I tried not to grimace. "And then what?''

"They'll have to choose someone else to fill a Council slot. The Charter does not permit Council members to . . . stay on after death.''

I looked away from the thing that was standing across the room pretending to be someone I knew. "What about Elnear? I mean . . . Shit, I don't know what I mean!'' My hand hit my leg in frustration; I winced. "I can't feel you. Are you alive or are you just data? Do you feel human? Do you feel anything at all any more?''

"Oh, yes . . .'' she murmured. "I wish you could know what I feel, Cat. You might understand it better than most people, because of what you are.''

I nodded, because I knew what she meant, better than she realized . . . maybe even better than she did. But I couldn't tell her that. "Maybe it's a nice place to visit. But I wouldn't want to live there.''

She smiled a little. "I'm only just beginning to grasp what it really is. My sense of individual identity may be no more than an artificial construct, for all I know . . . and yet I still feel quite human, somehow. Perhaps I'll always feel that way, because I interact as a coherent personality, all the time, with human beings at all levels of the system—just the way I'm speaking to you.''

"How do I look to you?'' I asked.

"Very far away . . .'' she said, and there was sadness in it again. "Perhaps my sense of humanness will fade, with time . . . perhaps it's wise that our service is limited by our lifespan. But I am not alone here inside, either, which I think will help me to remember why I exist and perhaps even who I am. I am a part of the Council in a very literal sense, and we are . . . of one mind.''

I thought about the shining beings I'd met inside the Council core when I'd been lost in inner space with Deadeye . . . and for just a second I went cold inside, as I imagined what it really would have meant if Stryger had become one of them. But then I thought about how it felt to make a joining. The Hydrans had been able to share a single mindspace with as many others as there was need for. But to share just one other person's mind totally was something that no normal human could ever do; it was almost impossible even for a human who was a psion . . . even for me. Something that might have been envy, but wasn't, stirred inside me. "Did you know it would be like this, all along?" It was almost more than I could believe, or wanted to. "That if you won you'd never be able to see anyone face to face again, or smell coffee or paint a picture or walk in the woods—?" The memories of all the things I'd watched her do that gave her pleasure filled my mind.

"Yes." She nodded. "I knew that much. I didn't know it would be like this—I couldn't really know. It's impossible to describe in human terms. But I knew there would be no coming back from it."

"You still wanted it." I couldn't make it a question, because the answer was obvious. "Weren't you afraid—of disappearing?"

"Weren't you afraid," she asked, "of what would happen when you let Stryger get his hands on you?"

"Yeah," I said. "I sure as hell was."

She laughed. "I sure as hell was, too. But Cat, someone described the process of augmenting the human mind as pouring indigo dye into a bucket, and then pouring the bucket into a vat, and the vat into the sea. . . . The dye is still there, no matter how diffused. It's rather like seeing God in all things. And I think that it's fitting, perhaps even the key to our survival as a species, that we stay a part of the systems we create, however we can: as cells, as organs . . . and, I hope, as souls. Because we have already set in motion our transformation, like it or not. Progress is always the process of leaving something behind. Every choice we make means that we are forced to give something up, as well; to sacrifice the thing not chosen."

I shook my head. "No regrets, then?"

"Oh . . ." The smile didn't quite work, this time. "A few. Phantom pains for my lost body. I'm told they will get worse, and then fade with time, as the past fades. But I am only my memories now, and so even my regrets are precious to me."

I looked away from her, disappointment rising up so suddenly in me that I couldn't speak. I'd come here to see Elnear, the living, breathing, human woman I'd gone through so much with, and for . . . to see her once more before the drugs wore off and I lost the ability to really see her: her mind, her soul. But because of those damned drugs I'd slept away three days of my life; I'd missed her, and now I'd never have the chance again.

"And what about you?" she asked, to my turned back.

"Lousy," I said, my hands tightening. "Really lousy."

"Are you angry?"

I shook my head.

"Disappointed, then—?"

I shrugged.

"Afraid of me?"

I turned back. "No . . ." I shook my head again. "I don't know." My voice sounded hoarse and thick. "I don't know how to feel, because I don't know what you are any more."

"Then you probably feel something like I felt when I first met you," she said gently.

I looked down again. Finally I said, "I just wish you'd told me. So I could have been . . . ready."

"We've both had painful secrets to keep, it seems." Chiding me, still gently. "What I knew about the real nature of the Security Council was not something that I was permitted to share freely. Those who do know feel—and I think justifiably—that the people of the Federation, the people the FTA is meant to serve, would rather believe that it is still run by identifiable human beings. And so they . . . we try to preserve that illusion. Now you know the secret too. You know it because I know I can trust you to keep it."

I looked at her image, my eyes unfocused, not saying anything.

"There is something I still need to discuss with you." Her voice got stronger, pulling me back. "Being on the Council leaves me in an awkward position, Cat. I am legally neither dead nor alive. I wanted to see you, not only to say goodbye, but also to discuss with you the disposition of my estate."

"With me?" I said.

"My personal holdings, including my controlling interest in ChemEnGen, will have to be overseen by a trusteeship in my . . . absence. I would like to name you to the board."

"Me?" I said again, sounding stupider than before. "I don't know sh— anything, about overseeing—"

She held up her hands. "That isn't necessary. Philipa will head the board. She will see that the actual duties are taken care of. I simply need individuals I know I can trust, to fill the other seats— I suppose that's why they call them 'trustees.' It would give you the freedom to live your life as you want to. You'd never again have to let someone like Braedee blackmail you into a job you hated."

I felt a smile start. "It wasn't such a bad job . . . But yeah." I

nodded. "Maybe I'd like that." *Freedom*. But more than freedom
. . . *security*. She smiled too as I looked back at her again. "You
have all the seats filled?"

"Do you have candidates?"

"Jule."

She hesitated, nodded.

"Jiro."

This time her surprise showed. But then she smiled, and nodded
again. "Thank you."

I shrugged, staring at her image. "I just want to know one thing.
Are you really happy, Elnear?"

"Yes," she said, and there was no hesitation in it. "Yes, I
am."

"Then I guess it'll be all right." I took a deep breath.

"What are your plans," she asked, "now that this ordeal has
finally ended, for both of us?"

I shook my head. "I don't know. I guess I'll go back to the
University, until I figure out what to do with the rest of my life." My
mouth twitched, not really a smile. I reached up, feeling for the patch
behind my ear; feeling my teeth clench. "But first I've got to find a
place where I can be alone and scream for a while." I tried to make
it sound like a joke, but it didn't.

Sympathy and pain that I couldn't feel showed in her eyes.
But then her face changed. She murmured, "I know just the place.
It's spring there, now. No one will bother you. It's a place that
can make you remember the good. . . . Will you let me arrange it?"

Surprised, I almost said *no*. But instead I thought about it, and
nodded. And as I did, I felt my body loosen with relief, letting go of
a fear that I hadn't realized I'd been holding all this time. I rubbed
my eyes with my hand.

"Goodbye, Cat," she said.

"Goodbye, Elnear." And then, because it was better than admitting the truth, I smiled at her, and said, "Think about me sometimes. Maybe I'll hear you."

She smiled too, and held out her hand. I even tried to touch it,
before she disappeared.

After she was gone I let myself out of Isplanasky's office. I walked
through the halls of the Federation plex for the last time, alone. When
I reached the display area, I stopped inside the crowd of tourists who

were staring at the mosaic of the People of Earth. I studied the faces on the wall, the faces around me, for a long time. Human faces. *I hadn't done it for them*. That was what I'd told Isplanasky. But somehow those faces weren't so hard to look at, this time. Somehow they'd changed; or maybe I had. "You're welcome," I said at last. No one turned to look at me as I went on my way.

EPILOGUE

I STAYED IN the cottage halfway up the mountainside for as long as it took—to learn to live with myself, and only myself, again. About once a week I had to walk down into the nearest village to pick up supplies. It was an independent crafters' commune, not a Federal outlet or a combine clave, and they didn't seem to care if I looked like hell or sometimes I couldn't make myself speak to them. I didn't want to speak to them, or even hear them speak to me. They might as well have been the hallucinations of my own sick mind, because I couldn't feel them inside my thoughts any more.

At first sometimes facing even fifteen minutes' mindless contact was more than I could stand, and I'd just go hungry. Sitting inside the one room, sometimes I wouldn't move all day. I stared at the silent, whitewashed walls, wishing they were black. All I could feel was pain. Some of the pain was physical, but that was almost a relief compared to the pain that wasn't. Sometimes I did scream. Once I called Mikah, ready to beg him to get me what I needed. Nobody answered the call.

But all the while I was healing. My battered body mended fast. The broken bones of my defenses mended a lot more slowly. In time the blackness inside me began to break up into shades of gray, telling me my inner eyes were finally adjusting to life in a darkened room. After enough time, I could even begin to see how far I'd come, in spite of everything, from the place I'd been when I first came to Earth. I started being able to look at the scars on my face and body for long enough to recognize that they were really fading . . . to look at the memories that strobed behind them directly enough that I could even begin to believe what had happened to me with Stryger wasn't the same thing that had happened to me back in Oldcity; to believe that this time it hadn't been random, meaningless suffering. This time I'd made a hard choice, for a good reason, and made a difference by doing it. And this time my survival hadn't been as random as my pain . . . this time I really hadn't been all alone in hell.

And slowly, painfully, I was able to see that even if Oldcity had been reality for me for seventeen years, it didn't make the life I had now a lie. Not the good parts of it; not the bad. I wasn't a victim any more. I wasn't a telepath any more, either. The drugs I'd used to blind me to the truth were the lie, just like they'd always been. Unless I wanted to live without my Gift forever, I had to face living without it now, for however long it took. But the truth was the bitterest drug I'd ever had to swallow; it burned my mouth every time I had to speak a word.

As my need died, day by day, I began to rediscover the world waiting for me outside. I heard birds calling, smelled damp earth and new grass, finally knew the color of the flowers and the sky. I tried to learn how to make music on the mouth harp Argentyne had given me along with one last kiss as we said our goodbyes. I watched spring turn into summer all across the valley below me, until finally I knew I was glad to be alive again . . . knew this world for a part of my heritage, a place that I had a right to love; a place I wanted to come back to again, on my own terms. And then at last I understood the real gift that Elnear had given me.

After the worst of the pain had died, I realized that what was left didn't hurt me the way it had before. That it let me reach out a little further before I ran into the wall. That maybe Jule had been right about what I'd done; that by helping someone else I'd helped myself, and the past had really gotten just a little further away for me.

One day I went into town when I didn't have to, because I wanted to hear a human voice that wasn't my own. And then I knew I felt human again, if not Hydran . . . and that I was ready to live like a human again, on their terms.

I contacted Braedee and made him take me back where he'd found me. On the way there, I made him fix my eyes. Neither of us said *thanks* as I got ready to leave the ship; but he said I ought to study chess. I told him I thought I'd stick to Square/Cubes.

The University was still in port where I'd left it, finishing up its session on the Monument. There was a tape waiting there for me, from Jule. I sat in my cabin and watched her smiling face a dozen times before I was ready to go out and start living the life of a student again.

My absence had been listed as being for "family problems." I had a hard time keeping a decent expression on my face as Kissindre Perrymeade told me I looked tired, and she hoped that everything was all right at home. She asked if I wanted to talk about it. I said *no*. She said she was sorry about what had happened between us just before I left. I couldn't remember what she meant, but I didn't say so. She offered to share credit with me on the session thesis she was finishing, because I hadn't had time to do anything for the course.

I shook my head, still having trouble even relating to what she was saying. I felt like I'd been missing for years, instead of months; the holomuraled walls of the museum hall seemed more real than she did. "No. It's all right. . . ."

"It would only be fair," she insisted, not understanding that I really didn't care. "You gave me the concept yourself. What you said before you left, about the Monument as a 'monument to Death'—"

"I said that?" I asked, and then nodded; remembering it, finally. I thought about the sunset at Goldengate, and the music of the wind, and what it had said to me. "I guess I did. . . . I'll see you later." I started to turn away.

"Where are you going?" she asked, with more gentleness than I would have expected.

"Gonna take a jump down to the surface. I want to . . . get the feel of the thing again before it's gone."

"Want some company?"

I looked back at her. "What about—" I broke off. *Ezra.* That had been his name. Her boyfriend. "Ezra?"

She made a face, and shook her head. "We're not speaking this week."

I looked away again. "I don't feel much like talking, myself."

"That's all right," she said.

I shrugged, and nodded.

We took the shuttle down together to Goldengate, and stood on the open plateau. It was barely dawn this time, and we were alone in the soft half-light. A handful of stars were still showing, and the arch of the Gate was a black silhouette that even my eyes could barely make out against the sky. The wind was still making mournful flutesong through the riddled stone, just the way I remembered it. I touched the mouth harp riding in the pocket of my jeans, finally remembering after all this time what something in its sound had always reminded me of.

I started away from the shuttle, the sandy dirt whispering under my feet. It was almost cold, and I was glad I was wearing Deadeye's sweater. Kissindre sat down cross-legged where she was, watching silently, but letting me have my space.

I sat on the rocks at the edge of the plateau, listening, feeling the wind, waiting as day broke and the light touched the arch and began to turn it gold. And I thought about the way this world had been made, put together out of ruined bits and pieces, forged into a work of art by a technology so far beyond ours that it still seemed like magic. *A monument to bad ends and broken dreams* . . . and yet that didn't seem right, when it seemed to be waiting through millennia just for something living to come here and touch it. Even the air I was breathing was a miracle; all the studies I'd ever seen said you needed a living ecosystem to produce an atmosphere a human could live in. But a human could breathe here, walk here, feel perfectly at home here . . . do everything except stay. So could a Hydran. I wondered if the Hydrans had known about this world, visited it, studied it. And I realized suddenly that it could just as well have been left here for them to find, as for the humans. Whether it had been meant for the Hydrans instead was probably a question no one had ever asked up at the museum. . . .

I tried not to let the bitterness take hold of me again as I thought it. I was still a halfbreed, even if my telepathy was gone—still made out of bits and pieces like this world was, but nobody's idea of a work of art. The two halves of me were so much alike . . . except for that one, fragile thing that made all the difference. In the way two peoples looked at life, and each other. I wondered how something like that could even have happened; what kind of cosmic joke I'd been made the butt of. I remembered Stryger asking me the same thing.

And because I couldn't face too much of that, I took the mouth harp out of my pocket and began to play, trying to make the sounds it made act like a song. The song that the wind made answered me, making me remember the symb; remember the good. There was more of it to remember than I'd expected.

I thought about Elnear then; about where and what she was now . . . about all she'd given up, and all she'd become. If I'd been given that chance, I didn't know if I could have taken it. . . . The part of me that wanted to be whole again, the Hydran part, had envied her;

but the human part had known it wouldn't be the same, and it had only been afraid. It was hard enough just living with what I knew already, just being one of a hundred billion random cells in the Federation's evolving supermind.

And yet knowing she'd had the courage to make that choice, and take that final step, still made a difference . . . as much difference, in its way, as what she'd done to help me survive in my own random life. She'd finally proved something to me about humans, and about the human side in me, that I hadn't thought anyone could make me believe again: that maybe they deserved some respect, after all.

And so did the ones who'd left this world here. I wondered what they'd been like, before they'd disappeared from our plane of existence hundreds of thousands of years ago. I'd told Stryger I didn't believe in a God; and I didn't—not any kind that he'd recognize. Probably not any kind that I would, either. But a race that could create this world, and then pull themselves into a hat and disappear . . . they could have played God a little before they left, done a little genetic tampering, planted some seeds and left them there to see what would happen. The Haves and the Have Nots. An experiment, a cosmic joke . . . the next generation.

The Hydrans had reached the stars first, but they'd depended on their Gift too much, and spread it too thin. When the humans got there after them, it had been easy enough to sweep their psi Net away like cobwebs. The Hydrans hadn't reached their transformation, and now they never would. Maybe they'd had it too easy. Maybe they'd never seen how much they'd been given . . . how much they had to lose.

Now the humans had built their own Net, and it was technogenetic, cruder but stronger. And now they were using it to climb inexorably up the same ever-steepening evolutionary curve. . . . I thought about Elnear again: about the chosen few already on the brink of something unknowable . . . and all the systems within systems below them, the individual humans who had become the core—the soul, Elnear had said—of an evolving meta-being they called a combine, creating their future almost without realizing it.

Maybe they'd never take the final step, either; maybe for humans it would always be too hard. Maybe the fear of Otherness that was always there, inside a mind that could never really put itself in somebody else's place, would always hold them back. Or maybe they'd make it just because they'd had to fight so hard simply to survive; because they'd never given up trying to bridge the impossible gulf between one human mind and another. . . .

I looked down at the fight scars on my knuckles, and out at the dawn again. Whatever happened to the human race, the Monument would be waiting here: a road sign, pointing toward an unimaginable future. Not a cemetery headstone, but a memorial to the death of Death.

I heard the soft scuff of someone's footsteps behind me; looked up as Kissindre stopped beside me.

"A credit for your thoughts," she said, almost whispering, with an embarrassed twitch in her smile.

I shook my head, smiling a little too. "Don't waste your money." She held her arms pressed tightly against her chest. She was wearing a thin, short-sleeved shirt, and I realized how much she was feeling the cold. "Sit down," I said, suddenly feeling selfish, and sorry for it.

She sat on the warming rocks beside me, and there was no tension in her body, no yearning, no anticipation in her mind. . . .

And I knew that. It wasn't much, but it was something.

I put my arm around her shoulders, but it was only to help her stay warm; something a friend would do. We sat together a while longer, like two friends, watching the day come in.